I0822156

· NIGHTINGALE SONGS BOOK TWO ·

# BALLADS OF SHADOW AND LIGHT

*by*

CHRISTINA MAI FONG

An Imprint of Acorn Publishing

This is a work of fiction. References to real people, events, establishments, organizations, or locales are intended only to provide a sense of authenticity and are used fictitiously. All other characters and all incidents and dialogue are drawn from the author's imagination and are not to be construed as real.

*Ballads of Shadow and Light*



Printed in the United States of America.

For information, address Oak Tree Press, 3943 Irvine Blvd. Ste. 218, Irvine, CA 92602.
An Imprint of Acorn Publishing.

Cover design by Damonza.

Book interior design and digital formatting by Debra Cranfield Kennedy.



ISBN—979-8-88528-010-5 (hardcover)
ISBN—979-8-88528-009-9 (paperback)

*To my mom and dad, Lily Mai Lee Fong and David Fong.*

*And to my sweet and kind baby brother, Daniel Fong.*

*Your support means everything to me.*

✦ ✦ ✦

✦ ✦ ✦

# BALLADS OF SHADOW AND LIGHT

✦ ✦ ✦

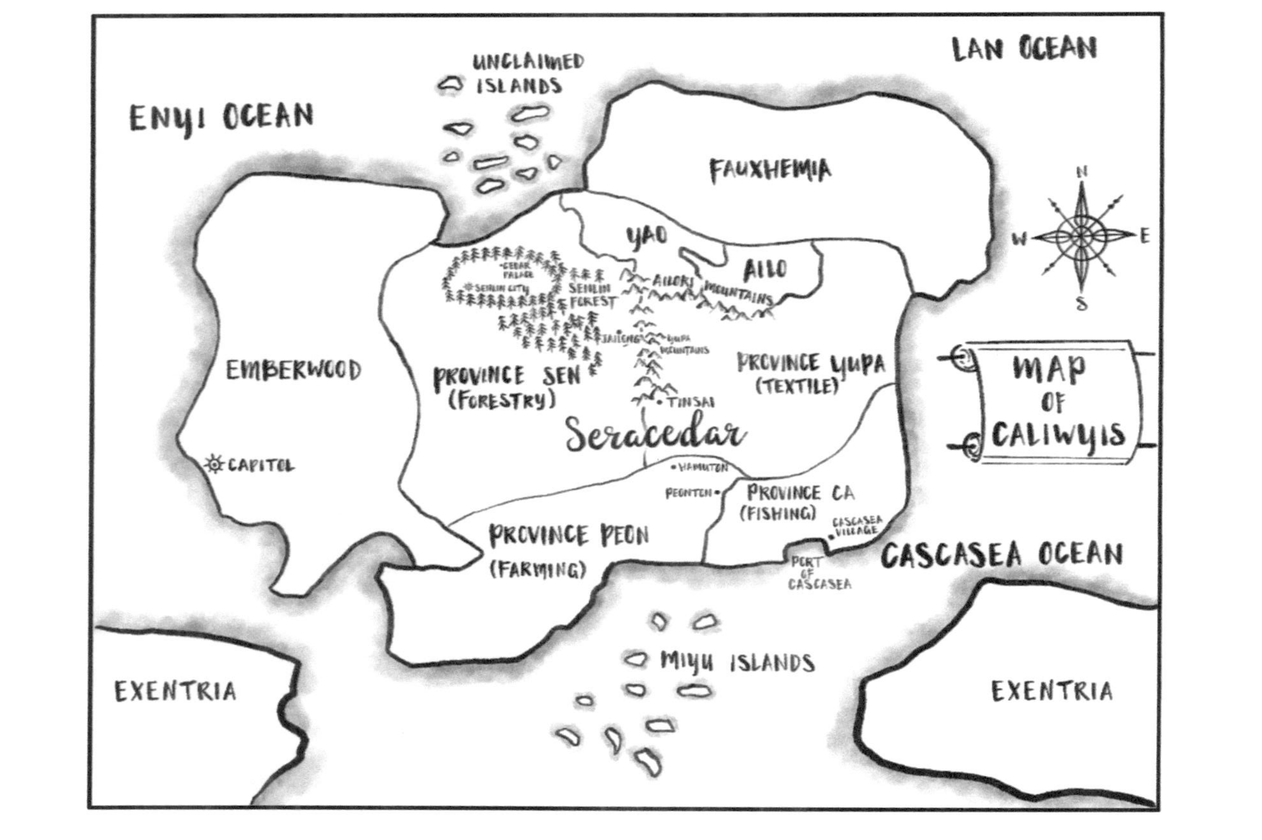

MAP OF CALIWYIS
LAN OCEAN
ENYI OCEAN
CASCASEA OCEAN
UNCLAIMED ISLANDS
FAUXHEMIA
N
S
E
W
EMBERWOOD
CAPITOL
YAO
AILO
CEDAR PALACE
SEILIN CITY
SEILIN FOREST
AILORI MOUNTAINS
YUPA MOUNTAINS
TINSAI
PROVINCE SEN
(FORESTRY)
PROVINCE YUPA
(TEXTILE)
Seracedar
HAMILTON
PEONTEN
PROVINCE CA
(FISHING)
CASCASEA VILLAGE
PORT OF CASCASEA
PROVINCE PEON
(FARMING)
MIYU ISLANDS
EXENTRIA
EXENTRIA

# CHAPTER 1

✦ ✦ ✦ ✦ ✦ ✦ ✦ ✦ ✦ ✦

From afar, the tiny village of Tinsai seemed suspended in the clouds that wrapped around the mountains like a hooded cloak.

I stopped walking and tugged at Aiden's arm. "I still don't know about this. The last time I tried to hide my face in fake boils didn't end well."

Aiden pressed one of the fake boils he'd pasted to my face, making sure the clay was securely glued to my skin. The clay dots had been strategically placed to hide my identity as well as the cursed mark of four on my cheek. "Don't worry so much, Rilla. You look hideous. I doubt anyone will take a close look at you much less want to be around you."

"What about you?" I asked.

Aiden had smeared his hair in soot, concealing his recognizable blond locks. I wasn't convinced it was enough. With his sword strapped to his belt and bow and quiver of arrows on his back, he looked like a warrior. "Should you hide your weapons?"

"I'm not the only traveler who carries weapons," he said. "There's no law against it. I don't think anyone will recognize me. Not many people have seen me without my bodyguard mask, and I doubt anyone could sketch my likeness on a wanted poster realistically. I'm much too handsome to be captured in a simple drawing."

A chuckle formed in my throat. Attempting to suppress the sound, I let out a snort.

He grinned. "Ah, I do love when I can make you laugh."

"Be serious," I said. "I know you said this is the last town we pass before we cross into Yao Kingdom, but we've managed to survive three weeks in the forest. Is it necessary to replenish our supplies here?"

"Yao Kingdom is enemy territory," he said. "We won't be able to hunt like we have been. We need to buy food. Besides, I'd like to find out the latest news of what's happening at the palace."

I nodded. He was right. "I just hope my fake boils don't wash away this time."

"Even if they do, we'll manage," he said. "Tinsai barely has any inhabitants. You'll see what I mean soon."

We continued walking and within minutes entered through the village gates. The romantic atmosphere of the village I'd seen from afar had been but an illusion.

The main road was desolate. The streets remained unpaved. Ditches and potholes littered the ground like scarred lepers. The paint on the buildings was chipped, colored in faded pastels mixed with soot and dust. Above the doors of the storefronts, drooping signs threatened to tumble to the ground. The washed-out words of the signs were faded to the point of being illegible. Hard to tell which stores were open or closed for business, or what they sold.

"What happened?" I asked. "Does anyone still live here?"

"A couple of years ago, these smaller northeastern villages on the border were overtaken by swarms of insects," Aiden said. "No one could go outside without getting covered and eaten alive."

I winced at the description, repressing the urge to gag. The sight of blood I could tolerate. Insects? Not so much.

Now that I knew Tinsai was close to a ghost village, my fears about being recognized as fugitives subsided somewhat.

"The pests ate up the crops, littered the streets, and passed on disease, killing off the majority of people here," Aiden said. "The palace was afraid of an epidemic, so these villages were quarantined. Now only a few survivors remain but only because they have nowhere else to go."

Many believed the curse of a disease lingered in the air of a quarantined village long after the sickness wiped away most of the inhabitants. They feared they might be haunted by the ghosts who'd died from the plague. I'd never bought into any kind of curse though. At least not the supernatural kind. The only curses that were real were the result of malevolent rulers abusing their power.

I shivered. "I had no idea. I heard about the pestilence but not the quarantine."

"The palace covered it up," Aiden said. "It was right before the failed coup. The rebels used this and other natural disasters to start rumors that Terran had lost the Will of Heaven."

"Like the tidal wave that damaged the Port of Cascasea," I said. A rush of sadness came over me as I thought of my hometown. "The sea market was never the same after."

So much death and destruction because of Terran's rule. It made me more determined to find the scepter and help Carrick ascend the throne to bring back peace and stability to the kingdom.

Aiden looked at me and furled his brow with concern. "That's right, you grew up on the southern coast. Was the tidal wave how your parents were killed?"

I shook my head, remembering I'd never told Aiden much about my family. We hadn't been allowed to speak back at the palace. But now he was my closest friend, and I couldn't imagine being with anyone else on this journey to find the scepter.

"They were killed by pirates after the flood. Terran hired mercenary pirates to kill Miyu, and he allowed them to pillage the coastal villages without punishment."

Aiden placed a hand on my shoulder. "I'm sorry."

The memory of killing Terran replayed in my head—the notes of the song that left my lips, the skin melting off the former emperor's body until all that was left were his bones. At least I had gotten my vengeance. And now I had the chance to help change history, to secure the future of the kingdom and make sure other girls grew up without worrying that a corrupt emperor would snatch away their dreams.

Aiden and I came to a street corner where two drifters sat on the pavement. They held tin boxes that contained a few spare Seran coins. Their unbathed stench traveled through the air, a mixture of rotting meat and sour pickles. Hordes of gnats clustered above them, and they scratched at their grungy hair, which was probably infested with lice.

I didn't have much money. Between Aiden and me, we had about a hundred Seran that Carrick had given us when we escaped from the palace. But it was more than enough to buy the supplies we needed, and once we crossed the border into Yao Kingdom, the leftover money would be useless. So, I put a coin in each man's container. As I did, I kept my head low, using a scarf and the hood of my cloak to veil my face as an extra precaution.

But they merely bowed their heads, accepting the gift. We passed them and continued to a newspaper stand. Other than the stand and its vendor, no one else was out and about.

Aiden handed the vendor a Seran coin and picked up a newspaper dated from a week ago. There was nothing more current. We moved to the side of the street and scanned the front headlines.

The first headline caught my eye.

## MORE REFUTATIONS TO PRINCE NELAN'S CLAIM TO THE THRONE

While many in the court of Cedar Palace and the Seracedar army have surrendered to the service of Prince Nelan, there is still a large faction that remains loyal to Prince Carrick. Carrick's supporters have escaped to the eastern part of Senlin City where Prince Carrick is reported to be gathering his forces to challenge his younger brother. Another group of rebels, growing in number, believe neither Nelan nor Carrick is fit for the throne, claiming it may be time for a new dynasty.

The rebel faction asserts the Sacred Cedar Scepter in Prince Nelan's possession is a fake, since the kingdom has yet to formally witness Heaven's light illuminating through him to grant him tin-chai amplification. If neither he nor Carrick can prove tin-chai amplification, they refuse to acknowledge either prince as Seracedar's true ruler.

Meanwhile, the remains of Princes Jalin, Poyo, Frill, and Quirl and their respective bodyguards were found in Senlin Forest.

"Damn," Aiden whispered, clenching his fists.

"Evidence reveals the bodyguards were branded and whipped before they were killed," I read aloud. "Nelan claims he has no knowledge of how this came to be, but he believes Prince Carrick's faction was responsible for these cruel executions."

Aiden's jaw was tight, and fury reflected in his eyes. "Those four princes were just kids, the oldest of them not even thirteen years old. And Nelan is intent on smearing Carrick's name."

I felt the onset of a sudden headache grinding at my skull. I massaged my temples. I remembered Carrick telling me how he had been forced to kill his other brothers before they killed him.

"Even if we get the scepter back for Carrick, there's no guarantee he'll receive tin-chai amplification," I said. "And what if we can't find the scepter? Or what if Nelan doesn't agree to surrender even if Carrick proves his right to rule?"

"I believe Old Grandfather Heaven will bless Carrick with the right to rule, and you have to believe, too," Aiden whispered. "Our only mission for now is to get to Emberwood. Focus on our goal. Once we're there, we'll figure out how to locate the scepter. Perhaps we can ask for an audience with the Emberwood king. If he agrees to stand by Carrick, and Emberwood Kingdom becomes our ally, then Nelan will feel pressured to step down."

"Why would the Emberwood king help us?" I frowned. "Given the history of Emberwood's break from Seracedar and our present-day political differences, the king wouldn't want to get involved. Besides, he believes Terran was responsible for the disappearance of his only son. King Ashbel would probably rather watch the fall of Seracedar and cherish it. And if that happened, he could even take advantage and seize control of Emberwood."

A strange look came across Aiden's face. One I couldn't quite make out.

"That wouldn't happen," Aiden said. "The king is content with his own kingdom. He's not power hungry."

"How do you know?" I asked. "My brother said there are some who support the reunification of Emberwood and Seracedar. King Ashbel might want to find the scepter for himself and attempt it."

Aiden frowned. "True, there are people in both kingdoms who believe reunification would benefit us all. Seracedar would become less fearful of modern technology and advance, and Emberwood would learn to cherish her roots and some of the old traditions instead of completely trying to rewrite and deny her history. It may happen one day, but King Ashbel won't be the one to do it. Anyway, we're straying off topic. Right now, we have to hope the king will be open to our appeal."

"All right, then." I said. "Do you have any ideas on how to do the impossible?"

"I was born in Emberwood. My parents had great influence in court, and if they are still alive, they could help me persuade the king."

I'd forgotten Aiden was an Ember. "You rarely speak of your family. You must be thrilled to be reunited with them after all these years. They'll be overjoyed to see you."

"Or angry I didn't return sooner," he said.

Come to think of it, I wasn't sure why Carrick hadn't allowed Aiden to go free. The two of them seemed to be more like brothers than master and servant. Yet I supposed I wasn't surprised. Carrick wasn't one to go against tradition, even for his friends.

"Well, you couldn't help being held as a slave in the palace, right?"

He made no reply. "We should get going."

We made a stop at a small general store that sold some food. The fruit smelled rotten, and black mold had developed on the apples.

We would still be able to hunt until we crossed into Yao Kingdom. Hunting for meat wouldn't be an option then. The Yao might think we were trying to hunt them.

Thankfully, the general store had dried fruit, nuts, and crackers. The crackers were probably stale, but it was better than going hungry.

Aiden also picked up a bag of what looked like black masks and a vial of liquid labeled "Camphor Oil."

"What's all that for?" I asked.

"We'll need it in Yao Kingdom," he said. "I'll explain when we get there."

After paying quickly for the goods, we left the store and proceeded into the town square, where we passed several wanted posters plastered to the street posts. Sure enough, there were portraits of Aiden and me.

Aiden whispered into my ear. "Don't be scared. No one will recognize us."

Despite his reassurance, I rewrapped my scarf tighter around the bottom half of my face, so only my eyes remained unhidden. Then I scanned the notice under Aiden's name.

## AIDEN LANG

Wanted for treason and the murder of His Majesty, Emperor Terran. His Highness, Prince Nelan, asks all honorable subjects to be on the alert for this dangerous criminal. He has the tin-chai to form fire with his hands. Compensation will be awarded for his severed head.

My gaze caught sight of the reward money. *Three million Seran*. I gasped.

The poster next to Aiden's showed a sketch of Androgy Haming. *Wanted for treason and the murder of His Majesty, Emperor Terran. Compensation will be awarded dead or alive in the amount of two million Seran.*

"At least I beat Haming, but we both have nothing on you," Aiden whispered.

I followed his gaze to my wanted poster.

## RILLA MARSEAS

Wanted for treason and the murder of His Majesty, Emperor Terran. Must be handed to the palace ALIVE, or no compensation shall be awarded. If captured, reward money shall equal five million Seran.

"Don't worry," Aiden said. "The soldiers will be reluctant to pass through here. The only inhabitants are those with no choice but to remain. I think we can stay the night as long as we're careful. We'll go to the monastery. The Crocuses and Lotuses are obligated to provide refuge to those in need. At least we'll have a bed to sleep in one last night before a long trek through Yao Kingdom. You remember our story, right?"

I nodded. "Brother and sister. I have a disease marking my face, so no one in any other town will let us stay."

We continued along the street. The sun was setting behind the hills. In the distance, a wide domed building that looked like the head of a truffle was nestled atop the ascending hill. That must be the monastery Aiden mentioned. Burnt-orange paint spots dotted the pale-brown umbrella rooftop. At least a hundred stone steps had been built leading up the hill. By the time we'd climbed them all, I was out of breath.

We entered through the large, iron gate into an outdoor courtyard paved with stone. Two bald monks dressed in sun-kissed yellow robes greeted us with humble bows. I couldn't tell if they were men or women. Their palms pressed together respectfully, fingers as straight as arrows pointed heavenward. Hanging around their meekly curved necks were long strands of dirt-brown beads, spheres the size of crabapples.

We walked into an entrance hall. Half a dozen monks were busy sweeping the hall, dusting tables, and polishing plaques. The smell of citrus, musk, and myrrh incense was so strong it made my head swim. I tried to breathe through my mouth instead of my nose.

I looked around at the gold-plated name plaques, wooden statues, and stone-carved figures of holy people from throughout history. One sculpture depicted the head of a woman bowing reverently in prayer.

Another was of a saint—also a woman—sitting cross-legged in meditation. Large tapestries filled the lengths of the walls. I stopped to study one of a lotus flower. Above it, a cedar tree in the shape of a cross bridged the gap between the flower and heaven.

I'd never been immersed in religion, though I did believe in and prayed to Old Grandfather Heaven. So I respected the religious traditions enough to have learned about them. The symbolism behind that tapestry was yet another reminder the Sacred Cedar Scepter was supposed to connect us with Heaven, with the emperor acting as a conduit.

A tall monk with round glasses came toward us. The other monks paused from their tasks as well and gave us curious stares. When I got a closer look at them, I realized they had smooth skin and no beards, and some had feminine features. These monks were women. No Crocuses, the brother monks, here. This was an order that consisted strictly of sister Lotuses.

The first thing I noticed about the tall monk was that I couldn't feel her wyis. Ever since I'd discovered Androgy Haming's wyis was like a torrent rather than the common steady trickle, I'd practiced the ability to read the strength of a wyis in most people I met. It was almost as though this monk didn't have one. Or she was hiding it. Maybe it had something to do with the practices of the monks to maintain their inner peace.

The monk was so controlled, I couldn't feel her breathing or her heartrate. That must have been contributing to the masking of her wyis.

"Welcome, my children. I am Dahlia Nin, the head of this order."

Dahlia Nin was unnaturally beautiful, with speckled violet eyes set on soft sugar-white skin. Her features made her look ethereal, like she wasn't human but artificially created, grafted together with perfect facial features. Her flawless skin looked synthetic and pliable.

It was hard to discern how old she was—she could have ranged anywhere from my age of almost seventeen to the latter end of her thirties.

Aiden held his palms together and bowed his head respectfully, addressing the Dahlia and the other Lotuses. "My sister and I are seeking shelter for the night. She has a rare skin condition. We've been denied at every inn in all the neighboring towns. But I promise the disease is not contagious. If it were, I would be pockmarked too, and as you can see, I am not." He flashed her a charming grin, turning his face from side to side.

*Old Grandfather Heaven forgive us for speaking lies to a Dahlia.*

"You are welcome in the House of Heaven," she said, politely bowing once more. "Rest assured, you are safe in this holy sanctuary."

The fading sunlight streamed through the window and glinted off a small piece dangling from the Dahlia's right earlobe. She wore an earring, and I couldn't help staring at the unique design. The earring was made of pure gold and shaped as a bird with the hilt of a sword in its mouth.

It was unusual for a monk to have an earring, especially one made out of precious gold. Lotuses and Crocuses were dedicated to living simply. But perhaps this order lived by a different set of rules.

Aiden bowed back to her. "Thank you and the Lotuses for your hospitality, Dahlia."

Not one to shrug off manners, I followed suit and thanked the Dahlia as well.

"Teer, will you ask the kitchen to prepare a meal for our guests?" the Dahlia said to a younger woman.

Teer had a smooth-shaven head as well. She didn't wear the robes of a holy Lotus but instead dressed like a woman of the world, clothed in a black and white kipa. Perhaps she was not a sister but someone who also sought sanctuary. She wore a gold pin. It was the same bird with a sword in its mouth as the one on Dahlia Nin's gold earring.

Teer regarded Aiden and worried her bottom lip. Two creases formed in her brow. Not quite a scowl. More like distrust and a flicker of fear reflected in her brown eyes. "Must we have a man stay here?"

Another Lotus stepped forward and cast Teer a chiding glance. "Do not question the Dahlia. We accept anyone who requires sanctuary."

"Yes," Dahlia Nin said. "It is the law of Old Grandfather Heaven for us to help anyone in need."

"I am uncomfortable with a man staying overnight," Teer said.

"I know you are new here, Teer, and you haven't yet learned our ways," Dahlia Nin said. "But if you are to successfully become a true Lotus, you must obey the rules Old Grandfather Heaven has dictated for us in the Tenets of Heaven."

Ah, so the woman was a Lotus-in-training.

"Now, please go to the kitchen as I asked," Dahlia Nin said.

The woman bowed, but her cheeks heated from the rebuke. "Yes, Dahlia. At once."

"The rest of you may continue with your work," Dahlia Nin said, dismissing the other Lotuses. To us, she clasped her hands together in a gesture of respect and bowed her head. "Follow me. I'll show you to your room."

# CHAPTER 2

✦ ✦ ✦ ✦ ✦ ✦ ✦ ✦ ✦ ✦

We followed the Dahlia through a corridor cloaked in darkness but for the faint light from the candles hanging on the wall. The catacombs were still. Sticky strands of cobwebs hit my face, and I brushed them away frantically, combing my fingers across my suddenly itchy scalp. My skin crawled.

A couple of roaches skittered across the floor, their cauldron-black bodies making me jump away and shudder. Like the rest of the town, the monastery was in clear need of tidying up.

At least we'd have a roof over our heads for one night, a nice change from sleeping on the forest ground. But we were only traveling further into danger, into a kingdom that saw us as enemies. Regardless, we had to get through this. For the sake of our kingdom's future.

We stopped outside a door, and Dahlia Nin jingled some keys and unlocked it. "Here we are." She opened the door and gestured inside.

Musty, dust-filled air greeted our noses. Aiden took a whiff and sneezed.

The Dahlia flashed an apologetic look. "I'm afraid we haven't been able to clean lately. Most of our order is only recently returned from a three-month mission to the neighboring orphanage."

I was reminded of my friend, Radi. She had been brought up in an orphanage in this province, not far from this village. She'd suffered so much—losing her family, forced into the palace, and turned into Terran's caged bauble. She was at Carrick's safe house now, and I hoped he continued to protect her. I prayed that Nelan wouldn't win and Carrick would defeat him.

My eyes stung at the thought of Radi and Carrick, but I blinked away the tears. I had to focus on the present moment, release all my worries tonight, and take advantage of the sanctuary at the monastery to get enough rest. Only then would I have the energy to travel through Yao Kingdom and then into Emberwood. I reminded myself that once Carrick was on the throne, Radi would be safe. Carrick would free all the novelties and baubles. Radi and those women would have a chance at a happier life. But it all depended on Aiden and me. We had to find the scepter.

"Teer will bring your supper soon," Dahlia Nin said. She bowed and closed the door behind her.

The walls appeared gray though I was certain the original paint was white. Other than one small cot and a washstand, the room was bare. There was a suspicious musty, sour smell, likely from mold growth. A suspicious sound, a grinding of sharp teeth or clawing of nails, came from somewhere in the ceiling. A rat. I wondered if it had friends. Goosebumps formed on my arms, and I shivered. But this room was still better than a cage at the palace. Or the hard ground of the forest.

"There's only one bed," I said.

"Guess we'll have to cuddle," Aiden replied with a coy bat of his eyes.

I blushed and averted my gaze.

He chuckled. "You should know by now that I'm only teasing. Don't worry, I'll take the floor."

Without complaint, he pulled out a blanket from his knapsack and laid it out on the cold, sickly-green tile. Then he lay on it spread-eagle, looking as though it were the most comfortable mattress in the kingdom.

He rolled to his side, facing me. "It will take about two more weeks before we reach the tail of Yao Kingdom."

I dusted off the bed and sat on the covers, leaning my back against the headboard. "I hope we don't get attacked. I won't be of much help to you."

Aiden had taught me some basic self-defense during our time in the woods. If we came up against a Yao, though, there was no way I could win unless I used my voice to kill our attacker. And I didn't want to kill anyone.

"I think you're stronger than you believe," Aiden said.

I scooched forward on the bed. "We have some time now. Can we practice some moves?"

"What kind of moves do you have in mind?" he asked, waggling his eyebrows.

I swatted his shoulder. "Be serious."

He grinned, then stretched, slowly sitting up on the floor. He reminded me of a lazy maocat. "All right. Try to tackle me."

I got off the bed, went to the other corner of the room, and gauged his casual posture. He sat with his back facing me. There was no way he could stand fast enough to avoid my attack.

I charged. He moved, faster than my eye could see, and flipped me over. I went down with a thud, my face to the ceiling. His hands pinned my arms to the ground.

His mouth tilted up cheekily. "Rule number one. Don't let your enemy know when you're about to attack. Your breathing changes right when you're about to make a move." He stood, towered over me, and extended a helping hand, which I ignored.

"I can pick myself up, thank you very much." I sniffed, trying to maintain what was left of my pride. I faked a wince and rubbed my ankle, pretending that I'd hurt it. "I think I twisted something."

I limped to the bed, sitting down to examine my ankle. Aiden quickly came to my side. I bit back a smile.

"Are you hurt?" The concerned words were hardly out of his mouth before I rolled over, wrestling him to the bed. His surprise rebuilt every ounce of pride I'd just lost.

"Rule number two," I said. "Never underestimate the powers of a damsel feigning distress." I laughed at his bewildered expression and let him up.

He held my gaze. His deep, laughing, golden eyes were beautiful.

A knock on the door sounded, and we both flew apart.

I cleared my throat. "Come in."

Teer stepped in. She held a silver tray with small plates of food. "Here is your supper."

"Thank you," I said.

Aiden took the tray. Balancing it in one hand, he took a pair of chopsticks in the other hand and dug into the rice and side dishes. He frowned. "No meat? Oh, right. The monks don't believe in eating meat."

"Correct, meat is banned in the monastery," she said. "Eating the flesh of any animal—land, sea, or air—goes against our moral code. Our guests are expected to follow our rules as well."

I glanced at the tray of food. There was a dish of bean sprouts cooked with shredded carrots and a second plate of snow peas stir-fried with textured bean curd, which had a consistency almost like meat.

Aiden poked at the pseudo-meat and sniffed it.

Teer bowed. "If you do not require anything further, I will bid you a good night."

She made her exit, but I caught a look of unease mixed with revulsion on her face as she regarded Aiden. She quickly closed the door behind her.

"Did you see the look she gave me?" Aiden asked. "I don't think she likes me."

He placed the tray on the bed, then framed his face with his hands. "I don't get it. Look at this face."

I poked his shoulder and rolled my eyes. "Just eat your supper, Mr. Charming."

Taking up my pair of chopsticks, I stabbed at my food. I munched on a bite of bean sprouts first. Not bad. Then again, I was used to a mostly vegetarian diet. Meat was expensive back at Cascasea Village. We had eaten fish, but it had been rare for us to eat any two or four-legged creatures.

"How long will it take us to reach Emberwood Kingdom?" I asked Aiden.

"We still have a few weeks yet," he said with a sympathetic glance. "If only we'd been able to travel across Province Sen, we'd be there by now."

Unfortunately, that hadn't been possible with the palace on our heels. Although Emberwood was to the west, and it would have been easier to take horses on the main roads there, it was exactly what Cedar Palace expected us to do. But Aiden and I had gone northeast instead, intending to cross into Yao Kingdom, travel to Yao's northern coast, and book passage on a ship to Emberwood.

I'd always wanted to travel the kingdoms of Caliwyis, but I'd never dreamed I'd be doing so as a fugitive from the palace, or with the mission of saving the future of Seracedar Kingdom.

"Do you think the Sacred Cedar Scepter really is in Emberwood?" I asked Aiden.

"I think we have to follow Androgy Solar's direction," Aiden said. "He wouldn't lie to us."

The memory flashed in my head of Androgy Solar, Aiden's mentor and Carrick's androgy, dying in Aiden's arms.

I had tried and failed to use my healing tin-chai to save him. All my life, I'd wanted to use my voice to become a healer, for my songs to help others. Though my tin-chai had other layers to it, the most important aspect was lost, replaced by the ability to kill. How would I be able to save lives now?

I sighed, the thought of this bleak new reality bringing an aching wrench into my heart.

"Tired?" Aiden asked.

Again, I thought of Solar. Of his dying words. *Find . . . wielder . . . in Emberwood.*

"I'm sorry I couldn't save Solar," I said.

He gave me a sad smile. "It isn't your fault." He placed a hand on my shoulder and gave me a knowing look. "And you *will* recover your healing ability. Believe in yourself. I believe in you."

How did he always know what to say to make me feel better? I didn't know what I'd do without his faith and optimism. Without him.

Still, anxiety crept up as I thought about venturing into Yao territory. What if I needed to use my ability to help Aiden and I failed him?

My stomach churned. I'd lost my appetite. I placed down my portion of food onto the tray and watched Aiden eat.

"I think I'm going to sleep," I said.

I got under the covers. Aiden snuffed out the candle, but instead of going to bed, he sat in a corner of the room and used his tin-chai to form a dimmer ball of firelight between his hands so that he could still see without the light bothering me. He eyed his empty plate, set it down, then picked up my uneaten food.

"What are you doing?" I asked.

"If you're not going to eat this, someone else has to. I volunteer myself. Good night, Rilla. Sweet dreams."

I shook my head, smiling. He never ceased to amuse me. "Happy eating, Friend."

# CHAPTER 3

✦ ✦ ✦ ✦ ✦ ✦ ✦ ✦ ✦ ✦

A loud banging woke me. I rubbed my eyes and sat up in the darkness. I heard Aiden sit up, too. He groaned. "Who is it, and why are you interrupting my beauty sleep?"

A voice called through the door. "It's Sister Lotus Jenlin. I'm sorry to bother you, but this is urgent."

Aiden struck a flame in his hand, lighting up the room. He dragged his feet to the door, looked through the peep hole, and opened the door.

The Lotus rushed in, her eyes as round as the full White Moon. "The two of you need to leave at once. Nelan's soldiers have come."

I flew out of the bed, grabbing the few belongings I had and my bag from the floor. Aiden snatched up his as well.

"Dahlia Nin has told them they cannot come into the monastery, but not even the servants of Heaven can control the corrupt tyrants from the palace."

"How did they know to come here?" I asked Aiden. "I thought the palace wouldn't bother coming to Tinsai when they're so superstitious of the pestilence and ghosts."

"They wouldn't unless they were informed," Aiden said.

We both looked at Lotus Jenlin, who hung her head with embarrassment.

"I'm afraid it was that Lotus-in-training, Teer. She has her own ideas and has been reluctant to abide by many of our rules. I apologize on her behalf."

"I knew she didn't like me," Aiden said. "But I didn't do anything to her. Why would she turn us in?"

"It's nothing personal," Jenlin said. "We don't ask about anyone's past, but I believe something must have happened for her to be so distrustful of all men. Now we must hurry. The Dahlia is buying you some time, taking the soldiers in circles around the monastery, but she cannot put them off forever."

To my surprise, instead of going out the door and through the corridors, Jenlin approached the cot where I'd been sleeping and jerked it away from the wall, exposing a narrow hole, big enough for a single person to squeeze through.

"We're going through the secret passageway," Jenlin said. "It will take you into the mountains."

I slid through the gap, into the space behind the wall to find myself at the foot of a spiraling staircase that slithered its way upward.

We climbed the stairs, taking two at a time. At the top of the landing, we reached a tapered passageway so constricted I had to hunch my back to avoid hitting my head on the ceiling. The floor was covered in a slimy film that smelled foul, and fetid water leaked from the roof in a steady *pit-pat, pit-pat.*

"These passages are accessible throughout the monastery," Jenlin informed us. "You aren't the first fugitives from the palace who the Lotuses helped to escape."

Aiden paused. "Who else did you help?"

"I'm sorry, but I can't give you their names," she said. "It would be violating the vows of our monastery. What I can tell you is what I told them. This passageway leads into the Yupa Mountains, and if you continue on the trail for a few weeks, it will take you to the tail of Yao. I assume you are seeking a way to Emberwood through Yao Kingdom."

"Yes, we're hoping to sail to Emberwood from the northern coast," I said.

Jenlin nodded. "A wiser strategy than traveling by land across Province Sen. The guards fear the forests inhabited by the Yao and would prefer not to cross into their territory. Unfortunately, this means it is a dangerous route. I have heard terrifying stories of Yao attacks."

The ceiling finally rose, giving us room to straighten our posture. Ghoulish shadows moved with us along the walls. The dense air heaved with an acrid stench of decay. We passed the source—the festering clump of a dead rat. Flies hovered above the carcass like a cloud of steam over a boiling teapot. I hurried past, holding my breath.

Muffled voices sounded from the other side of the walls. The murmurs grew louder until I could hear every word. It sounded like we were right next to them. Jenlin gestured, placing a finger to her lips.

". . . insist I had no idea."

A man spoke. "Dahlia Nin, do not patronize me. I thought the servants of Heaven could not lie."

"I speak the truth, young man," the Dahlia said. "They said they were brother and sister. She did not look like the fugitive girl on those wanted posters, and the boy did not form fire with his bare hands."

The Dahlia wasn't lying. She'd never seen me without my scarf, and Aiden hadn't used his tin-chai in front of her.

"They tricked you, Dahlia," the man said. "And now they have escaped. Emperor Nelan will not be happy if you helped them in any way."

Emperor? That bastard had already declared himself as sovereign?

"Tell me what direction they went," the man said. "We need to know where they intend to go."

"I can assure you I have no idea," the Dahlia said. "But I think they did mention needing to buy horses in the next town eastward. Perhaps they mean to travel through Province Yupa and escape to Fauxhemia Kingdom."

If I ever saw Dahlia Nin again, I'd have to thank her for helping us divert the guards.

"If you mean to trick us, I will personally ask our emperor for the authority to execute you and your entire order."

"I assure you I have no intention of risking that," Dahlia Nin said. "But I am only trying to help. That is why I suggest you not waste any more time searching our tiny monastery. They're probably miles from Tinsai by now. Your emperor will certainly be displeased if you let them get away."

The man swore. Then boots stomped away.

"I hope we haven't caused trouble for Dahlia Nin and all of you," I whispered to Jenlin.

"All for the glory of Old Grandfather Heaven," Jenlin said. "If Nelan is searching for you, then I know you are on the side of good. Now hurry. This way."

She came in front of us, leading the way, and picked up her pace.

Through a series of winding tunnels, we walked. The muck on rotten wooden frames slowly blended into formations of rock. The caverns wormed into darker, deeper territory, signaling we were well into the mountains now. The walls arched upward. Pointed spikes of large stalactites threatened to stab our faces if we weren't careful. A flurry of black fluttered past my face. I stumbled back, clutching at my chest. My heart raced.

A shrill screech mingled with the shriek that escaped my own throat. Aiden reached out to steady me and tilted his chin up. My gaze followed his. Hundreds of black-winged beasts perched upside-down on their roosts, countless points of red glaring down at us.

If they decided to swoop down all at once, my petrified heart might shatter into thousands of shards. A draft of cold wind flooded in, penetrating the stifling, musty air in the cavern.

Then I saw a smidgeon of sunlight. The end of the cavern was in sight. As we came to the cave's opening, Jenlin stopped. "I must leave you here. I don't know if Dahlia Nin's strategy worked, but hopefully the guards have taken the bait and won't be following you into Yao Kingdom. I pray Old Grandfather Heaven protects you from the Yao shifters."

We bowed in parting.

"Thank you," I said.

"If Old Grandfather Heaven allows it, may we meet again," Aiden said.

We watched the Lotus's retreating figure. Then we faced the opening of the cave and trudged on, progressing further into the unknown. There was no turning back.

# CHAPTER 4

✦ ✦ ✦ ✦ ✦ ✦ ✦ ✦ ✦ ✦

We traveled at a quick pace for the first two days, stopping only to hunt and eat the wild birds we caught. We had to save the dried food we'd bought from Tinsai for when we reached Yao and could no longer hunt. It would take us another week and a half, at least, to reach the tail of Yao on foot if we moved quickly.

As we hiked up the narrow mountain trail, I took in the entire mountain range ahead. The serrated peaks of the profile forming Yupa Mountains created sharp, jagged pikes like a kaigon's back. They jutted into the glacier-blue sky speckled with white, willowy puffs shaped like moonrabbit cottontails and chubby shuroo cheeks. Silvery-white tiaras crowned the high-tipped crests, the snowdrops glistening as bright as fiery diamonds under the sun.

We followed the path of the river as it wended and weaved its way through a crackly wildwood bed along the mountainside. Daisies, hyacinth, and wild basil were scattered over the jade carpet of grass. A freshness washed the air with scents of cucumber melon and cool mint, banishing the remaining sullenness of winter.

When we were sure we were far enough away from the monastery and the soldiers were not on our tail, we relaxed, going at an easier speed that allowed for longer rest times, and when we weren't climbing the narrow, mud-strewn trails, Aiden and I trained.

I struggled to keep up with Aiden, who never seemed to tire. Every muscle and bone in my body was heavy and sore, and I discovered aches in muscles I didn't know I had. I forgot to be scared of how high we were in these mountains. Aiden made sure of that, always tossing out jokes and somehow able to distract me as we crossed narrow passes and rickety bridges. But his demeanor changed whenever he coached me, and for the first time, I realized how merciless he could be.

On our last morning before entering Yao Kingdom, Aiden and I woke to train. A songbird sang from within the shrubs. It hummed a morning medley with spirited gusto.

I held a training sword made of wood that Aiden had made to help me practice. He was teaching me to put more force into my training sword when I swung and to be less predictable in my attack. He corrected my form, straightening my arms and torso. "Use the power in your core."

I struck the sword down and let out a hearty yell. The bird chirruped a frantic alarm and flew away in a frenzy. I was sorry to interrupt its song. Aiden unsheathed his sword and demonstrated, cutting the air with his blade in a downward motion. The force generated a wind that hit a nearby tree, causing its branches to sway and leaves to rustle. "Remember, most of your power comes from your hips and torso. Try to attack me."

I struck the sword out, yelling a guttural sound. Aiden ducked effortlessly and grabbed my wrist, causing me to drop the wooden sword. He tossed me to the ground like I weighed no more than a sheet of parchment.

Stunned, I lay facedown in the dirt.

"Again," he yelled.

My breaths came in heavy pants. With a groan, I forced my wobbling jelly legs to stand. In all fairness, I had told him not to go easy on me because I was a girl. I wanted to be treated as his equal. And he'd done that. With each day that had passed, I sensed myself moving a bit quicker, and the moves Aiden taught became a little more complicated, forcing me to exert even more effort in my training sessions.

I picked up the training sword from the ground and ran at him, powering the sword down through the air. Again, he easily evaded my attack, somersaulting backward. This time, he used his foot to kick the training sword out of my hand. I stumbled in surprise, stopping before I collided into a tree.

He pretended to be affronted. "I already told you I'm not the kind of fellow to offer up his charms so easily. You may want to get your hands on this . . ." His hands extended, arching to showcase the entire length of his body. "But you're going to have to work for it."

I tried unsuccessfully to hide my amusement, but a gurgle of laughter erupted from deep within my chest. "You are *so* inappropriate."

"I suppose this is the result of having to suppress all my clever witticisms for ten years," he said, then stopped to quirk an eyebrow. "No, I'm pretty sure I said them anyway. Carrick just hit the back of my head when I got too annoying, or he chose to ignore me all together."

His expression straightened, and he once again took on the role of a strict instructor. He gestured to my head. "You have this habit of cocking back your head before you're about to attack. Takes away the surprise when your opponent can anticipate your move."

I curled my fists. Would I ever get it right?

"You will get it," Aiden said. Somehow, he always knew what I was thinking. "We'll keep working on it."

I leaned against a cottonwood tree. Aiden sat next to me and fished out a canteen of water from his knapsack. He took a sip and peered above the rim to assess our surroundings.

Lifting my gaze to the bare trees, I observed how their exposed branches looked like prayerful palms reaching toward the grayish blue sky. The wind brushed through the golden leaves on the ground, lifting them into the breeze. They reminded me of dancing flutterflies.

I shivered. The higher we'd climbed into the mountains, the colder it became, a reminder that although winter was at its close, spring had not yet come fully to life. Sunlight scattered like stardust upon the awakening dale. The lisping brook bubbled and gurgled, weaving a serpentine path through the crinkly crimson bed of fallen leaves. Patches of frost crystallized along the sides of the bank.

"We're about to cross into the tail of Yao," Aiden said. "We should discuss more tactics in case we're attacked. Be alert and stay close to me. Use your wit. Brains are far more effective than brawn in nine cases out of eleven."

"You made up that statistic just to make me feel better."

"Hmm . . . it's an educated guess. The gist of it is the truth. I've never met a Yao before, but I hear they're cunning. Especially a fox Yao. That's why it helps if you're cunninger than them."

"More cunning, you mean," I said.

He grinned. "That's what I said. Cunning-*er*."

"I've heard stories about the fox Yao," I said with a look of disdain. "That in their human form, the women trick men into their beds and eat their hearts to maintain their youth. And they have nine tails, which make for deadly lashes in a fight."

"Looks like you don't believe those stories."

"Those stories were made up by Shyan men," I said. "The same Shyan men who tell stories of how the Miyu are to be feared. I always think of how those men were the ones who attacked the Miyu first. How they took over the kingdom of Yao, made them hand over their gemstones in their mountains as tribute."

I tipped my head back, staring up at the sky. "But perhaps all the attacks against Shyan who have crossed into Yao Kingdom happened because the Yao were trying to protect themselves."

"I agree." Aiden leaned back against a tree, hands behind his head. "Nevertheless, the Yao and the Miyu are angry, and they don't care if we personally mean no harm. To them, we are no different than Terran. They will not show mercy to us, so don't take those stories too lightly."

He did have a point there.

"We'll have to watch out for the sleep-inducing fog," Aiden said. "Fox Yao create it when strangers get too close to their lair. Just like with alcohol, some people are less susceptible to its effects than others, but there's no way of telling who will be less affected."

"How do we make sure we don't breathe it in?"

Aiden handed me a black mask that tied behind the ears. It was from the bag of masks he'd picked up at the general store earlier. "These will filter the air. It won't completely stop us from breathing in the fog, but it will slow down the effects, giving us more time to fight or to run."

He took out a vial of liquid. Camphor oil. "The Yao won't be able to track our scent if we wear this. It weakens their sense of smell."

He smeared it on his neck and arms, and I did the same.

Then we sat in silence.

Aiden looked deep in thought. "I can't help thinking about Androgy Solar again, going over his last words."

"I'm sorry. I know you were close to him, and it must be hard."

"Yes, but that's not what I mean," Aiden said. "I was so sure he told us to find the wielder in Emberwood."

"Wielder, yes." I nodded. "That's the word he used."

"But I've been thinking. What if he actually said the name of the person who stole the scepter? Like Welder?"

"Who?"

"General Welder. He and another man, Captain Montier, were involved in leading the coup against Terran, but when that failed, they fled together. They were headed for Emberwood. When Jenlin mentioned that she'd helped fugitives from the palace before, I thought of them. Always suspected they may have escaped to Emberwood through Tinsai and Yao Kingdom. Also, I remembered suspecting Welder of being one of Empress Limera's lovers."

The empress had revealed that one of her former lovers had stolen the scepter from her. I gasped. "Do you think this Welder took it?"

"It's a possibility," Aiden said. "Especially if Solar said *Welder*, not *wielder* like I'd first thought."

I nodded. This did make sense. "You kept asking Solar for the name of the man, but he kept repeating *wielder*. I think you may be right. It does sound like *Welder*."

"And if Welder and Montier were the fugitives the Lotuses helped to escape, then they would have fled to Emberwood," Aiden said. "We should find Welder there."

"If he ever made it," I said.

Aiden's eyes shone with determination and hope. "He and Montier would have made it. They're survivors. And we are, too. We'll find them."

By nightfall the next evening, we were deep in the tail of Yao Kingdom. The forest had grown thicker and darker, and the trees seemed to meld together into one formidable beast. Dangling boughs twisted like the tentacles of a giant sea monster reaching to grab us. Damp moss clung to rotting wood, bringing with it a rank odor, decaying and pungent. A ghostly-white mist enrobed all it touched with its gossamer cloak. An eerie silence drifted through the breeze. Nothing stirred. Nothing shifted. Nothing dared to even breathe.

This didn't mean nothing was out there. We both put on our masks in case we ran into sleep-inducing fog, which Aiden said had a sweet smell and was almost invisible, distinguishing it from regular fog. As we settled down for the night, I shivered, feeling as though dozens of pairs of eyes peered through the bushes, simian-like and glowing demon-red.

"Get some sleep," Aiden said. "I'll take first watch."

For the longest time, all I could hear was the frantic pounding of my heart, but I forced my eyes shut. I meditated on silence and tried not to think about anything but the blank spaces in my mind.

The next thing I knew, Aiden was shaking me awake for my shift. I must have drifted off for awhile, but I didn't feel the least bit rested.

"Sorry," he said. "Wanted to let you sleep longer, but I can't stay awake."

His eyes drooped shut even as he spoke. Why was he so tired?

"It's fine . . ." I started, but Aiden had already crashed down on his blankets and was snoring away as though we were on holiday at the beach instead of in the middle of a forest where a Yao could ambush us any second.

I stared into the darkness. Shadows played in the trees, creating a netherworld between night and morning, which I imagined to be frequented by monsters, their bloodstained fangs glistening with silver-tipped drops of saliva.

Anxiety rolled over me. My overactive imagination played tricks on my mind.

Then I saw a mist rolling up from the ground. Barely visible. A sweet smell like cinnamon sugar filled the air. Sleep-inducing fog.

I made sure my mask was on tight, then shook Aiden. But his mask had slipped down, exposing his nose. No wonder he was out cold.

A boy emerged from the fog like a specter. He was young, no more than eight, half my height, and lanky. He walked right into the middle of our campsite. His hair stood out, stark white, and three tails wagged behind him under the silvery glow of the autumn White Moon.

A white fox Yao child.

I jerked to my feet and raised my fists.

"Hello," he said. "Sorry, but I don't think he'll be waking up soon."

# CHAPTER 5

✦ ✦ ✦ ✦ ✦ ✦ ✦ ✦ ✦ ✦

I froze, the hairs on my arms rising.

"How do you do?" Again, he greeted me with politeness, as though we were familiar acquaintances. He spoke with a slight accent and with the slowness of someone who was practicing a foreign language. "I apologize for the fog. Mama doesn't like strangers coming near our house, but I guess it didn't do nothing to you. Don't worry, it wasn't a big dose. Your friend should wake by morning."

The boy seemed not to sense my fear. He had adorable chubby cheeks and a wide, animated grin. His eyes were wide and innocent. His features almost made me forget the danger that his kind posed.

He hugged his gray, moonrabbit fur coat closer to his body and patted his belly. "Do you have any food? I'm so hungry I could eat about twenty . . . twenty . . . what's the name of that animal you Shyan like to ride around?" He paused, thinking. "Oh, I remember. Horses. I could eat twenty horses."

I hesitated, taken aback, before replying. "Umm . . . sorry, I only have some dried cranberries."

The boy wrinkled his nose. "Awww, never mind then. I don't like fruit." He propped himself on a rock. His burlap trousers made a soft swishing sound as he swung his legs to and fro. It seemed like he couldn't stay still. "That's weird. I can't smell you. I guess that means Mama won't be able to smell you, either, so it should be safe to talk for a bit. I've never met a real-life Shyan before. This is the first time I can actually practice speaking Shyan."

His eyes were giddy with excitement and curiosity. "By the way, my name is Wyle."

*Should I give him my name?* I wasn't sure I wanted to. But he didn't ask.

"I've always been curious about outsiders. So, what're you doing here?"

"Just passing through," I said, still caught off-guard by the boy's friendliness.

"Where are you off to?" His sharp ears perked, and his pointed nose twitched.

"Emberwood Kingdom."

"Oh, that's glib," he said, his slate-blue eyes growing as round as a pie.

"Excuse me?"

"Glib," he repeated. "It's the word I say when I think something's interesting. I've always wanted to meet a Shyan to see if you're as horrible as Mama says. She swears you're all fools. Believe you're stronger than you are. But you don't seem like a fool. Although you don't talk much."

"Well, thank you, I think."

"I'm so jealous," he said. "You get to travel to other places. Mama never lets me go anywhere or do anything fun. We're foxes, the most prominent and respectable of all Yao clans." He raised his voice a pitch, imitating his mother. "Therefore, we must train our bodies and our minds to become the leaders of our kingdom."

My gaze darted around the area. "Where is your mama?" My stomach gurgled from nervousness. *Old Grandfather Heaven help us if she's here.*

"At a meeting with the Council of Southern Yao Clans," Wyle said. "I usually go with her, but I pretended to be sick so I wouldn't have to go tonight. The bear and the daowolf clans always fight about the boundaries of their hunting grounds. And the kaigon clan sulks because they think they should have more power than Mama. But our family has always been the leader of the Southern Clans, so it's Mama's job to settle disputes. The meetings last forever." He groaned, then stretched and breathed in the night air.

A breath of relief whooshed out of my lungs. Thank Old Grandfather Heaven his mama wasn't home.

He smiled sheepishly at me. "I did promise not to leave our den before she left, but I was so bored. It was fun talking to you, but I should probably get home before she comes back. And you should probably leave, too. She wouldn't like it if she knew—"

A sudden crash in the trees made us both jump.

"Uh-oh," he whispered. "The meeting must've ended earlier than I thought."

A wisp of white smoke curled into the air. It whirled around like a tornado before coming together to form the translucent image of a white female fox. Her fur was lustrous and iridescent, as though she were made of light from the White Moon itself.

Her back was arched, fur bristling, and dark blue eyes glinting at me furiously. Nine tails whipped through the air. They waved and whistled like a windstorm blowing through the trees.

The boy jumped, standing straight as a book spine. He bowed to the creature. "Mama." He laughed nervously and said something to her I didn't understand.

His mama's chilling voice filled the air, sounding like the echoes of a wailing ghost. I didn't understand a word of what she said, but it sounded horrifying.

The boy hesitated, looking back at me. "Mama, you're not going to kill this girl, are you?" He spoke Shyan. "She didn't do anything to hurt me. It was my fault for wandering from home."

One of her tails lashed out at me. I whirled away, barely avoiding a strike in the face. But the tail caught me on the shoulder instead. Tears stung my eyes, and I bit back a cry.

Before I could react, she wound another tail around my torso. A third tail bound my arms. She lifted me into the air.

Aiden still slept. The camphor oil must have masked his scent. Unaware of him, the fox Yao whisked me away.

I bobbed up and down like a tossing wave. I couldn't see anything but a blur. My body whacked painfully against the terrain as she carried me through a dim passage of tunnels. My head swam, and the world around me whirled like a carousel.

She flung me onto the ground, and pain radiated down my back. I blinked, trying to clear my vision. I was in a small den. In the center of the room, dozens of twigs were spread in a circle on the ground. The circle of twigs surrounded a mound of sparkling diamonds. A separate pile of bones lay in the opposite corner. I made out the skull shapes of rodents, moonrabbits, and humans. Shyan? I gulped.

Mama Fox bound my legs and hands with ropes made of fur, likely preparing me to roast over a fire.

The kit hung back in the corner. His mama bared her teeth and snarled. Her lean, lithe body swirled around the air and suddenly morphed into the form of a woman. Translucent skin and wild, snowy hair gave her an almost ghost-like appearance. Her fur also transformed around her body, clothing her in a flowing white gown. Long, fluid sleeves ran from her arms to the ground. The fabric seemed endless, like it would swallow someone up if it wrapped around them.

She addressed me in Shyan. "You have wandered where you are not wanted." Her voice no longer sounded like a wail but was rich, warm, and velvety. However, her words were far from warm. "Now you must pay the sacrifice. My son and I will feast on your heart tonight."

"But Mama, I don't want to feast on her heart," the kit said, trying to step in front of his mama. "We just became friends. Besides, Shyan hearts are icky. They have this mushy texture I don't like."

"Hold your tongue." She took him by the earlobe and dragged him to the side. He stumbled, whimpering. She scolded him in Yao, then pushed him down, forcing him to sit with his face to the wall. He massaged his red ear, folded his arms across his chest, and pouted.

She pointed at me and spoke to her son in Shyan. "You are never to be friends with a Shyan. They killed your father. They're self-righteous beings who believe they have the right to rule over us and steal our treasures. Then they turn around, calling us wicked and scheming when we refuse to cooperate. The Yao are honorable. We would allow even our worst enemy to die with dignity. The same cannot be said for Shyan, who humiliate their enemies before killing them, just as they did to my husband."

My skin heated from my neck to my ears. Never had I felt so embarrassed to be a Shyan. My legs shook. "I have nothing to say that would defend the actions of my people. It's true that we have committed atrocities against the Yao. But I mean you no harm."

"Hah!" She spat. "The only reason a Shyan comes to Yao Kingdom is to kill and steal from us."

"I promise that's not why we're here," I said, trying unsuccessfully to repress the tremor in my voice. "We are just traveling through."

Her eyes flickered dangerously. "*We*? You have a companion?"

*Fainting faela!* I bit my lip, cursing myself for slipping.

She sniffed the air, and the dark brown of her pupils transformed to blood red. "You must have masked your scent with camphor oil."

She turned to her son, who was still cowering in the corner. He moped, head hanging, but his ears twitched as his mama barked an order. "Make sure she doesn't touch our diamonds. I'll be right back. We'll be dining on two Shyan hearts tonight."

She morphed back into her fox form and floated out in a whoosh of fury.

The fox child untied my bindings and cast them away from me. "Come on. You have to get out of here before she comes back."

I massaged my wrists and straightened. "You're letting me go?"

"Yes," he said. "Mama hates Shyan, but Baba told me before he died that not all of you are bad. He told me to look at the person, and I think you're all right."

Bless the child for his innocence.

I followed him through the tunnel.

We emerged from the ground but had only taken a couple of steps when Wyle let out a shriek.

"What's wrong?" I glanced at the boy, who pointed to his feet. They had turned into paws.

"I stepped in a puddle of water," he said. "Salt water makes foxes change into their animal form, and we can't change back until we're completely dry. Until I become an adult like Mama, I'm much weaker and slower in my fox form."

"Why is there salt water here?" I asked. A bucket of water splashed down from a tree, dousing Wyle. He completely morphed into his fox form, a tinier three-tailed version of his mama.

"Fainting faela, what's going on?" I gasped.

A sudden blast of fire rained down, nearly singeing my hair. Above our heads, a bright golden kaigon Yao circled us, eyeing the fox pup next to me.

"Oh, no," Wyle cried. "It's a kaigon from a rival clan."

The kaigon said something to Wyle in Yao. Another blaze came crashing down, and I grabbed the kit, lunging out of the way. The kaigon shot another ball of fire. I cradled the fox kit in my arms and rolled behind a large boulder, barely avoiding the scorch.

"Translate," I told Wyle. "Why's this guy trying to kill you?"

"If he kills me, Mama won't have a successor. The kaigon clan will seize power. He's been waiting months for a chance to get me alone without mama and in my weakened fox form."

The kaigon flapped its wings, and his booming voice filled the air. He spoke in Shyan now. "I didn't expect to see a Shyan maiden tonight, especially one determined to help a fox child. You might as well give up, girl. If there's anyone I hate more than the fox clan, it's a disgusting Shyan. The only question is, do I kill you first, or the child?"

"What're we gonna do?" The kit panted. His stricken blue eyes gazed at me.

If only I could have a chance to sing long enough to not become roasted.

"There's no use hiding," the kaigon said. "Come out now." He blew out another stream of fire, blasting the boulder where we hid. The intense heat blistered my skin. I pulled back my hand from the rock and gasped. We wouldn't be able to withstand another blast.

I placed Wyle on the ground. "Stay here."

"What are you doing? We can't surrender."

"Trust me."

I revealed myself from behind the boulder.

"Hey, kaigon," I yelled. "You can take me first, but I've heard the Yao, especially the kaigon clan, are all honorable and allow even your worst enemies to die with dignity. So, would you allow me one last request before you kill me?"

The kaigon landed twenty feet away from me. He shifted back into a man. "True, we are honorable. What is your request? If it's in my power, I'll grant it."

"I'd like to sing a final song to say goodbye to this life."

He nodded. "I see no harm in that. Proceed."

I sang.

*"Wealth became his ev'ry need*
*Friends became the enemy*
*Helping hands met with hostility*
*Destroyed by the edge of his blade."*

The kaigon clutched his ears and writhed.

I continued singing.

A family of moonrabbits dashed from one bush to another, into my line of sight.

I tried to block out the family from my thoughts, but my tin-chai felt different from when I had used my healing power. Whereas before I could hone in on one person and focus my power on them, I felt my tin-chai flaring up like a wildfire, ready to ravage the forest and everything in its path. I had no control over it.

The moonrabbits dropped to the ground.

I stopped singing and shouted, "No!"

Next to the family of moonrabbits, the kaigon, a mere frame of the monster he once had been, lay motionless on the ground. But the four moonrabbits were my only concern now.

I ran toward them and fell on my knees. A mother and her three babies—all of them bled, their bodies twitching.

The last time I'd sang to heal, I'd failed to save Solar. But maybe my power had been restored since then.

I sang, trying to muster my healing power. But the words that left my lips sailed into the air and disappeared like phantoms.

I tried again. And again. It was no use. I had lost my ability to heal.

One by one, the moonrabbits stopped moving. I stared at their wounded bodies. Tears streamed down my face and hit the ground.

I was a death bringer now, not a life giver, and I brought death through the very thing I held dearest to my soul. Music.

I dug my nails into the earth and sobbed. The emotions were so overwhelming, my whole body shook. Pain sliced through my back and my arms, and I realized I was burned and bleeding, a combination of wounds from getting lashed by the fox Yao's tails and burned by the kaigon Yao's fire. My vision swam, threatening to black out completely.

Someone placed a hand on my shoulder. I gazed up into Aiden's face.

"I may never be able to heal again," I whispered. The black dots took hold of my vision, and I let myself pass out.

# CHAPTER 6

✦ ✦ ✦ ✦ ✦ ✦ ✦ ✦ ✦ ✦

I opened my eyes, slowly coming to awareness. I lay propped against a tree. Comfortable, woolen blankets were wrapped around my body. Sun spilled from between the trees, the light reaching my eyes.

I scanned the surrounding forest. This was the campsite Aiden and I had set up. Aiden sat a few feet away from me.

"Thank goodness you're awake." Aiden rose from where he'd been stoking the fire and approached me.

Pain shot through my brain. I winced. There were aches in several places on my body, but the burns on my shoulder and arm smelled like menthol from carob bark balm. Aiden must have applied it for me.

Aiden kneeled by me. "You've been sleeping for over a day."

That explained the headache. The vision of the dead moonrabbits played in my mind. I'd killed them. I let out a shaky breath, and the sting of tears rose to the rims of my eyes.

But at least I'd saved the fox child. Hadn't I?

I looked around. "What happened to the fox boy and his mama?"

"You mean Wyle and Sago?" Aiden gestured behind him, and I saw the foxes.

The fox boy, Wyle, cried out from behind Aiden. "Rilla, I'm here."

He ran to my side and gave me a hug, making sure not to disturb my bandages. His mama, Sago, stood politely a few feet away. Her voice was twinkling and melodic as she addressed me. "Thank you for saving my son."

Sago was completely different than she was when we were in her lair. She wasn't exactly smiling, but I sensed respect in those shimmering cobalt eyes.

"Wyle and Sago were waiting for you to wake up so they could thank you," Aiden said. "Imagine my surprise when I'm violently shaken awake from a drug-induced sleep, realize a fox Yao has me in her clutches, and just when I think I'm about to become fox fare, we stumble upon you slaying a kaigon Yao. Sago was impressed and grateful, so she decided not to eat us after all."

Sago came closer to me, extending her hand to my forehead. Her skin was cool on my skin. "You've been burning with fever," she said. "But you seem to be getting better, thanks to the medicine I gave you."

She returned to the fire. A cauldron sat above the flames. Sago stirred something within.

"I have gathered some herbs that will help you recover your strength," Sago said. "I quite apologize for the cuts my tails left on your body, but I used the carob bark balm Aiden provided on the most severe lacerations. I hope they don't leave lasting scars."

"I think the burn marks from the kaigon were more serious," Aiden said. "Still, you took quite a beating."

"Again, I am truly sorry," Sago said. "I am distrustful of most Shyan who venture here. Many of them only want to steal our gemstones. Yao gemstones are the conduit for a kind of blood magic, you see."

"Blood magic?" I repeated. "I've never heard of it."

"I have," Aiden said. "Though I haven't seen anyone use it. If you wear the gem and place three drops of someone's blood upon it, you can use your wyis to channel their tin-chai. It even works for non-

Shyan and for stealing other kinds of magic."

I frowned. "What do you mean?"

"If I stole your blood, I'd be able to use your tin-chai," Sago said. "But if you stole my blood, you'd be able to use Yao magic, transform into a nine-tailed fox and use those tails to fight. And if either of us had an Ailo's blood, we'd be able to turn ourselves into rocks or trees or whatever form that Ailo takes."

"Ah, so I could perform any kind of magic in this world, depending on whose blood I had, even if I am not of the same race as them," I said.

"That's why Yao gemstones are rare and can only be bought illegally," Aiden said. "And it comes with a cost. If someone uses it with evil intent, it causes devastating side effects to their health. The emperor and empress collected the gems because they wanted to use the magic, but they never could figure out how without endangering themselves."

Sago's eyes shone with fury mixed with sadness. "My husband was killed by a Shyan poacher who tried to steal our family diamonds. At the end of the war between our kingdoms, we agreed to pay tribute with regular gemstones if we could keep our family gemstones. Yet, the Shyan remain greedy. Many of my friends were also victims. Your Emperor Terran did nothing to stop the poachers, and he even declared us dangerous and uncouth for defending what belongs to us."

"I'm sorry, Sago," I said. "No wonder you were distrustful of us."

She gave me a reassuring smile. "And yet I forget not all Shyan are as terrible as those fools in Cedar Palace. I did not see the scar on your face at first glance, only after you killed the kaigon. You are the girl who killed Terran. Your reputation has traveled to these woods. The girl with the magical voice that heals and kills. The Shyan might regard you as a threat, but when we Yao read about you, we were impressed."

I glanced away with sadness. I thought about the moonrabbits that had died before my eyes. And about Solar. "The magical voice that only kills now. I can no longer heal."

"You will again," Aiden said.

But even his optimism wasn't enough to pull me out of my slump today.

"Your voice is powerful nonetheless," Sago said. "It is you, not your magic, that makes it so. If not for your bravery, that kaigon would have killed my son. I am eternally grateful to you, and I must ask you how I can repay you."

"There's no need to repay me," I said. "I only did what was right. But I do hope we can be friends from now on."

"Yes, of course," Sago said. She ladled some of the liquid from the cauldron into a bowl and brought it to me. It was a black concoction and smelled foul. I knew it would taste ten times worse. But my brother had always said the more bitter the herbs, the more potent the cure.

I took a whiff, wondering if I could guess what was in it. "Yonlin leaves and goldfeng husks."

"Ah, so you have some knowledge of medicine," Sago said.

"My dream is to be a healer," I said. "Was. It *was* my dream to be a healer. Before my voice lost its purpose."

A concerned look passed over Aiden's face. "Your healing tin-chai will return. I don't believe it's lost forever."

"You don't know that," I said.

He opened his mouth, probably to argue more, but Sago laid a hand on his shoulder.

"There is no use speaking of that now," she told him. "The girl needs to take her medicine and rest."

I drank down the bitter concoction, and Sago took the bowl away from me. She smiled kindly. "Sleep now. Everything else can wait."

As if her words had magical power, my eyelids grew heavy, and I drifted into slumber.

# CHAPTER 7

✦ ✦ ✦ ✦ ✦ ✦ ✦ ✦ ✦ ✦

It took almost a week for me to recover my energy. My appetite returned, and I was able to join Aiden, Sago, and Wyle for supper around the fire.

Aiden grilled three wild birds he'd shot earlier, and he made a soup of mushrooms and vegetables. Sago and Wyle shared a meal of raw hearts from the birds that were on the grill. Despite how unappetizing that looked, my stomach growled as I smelled the grilled meat.

Sago filled a cup with water and passed it to me. "I believe you've recovered enough for us to begin our journey to the coast, which will take us about ten days."

I took the water from her. "We?"

"Wyle and I will be accompanying you on this leg of your journey." She filled another cup and gave it to Wyle. "Aiden has already told me that you are passing through Yao Kingdom to the northern shores in hopes of finding a ship to Emberwood. I can help you."

Aiden grinned. "Sago has agreed to be our personal protective escort."

"These woods are dangerous for Shyan, as is the rest of Yao Kingdom. But if I am with you, the other Yao shall not bother you."

"I'm so excited," Wyle said. He forgot he was holding the full cup, and water spilled to the ground. "It's been so long since I got to see the ocean."

"Sago also said she knows someone who can take us to Emberwood." Aiden slurped some soup from his bowl.

Sago wiped food off Wyle's chin with the corner of her sleeve. "The Yao on the coast may not be as vicious as we are here in the woods, but they still dislike the Shyan. It may be difficult for you to find someone who will take you aboard their ship. I have a friend who will help you if I ask him for the favor. He owes me."

I took a small bite of meat. "Thank you. That is very kind and will make our mission somewhat easier."

"It's the least I can do after nearly killing you. I don't understand Shyan politics completely, but Aiden has been trying to explain some things to me."

Aiden took a big bite and chewed with his mouth open. "I told Sago that we're trying to help Prince Carrick defeat Prince Nelan. And we're trying to locate the Sacred Cedar Scepter in Emberwood."

"Here's where I'm having some confusion," Sago said. "Aiden says Prince Nelan has control of the palace and has declared himself the rightful emperor. But if he doesn't have the scepter, then he has no legitimate claim. Why would anyone believe he has the right to rule?"

Aiden took a gulp of water before replying. "Nelan has a fake scepter, but rumors are spreading of his deceit. He's losing supporters. Still, he's got staunch followers willing to lie. They claim they saw a light illuminate within him when he touched the scepter, evidence of tin-chai amplification. The only way to prove he is lying is to find the true scepter."

Sago furled her brow. "I see."

It was Wyle's turn to frown. "I don't get it. If you find the scepter and take it to Prince Carrick, does that mean he gets to become emperor?"

"Yes, if he proves he has the right to rule." I carved my grilled meat.

"But that's up to the scepter to decide. It grants power to the chosen ruler through the amplification of that man's tin-chai. Some say it happens as soon as the future emperor touches the scepter."

"I've also read in the historical records that one or two emperors did not get the Will of Heaven right away," Aiden said. "In these cases, the scepter had passed them over the first time, but it was the second or third time before their tin-chai was amplified. Usually it was because the current emperor turned out to be corrupt, and Old Grandfather rescinded his right to rule."

Wyle shifted his position and flexed out his legs. "How do you know Prince Carrick is going to have his tin-chai amplified? What happens if he's not meant to be the next emperor?"

Aiden flung the bones of his remaining supper onto the ground. "Carrick is an honorable man. No one else is worthy of the throne. Only he can restore peace and stability to Seracedar."

"Still," Sago said, "if he is indeed the chosen ruler, shouldn't the scepter naturally fall into his hands without anyone else doing the work to find it for him?"

Aiden scowled, and I knew he disliked where this conversation was headed. He'd advocate in Carrick's favor no matter what.

I interrupted before his temper got the better of him. "The scepter was stolen out of the kingdom, and Carrick is too busy defending his part of the city and his supporters to search for it himself. I think that just because someone needs help, it doesn't make him any less worthy."

Sago pulled back her sleeves and washed the tips of her fingers in a bowl of water. "Point taken. I hope your intuition proves correct then, and Carrick is worthy enough to earn the right to rule."

"I may not say my prayers as much as I should," Aiden said, "but I believe in Old Grandfather Heaven's judgment. He will find Carrick to be worthy."

Sago shrugged. "We Yao do not worship your Old Grandfather

Heaven, so it's difficult for me to comprehend how a deity could predestine a man to become a ruler. Rather, I believe in judging the character of individuals on my own. You seem to be loyal friends with Carrick, and I'd hate seeing you put your trust in the wrong man. I certainly hope he doesn't follow in his father's footsteps."

We sat in silence for awhile, and Wyle yawned and dozed off. He leaned against his mother.

"If Old Grandfather Heaven doesn't find Carrick worthy of the throne, then why would I have risked my life for him all these years?" Aiden asked quietly. He stared into the fire, seeming to address it instead of Sago. "I have no choice but to believe in Carrick and Old Grandfather Heaven's will."

Sago glanced at him. "I did not mean to offend you. It is in my nature to be suspicious, but perhaps I overstepped."

Aiden's gaze gentled. "You did not overstep. If I were an outsider, I'd probably be asking the same questions." He stood. "Excuse me. I'm going to take a walk. I need some exercise."

"Oh, dear," Sago said, watching Aiden's retreating figure. "I should not have asked so many questions."

"It's not your fault," I said. "Aiden has been by Carrick's side for many years. Carrick saved his life, and Aiden feels he owes Carrick a lot. I don't think it ever occurred to Aiden that Carrick might not receive the Will of Heaven, and if he does not, Aiden would feel as though he failed him."

"You seem to know Aiden very well," Sago said.

"Yes, he's come to be my best friend." I knew where Sago's mind was headed. "But we're only friends. Nothing more."

She gave me a knowing look. "If you say so."

"It's true," I said. "Besides, Carrick declared his love for me. He needs me. I would never betray him. Nor would Aiden. We both owe Carrick a lot."

"Needs you?" Sago repeated. "Do you love him?"

I wrinkled my brow. "You do ask a lot of questions."

Sago simply smiled. "Only the important ones."

"Carrick saved my family so the palace couldn't use them as leverage against me." I adjusted my position, tucking my legs under me. "We've been through a lot together. And what girl wouldn't fall in love with a prince like him? It broke my heart when I had to leave him, not knowing if I'd ever see him again. I would do anything to help him. So yes, I think I love him."

"However?"

I blinked at Sago. "Why would there be a however?"

"You said you think you love him," she said. "I sense hesitation."

"If I sound hesitant, it's only because things are complicated. I never thought we'd have a chance to be together. First, because I was in the showcase to become Terran's faela. But now? I believe in his destiny to become the emperor. But I wouldn't be happy in the palace. I don't want to become an empress or compete with all the faela in his harem for his love."

"I see." Sago nodded.

"And . . ." Why couldn't I stop talking? "When I was with Carrick in the palace, a part of me found it flattering to be needed by a prince. To affirm the goodness in him whenever he needed to hear it. But it also felt like I couldn't let him see the real me. I always had to be who he wanted me to be—a girl who believed in him and who never had any darkness of my own. I had to be perfect. It felt . . . burdensome."

I couldn't get over the memory of being at my lowest point when I was in the novelty cage. I hadn't been able to remain optimistic for him, and he'd scolded me for it, then walked away. He had expected me to be his light, but when I needed him to be my light, he'd only given me his shadows.

I shrugged. "In any case, even if I do love him, I know I will never marry him. I can't sacrifice my freedom, not even for love. But that won't stop me from helping him take the throne. Searching for the scepter makes me useful, like I'm part of something bigger than myself. I'm not just doing it for Carrick but also for my kingdom. Carrick is the only one who can restore peace."

Sago hugged her arms to her chest. "And what will you do after you accomplish this mission?"

"If I can no longer heal, then I must find another purpose. One that lets me live for something outside of myself." I stared into the fire, surprised by my own answer. I'd never thought about life beyond the palace and after this mission. When I'd been taken to the palace, I thought I'd be trapped there forever. "Honestly, in these past few weeks I've traveled with Aiden, I feel like I've been bathed in light. Even though we've been on the run, the darkness of the palace feels like it's getting further and further away. I think I'd be happy traveling the world for the rest of my life, meeting new people and helping them in any way I can."

Sago kept her gaze on me as though trying to read into my soul. "So, is marriage a part of your plans at all?"

"Not if it makes me feel confined. Marriage sounds like a burden."

She nodded slowly and shrugged. "Well, don't discount falling in love yet. A life traveling the world doesn't mean you can't fall in love, too. Besides, real love shouldn't feel burdensome. If that's how you feel with Carrick, then I don't think he's the one for you. Perhaps a friendship where one feels bathed in light could lead to something more."

Her implication could not be more obvious. But it was too dangerous to think about, and I could not let myself go down that road. I didn't need to complicate my jumbled emotions further.

I faked a yawn. "Sorry, Sago. I'm getting sleepy."

She grinned as though she knew I was trying to end this conversation. "All right, child. Get some rest."

Although I'd told Sago I was going to bed, sleep eluded me. Maybe it was because I'd been sleeping so much the past two days. Or maybe the light from the full Turquoise Moon kept me awake. Whatever it was, I could not turn off my mind.

Long after Sago and Wyle had gone back to their den, I heard Aiden return to the campsite. I opened my eyes a smidge, not wanting to give up my charade of being asleep. Aiden sat on a stone by the campfire. He bowed his head, seeming to be deep in concentration. He formed a small orb of fire in one hand, and something else was in his other hand. Colored glass. He blew on the glass, shaping it.

The light from the fire illuminated several shards on the ground next to him. Tiny glass beads. Why did they look familiar?

It couldn't be. The beads were from my pendant, the precious keepsake I'd inherited from my parents and taken with me to the palace. I inhaled a sharp breath and sat up.

Aiden lifted his gaze and saw me. His cheeks flushed. It was the first time I'd ever seen him embarrassed. "I thought you were asleep."

"How did you get the beads from my pendant?" I stood, walked toward him, and examined the beads next to him. They had once formed a tiny ship suspended within a glass globe until my necklace chain broke, scattering the beads across the ground of the Summer Gardens. It looked like Aiden had melted them down, allowing them to meld together as they cooled.

"My necklace smashed to pieces the day I stumbled on Radi's bauble cage," I said. "I didn't have time to collect the beads."

"I know," he said. "I saw you wandering into the Summer Fields. Thought you might get in trouble, but you managed to save yourself without my assistance. I picked up the remnants of your pendant from the ground. I didn't want anyone else to discover it and make the connection you'd been there."

"Oh," I said, my eyes widening. "That didn't even occur to me."

I had only been thinking of Radi then. Again, Aiden had kept me safe, and I hadn't known it until now.

"Besides, you were always playing with it around your neck, and I sensed how precious it was to you." Aiden still averted his gaze, his cheeks flushed. "It was impossible to recreate the ship inside the globe, but I thought I could make a new ship out of the same beads. Better than nothing, right?"

It dawned on me how much Aiden had done for me. When I'd taken the arrow for Carrick, Aiden had tended to my wound. He had visited my novelty cage every day to keep me company, to encourage me not to give up hope. In my loneliest moments, when I thought I'd been abandoned, Aiden had always been there. He'd protected me even though I hadn't known his name. He'd stayed with me when I needed him most.

I took a closer look at the new pendant in Aiden's hand. Though it wasn't quite finished, it was coming together into a dazzling piece of artwork like a stained-glass window in a monastery.

Aiden flashed me a rather sheepish look. "It will take a few more days to complete."

"It's beautiful," I breathed, noting the tiny hole at the tip of the ship where a chain could pass through. Now I would be able to wear it around my neck without worrying about it breaking again or about the beads spilling out. They were forever melded together.

He gazed sideways at me and self-consciously tossed his disheveled bangs away from his face. "I wanted to give it to you as a surprise, but I guess at some point it was inevitable that you'd wake up while I was working on it."

A sudden thought arose. "Is this why you've been staying up every night and taking over my share of the watch sometimes?"

"Partly," he admitted with a grin, "But mostly because I find it amusing to watch you drool in your sleep."

I gave him an indignant look. "I do not drool."

"It's all right. I find it endearing." He stopped fiddling with the glass and regarded me thoughtfully. "You know, it's a pity. If Carrick hadn't fallen in love with you, I would have tried to seduce you." My eyes bulged, and he laughed. "Look at your face. I'm teasing."

I frowned at him, thinking of my earlier conversation with Sago. "I wish you'd stop joking like that. I know you're jesting, but strangers might think you're flirting with me."

"What does it matter?" he asked. "Strangers don't care about us. Once we're back at the palace, I'd never joke like this. But now we're free to do as we please, and it's fun to tease you."

"If you won't flirt with me in front of Carrick, then why do you do it when we're alone?" I asked. "Aren't you afraid I might start taking you seriously?"

"You know better than that," he said. "We both know I cannot fall in love with you when you are promised to Carrick."

Why did I sense a question in his voice as though he were warning himself more than he was speaking a fact?

"I'm not promised to Carrick," I said.

"But *I* did make a promise." His voice was a low murmur. I almost missed it. Then, as though that moment of seriousness had never passed, he sent me one of his devastating, devilish smirks. "I'm glad we're friends and not lovers. Friendships last forever. Romance only complicates things."

My heart clenched. Was it disappointment I felt? Couldn't be. Though I'd confessed to Sago that I would never marry Carrick, I still loved him. Didn't I? But the feelings I'd had for him in the time under the Lavender Moon were no longer so potent. I realized they had continued to fade further the more distance I placed between myself and the palace.

Was I so fickle that my love could wither this quickly? But even if it had, it didn't mean I could replace Carrick with Aiden so easily.

No, I decided. I didn't feel anything for Aiden other than friendship.

Aiden did some sort of flickering trick with the fire in his hand, holding it over another piece of glass, and added it on top of the ship's bow. Although his actions were precise, he seemed a little absent-minded, deep in his thoughts.

Tears welled in my eyes. I hadn't fully grasped how much his friendship meant to me until now.

"I'm glad I know your name now." My voice choked up, and my cheeks heated. "I'll never forget your kindness and your warmth. I will always remember you as long as I live, and I hope we'll always remain friends."

He looked up again, eyes wide. His teeth flashed as he gave me a lopsided grin. "I hope so, too. I certainly wouldn't be losing precious sleep trying to put together a glass ship if I knew you were to forget me by morning. That would be awkward."

Just like that, any discomfort that had been in the air vanished, and as always, we sat at ease with each other in companionable silence. I watched as Aiden worked. He was talented, easily shaping the glass, cutting it down so the ship was intricate and detailed.

As he crafted the pendant, I hummed a song to fill the silence, making sure to keep my wyis out of it. It was a tune Aiden had often requested when I'd been a novelty—*The Lady of the Sea,* a sad, soulful song.

> *"The lady of the sea waded through the tide*
> *To seek the one comfort she could find*
> *At long last the sea yielded to her request*
> *The weeping waves heaved one final sigh.*

*"The lady of the sea saw her love again*
*He called her name, and she took his hand*
*They waltzed into the sunset, ne'er to look back*
*At the treasures left buried in the sand."*

"I love that song," Aiden said. "It's so hopeful."

"Hopeful?" I gaped. "The song is about the grief and loneliness attached to loss. The lady of the sea commits suicide because she can't get over her grief."

"Based on your interpretation, maybe," he said. "But not on mine. To me, the lady of the sea was able to move on. She may have lost her first love, but she didn't give up on love. Eventually, she found love again."

Never in my wildest dreams would I have come up with that interpretation.

I shook my head in awe of him. "Only you could turn sad lyrics about death into a joyful tune of healing."

He smiled at this. The fire in his hands faded. He yawned and stretched. "I think I'm done for tonight. It will take me a few more nights to finish."

He placed the melded glass and the still unfinished glass beads in a tin box, then stashed it in his knapsack.

"Thank you," I said. "I don't know how to repay you."

"Actually, there is something I want from you."

I nodded. "Name your price."

"I want you to promise me you won't give up on your dream."

I was so surprised by this request that I could only stare at him.

"Tell me you won't give up on reclaiming the power of your voice. I know you still have your healing ability within you." He rose from his seat and patted my head. "It's getting late. If you aren't going to sleep, then maybe you can take guard duty so I can get a few hours."

I nodded. I was still nowhere close to feeling sleepy.

He sat on his makeshift bed, then paused and faced me once more. "I want you to know, Rilla. To me, you're worth more than a million sleepless nights. Whatever it takes to keep you safe and happy."

He pulled the covers over himself and closed his eyes, leaving me to my own thoughts.

# CHAPTER 8

✦ ✦ ✦ ✦ ✦ ✦ ✦ ✦ ✦ ✦

Over the course of the next ten days, we made our way across Yao Kingdom. It was a grueling trek through the forested terrain, but I was looking forward to reaching the coast. When I'd been taken from my home, I honestly thought I would never see the sea again in this lifetime. I was certain I'd die in Cedar Palace and never cast another footprint into the wet sand or feel the waves flush over my skin.

I was thankful Sago and Wyle were there to act as our navigators. Sago's presence alone kept all other Yao from bothering us. We came across many. Although they cast us unfriendly looks, they limited their contact and spoke little. Most chose to only interact with Sago. Sago made sure we had permission from the local Yao who owned the territory whenever we set up a campsite. They never refused her. Nine-tailed foxes were highly ranked in the Yao hierarchy, and Sago was well known throughout the kingdom, having come from a prominent family.

I did worry that Sago was risking her reputation by traveling with Aiden and me, that the other Yao would challenge her for being friendly with Shyan. But Sago reassured me that no one would question her, especially because she spread the news that I had killed the kaigon Yao. That kaigon had been suspected of killing some children of other Yao clans, though there had never been proof.

Aiden continued to train me in self-defense with the training sword when we weren't hiking, and Sago watched, sometimes adding her own comments and showing us her fighting style. Wyle practiced alongside us. His mama made him. Though the poor child often complained, his mama wasn't having any of it.

"You need to get stronger and make your first kill if you're to grow your other tails," Sago said. "That will make me so proud, and you do want to make your mama proud, don't you?"

Wyle sighed. "Yes, Mama."

On the morning of the tenth day since leaving Sago's den, I woke to softly falling rain. The drops tickled my skin like the brush of flutterfly wings. The sky was slightly overcast, and the air was crisp and cold. We'd come to the base of the mountains. Traces of snow still clung to the peaks towering above us. Birds twittered in harmony, a chorus of praise. I breathed in a hint of salt. We must have been nearing the coast.

After a breakfast of fried trout and berries, we packed up our campsite and made our way eastward toward a small fishing village.

Sago gestured to the horizon. "My friend lives in Tamika Village. He'll most likely let you book passage on his ship to Emberwood first thing tomorrow. Or, if his ship is too small for the voyage, he'll know someone who can take you."

I'd become fond of the foxes, and I would be sad to part ways with them when we reached the coast. Sago had become rather like a protective mother to me, and Wyle was such an adorable kit. But foxes did not take to water well, so they couldn't come with us. Also, though Sago had put her trusted friend in charge of the Southern Yao Clans while she was away, she had to return to her responsibilities soon.

We finally heard the distant cry of gulls. Aiden increased his pace. "Come on. I can smell the ocean."

He was right. The quiet rain that misted on my skin smelled like home. The ocean was within reach.

Through another grove of trees, a clearing with a hill appeared. I ran up the hill, and just beyond, the blue-gray sea roared against the milky sands of the beach. White gulls called out, dipping their beaks into the water in search of food. I breathed in the salty air.

Laughing with joy, I ran down the hill, casting away my shoes. The wet sand sank beneath my feet like melted wax. It squeaked under my heels. I headed straight for the water, soaking my feet, drenching my clothes. The water was freezing. Behind me, Sago yelled that I was insane. But I didn't care. All I felt was the exhilarating rush of being in the sea again. I let this feeling of light and freedom replace the darkness and corruption that had once filled me at the palace.

Wyle shouted behind me. "That looks fun." He raced toward the water, but his mama grabbed his arm, stopping him.

I dunked my head underwater. The silken texture of the water lapped softly against my skin. Soft grains of sand tickled the bottoms of my feet, and the warmth of the sun sprinkled gentle kisses upon my face.

A splash sounded beside me. I twirled around and saw Aiden in the water. He'd removed his shirt. I blushed as I caught sight of his broad chest and the tattoo of a flaming torch emblazoned on his skin. It reminded me of the first time we'd met at the palace when I'd gone skinny dipping at the lake.

A broad grin threatened to split his face in half. "I don't remember the last time I've been to the ocean."

"Isn't it great?" I exclaimed and dreamily sighed.

"Better than great. Especially because it's payback time."

Before I had time to blink, a surge of water hit me square in the face. I spluttered in surprise. "Hey!"

He remained unrepentant. "This is for splashing me on the night we first met."

Again, he lapped up water with his hands and shoved it at me. I laughed and screamed, turning my head to the side, then barreled at the water with my palms, spraying it in Aiden's direction. Droplets flashed down my hair and the side of my face as I took pleasure in hearing the ripples of the splashing waves.

"Enough, I surrender!" Aiden called out. He coughed and sputtered as a ringlet of water from my hands caught him square in the face.

"That's right," I told him, laughing. "Never mess with a girl who grew up near the ocean."

We swam back to shore.

Sago pulled back, shuddering at the sight of us and the water dripping from our clothes. "What can you possibly be thinking? Look at you two. You'll likely both catch colds in this state."

She took her eyes off her son for a second, and Wyle seized his chance, inching closer to the water. A surging wave hit the shore, splashing on his feet. They instantly changed into white paws.

"You disobedient boy," Sago cried, snatching him back. "I told you not to get wet. Now look what you've done."

"Aww, I didn't mean to, Mama," Wyle said. "I've never touched the sea before. I just wanted to experience it once."

"Quiet. Now I have to dry you off. Come along, and no more nonsense."

Sago took Wyle down the shore to a cove hidden by high rocks. I imagined the child was in for quite a scolding.

"I wonder if that happens to all Yao or just the foxes," I said.

Aiden lit a fire. "I believe it's the land Yao, not those who come from the sea or the air."

Both of us tried to dry ourselves as much as possible. Aiden had a pensive look.

"What are you thinking?" I asked.

"Just wondering about Montier and Welder," he said. "If they had to trek through Yao Kingdom, they must have faced the same trials we're going through. But we've got Sago's help."

"Do you think they made it to Emberwood?"

Aiden skewered two fish he'd caught earlier and set them above the fire to grill. "I've always been a positive person, so I'm going to continue believing they did despite the odds."

Sago hiked back up the shore toward us. But she was alone.

As she took a seat next to me by the fire, I asked, "Where's Wyle?"

"Oh, he was talking all about how he wants to join you on a grand adventure, so he doesn't have to listen to me anymore," Sago said. Her tight-lined lips were stretched with annoyance, and her brow folded, forming two vexed lines between them in the shape of a wide V. "Frankly, he's been incredibly impertinent. He's crying and throwing a fit. I told him to stay behind at the cove to think about what he said, and when he's decided to change his attitude, he can return."

I didn't think an overprotective mother like Sago would ever leave her child by himself in unfamiliar territory. Was something wrong with her?

I read Sago's wyis. Funny, but I could barely feel Sago's wyis today. It was so weak.

"Are you feeling well?" I asked her.

Sago gave me a puzzled glance. "Yes, why?"

"Your wyis is extremely weak."

"Well, I am quite tired, I must admit," she said. "Disciplining my son is a trying task. But let us not speak of him right now. What are you two talking about?"

"We were speaking of our friends who escaped the palace a few years ago after the failed coup," Aiden said. "Montier and Welder. I spoke of them to you before. Even if they made it to Emberwood, they could be anywhere in the kingdom. I have to figure out a way to narrow the search."

Sago's eyes sparkled. "Yes, I remember now. I wonder, though. If they stole the Sacred Cedar Scepter after that coup, why wouldn't they have revealed it? They could have discredited Terran long ago."

"That's a good point," I said and looked to Aiden for his opinion.

But he frowned at Sago. "I never mentioned we suspected either of them for stealing the scepter."

"It does not take much to piece everything together," Sago said with a laugh. She glanced down at the shore. "Excuse me, I should go see to my son. I don't want to leave him alone for long."

She left us. I watched her walk away and frowned.

"Did something seem strange about Sago?" I asked.

"I was thinking the same thing," Aiden said.

"Her wyis was barely decipherable," I said. "Like someone who is suffering from illness or extreme fatigue."

Aiden's gaze flickered to the shore, opposite the direction Sago had headed, and he gasped. "How could I have been so stupid?"

I allowed my gaze to travel where he looked. Sago walked together with Wyle.

Aiden swore. "Torched timbers. We've been tricked. That had to have been Androgy Haming."

Sago and Wyle reached us. As the fire illuminated their faces, it was clear whatever had transpired between them had not involved Wyle crying. There were no tear streaks on his face. If anything, I thought maybe he looked a little sheepish.

Sago took one look at us and frowned. "All right, what's wrong? You two look like you've seen an evil spirit."

"An androgy we knew from the palace came here impersonating you," Aiden said. "Androgy Haming has a face-changing tin-chai. He's searching for the scepter, too, and he must have been following us all this time."

"He has a unique strong wyis," I said. "But he must have figured out a way to suppress it, make it less intense, so one who could read wyis like me wouldn't be able to detect his identity."

Aiden swore. "He was fishing for information, and we fell for it. Now he knows we're looking for Montier and Welder to find the scepter. We have to get to Emberwood before he does."

"The town is not too far," Sago said. "Since Haming is able to change into a Yao, he won't have a hard time finding passage to Emberwood. But the cliffs are rocky, and it's too dangerous to climb until morning."

"But what about Haming?" I said. "If anyone is able to climb rocks in the dark of night, he is."

"None of the sailors would agree to set sail at this time of night. Haming won't be leaving any time soon unless he steals a ship, but I doubt he would. There have been plenty of ships that disappear on the way to Emberwood. It takes an experienced seafarer to know how to avoid the dangers. We'll keep especially alert for Haming when we get into town. For now, we should get some rest."

# CHAPTER 9

✦ ✦ ✦ ✦ ✦ ✦ ✦ ✦ ✦ ✦

The sun chased away the darkness as wispy strands of light touched upon the infinite line where the sleepy-eyed sky met the glistening gray waters. Blushes of pink and purple bent down from the horizon, kissing the smooth plains of the sea. The soft hush of the waves hummed a sweet lyrical lullaby as they swept across the shoreline.

I yawned and stretched, sitting up and looking around to see if my companions were awake. Wyle was still asleep, but Sago, who had kept watch during the last leg of the night, and Aiden were awake. They spoke to one another in low murmurs.

I rubbed my eyes. "What are you two talking about?"

"I'm sorry. Did we wake you?" Sago asked.

"It's all right," I said. "We should get an early start to Tamika Village anyway."

Aiden grinned. "Well, before we go, there's something we have to give you." He reached behind him under his makeshift covers and then presented me with a sheathed sword. "No more training swords. I thought you could use a real one."

I took it from him. It was light, which I hadn't expected. I unsheathed it, and the blade glinted. It was sharp, but the material didn't look like iron or steel.

"Thank you. But where did you get this in the middle of Yao Kingdom?"

I'd been with him the entire time and hadn't seen him get the sword.

"Sago knows a daowolf Yao who specializes in weapon making," Aiden said. "She got it from him two days ago before we left the last campsite. The reason it's so light is because it's made out of the discarded fangs of daowolves. That also makes it stronger than any kind of metal other blades use."

"I hope you didn't spend too much on it," I said. "If it's too expensive, I can't accept."

"Don't worry," Sago said. "That daowolf is a friend, and I made sure Aiden got a good deal."

"Besides, I can't be the only one with a real weapon," Aiden said. "I might need you to save me one day. It's self-investment. And that's not the only gift."

"Something else? But this sword is already more than I could ever ask for."

"You can't refuse this gift," Aiden said. "I spent way too much time on it."

He extended his closed hand and then opened it. In his palm was a necklace with the ship pendant Aiden had been working on for me.

"It's finally done," Aiden said.

I took it and examined the craftsmanship. In the middle of the ship, something sparkled brighter than glass.

I gasped. "Is that a diamond?"

"Indeed." Sago smiled. "I saw Aiden making this pendant for you, and I asked if I could contribute. It's one of our family's diamonds."

"I can't possibly accept your diamond," I said. "It's too precious."

Sago pursed her lips in feigned displeasure. "If you don't accept, I'll take great offense. I consider you part of my family now, and after you saved Wyle's life, I want to give you something to remember us by. When you look at this pendant, may you think of all the people it represents. All the people who love you."

Tears prickled my eyes. "Thank you both." I held it out to Aiden. "Would you help me put it on?"

He took the necklace and fastened the chain around my neck.

"Make sure you keep it hidden under your collar," Sago said. "As I said, many covet these stones for their use in blood magic."

I nodded and slipped the pendant under the lapel of my gown. "Have you ever tried to perform blood magic, Sago?"

"No, I never had the need," Sago said. "Why? Do you want to learn?"

"It might come in handy," I said. "But is it safe? I mean, Aiden did say there are repercussions, that it could have devastating side effects on your health, and that's why Terran and Limera couldn't use it."

"Because they had evil intent," Sago said. "A pure soul will have no problem harnessing the magic at no cost to their health. However, it's tricky. It requires one to draw their wyis through all four channels—ha, ji, dai, and kai. And then, on top of that, one has to focus their wyis into mingling with the wyis in the other person's blood. Those with limited experience will find themselves drained and unable to use the magic they borrowed for long."

"Now that you've brought it up, let's try it," Aiden said.

Before I could stop him, he took out his knife and pricked his index finger. Blood welled out.

"What are you doing?" I exclaimed.

"Being your first experiment," he said. "I've never drawn my wyis through more than two channels, but I know you've used all four."

I hesitated. "That was only once, and I was under a lot of stress." If I hadn't done it, Emperor Terran's tin-chai would have turned me into a terracotta figurine. "I'm not sure I can do it again."

He pouted. "Please don't reject my blood."

I grimaced at him and brought out the pendant. Aiden let three drops of his blood fall upon the diamond.

"Focus on your wyis," Sago said. "Draw it into all four channels and into Aiden's blood."

I concentrated on my wyis, honing it as though I were drawing an arrow through a bow. I felt Aiden's wyis in that small amount of blood. Sweat poured from my brow and drenched my back. A lick of fire formed in the palm of my hand. But just as quickly, it died. My head swam, and I fell backward, dizziness overtaking me.

"Are you all right?" Aiden asked. His arm came around my shoulders, supporting me.

The dizziness faded. Aiden's and Sago's concerned faces hovered over me.

"I'm fine now. But you're right, it does take a lot."

"You had it, though," Aiden said, grinning. "And you didn't use up my blood, so you could try again."

Sago nodded. "With more practice, you could keep it longer."

"No more for today," I said, my gaze looking to the sky. The sun was higher on the horizon, and morning was well upon us. "I think we should get going."

"You're right," Sago said. She tended to Wyle, shaking him awake.

Aiden continued to grin at me.

"What?" I asked.

"You're amazing, you know that?"

"I wouldn't be amazing if I didn't have my best friend here."

"Oh, stop. You're making me blush." He fluttered his eyes and brushed me off with a wave of his hand, making me laugh.

We packed up quickly and headed across a rocky part of the beach. Sago was right. This would have been impossible to trek in the dark of night. Instead of fine sand, the ground was covered with large, unstable stones that wobbled beneath our feet. We had to concentrate to keep our balance. One stumble might result in a twisted ankle.

But once we crossed the rocky ground, the beach transitioned into sand again, and it was an easy walk down the rest of the shore.

We came upon the lonely, sleepy Tamika Village, even smaller than Cascasea Village. Half a dozen dinghies were tied to the pier, their hulls silently nodding to the rhythm of the sea's waltz. Heavy accumulations of black-green algae and rust marked their bottoms. I spotted several bigger ships farther down the pier, vessels merchants used to carry cargo on longer voyages. They were like the ship my baba used to own when he'd gone to Emberwood to trade. Baba had always promised one day he would take me traveling all around the world. I touched the ship pendant that hung from my neck. The last time he sailed to Emberwood, Mama went with him. And when they returned, the pirates killed them.

I shuddered at the memory. Back then, I had blacked out in a red haze, not knowing I'd killed the pirates with my tin-chai. If I hadn't killed them, they would have taken me and sold me as a slave.

Wearing this ship pendant made me feel as if my parents were traveling with me now.

I watched Aiden's back as he walked ahead of me. I was eternally grateful he had saved the only treasure I had to remember Mama and Baba. Maybe it was a strange notion, but I wondered if they had asked Old Grandfather Heaven to bring Aiden to me.

Aiden spun around and sent me a curious look. "Are you all right?"

"Sorry, just daydreaming." I rushed to catch up.

We continued down the pier. An old fisherman sat alone on the edge of the boardwalk, casting his fishing line into the dark water. Though his eyes were closed, and his head drooped on his shoulder as if he were taking a snooze, small individual circles of smoke came off his lit cigar and rose in the air.

"A gull Yao," Sago whispered to me. She wrinkled her nose at the sight of the cigar. "Only gulls love smoking those filthy things they get from Emberwood."

We followed a dirt path that led from the pier to the town. The trail was strewn with wildflowers, bright yellows and magentas clustering like bursts of fire.

"Do you think anyone here will recognize us as fugitives from the palace?" I asked.

"I wouldn't worry too much," Sago said. "They're all Yao here. If they know you're wanted by the Shyan government, they would more likely hide you than turn you in. Besides, they won't bother you with me here."

"Are you sure your friend will take us to Emberwood?" Aiden asked. "What if he's not in town?"

"He retired from sailing years ago and just lives on his ship now," Sago replied. "But like I said, he owes me a favor. And if he won't take you, he'll know someone who will."

The waves crashed over the shore in a steady rhythm as we walked to the harbor on the other side of town.

We followed Sago down the docks, and she waved over some dockworkers. She spoke to them in Yao, and they made a reply.

Sago translated for us. "I asked if they know where Sei is, and they said he should be aboard his ship, right next to the *Lullapiper.*"

A fishing vessel was docked to a wooden post. On the side of the ship, three characters were written in Yao. The characters were familiar and unfamiliar at the same time. The last character looked like the word for "bird" in the ancient Shyan language, but the other characters were more rounded and had more short strokes than what I'd been taught to read.

Sago watched me with a smile. "It says *Lullapiper.*" She must have noticed me studying the sign.

"I didn't realize how similar the written Yao language is to ancient Shyan," I said.

"Given that our kingdoms have been neighbors for most of history, it shouldn't be a surprise," Sago said. "Actually, the spoken Yao language is close to the speech of the ancient Shyan before the influence of the conquerors from Exentria took over your kingdom and renamed it from Shyan to Seracedar. This was, of course, the start of the Ponzu Dynasty."

I studied a bit of that history when I was still in school, but I didn't retain the knowledge after I passed my exams.

"Wow, Sago, you sure know a lot about Shyan history," Aiden said.

"My father always said it's wise to know your enemies better than they know themselves," she said.

We went past the *Lullapiper*, but there was no ship next to it. The space in the water was empty.

Sago frowned. "That's strange. Maybe his neighbor knows his whereabouts." She walked closer to the *Lullapiper* and called out in Yao. I'd heard her speak enough in the past few weeks to other Yao to know she had said, "Hello, anyone home?"

A rank, fishy odor, mingled with alcohol, wafted from the ship. A fin popped out of the shallow water to the right side of the boat. A shimmering gray body appeared below the water and morphed into a man. The man rose from the water, but he was too far away for me to get a good glimpse of his profile.

The man called out in Yao.

He climbed onto the side of the boat and disappeared into the cabin.

"He said, 'Just a minute,'" Wyle said. "He needs to put on some dry clothes."

Aiden frowned. "That voice. I swear I've heard it before."

A moment later, the man reemerged. He wore a waterproof black robe made of Sea Kaigon Silk. It was said that this special silk was originally created by the Miyu, who sold it to land dwellers back in the days when they still thought it safe to mingle with us.

The man came toward us. His black hair stood in stiff spikes on his head. Except for the hair on his head, he was clean-shaven. His eyes were narrow slits, and he had thick, black eyebrows. Shrewdness was reflected in his dark irises. It wasn't maliciousness that I sensed in his presence but a certain edginess, as though he was ready to battle at any moment.

He saw Sago and Wyle, and he smiled, his muscles relaxing somewhat. His teeth glinted under the light. Sharp, pointed teeth. He opened his mouth to speak, but then his gaze traveled to Aiden. His laidback expression transformed into one of surprise. "Aiden Lang, is that you?" He spoke perfect Shyan. No accent.

Aiden's jaw dropped.

"Captain Montier?" Aiden said. "I knew you sounded familiar. But I didn't know you were half Yao."

Montier? He was one of the two men we were looking for.

"Well, I'll be," he said. "It's nice to see you again, Aiden. Just to let you know, I'm no longer known as Montier here. The name's Daki now."

Aiden's eyes still bulged in shock. "What are you doing here?"

Daki's grin spread wider. "Living. Something I wouldn't be doing if I were back in Seracedar." He took note of me. "Now let's not be rude to your friends. Aiden, please make the introduction."

"This is Rilla," Aiden said. "And Sago and Wyle of the Southern Yao Clans."

"It's nice to meet you," I said.

"The pleasure is all mine." He bowed, then faced Sago and Wyle and bowed again. "The Fox Clan from the south. I have heard of your family. It's an honor."

I had already taken note of his friendly smile and kind face, but now I noticed he also had a mature and experienced air about him. I'd say he was in his late thirties at most.

Sago returned his bow. "Mr. Daki, we are looking for Sei in hopes that he might be able to help Aiden and Rilla book passage to Emberwood. I was told his ship was docked next to yours, but he's not here. Do you know where he went?"

"I heard his ship set sail before dawn this morning," Daki said. "But I've no idea where he was off to. Sometimes he does take short fishing excursions, but he's usually back before nightfall."

"We're in a bit of a hurry," Aiden said. "I'm not sure we can wait. It's a long story."

"Perhaps I can take you then," Daki said. "But maybe you should come aboard and tell me what's going on first."

I felt for his wyis, but it was normal for a male in his prime. Nothing was off or indicated that this was Haming in disguise.

"Just one question," Aiden said. "Do you remember how we met?"

"Prince Carrick wanted you to test out my kite invention so he could use it," Daki said. "You didn't even last a minute. I still remember how you turned green in the face. Why?"

"One can never be too sure, especially with a face-changing androgy on our heels," Aiden said. "But that's all part of the long story I'm about to tell you."

"I'll stay here on land with Wyle," Sago said, eyeing the ocean warily. "You go ahead."

"Be on guard for any sign of Androgy Haming," Aiden told her. "He could be anyone now. He must be here, trying to find a ship, too."

We crossed the plank that took us on deck, and Daki led us into the main cabin. Here, we descended a narrow staircase. Below deck, I bent my head to keep it from knocking against the low ceiling. The cabin wasn't large, but there was enough room for a bed and a round, wooden table. On that table, there was a glazed jug labeled "Rice Wine" and a blue and white dish with a pile of roasted nuts.

Daki gestured for us to sit around the table. "Peanuts, anyone?"

We declined, but he wouldn't let us refuse the wine. He poured it into three cups, one for each of us.

Daki took a sip of his wine. "Now, what brings you here, and why must you go to Emberwood?"

"We are on a mission to find the Sacred Cedar Scepter and take it back to Prince Carrick," Aiden said. "Prince Nelan has taken control of the palace and the army, but he carries a fake scepter, and word of his deception is quickly spreading throughout Seracedar. We have reason to suspect the real scepter is in Emberwood. Would you be able to take us there?"

"I will assist you in every way possible," Daki said with a nod. "I have heard the news of Terran's death and the chaos that has ensued. Carrick is the last prince who offers hope to Seracedar, and I gladly give him my support and loyalty."

Daki offered to pour another round of rice wine, but I declined. "Perhaps some tea then."

Behind Daki was a small open stove. He placed a kettle on a rack above the flames and boiled some water.

"There's something else," Aiden said. "We think Welder may have stolen the scepter out of Cedar Palace when you both escaped after the coup. I know he traveled with you for a time. Did you ever hear from him after you parted ways? Or do you know anything about the scepter?"

"General Welder took the scepter? After we fled the capitol, we traveled together as far as this shore." Daki shook his head, his brows drawn together in bewilderment. "If he did take it, I never had any notion. However, Welder had a powerful tin-chai. He could disguise any object or person to look like something or someone else. From changing his own appearance to camouflaging any inanimate object, he would have been able to pull off any heist. It's possible he changed the scepter and smuggled it out of the palace as a dagger or even a sash around his robe. I wouldn't have been able to tell. He decided to continue on to Emberwood while I stayed here. But I'm sorry to say I haven't heard from him since. Are you sure he has the scepter?"

"Androgy Solar hinted as much before his death," Aiden said. "Solar told us to find 'wielder' in Emberwood. It was only later I realized I may have misunderstood, and he could have meant to say Welder. I was hoping you'd be able to confirm."

"And what about his personal life?" I asked. "Did he ever talk to you about that? Before Empress Limera died, she said her former lover tricked her into revealing where she kept the scepter. Aiden mentioned that Welder may have had an affair with her."

Daki's eyes widened. "Yes, Welder did confide in me that the empress had invited him to her bedchamber, and he had plans to use the opportunity to gain her trust. I advised him against it. It was a dangerous game, especially knowing Limera's tin-chai to discover secrets. But he assured me he knew what he was doing. In the end, Limera didn't learn the plans of the coup from sniffing out Welder, but from one of the faela."

Aiden clapped his hand on the table and beamed. "Then we definitely have our man. Do you know where in Emberwood Welder was headed?"

"The capitol," Daki said. "He was going to the king to ask for sanctuary in Emberwood and hoped to become a permanent citizen. If he made it there, then Linlang Palace should have record of his whereabouts."

"Why didn't you go to Emberwood with him?" Aiden asked.

"Emberwood has always had a good relationship with Yao. You wouldn't need to hide your Yao side there."

"I suppose I've always hoped to return to Seracedar one day," Daki said. "I still consider it my home."

The kettle let out a hiss. Daki took it away from the fire of the stove and set it down on a wooden block. From the cupboard, he pulled out a large teapot and a white bag. Inside the bag were dried tea leaves, though they were more oval-shaped than I was used to.

"Anemone leaves," Daki said. "A special kind of leaf found in deep waters. Shatooth Yao like using them for tea, and usually, only we shatooth Yao can dive deep enough to gather the leaves. You'll like it. The tea is sweeter than what you usually drink."

Daki added the leaves to the teapot, then poured the boiling water into it, letting it steep.

Aiden regarded Daki thoughtfully. "I never had a suspicion you were half Yao, but now it makes sense why you were a captain in the Seracedar Navy. A shatooth. Who would have guessed?"

"My mother was a Yao, something no one knew except Prince Taimin, Carrick's older brother and my commander," he said. "When Prince Taimin discovered my secret, he allowed me to stay in my position rather than expose me. For this, I was eternally grateful to him."

"Forgive me," I interrupted, "but I'm afraid I don't know much about palace politics. Which of Carrick's brothers is Prince Taimin?"

"The second in line for the throne until his death after the coup," Aiden said. "Terran placed him in charge of the attacks on the Miyu. As far as I know, Taimin was one of the only brothers Carrick got along with, but he was several years older. Carrick had no idea Taimin was planning a coup."

Daki poured the tea into my cup. I took a sip. Indeed, it was slightly sweet and spicy like cinnamon. I liked it.

"Prince Taimin didn't agree with the war on the Miyu," Daki said. "He thought it was all morally abhorrent. When he protested, Terran threatened to send him into exile. He planned the coup for years, but Empress Limera discovered his plans and warned Terran."

Daki scowled and ruffled his damp, black hair. He took a sip of tea before continuing. "Many of those involved were captured and later executed. Before Prince Taimin's arrest, he arranged for Welder and me to escape. He did so much for us that I sometimes feel like a traitor for not staying. I came here, the birthplace of my mother. Used the Yao name she gave me, Daki, to fit in here. But I have always vowed that one day I'd return to Seracedar and help restore peace and prosperity. Now that Terran is dead, I intend to make good on that promise. Nelan cannot be allowed to continue his father's dismal legacy. I will help you find the Sacred Cedar Scepter for Carrick."

I took another sip of tea. "When can we set sail?"

Daki opened his mouth, but his reply was cut off. A man's angry scream reverberated through the air.

We all exchanged glances, startled.

"That sounded like my neighbor, Sei," Daki said.

We rushed out on deck and found Sago and Wyle on the dock. Sago saw us and gestured to a bald, overweight, middle-aged man who was letting out a string of curse words in a language I didn't understand.

"We found Sei," Sago said. "He just returned, but he was in town doing business at the market. Turns out someone stole his ship."

Sei shook his fists at the sea.

"Sei," Daki said. "Is there something we can do to help? Do you have any idea who did this?"

Sei's gaze collided with mine. His eyes narrowed, and he growled. "*You* must have stolen my ship."

# CHAPTER 10

✦ ✦ ✦ ✦ ✦ ✦ ✦ ✦ ✦ ✦

The man's sudden rise of anger made me step back in surprise. Did he recognize me from the palace's posters? Aiden stepped defensively in front of me.

"You must have had something to do with this, rotten thief. Where are your cohorts?"

"What?" I stared at him.

Sei pointed his finger, shaking it at me in fury. "I never forget a face." His forehead was crinkled, grizzly brows drawing together like a caterpillar. He looked at Sago. "This girl and three others were here before dawn looking to borrow a boat, but of course, I refused. Especially since they were rude and woke me up. Besides, I don't do no favors for Shyan. They must have made off with my boat when I went to the market."

"That's impossible," Sago said. "Rilla couldn't have been here before dawn. She was with me, Sei."

Wyle stood in front of me in a defensive stance. "Mama's right. Rilla's no thief. She saved me from a kaigon."

"I can vouch for Rilla as well," Daki said. "There must be some mistake."

Aiden's eyes widened. "It must have been Androgy Haming again.

Instead of pretending to be a Yao, he face-changed into Rilla to give us trouble."

Sago regarded Sei. "A face-changing Shyan from Cedar Palace has been following Aiden and Rilla. He must have impersonated Rilla."

Sei scowled. "Well, someone needs to answer for this. My ship is my home. Where am I supposed to live?"

"I'll build you another ship, my friend," Daki said.

"How are you going to do that?" Sei asked.

"I have my ways," Daki replied. "I promise you'll have a new one by evening."

"What?" I said. "By this evening?"

"Daki has a creation tin-chai," Aiden whispered so only I could hear. "He can transform the elements into any transportation vessel imaginable and do it in a few hours."

"These damn Shyan," Sei said. "Always taking what doesn't belong to them. If I wasn't so fat and slow in my wanpo Yao form, I'd chase them down."

He did look like one with the extra folds around his neckline and waist.

"I already lost my family's gold to pirates last spring," Sei said, fists curled at the sky. "And now this."

Aiden frowned. "Mister Sei, you said there were several Shyan looking for a boat, correct? Besides the one who looked like this lady . . ." He indicated me. "What did the others look like?"

"Three females," Sei said. "Lotuses, you call 'em. Those religious ones are the worst kind of Shyan if you ask me. Hypocrites, the lot of them. Holy sisters, my wanpo sac."

"Sei," Sago cried. "Watch your language in front of my son."

"Mama, what's a sac?" Wyle asked.

"Never you mind," Sago said with a glare at Sei.

"I'm going to the inn to see if anyone else saw anything," Sei said.

When he had gone, Aiden gave the rest of us a concerned look. "Why would Lotuses be working with Haming?"

"Puzzling, indeed," Daki agreed. "I wonder if—" He broke off, and his gaze narrowed. The whites of his eyes became completely red. His nose twitched as he sniffed the air.

I took two steps back in alarm as the man jumped up in a frenzy.

"What's going on?" Aiden asked. "Are you all right, my man?"

"My shatooth senses smell blood," Daki said, looking over his shoulder at us. "Something is dead or dying in the water." He sprinted forward down the pier.

I thought I heard a cry in the distance. I glanced out at the horizon and saw a dark speck that looked like the frame of a ship. But I blinked, and it was gone. Had I imagined it?

Aiden grabbed my arm, returning my attention forward to the pier. "Come on."

We followed Daki through the docks and onto the beach. When we reached the shoreline, Daki waded deeper into the water until it came to his knees. The rest of us waited on land, watching him sniff the water and swim into the tide.

Then he dove down into the sea. When he resurfaced, he carried someone in his arms and came back onto the shore.

Daki laid a body onto the sand. It was a Miyu. Her bloodied torso was frothing, dissolving into sea foam. Her tail was missing. Her cloak, which was said to contain her soul, was wrapped around her shoulders. Her golden hair clumped together, draped over her shoulders like slimy seaweed.

Sago tried to shield Wyle's gaze, but it was no use. The boy had already seen her. He buried his head in his mama's shoulder, his body racked with sobs.

"She looks like a sentinel in charge of protecting royalty," Daki said.

"Who would do this?" I asked. I bit down my anger.

"Likely mercenary pirates from Exentria," Daki said. "They love pillaging the coast and taking from the fishermen. Only they would be cruel enough to chop off a Miyu's tail. They can sell it for a hefty price on the black market. Miyu tails have incredible healing properties."

Pirates. Like the ones that killed my parents.

As I stared at the blood-soaked Miyu, I couldn't stop a gushing breath from escaping my lips. Grief poured into my veins, all the way to my fingertips, making them tingle with pain.

A hand touched my shoulder. "Are you all right?" Aiden's warmth was calming, and I leaned into him.

I shook my head. "Not really. Why must there be so much evil in the world?"

Without answering, he took my cold hands into his and simply held them.

"She will turn to sea foam now," Sago whispered.

Already, white froth, tinged with gray and blue, lathered over the Miyu's skin. Her face was quickly dissolving, transforming into the color of the tipped waves.

Daki whispered a prayer, a hymn that flowed to the lull of the tide, over the Miyu's body, and pushed it toward the ocean, where the waves took the Miyu out to sea again.

"How did she even end up here?" Aiden asked. "We're far from Miyu territory."

"Maybe the pirates took her from her home then killed her here," Sago said.

Daki's gaze dropped to the sand. He picked up several small, white, spherical objects.

"Pearls?" I said. "Are they Yao family pearls?"

"No," Daki said. "Pearls are not among the precious treasures that belong to Yao. These three are from the Miyu. Miyu tears transform into pearls. With these, I might be able to see what happened to her in her final moments. Miyu pearls hold their memories."

He held on tight to the pearls and closed his eyes. Three seconds later, he opened his eyes again. "All I saw were the faces of the pirates looming over her. They definitely killed her. That doesn't tell us—" Daki broke off. His nose twitched. "Do you smell that?"

Unlike when he'd smelled the Miyu blood, this time I did smell something. Something was burning. A fiery blaze lit up the sky in the distance.

Daki gasped. "My ship!" He took off in a sprint.

But it was too late. When we reached the ship, all we could do was watch it burn into ash.

# CHAPTER 11

✦ ✦ ✦ ✦ ✦ ✦ ✦ ✦ ✦ ✦

Although Daki was saddened by the loss of his ship, it would have been more of a tragedy if he wasn't capable of building another one with his tin-chai.

"At least I don't have many valuables," he said. "But it will take the night to rebuild another ship, in addition to the one I promised Sei. I'm sorry. I know you wanted to leave sooner rather than later, but we've no choice but to delay."

"How long?" Aiden asked. He worried his lower lip, impatience covering his face.

"At least another day."

Aiden groaned. "Just our luck. Now Haming is far ahead of us. Be on the lookout for those Lotuses who were with him. They may have been the ones to burn your ship, probably instructed to delay us. Eventually they'll reveal themselves, and we'll have to fight."

We left Daki at the docks and followed Sago and Wyle to the only inn in town. Daki promised to meet us in an hour for supper. We waited at the cantina downstairs. Other than a few drunk fishermen, we were the only ones here.

Sago took a sip of tea. "Even if that androgy gets to Emberwood first, it doesn't guarantee he'll know where to find the scepter."

I tapped a finger on my chin, thinking. "But now he does know we suspect General Welder has it. I wonder what he plans on doing with the scepter if he finds it first."

"Probably trick people into believing he's achieved tin-chai amplification and the right to rule." Aiden crammed a spoon of seaweed and rice into his mouth. He'd ordered a snack to enjoy before supper. In addition to seaweed and rice, there was an order of roasted garlic topped soybeans and fried meat pies. I was amazed Aiden didn't choke on the huge bites he took.

Sago gave Wyle a chiding glance as he copied Aiden and stuffed his mouth full of food.

"Slow down there, both of you," Sago said. "No one's going to steal your food."

The door to the dining hall opened, and in walked Sei. He looked pale and uncomfortable, and sweat soaked through the shirt on his back. When he saw us, his grim frown deepened.

I scanned the cantina. The drunk fishermen had disappeared. There was only one door that led outside, and I hadn't seen them leave through it. We were now the only ones in the restaurant, along with the innkeeper, who kept his cloak over his head and continued wiping down the tables, ignoring us.

"Sei," Sago called. "I was hoping to see you here. Good news. Daki says your boat will be ready in the morning."

"That's great," he said, shifting his gaze left and right.

The innkeeper stopped his work and greeted him. Sei whispered something to the man, and the innkeeper slipped back into the kitchen, out of sight.

"Something wrong?" Sago asked. "You look distracted."

"I'm fine," he said, then spoke something in a different language to her.

Without another glance at us, he strode to the back of the cantina and opened a door into a private tearoom.

"Something's wrong," Aiden whispered.

"Yes," Sago said in a low whisper. "He said in Yao that *they* are listening. Said he's messed with the wrong people."

"Who are *they*?" Wyle asked.

A thud came from the private tearoom. It sounded like someone had been thrown against the door.

"There's someone in the room with him," Sago said.

We moved to the door.

Aiden tested the handle. "It's locked." He unsheathed his sword. I withdrew mine as well.

Several shouts echoed, followed by the sound of a fight.

"Wyle, go find Mr. Daki at the pier, and tell him to come immediately," Sago said.

Wyle nodded and ran.

Sago charged at the door to the private room. She evaporated into a mist, shifting herself into fox form, and her nine tails whipped out, slamming against the door and smashing the wood into smithereens. She shifted back into human form and burst into the room.

Aiden and I followed.

Sei was there, but he appeared perfectly fine. He stood with the drunk fishermen from earlier. But they weren't fishermen. They took off their hats, exposing their bright-colored hair, a unique characteristic of Exentriks. Neon blue, bleached white, and bright pink. These men were mercenary pirates from Exentria. The white-haired pirate was so tall, his head nearly touched the ceiling. The neon-blue-haired man had a rotund figure, and the pink-haired man's neck sloped like a swan.

Were they the same pirates who had killed that Miyu? As I read their wyis, it was the tall man's wyis that stood out. It was dark. As if some other being existed within him.

The presence of several other wyis flashed around me. A Lotus was in the room. I recognized her face. She had been at the monastery where we'd stayed in Tinsai Village.

Two more wyis flickered behind us.

I whirled around. A Lotus came into the room and slammed the door. There were two other people. One was the innkeeper. He shed his cloak, and the light revealed his face and shaven head. Not a he, but a she. Another Lotus. It was Teer, the sister who had informed the guards that Aiden and I were at the monastery. I could feel her wyis but not the wyis of her companion.

I squinted, trying to make out the face. Her earring glinted in the light, and as she came forward, I realized it was Dahlia Nin. No wonder I couldn't read her wyis, the intensity of her spiritual energy. I hadn't been able to back at the monastery either.

"Surprised?" she asked. "I expect you're wondering why you can't read my wyis, Rilla."

My mouth fell open. How did she know?

"Don't expect to be able to identify me that way anymore," she said.

Her features morphed, and instead of the Dahlia, there stood Androgy Haming.

"You disguised yourself as a Dahlia back at the monastery," I said. "You've been tailing us ever since then."

"I had to find out what you knew." Haming's breathing was shallow, and sweat dotted his brow.

"Master," Teer said. "Are you sure you are well enough to travel so soon after—"

"Silence," Haming said.

Aiden smirked. "I thought you would have taken off to Emberwood on Sei's ship by now. If you'd stayed just for us, that would've warmed my heart. But I see you don't look so well. What, did you eat something rotten? I've heard seasickness is ten times worse when you've got the runs."

Haming scowled and opened his mouth to reply but stopped and closed his eyes as though he had a headache. He looked weaker than when I'd last seen his true form after the battle with Emperor Terran and Empress Limera. Several scars marred his face.

One of his eyes twitched as he regarded Aiden. "Impertinent boy. I told you if we met again, we'd be enemies. I warned you not to get in my way, but you didn't listen. I'm afraid you've left me no choice but to remove you from my path."

He motioned to the Lotuses. "Make sure they don't get away. Destroy the ship the shatooth Yao is building."

Sei cleared his throat. "My ship is waiting for you offshore three miles away, just as you wanted. But as I warned you before, it's a bit of a swim."

The tall pirate bowed to Haming. "Not to worry. The rest of our crew is waiting on the beach to assist you there as long as you've got our gold."

Haming leaned on Teer as though it pained him to stand. He waggled a finger at the pirates. "I've got your gold, don't you worry. But after tonight, our transaction is finished. Make sure no one traces you back to me or the holy sisters."

"Take the wanpo Yao to collect his prize," Teer told one of the other Lotuses. "I will take Androgy Haming to the ship first, and you can join us when you're finished."

Sago growled at Sei. "Traitor."

Sei regarded Sago. "Sorry, but they promised to give me the price of my ship in gold if I cooperated."

Haming and the Lotuses veered for the exit.

"Not so fast," Sago said. She and Aiden lunged for Teer and Haming, but the pirates blocked the door, swords drawn. The tall pirate used his wyis and cast a surge of energy out of his palms, which threw Aiden and Sago back.

Aiden pointed his sword at them, and Sago revealed her nine tails.

It was too late to stop Haming and the Lotuses. They strode away with Sei close on their heels.

The tallest pirate leered at Sago. "I'd love the chance to spar with you, pretty fox."

"Out of my way, you oaf." She shoved at him, but he ducked, avoiding contact.

He smirked and slapped her behind.

"Show me those pretty, white tails," he taunted.

Sago growled. She lashed out at him with a tail, but he spun away. Sago chased after him, leaving the two other pirates circling Aiden and me.

"Come with us quietly, and we won't have to hurt you," the round-bellied pirate said. "Haming already paid us, and Emperor Nelan will pay a huge sum if we bring both of you back to him."

Aiden pointed his sword at them. "Nelan is not my emperor."

The swan-necked pirate scoffed. "We might have to keep the novelty alive, but that's not the case for you."

He charged at Aiden with his sword. Aiden deflected. Their swords clashed, and their battle cries resounded in the air.

I stepped backward.

The round-bellied pirate looked me over.

"I can see why Nelan wants you returned despite that cursed four on your face," he said. "A delicious novelty like you might definitely be worth that million Seran."

"I am not a novelty." I spat. "Never again." I pointed my sword at him.

"We'll see about that." He lunged. I jumped out of the way, and he nearly tripped over his own feet. He came for me again. This time I was too slow. He knocked away my sword. His hands pinned my arms behind my back. He was strong. I knew I didn't have a chance to break free, but he was bulky and clumsy. Instead of struggling, I let myself fall limp and heavy into him. He stumbled from my sudden weight.

I couldn't risk using my voice to kill him. What if I couldn't control it again? I'd killed those moonrabbits, and I didn't want to hurt anyone else. I looked around and located a wooden beam on the ceiling.

I sang two notes, aiming at the wooden beam above us. *Please work this once.*

I focused on the beam. The wood bent to my will. It was working. With a loud thwack, it hit the man's shoulder, forcing him to release me.

He yowled in pain. "You little bitch. I may not be able to kill you, but I can hurt you in places no one can see."

I sang louder.

He leapt at me, coming for my neck. "Stop that bellowing!"

The beam hit his head. The man froze, staring at me with a look of shock. Blood poured down his bald scalp, and he crashed to the ground. He struggled to get up.

I grabbed my sword from the ground. Pirates like him had killed my parents, taken them away from me forever. I wasn't going to let him do that to anyone else.

I gutted him once through the chest, then again. Rage overcame all my senses. Over and over, I stabbed him. Through the red haze, Aiden's voice carried to me.

"Stop, Rilla. That's enough."

Aiden's hand touched my shoulder, and I snapped out of my daze. The round-bellied pirate lay on the floor, blood oozing from his body. His eyes were open, but he was dead. I dropped my sword.

His companion lay a few feet away, the deep slash of a sword splitting open his gut. Aiden had managed to kill him.

From the cantina came the sound of wood smashing and splintering. Sago and the tall pirate rushed at each other.

All the tables were overturned and dishes were smashed. Sago chased the pirate upstairs, where the inn's rooms were located. Panicked shouts came from the lodgers. Fear lit in their eyes as they fled their rooms and ran out of the inn.

"I'll stay and help Sago," I told Aiden. "But you need to get to Daki. The Lotuses were going after him, and Wyle could be in danger, too."

Aiden hesitated, but then nodded. "Be careful."

"You, too."

I rushed upstairs. Sago had made a full transformation into a nine-tailed fox. She faced her opponent, who perched on the balustrade of the stairway. The pirate was no longer in the form of a man but of an eight-winged crow. Was he part Yao?

I read his wyis again. It was sinister and crazed, even more powerful than my initial reading. There was an uncontrollable desire to consume and to raze. It made me cold. I had never felt anything like it.

"Watch out," Sago shouted. "He's not a Yao like me. He's possessed by a dinin. An evil spirit."

The creature flew from the balustrade, keeping itself close to the ceiling above the cantina. It screeched, a sound so deafening, windows shattered. I covered my ears. He flapped his wings, creating a wind with such force that it was difficult to maintain my foothold. I hung onto the bannister.

Next to me, Sago whipped out her tails, but the force of the wind blew her back. Pieces of wood and debris from the stairs and tables flew at us. A glass shard grazed her shoulder, and she winced.

I took a deep breath in and out, trying to calm myself. *Old*

*Grandfather Heaven, if you're there, please help me take down this creature.*

A song played in my head as clear as if someone were humming it before me. I aimed my wyis at the air and sang above the roar of the wind. The words came to me instantly, words I didn't know until they formed on my lips.

> *"Holy deities surround us now.*
> *Expel this evil that abounds.*
> *Hear the words of my sanctified spell.*
> *Exorcise this dinin!"*

The wind reversed direction, blowing toward the eight-winged crow. The bird squawked and flapped its wings but couldn't stand against the wind. Its body exploded in a cloud of black smoke and turned into the form of a man once more. The pirate flew backward, colliding into the wall. He hit his head and fell unconscious to the ground.

Sago wrapped one of her tails around the man and snapped his neck. She turned to me in wonder. "Where did you learn how to exorcise the dinin?"

"I didn't," I said. "The words just came to me."

"That must be a part of your tin-chai then," Sago said. "The deities have blessed you with powerful magic through your voice and your words. If you hadn't exorcised the dinin, he would have finished both of us off."

She looked around the inn. Worry lines folded her brow. "I must find my son. I hope he found Daki before the Lotuses did."

"Aiden is already headed for the docks," I said. "Let's go. If those Lotuses have powerful tin-chai, Aiden and Daki might not be able to defend against them on their own."

Sago gestured to me. "Get on my back."

I climbed on, and she jolted forward. I grabbed onto the scruff of her neck to keep my balance. She moved so quickly, it was almost as though we were flying.

The sky was dark except for the glow of the Turquoise Moon, and it was hard to see. But before we came to the pier, Wyle bounded out of the shadows toward us.

Wyle shouted. "Mama!"

I jumped off Sago's back, and she shifted back into human form. She caught Wyle as he jumped into her arms and transformed into his human self.

"Are you all right, darling?" She inspected him for wounds.

"I'm fine, Mama. Stop it." He brushed her off and pointed farther down the shore. "You have to help Mr. Daki. The Lotus did something to him."

Terrified screams resonated in the air. I searched the shoreline to where Wyle pointed. Squinting through the darkness, I made out the figure of a man.

"Daki," Sago said. She addressed her son. "Wait here."

She sprinted down the beach toward Daki. I followed, running as fast as I could. By the time I reached Daki and Sago, I was out of breath.

Daki collapsed into the sand. Sago kneeled next to him.

His eyes were vacant and unseeing, his face contorted in horror and sorrow. "Don't make me leave. No!"

"What's wrong with him?" I asked.

Daki stared at his hands as though they were covered in filth. "No! Please, no! You can't abandon the cause now."

"He's in some kind of trance." Sago took Daki by the shoulders and shook him. "Wake up. Whatever you're seeing isn't real."

Daki still didn't hear her. She slapped him. That did it. He jolted, and his eyes lost their glazed over sheen. Slowly, he looked away from his hands, then up at us. His gaze refocused, but his eyes still gleamed with tears.

"Prince Taimin," he said. "I couldn't stop him."

"What are you talking about?" Sago said.

Confusion filled Daki's features. "The prince ordered me to leave. The guards were coming, and the prince... he killed himself. I couldn't stop him. Holy deities, it feels like it just happened."

"That was two years ago," I said. "You're in Yao Kingdom now. Something must have triggered you, put you in a trance."

Clarity filled his eyes. "That's right. I remember now. A Lotus attacked me as I was building the new ship. Then I had the worst headache, and suddenly, I was reliving the day I fled the palace. I think the Lotus cast some kind of spell on me. Where is that unholy sister?"

A blast of fire lit up the dark sky. I directed my gaze toward the source. On the pier, Aiden and the Lotus were locked in battle near the docked ships. Aiden threw another blast of fire at her, but she dodged it.

"They'd better not destroy the work I did on my new ship," Daki said with a growl.

"At the moment, we have more to worry about," I said. "If her tin-chai casts such powerful illusions, Aiden is in trouble."

"Let's go," Sago said to me.

Daki attempted to stand.

"Not you. Whatever she did to you, I don't want it getting worse. Watch Wyle for me." Sago pointed to where we had left Wyle. He had obeyed her and stayed put, watching us from where he stood.

Daki nodded.

Sago and I took off for the pier. As we neared the framework for Daki's new ship, I almost stumbled over a dead body.

Sago breathed out a horrified gasp. "Sei."

The man's face had been frozen, his eyes covered in frost.

"Who did this?" Sago demanded. She searched the shadows. "Come out, you coward."

"I'm no coward." A Lotus revealed herself, the same sister who had been with Teer and the pirates at the inn. "The man was stupid. I paid him the price of gold I promised, but then he tried to kill me. I suppose he felt guilty for betraying you."

She sneered at Sago. "A pity you'll be joining him soon."

# CHAPTER 12

✦ ✦ ✦ ✦ ✦ ✦ ✦ ✦ ✦ ✦

The sister lifted her hands, and I noticed a marking on the backs of them—a bird carrying a sword. This was the same symbol from Teer's pin and Androgy Haming's earring when he pretended to be Dahlia Nin back at the monastery.

Before I had time to make sense of this, the Lotus clapped, and two icicles formed in the palms of her hands.

"I thought Lotuses were forbidden to use their tin-chai once they entered the monastery," I said.

"I am allowed to break the rules for the greater good," she said.

Sago nudged me. "Go help Aiden. I can take care of this one."

She whipped her tails out at the Lotus. I made haste, running for Daki's ship. On deck, Aiden fought Teer. I climbed aboard, but as I approached them, Aiden fell to his knees. A terrible look crossed his face, and his eyes glazed over.

"Ah-fu, Ah-mu," Aiden cried out. "I didn't mean to abandon you."

*Ah-fu and Ah-mu?* Baba and Mama. Embers spoke a slightly different dialect of Shyan. Aiden was calling for his parents.

He clutched his hands at his temples and groaned. "No. No!"

Aiden wore a look that was consumed with guilt, one like Daki wore when he could not stop Prince Taimin's suicide.

I pointed my sword at Teer. "Stop whatever you're doing to him."

A spark of pity ignited in Teer's eyes. "I don't want to hurt you, but I will do what I must for the greater good. It's what my master taught me."

A sharp ache formed in the side of my head, and images filled my mind. I saw Lady Arlyn dying in front of me. That memory was replaced with the images of me singing, discovering my power could also strike people with disease and kill them. I pictured the innocent trifles and androgies at the palace who had succumbed to disease as they heard my song.

"How many others will die because of you?" Teer's voice filled my senses.

"Stop," I shouted. "I know this is your trick. I'm not falling for it."

But the guilt nibbled and gnawed, making my chest clench tightly.

"No!" I heard myself shout. I broke out of my trance. "Stop playing with my head."

I sang to the sea. Tendrils of water floated up and wrapped around Teer. She smiled. "Oh, you're more powerful than I anticipated. Not many are able to break free of my tin-chai."

"Shut your mouth," I said. "I'll kill you."

"Go ahead. It only proves you'll never be the healer you dream of becoming. You're a failure."

Now I saw Solar's battered body the first time my healing power failed.

I shook my head, and the images faded. "I told you to stop."

I had to keep talking, distract myself from the images and figure out how to defend against her tin-chai. "How is working for Haming and killing people for the greater good?"

"You wouldn't understand," she said. "Unless you were one of us."

Pain etched into her face, and a shadow of something dark reflected in her gaze for a second. Just as quickly, it disappeared. But it was enough to tell me something horrible must have happened to her. That was the haunted look of someone who had experienced trauma. I'd seen it before in Lady Arlyn when she told me about the bauble cages at the palace. But what did Teer mean by *one of us*?

"Enough talk," she said. "If you do not support our cause, then you are the enemy. You are a killer. I can see the guilt consuming you for killing that family of moonrabbits."

The images flickered in my mind again. I shook my head, trying to dislodge them. "It was an accident. I didn't mean to."

"Doesn't matter if you didn't intend to kill them. You are a killer all the same. One day, you'll make the same mistake. You'll use your tin-chai, meaning to control the elements, but instead, you'll destroy innocent people. Your friends. You have no control over your tin-chai, and you never will."

More pictures played in my mind. Aiden and Carrick lay before me, their bodies bloodied and broken. Evidence of disease scarred their skin.

"No, this isn't real," I said. "They aren't dead."

"Not yet, but they will be if you stay around them long enough," Teer said. "Your tin-chai will bring about their death, even if you claim it to be an accident."

Tears brimmed in my eyes and fell down my cheeks.

What if I did accidentally misuse my tin-chai and harm the people I cared about?

The Lotus took a step toward me. The water I'd lassoed around her had loosened and retreated from her body.

*No. Focus.*

I sang again. But the sea continued its gentle caress on the shore, unaffected by my voice. Something was wrong with me.

Without further warning, Teer came at me with her sword. I deflected her blow with mine. She was strong, much stronger than I was. She forced my sword closer to me, the blade descending upon my neck.

Suddenly, she let up. Her body lifted into the air. A white tail was wrapped around her torso and restrained her arms. She screamed. She dropped the sword, and it tumbled to the ground. Sago?

The sounds of battle rang behind me. Sago was still fighting the other Lotus. My gaze followed the white tail. Wyle stood five feet away in fox form, the miniature version of his mother. Two new tails sprouted behind his back in addition to his original three. He looked ferocious.

He tossed the Lotus back and forth, slamming her into the ground again and again until her screams faded into silence. He let Teer fall to the ground, then collapsed, morphing back into the form of a boy. I rushed to him. His breathing was normal, and I didn't see any injuries. He must have fainted from exhaustion.

Several feet away, Aiden stood from where he had been kneeling. His eyes were clear, an indication he'd snapped out of the trance. Behind me, Daki and Sago had managed to subdue the other Lotus as well. Sago had used her tails to bind the sister's hands. Now, she could no longer form icicles without impaling her own palms.

Daki tied a rope around the Lotus's hands, allowing Sago to pull her tails away.

Sago rushed to her son and gathered him into her arms.

"He's fine," I said. "Just tired. He saved my life this time."

"I'm so proud," Sago said, beaming. "I caught a glimpse of the fight and saw that two more of his tails had finally come in."

I nodded, trying to look calm and not cause concern, but my body was still trembling. I walked away from Sago and touched my throat. Why hadn't my tin-chai worked? What was wrong with me?

Aiden touched my shoulder. "Are you all right?"

"I couldn't use my tin-chai at all," I said. "I tried to control the water, but it stopped bending to my will."

"Try it again now," Aiden suggested.

I sang a phrase. The water stirred. Hope flickered in my chest. But the images flooded my head again. Of Aiden and Carrick, their bodies ridden with disease. Teer's taunting voice echoed in my mind. *You'll kill innocent people. Your friends. You will fail to be a healer.*

I took a deep breath, my words choking in my throat. The water lay motionless.

"You were doing it," Aiden said. "What happened?"

"I don't know." Tears brimmed. "I can't maintain my focus."

He nodded. "Maybe later then. You don't need to pressure yourself."

We returned to the others. Sago cradled her son in her arms. Wyle remained fast asleep. Snores emerged from his throat. Sago chuckled with fondness.

Daki dragged the bound Lotus and tied her to a post. He walked over to Teer and placed a finger under her nose. He shook his head. "Dead."

Aiden spun around to face the surviving Lotus. "What is Haming planning? And are all the Lotuses and Crocuses in league with him? I want to know everything you know."

She bared her teeth in a smile. "Too bad you'll have to figure it out yourself."

Her fingers turned to frost, and before anyone could do anything, the rest of her body chilled, crystals of ice forming on the surface of her skin and brows. Her eyes remained open, still staring rebelliously at us. She shuddered once, then stopped moving completely.

Aiden felt her pulse. "Dead. Damn it, she didn't tell us anything."

"Actually, look at this marking on the back of her hand," I said. "I noticed it earlier. It's the same as a pin Teer wore."

I took two steps toward Teer's body and pointed to the pin

fastened to the front of her cloak. "Dahlia Nin—Androgy Haming—wore an earring with the same design."

"What do you think the symbol means?" Sago asked.

"A symbol for a secret association perhaps," Daki said. He rolled up his sleeves. On his upper arm was a tattoo of two crossed swords. "The leaders of the Zhynites had this tattoo so we would recognize one another even if we'd never met in person before. Only a select few knew what it represented. I suspect Haming's followers have formed a new secret society and identify with their symbol."

"That means he's got more than just these Lotuses working for him," Aiden said. "If they're scattered across Seracedar and pretending to be Lotuses, they've probably got a plan to take the throne. All they need is the scepter."

Daki nodded. "I'll need until morning to finish the ship. We'll get rooms at the inn tonight. Let's prepare to set sail for Emberwood as soon as I'm done."

# CHAPTER 13

✦ ✦ ✦ ✦ ✦ ✦ ✦ ✦ ✦ ✦

Feathered wisps of clouds floated through the bright blue sky, and tendrils of golden light filtered down on the crescent of beach. Aiden and I stood on the pier with Sago and Wyle.

Daki waved at us from aboard his ship, then jumped down to the docks. "I'm ready when you are."

I hugged Wyle goodbye.

The kit's eyes filled with tears. "I wish I could go with you. I want to have an adventure."

"You're too young to leave," Sago said. "Maybe one day we'll travel to other kingdoms."

"I'm sure we'll see each other again," I said.

"If you come visit Yao Kingdom again, be sure to find us," Sago said.

We turned to board the ship. Daki hesitated behind us. He stared into the horizon and into the clouds. A frown played on his lips as though he were in deep concentration.

"Is something worrying you?" Aiden asked him. "I hope a storm isn't brewing."

"Oh, no, it's the perfect weather to sail," Daki said. "But I'm still thinking about that slain Miyu. It was disturbing and takes me back to when I was fighting against them." He shook his head as though trying to dislodge the memories. "Forgive me. We should get going. Perhaps this new adventure will distract me from my dark thoughts."

Sago hugged Aiden, then me. "I wish you both the best, and I hope you accomplish your mission."

Tears pricked at my eyes. "I hate goodbyes."

"Oh, stop that," Sago said. "This isn't goodbye forever. It's simply a see-you-later."

I nodded, not trusting myself to not break into sobs. Aiden and I followed Daki and climbed aboard his newly built ship.

We set sail. As the pier grew smaller, I continued waving to Sago and Wyle until they were mere specks.

I walked on the main deck and gazed out at the ocean. Happy dofei fish flip-flopped at the side of the ship, their friendly grins beaming up in greeting. The sun beamed high in the sky, casting golden rays upon the shimmering water.

The waves rippled and bobbed against the hull, the sound like a hypnotic lullaby.

I allowed myself to relax, feeling the tension release from my shoulders. I sat and let myself take in the sunshine, and eventually, I drifted off to sleep

When I woke, I rubbed at my eyes and looked around. We were in the middle of the ocean, no land to be seen for miles. I must have been sleeping for at least a few hours.

Aiden and Daki conversed at the stern. Aiden grinned at something Daki said. He had such a dazzling smile. Being around him felt like basking in the sunshine after a long winter.

His gaze drifted and he saw me observing him. He waved and approached me, and suddenly I was conscious that I'd been staring at him. Why was I flushed, and why was my heart beating faster? It wasn't as though I hadn't admired his smile and charisma before.

"You're finally awake," Aiden said. "Daki says the weather is perfect right now. If all goes well, we should arrive at the Emberwood harbor in two days. Leihu Port is on the north side of Emberwood. We'll need to travel another three days by land to get to the capitol of Huohua, where Linlang Palace is."

"Will it be difficult to get into Emberwood?" I asked. "What if they don't let us in? And what if the Cedar Palace guards are there waiting for us?"

Aiden brushed a hand through his hair. He didn't look worried at all. "It's easier for Seracedareans to enter Emberwood than it is to leave. And Cedar Palace guards would be hesitant to cross the border into Emberwood. They'd no longer have legal authority to arrest anyone or force them back to Seracedar. Unless they use illegal means like smugglers and slave traders."

A dark look crossed his face. I remembered that slave traders had brought him to Seracedar.

"What do we do once we get to Linlang Palace?" I asked.

"Access Emberwood's records. We can find out if Welder sought Emberwood citizenship, or at least we'll know his whereabouts."

I pursed my lips, thinking about this plan. "Wouldn't those records be under lock and key? I'd imagine only certain people would have access to them."

"You'd be right. Only the records keepers and those with permission from the king and queen are privy to that information."

"Mind sharing how we're going to get permission from the king and queen to access those records then? Or are we going to sneak in illegally?"

He stretched out on the bench next to me, reminding me of a lazy maocat. "I'll tell you when we get to Emberwood, but I can do it without breaking any laws this time."

"Do you have connections to the crown through your family?" I asked. "I remember you said they have some influence in the Emberwood court."

"Good memory," he said. "Yes, my plan does involve my parents' influence in court."

"They must be aristocrats then. When you were under Teer's tin-chai illusion, you were calling for them. Ah-fu and Ah-mu. If I'm not mistaken, that's how Embers address their parents, right?"

"Mm-hmm."

Was he not going to say anything else?

I shook my head and rolled my eyes. "You're being so enigmatic. Why don't you ever talk about Emberwood and your childhood?"

"I have a reputation to maintain as a man of mystery." He closed his eyes, leaned back, and tilted his chin upward to embrace the warmth of the sun. "I'll tell you more about Emberwood later. Right now, I want to relax and enjoy one moment of not having to fear for my life."

I settled back into the bench, but not two seconds passed before Aiden rolled to his left side, then to his right. He sat up. "I didn't realize relaxation was so boring."

I bit back a secret smile. He had never been one to sit still for long.

"Did you recover your tin-chai yet?" he asked. "I mean, not the healing layer, but the layer allowing you to manipulate the elements. Did Teer do something to inhibit your tin-chai?"

"I—I don't know," I said. "One minute I had the water controlled, had it tied around her, and the next, my voice no longer had an effect on the water."

"Well, sing now and try to bring a tendril of seawater aboard," Aiden said.

I looked out to the sea. A song formed. I sang out two notes. The water rose from the sea, but that second of triumph was quickly replaced by Teer's mocking voice. The same images Teer had conjured earlier now replayed in my mind. Aiden and Carrick lay dying before me. It was my fault.

The water sank back down into the sea.

"It's not working," I said.

"Try it again. You almost had it."

Once again, I tried, but my stomach fluttered, suddenly queasy. I fled to the side of the ship, and threw up into the water. Aiden came up beside me.

"I told you I can't," I said. "Teer must have done something to me."

"But she's no longer here," Aiden said. "Do you think it might be a mental block?"

I whirled to face him. "Are you saying it's my fault I can't control my tin-chai? That I'm to blame?"

Aiden put up his hands in surrender and shook his head. "No, that's not what I'm saying. I'm trying to help you figure out why this is happening. But the fact you think I'm blaming you tells me that you blame yourself. I think your self-doubt is the reason your tin-chai is failing you."

I clenched my fists and tried to bite back my rising temper. "So, you do think I'm a failure."

"Grieving gargoyles, lady," he said, exasperation on his face. "Do you even hear yourself? Never in my life would I believe you're a failure. I think all the layers of your tin-chai are still in you, and if you would only believe in yourself, it would come back to you. I can't believe we're even arguing about—"

He broke off as sudden shadows crept in all around us. He lifted his gaze to the sky, as did I. The darkness hadn't come from any cloud coverings, though. The sun still shone, and the sky was a perfect blue.

But around the ship, a wraith-gray mist formed. It came fast out of the waters. A serpentine shape slithered toward us. The menacing mist rose, two narrow eyes on either side of its head blinking with ominous intent.

"What is that?" I asked.

Daki swore and came toward us. He peered into the waters. "A water kaigon."

"A protective spirit of the Miyu," Aiden said. "I think we're under a Miyu attack."

# CHAPTER 14

✦ ✦ ✦ ✦ ✦ ✦ ✦ ✦ ✦ ✦

To the right of the kaigon, an ethereal body appeared below the water, swimming for the side of our ship. I made out the shape of a woman with a large fish tail. Her skin was iridescent, causing the sea around her to appear silver. She was curvaceous but muscular and strong. Beautiful. A red cloak was draped around her shoulders. She emerged from the water, her head and torso facing us. Her gaze narrowed on us.

"We don't wish you any harm," Daki called to her.

"Unfortunately, I cannot say the same to you," the Miyu said. "You cannot be allowed to sail further."

"What have we done to earn such animosity?" Daki asked.

"Do you really not know?" She tossed her head back and laughed. "Ignorant Shyan. Your emperor wanted to erase the Miyu tribe from existence. How could I not hate the Shyan sailors for what they did to us? For killing my sisters, stealing our land and our pearls, cutting off our tails for profit? If I had the power, I would conquer your kingdom. Control and enslave all the males. Your poor women would certainly benefit from being freed of you, too."

How did she know we were Shyan?

"You must be mistaken," Daki said. "We are from Yao Kingdom, and we're only trying to sail to Emberwood."

The Miyu scoffed. "Typical Shyan behavior. Spouting lies to get what you want. But you can't fool me. I already know who you are. I made a deal with someone who regards you as a nuisance. He will give me what I want if I get rid of you."

"Androgy Haming," Aiden said. "It was him, wasn't it?"

Instead of confirming, she petted the watery head of her kaigon. "Darling, shred this ship to bits."

The kaigon reared up, building in size. The creature screamed, forming a wind so strong it threatened to capsize our ship. It took everything in me to maintain my balance and not let the wind knock me over the railing.

Daki grabbed the helm, trying to steady the ship. "We have no choice but to abandon ship, and we're already too far from Yao to attempt to return."

Aiden kicked open the storage chest behind the helm and grabbed our knapsacks filled with our basic necessities. He tossed one to Daki and another to me. "I assume you've got a plan, Daki?"

"Remember the kite you tested back at the palace?"

Aiden groaned. "You're kidding. We have to fly on those death traps?"

"Fly?" I echoed him, and my heartbeat flew into my throat. "Are you sure about this?"

Never in my life had I been higher in the air than I was able to jump.

"Unless you two have any better ideas." Daki lifted one hand to the sky and pulled strands of cloud and mist from the air. The wisps of cloud gathered like threads, spinning into four triangles. They weaved together into one gigantic diamond. A kite. More mist joined together, forming the tail. Daki made another one the same way. Using the tails, he tethered the kites to the side of the ship. They seemed light and delicate, shaped like koi fish. But as they flapped in the wind, they stood strong, showing no signs of folding in.

"Hurry and strap this around your waist before they take off without us," Daki said. He shoved a buckle, which was attached to the kite tail, at me. "I only have enough wyis to make two."

Aiden nodded. "I'll share a kite with Rilla."

"I hope you remember how to fly one," Daki said. "Under these conditions—"

"I'd rather never fly again, but there doesn't seem to be a choice at the moment," Aiden said. "See you on the other side. Dead or alive. Preferably the latter."

Aiden attached our buckles to an adjoining strap, and to this strap, he attached the kite. This way we were joined with my back strapped to Aiden's front. He strapped our knapsacks onto his back, then untied the kite's tail from the ship's railing. We were propelled into the air. Aiden wrapped his arms around my waist.

The water kaigon roared, taking the form of a swirling cyclone. We had to fly higher, or it would take us down.

Aiden tugged on the kite's tail, and it went higher. Depending on which way Aiden pulled the tail, he was able to drive us left or right, up or down. The up and down motion made me queasy. This was the first time I'd been this high in the air, and it took all my courage to keep my eyes open. I didn't want to look down, but I also didn't want to lose sight of the kaigon chasing us.

The kaigon blew out its steamy breath. The winds picked up. Daki flew in the opposite direction from us. The force of the wind was so strong, it was hard to breathe. The ocean spray stung my skin. The kaigon's cyclone struck our ship. Splinters and debris flew in all directions. A piece of wood came flying at us. I shrieked and ducked, but not fast enough. The fragmented plank grazed the side of my head. Pain laced through me. A trickle of warm blood trailed down my cheek.

Aiden swore. "Hang on." He pulled on the straps, directing the wings of the kite above the flying debris. The waves forming the kaigon's talons rose, threatening to envelop us. The kaigon reached into the air. The tip of its watery claws struck my shoes, but we soared upward and spiraled away from its reach.

Finally, we rose above the clouds. The sky was blue once more. The kaigon and the ship grew smaller until they became distant dots on the horizon.

"Do you see Daki?" I asked. "I hope he got away safely."

"There." Aiden pointed westward. "Scorch the three moons, something's wrong with his kite."

Indeed, Daki was spinning, descending quickly.

"Can we do anything to help him?" I asked.

"He's heading toward that island," Aiden said. "We're too far away to be able to do anything, but don't worry. Daki's experienced. He'll know how to land, even if the circumstances are not favorable."

Aiden redirected the kite's wings, and we set off for the island.

The isle was in the shape of a slivered moon. A tiny strip of land, a sandbar, connected the tips of either side of the crescent. As we made our descent, I realized the sandbar was actually made of coral reef. It acted as a barrier between the sea and a beautiful lagoon that lay in a private alcove, hidden by lush jungle foliage.

Our kite glided through the air in a smooth descent until our feet touched the golden sands of the shore. My legs wobbled. Thank Old Grandfather Heaven we made it. I didn't know what was scarier, flying at harrowing speeds at such extreme heights or almost becoming food for a water kaigon.

We unhooked ourselves from our kite.

I worried my bottom lip. "Do you think the Miyu will follow us onto the island?"

"Let's hope not," he said. "But right now, I'm more concerned about that cut you got. Let me see it."

He searched through his knapsack and pulled out camphor oil and cotton dressing. He applied the balm on my cut. I bit my bottom lip to stop myself from making a sound and tried not to look at him. I was still mad and hurt that he'd said it was my own self-doubt causing my tin-chai to fail.

"That should do it," he said as he finished dressing the wound.

Though I sensed his concern, he was curt with me. Our heated discussion had been cut short by the Miyu's interruption.

I sniffed. Admittedly, maybe he had a point. But I was too proud to apologize. Still, if I did have a mental block, I couldn't overcome it overnight. He expected too much of me.

It didn't seem like he was in any hurry to make amends with me either. He stood and circled away from me, scanning the beach. "Let's search for Daki."

I spotted a piece of blue and white fabric about twenty feet away. "Is that part of Daki's kite?"

We came to the discarded bag.

"And that's his knapsack," Aiden said.

It was open and still fully packed. More shredded pieces of the kite and tail were scattered around the shore. But there was no sign of Daki. If we couldn't find him, we'd have no way to get off this island.

"Do you think he made it?" I asked.

"He's alive," Aiden said. "If he wasn't, we'd find his body. Let's head to the lagoon. Maybe Daki went there for water; although, I wonder why we didn't see him during our descent, and why he didn't wait for us to land."

We trekked through the jungle terrain. The air was muggy and humid. Sweat poured down my face, adding to my already drenched clothes. The fabric stuck to my skin, and my shoes made a sloshing sound. My feet kept sinking into the swampy earth. I had to pull each foot out of the mud with every step.

Aiden followed close on my heels, but his footsteps were soft and effortless. I felt like a bumbling ungbeetle next to him.

No signs of animal life stirred; no birdsong twittered in the bushes; not even a breath escaped through the still trees. An earthy fragrance permeated the air.

Aiden stayed quiet as we hiked. It was unlike him, so I knew he was piqued with me. Our earlier conversation lingered, the invisible tension so taut it weighed heavy on my shoulders. I didn't like this awkwardness.

The silence gave me time to think, though. Maybe I was the one at fault.

He'd only been trying to help me figure out why my tin-chai wasn't working.

I took a false step and slid but caught my balance before I fell.

Without a word, Aiden extended a hand, helping me safely climb down a steeper part of the path. Once we'd cleared it, he walked ahead again.

"I'm sorry," I blurted out to his back.

He stopped.

"About earlier. I didn't mean to lash out at you."

He made no reply and still didn't look at me.

"I was being unreasonable," I continued. "I know you were pushing me because you care, and I'm sorry for being a brat."

"Is that all?" There was a hitch in his voice, like he was struggling not to laugh.

"I'm sorry for twisting your words."

"And?"

The cad! I smacked him on his shoulder.

He turned and grinned.

I scowled. "And you'd better say we're friends again and start talking to me, or I'll never speak another word to you as long as we live."

"It'll take a lot more than that little argument for me to stop being your friend," he said. "It's too hard to stay mad at someone so cute. Plus, you don't know how difficult it was to not talk."

He reached out and pulled me into a side hug, then tried messing with my hair.

I pushed his hand away. "My hair's already a fright. I don't need you to make me look any worse."

"Well, I disagree. I love your hair. You couldn't possibly get any prettier."

I averted my gaze before he saw my blush. Even though I knew he was flirting for fun again, my heart raced. I walked faster.

We passed through the shadowed green brush. The gushing laughter of a waterfall echoed ahead, pounding like drums in a festival parade. Aiden parted the dangling vines to reveal the lagoon, which lay sparkling and welcoming in the afternoon sun, still except for where the torrent of water cascaded into a circle of white, bubbling foam. The waterfall spilled off the side of a hill. Jungle foliage veiled the pool on all sides, a private niche waiting for wandering explorers to unveil.

I was so excited to see the lagoon, I forgot all about the slippery mud beneath my feet. I ran, and my shoes slipped and skidded.

I shrieked and braced myself for impact.

Aiden grabbed my waist, steadying me. I rotated myself toward him and found my balance again.

"Thanks," I said.

His gaze remained on mine. My heart pounded faster. His head lowered as though he were about to kiss me.

I gasped and shifted away from Aiden, but I lost my balance and plummeted facedown in the mud.

Moaning, I pulled myself up, but my hands slipped in the mud. I shrieked and fell on my back. Cold, slimy mud covered me from my hair to my heels.

Aiden snorted, barely masking his grin. "Sorry, but you look like something a maocat spit up."

I scowled at him. "I could have been seriously injured."

His amusement faded, replaced with concern. "Are you hurt? I'm sorry. How tactless of me."

He extended a hand toward me. I hesitated for a moment. On impulse, I grabbed his hand and dragged him down into the mud with me. He sat, stunned, fresh mud soaking through his clothes.

I laughed and patted his cheek, leaving a muddy handprint. "Thanks for joining me. You're a supportive friend."

"I can't believe you did that." He gathered a clump of dirt and smeared it on top of my head.

I tossed another handful of mud at him. It landed square in his chest.

"Stop, I surrender." Aiden pretended to wave a flag indicating his defeat. "We shouldn't be wasting any more time. We need to clean up and look for Daki."

I nodded, still laughing. He took off his muddied shirt and deposited it on the bank. I looked away lest I be tempted to stare at his bare chest. Peering into the water, I saw my reflection. I looked hideous. My hair was tangled, and dirt caked my face like war paint.

I caught Aiden's grin in the pool, and he said, "Go ahead and take your turn. I'll take a quick hike up the falls to see if there's any sign of Daki. Will you be okay alone?"

"I should be fine. I don't see any evidence of the Miyu."

"I won't wander out of hearing distance. If you need me, holler."

He started out a few steps before turning back. "Feel free to strip naked. I can't promise I won't peek though." He waggled his eyebrows, making me laugh. I knew despite his teasing, he was still a gentleman.

The climb to the top of the falls wouldn't take too long, though. Judging by the height of the waterfall, somewhere between fifty and seventy feet, I'd have enough time to bathe quickly and clean the mud from my clothes. My undergarments were still clean, so I would put those back on while I waited for my outer garments to dry.

I stripped down and hung my undergarments safely over some branches; then I carried my dirty clothes as I waded into the water. I stayed on the shallow side, scrubbing out the dirt from my gown and laying it out to dry. Then I headed for deeper waters. The water felt cool on my mud and sweat-polluted skin. I dunked my head under. The cut on my head stung. Careful to not touch it too much, I washed away the blood caked in my hair.

As I washed the mud away from my face, I replayed the mud fight I'd had with Aiden, and I smiled. Then that thought led to what happened after, when it felt like he was about to kiss me. I was feeling things for him I shouldn't. Aiden was my friend. I couldn't feel anything more for him, or I'd risk ruining what we had.

It wouldn't do to think about romance with anyone at the moment. The task at hand was to find Daki and get off this island.

I scrubbed my face and arms, getting rid of all traces of mud. Finally, my skin felt clean again.

Amidst the rush of the waterfall and the splash of the pool, I thought I heard a few notes of music. Was it my imagination? I peered around for the source. It seemed to be coming from within the waterfall. I stood quietly, waiting to hear it again, but all was still.

Yet, I was sure I had heard something. The melody echoed in my mind. It had sounded like a pan flute. I played the song back, and this time, the lyrics formed in my head.

*"United in love, the two shall become one.*
*He shall be fire who bears the flame,*
*And she who sees life's future present*
*Shall further give or take away."*

The words felt familiar, like an old folk song I'd heard long ago but forgotten. Maybe Mama had sung it before. As for the pan flute I'd thought I heard, it was probably just my overactive imagination. This wouldn't be the first time my mind composed a new tune.

I made a mental note to research the origin of the lyrics. I took a step for the bank, eager to dry off.

"Hey Rilla!" Aiden's voice interrupted my thoughts. I gasped. Was he back already?

I looked around but didn't see him. On guard, I crossed my arms over my chest and submerged myself deeper into the water.

"Over here, Rilla," he called again. His voice came from overhead. I peered up, and there he was, gazing at me from a ledge near the top of the falls.

I glared at him. There went my assumption that he was too honorable to peek.

"I can see something," he yelled.

"Well, stop looking, then," I shouted back.

"Why?" Aiden pointed to the waterfall. "There's a cave behind the falls."

He was high up and probably couldn't see that I was naked beneath the water. My cheeks heated at my mistake.

"I hiked up here only to find that there's a path of ledges all the way down behind the waterfall to the cave entrance," he said. He waved something in the air. "It doesn't look like it's accessible from the lagoon, though. I found Daki's goggles outside the mouth of the cave. I think he went inside. I'm going to dive down to you, and then we can head back up here together."

"Wait, I'm not dressed!" I shouted, but it was too late.

He'd already catapulted himself over the ledge, gliding smoothly into the glassy surface of the lagoon.

I struggled to get to the bank and my underclothes. I'd barely reached the shallow end when he emerged. I sank deeper into the pool, knees hitting the bottom so the water covered me below the neck.

He shook the water from his golden locks, sending spray into the sky. The drops glinted like diamonds in the sunlight. His tattoo stood out on the chiseled muscles of his bare chest. He was gorgeous.

"So glad to be rid of all that muck," he said, sending me a beam.

"Don't come any closer," I said.

He froze. His eyes widened as big as apples, and his gaze traveled slowly from under the water to my face. "Rilla, are you—"

"Yes."

"*Really*?" There was a laughing tilt to his voice, and his eyes sparkled. "I know I told you to feel free to strip naked, but I didn't actually think you would." There was no sign he viewed this moment with the same awkwardness I did. Had I called Aiden a gentleman? I took it all back. He was shameless.

"I guess I should have known, since you were naked last time, too."

I heard the grin in his voice. How dare he mention our first meeting, when I'd gone skinny-dipping with Radi at the palace lake? Shameless man.

Yet, I was dying of embarrassment.

"Will you turn around and let me get dressed?" I furrowed my brow and glared.

He clapped his hands over his eyes, still wearing that infuriating smirk. He turned around. I stalked out of the pool.

I grabbed my underclothes.

"Hey Rilla," Aiden called. "Nice backside."

I whipped my head around in outrage, but Aiden was still facing the other way with his eyes closed.

He laughed. "Made you look, didn't I?"

"Cod head," I muttered under my breath.

Although my clothes were still wet, I put them on anyway. They would have to dry as we walked.

"You can turn around now," I told Aiden. Then I forged ahead before he could get out of the water. I heard him trailing after me.

"Wait a second," he said. "Let me dry off a bit."

I stopped. He shook off the water from his body, picked up his shirt from where he'd deposited it on the bank, and put it back on.

We hiked silently up the hill. My feet sloshed and slunk into the marsh, and as the path grew steeper, the muscles in my inner thighs strained and protested.

Finally, we reached the top. The rapids gushed down like spit from a giant's mouth. Through the misty spray, I found the outline of the entrance to the cave Aiden described. The falls hid a path of overhanging ledges that led diagonally downward to a small opening in the cliff. The cave entrance was at the same level as the lagoon, with the water flowing out of the cave. Several rock pillars made it hard to access. One would have to swim through the falls and navigate around the rocks to the cave, a feat that an expert swimmer could take on, perhaps. But it was easier to use the pathway of ledges.

Aiden led the way, jumping gracefully from ledge to ledge. I stared warily at the steps. They seemed so far apart. Could I make those jumps?

I shook my head, dislodging the doubt. I was strong. I'd survived the showcase and being locked in a novelty cage. I'd taken down Emperor Terran and Empress Limera. If I'd been able to do that, I could conquer hopping a few ledges.

"Come on, Rilla," Aiden called. "You can do this."

I heaved my full body weight forward, pitching myself to get to the next step. I wavered a bit before catching my balance. It wasn't as hard as I'd thought.

Again, I repeated the motions, propelling myself to the next ledge, then the next, my confidence growing. It was evident my physical stamina had improved after training with Aiden and surviving in the wild these past few months.

Finally, we were at the bottom.

Aiden continued into the cave. I followed, nearly bumping into him when he suddenly stopped.

"What?" My gaze drifted to where Aiden was looking. There was no more land to walk on. A series of water passageways greeted us. A boat, tied to a post, swayed in the water as though it were waiting for its next passengers.

"Someone else must be on this island. Or they were," I said.

Aiden regarded the boat. "It looks well kept. It would only make sense if the owner was still on the island or had recently passed through."

A horrible thought occurred to me. "What if they are here, and they took Daki?"

"I say we see where the passageway leads and find out." Aiden stepped into the boat.

I hesitated. "Are you sure? We don't know who they are. What if we run into pirates again?"

"Exactly," he said. "Daki might need our help."

He was right, as always. I took a deep breath, trying to cast away my doubts. Even though it was a risk taking a boat that didn't belong to us into the cave where an enemy might be waiting, we did need to find Daki. This boat was the only way we could navigate through these tunnels.

I sat opposite Aiden. He took the oars and rowed slowly. His narrowed gaze was focused, cautious.

"Keep your guard up," he said.

As if I needed the reminder.

Though we were in a cave, there were holes in the stone canopy where the sun was able to shine through. The patches of light cast ominous shadows on the walls. I shivered and hugged my arms to my chest.

"Look," Aiden said. His attention was on a spot of the canal bank touched by a ring of light. The sunlight glinted off something white and shiny. Dozens of white beads lay scattered there. Pearls.

Were they Miyu pearls? Or regular pearls that pirates had stolen?

We came to a landing, where the water canal ended. The entrance to a grotto. The top of the cave towered above us. It was a wide space, large enough for a band of pirates to hide a ship and their treasure.

I climbed out of the boat after Aiden. More pearls littered the floor. But there was no other treasure. No gold coins or precious gemstones. Nothing to indicate pirates had made this place into their lair. The skeleton wreckage of two overturned hulls loomed in the cave like the mouths of monsters. Buried under the rotting wood, rats scurried to and fro. I shivered and stepped back. Goosebumps rose on my flesh.

Bones and skulls, off-white and graying with decayed matter, littered the ground. This must be what the rats were feasting on. There were some smaller-sized skulls. They had probably belonged to animals. But many of the bones were larger. Hard to tell if they had been Shyan, Fauxhemian, or Exentrik. I didn't want to be added to the pile.

A few more pearls were scattered among the wreckage and the remains.

"There are only two ways these pearls could have ended up here,"

Aiden said. "Either this is where pirates stashed their hidden treasure, or these pearls were once Miyu tears. But something tells me this may not be a pirate's den, which means . . ." He trailed off, casting me a bleak look.

My heart sped up, and anxiety coursed through my veins. "This could be a Miyu's lair. What if it's the Miyu that attacked us?"

"Well, there's one way to find out," Aiden said. "Touch a pearl. Remember? Daki said they hold the memories of the Miyu who created them. You'll have to do it so that I can stay alert in case the Miyu sneaks up on us."

A fat pearl sat atop a rotting wooden box. Despite the dread of discovering the truth, I had to touch it. I had to know. I brushed my fingers across the smooth, white surface. Instantly, images flooded my mind.

I was present in the body and mind of a young Miyu girl. Her name was Hara. The memory played as though I had become her.

*I stand in the center of a stone circle. I twitch my tail, keeping myself balanced in the water, but other than that, I try to keep my body completely still. My* shinu, *teacher, watches me from several feet away. She's waiting for me to make a mistake.*

*"Concentrate, Hara," Shinu Lairu says, her expression stern. "Summon your water kaigon."*

*I let out a pulse of my wyis. Bubbles of water accumulate around me, forming the outline of a kaigon. But I can't hold my wyis. The bubbles dissipate. I wince and hang my head in shame.*

*"I'm sorry. I broke my focus."*

*Shinu Lairu slaps me. The pain is a reminder of my constant failure and disappointment to my people. "How many times must you repeat this lesson?" she says. "Why can't you be more like your sister? Thank Goddess Mi you aren't next in line to be queen."*

The memory broke. I glanced at Aiden. "It's the Miyu that

attacked us. Her name is Hara."

"Keep going," he said.

I touched another pearl.

A new memory appeared in my mind. I was present in Hara's body again.

*I tug my red cloak closer to my body as I stand on the shore of this despicable island, and I prepare for my sister, the Miyu queen, to lecture me. But she no longer intimidates me. We're not children anymore. I stare at the tiara of pearls adorning her head. If only I'd been born three minutes earlier, I would be the older twin, and that tiara would belong to me.*

*Behind my sister, three Miyu royal sentinels stand guard, waiting for my sister's command. If they think they're going to stop me, they're delusional.*

*My sister scowls at me. "I know what you've been doing, sister. How you've been wrecking ships. Enslaving the survivors who get stranded on this island and then killing them. This behavior must stop."*

*"I'm simply demonstrating how easy it would be to control the Shyan males," I say. "Why should I stop? Their hearts are evil. If we do not use our magic to control them, they will always pose the risk of conquering and controlling us."*

*"The Shyan emperor is cruel—that is true," the queen says. "But we cannot use our magic for evil, or we'll be no better than he is. You haven't just killed Shyan sailors. You've been wrecking the boats of innocent fishermen no matter what kingdom they sail from."*

*"They're all men," I say. "In my eyes, there's no difference between them. They are liars."*

*"Careful, sister, lest your broken heart becomes a bitter one," she says. "I care too much about you to see you go down this road. Either return home with me willingly, or I'll have no choice but to use force."*

*The Miyu sentinels behind her step forward, encircling me. I smile.*

*Better to pretend to be compliant for now. I'll have time to make a move later.* "*There's no need for that. We are family, and you are my queen. I'll obey your orders.*"

I went through a few more pearls and saw Hara's childhood memories, each lasting just a few seconds. Some were of her playing with her older sister. I went through her memories of her sister's coronation and of her niece's birth. I felt her excitement to be holding her baby niece for the first time.

In another memory, a man wore a contraption on his back, something in the shape of a diamond, acting as wings. A kite? In his hands, he held a bamboo flute.

Hara shook her fists and cursed at him as he flew away from the island. But as the man fled, the flute slipped from his fingers and landed in the ground next to Hara.

I pulled away from the pearl. That man had used Daki's kite to get away. What was he doing with Daki's kite?

I hadn't recognized his face. Probably another man Hara had shipwrecked.

I came to another pearl. In this memory, I was a younger version of Hara. She was a teenager.

*I surface from the water, carrying the unconscious man. I swim to shore as fast as I can. I have to save him.*

*As I reach the sand of the shoreline, my tail splits apart and becomes legs. I place the man on the ground and breathe life back into him.*

*Why don't I want to kill him? I should. His emperor has brought war on my people. But I think I am in love.*

I took my fingers off the pearl, and the images faded.

Aiden placed a hand on my shoulder. "Did you see anything useful about Hara?"

"She didn't seem evil in all the memories," I said. "She fought in the war Terran started against the Miyu, but she saved one of the sailors from drowning. She was in love with him. I don't know what happened between the war and now, but she's responsible for wrecking ships in this area. The surviving men end up on this island, and she'll enslave them before killing them. Also, I saw a man escape from Hara using one of Daki's kites. It wasn't Daki, though."

Aiden furled his brow. "How did he get Daki's kite? Well, never mind that now." He stared into the darkness of the cave. "As much as I'd like to leave this place and the island, we still have to find Daki. Stay alert. I'm not particularly eager to become the man-slave of a fish."

# CHAPTER 15

✦ ✦ ✦ ✦ ✦ ✦ ✦ ✦ ✦ ✦

We ventured farther into the lair, keeping out of sight by hiding behind the wreckage of the ship. Two cages stood upon the broken hull of another ship. The bars of the cages were white, and as we approached for a closer look, I realized they were made of bones. Cleaned bones. The skeletons of unfortunate souls who had sailed too close to this Miyu. Skulls lay scattered on the sand amongst more pearls. These skulls seemed to have been laid out for decorative purposes, unlike the decayed ones under the wreckage of the ships.

I shivered, suddenly chilled. Within the first cage, a colorful bird was perched on a swing. It saw me and flew toward the door, flapping its wings frantically. The poor thing probably wanted to be free from its prison.

I cast it an apologetic glance. Maybe I imagined it, but the bird seemed to have an annoyed expression.

I peered into the second cage. In this one, a sleeping girl lay on some blankets. She appeared almost ethereal. A mound of pearls lay around her cage, and a few were scattered along her sleeping form. Some were even stuck in her gown and on her cheeks. She had the same long black hair as Hara, beautiful thick locks that fell to her waist. Two tattoos were inked on the girl's upper arms, one of which depicted a sea kaigon.

"She's a Miyu, too," I whispered to Aiden. "What if she wakes up and sees us?"

"If Hara imprisoned her in that cage, then I don't think she's our enemy," Aiden said. His gaze fell upon the pearls. "Guess there's only one way to find out her story."

I bent down and plucked one up from the ground. My surroundings blurred as I journeyed into the girl's mind.

*I hear the most pain-stricken scream. The pirates have surrounded Sentinel Jaiku. They stab her. Then I hear myself scream.*

*"Stop, you murderers," I shout. "Don't hurt her."*

*They don't listen. Over and over, they stab her. I scream again, and tears pour down my face. I can't save her.*

*Aunt Hara holds a knife to my back. I freeze, unable to process that this is happening. I stare at her in disbelief. "How could you do this? You're my aunt. And I am the princess of the Miyu. You're a traitor to the crown."*

*"My dear princess," Aunt Hara says, "don't take it personally. You are simply a means to getting what I desire. My sister will cede the throne to me if she wants to see you alive again. Now, give me your cloak."*

*Aunt Hara wrenches my cloak off my back. I grab for it, but she's too fast. She thrusts a flattened palm into my chest. A stream of her wyis bolts into me, and the pain is overwhelming. I fall to the ground and feel myself losing consciousness.*

I dropped the pearl.

Aiden touched my shoulder. "What did you see?"

"She's the Miyu princess," I said. "Hara is her aunt. Hara also worked with the pirates and the Lotuses back in Yao Kingdom. She allowed the pirates and Lotuses to take the princess's sentinel and kill her. Then Hara kidnapped the princess."

"I suppose you've seen my memories through my tears." The

girlish voice made me jump. The Miyu princess was awake. "I'm Princess Amika, crown princess to the Miyu tribe. I apologize on my aunt's behalf. I know she destroyed your ship, and you were forced to land on this island."

"Your aunt told you this?" I asked.

She shook her head no. "I gathered this much from the conversation between Aunt Hara and your friend before she changed him."

Aiden perked up. "Daki? What do you mean, *changed* him?"

"Unfortunately, that's him." Amika pointed to the other cage that held the bird whose wings flapped as if to gain our attention.

"Aunt Hara is known to change sailors into birds and other creatures before she hunts them down and eats them," Amika said. "My mother disapproves, but Hara does what she wants. I didn't know how bad she had gotten until now."

"Is there any way we can change Daki back into a man?" Aiden asked.

Amika nodded. "Several ways, but I'll only tell you if you help me escape."

I tested the lock of her cage. "Where did Hara hide the key?"

"There is no key to this cage. Only a Miyu's wyis can open it. Unfortunately, without my cloak, I'm powerless and my wyis is low. Can't transform into my Miyu form, or summon my sea kaigon." She extended her arm, showing us the sea kaigon tattoo. "If you can get my cloak, I'll be able to escape from this cage and help your friend. I'm afraid I don't know where my aunt stashed it."

Aiden weaved his way among the planks and debris. "I don't see it."

"Check behind that crevice." Amika pointed to a pillar of rocks. "She keeps some of the treasure she's found over the years in a box."

I was closer to the crevice than Aiden was, so I went to look. In the space behind the rock, there was a chest made of bones. I grabbed it, but it was heavy. It wouldn't budge.

Aiden came over and helped. Together, we pulled it across the ground toward us.

"I'll keep guard for Hara," Aiden said. "You search the chest."

I opened the lid. Gold pieces and glittering gemstones filled the box.

Again, the song that had played when I'd been in the lagoon came into my mind.

> *"United in love, the two shall become one*
> *He shall be fire who bears the flame*
> *And she who sees life's future present*
> *Shall further give or take away."*

Something made of wood lay beneath the gems and coins. A cylindrical object. I stooped down and picked it up.

A bamboo flute? Just like the one I'd seen that man drop in Hara's memory.

The flute was exquisitely made. Crafted for a true musician. A pattern and the initials J. W. had been carved into it. Carving the owner's initials on instruments was a popular trend among rich aristocrats. I could easily imagine a courtier carrying this and playing it under the light of the Lavender Moon for his own enjoyment and to entertain his fellow aristocrats.

I pocketed it and continued rummaging through the chest. But the cloak wasn't there.

I shook my head at Amika. "I can't find it."

"She must have it on her then." Amika shook the bars of her cage and groaned. "Of course, she does. She'd never allow anyone to help me so easily."

Footsteps sounded behind us.

"She's coming." Aiden pulled me behind a rock, and we crouched out of sight.

Hara approached. Her long black hair flowed down to her thighs. She had a voluptuous frame, full breasts, and sharp, gray eyes the color of a storm. And she wore a red cloak.

Hara went up to Amika's cage. "Hello, dear niece. Sorry to have left you for so long. I was trying to find two Shyan who are visiting my little island. You wouldn't have happened to see them, have you?"

Amika came up to the bars and glared at her aunt. "No. Now give me back my cloak."

Hara made a disappointed clicking noise with her tongue. "You know how much it hurts to know you're lying to me." She faced Daki's cage. Her wyis formed a tendril of dark energy in the palm of her hand. "Your new Shyan friends better come out of hiding now, or I'll be forced to kill this nuisance of a man in front of them."

The tendril twisted around Daki and squeezed. He made a pained noise.

"Stop. Release him." I dropped my knapsack, getting rid of the extra weight, then unsheathed my sword and came out of hiding. Aiden did the same, pointing his blade at her.

Amika grabbed the bars of her cage and shook them. "Aunt Hara, leave these people alone, and unlock this door now."

With her free hand, Hara lifted a red cloak. Not the one she wore, but a second. The grimace on Amika's face implied that the cloak was hers. "I have your cloak, child. Did you think I would leave it laying around where anyone could take it?"

"I don't understand why you're doing this," Amika said.

"I want what's best for our people, niece. A world where we are no longer threatened by Shyan rule. So, I take great offense that you'd ask them for help rather than wait for me to return this to you when I'm ready."

Her grip on Daki tightened. He squawked a choking sound.

"Give me back my cloak, and stop hurting him." Amika growled.

Hara released Daki. His bird form fell back on the ground, and he released several more squawks, gasping for air. "See? I'm not an unreasonable woman. As for returning your cloak, I already said I would. Just not now."

With no warning, Hara flicked a wrist toward Aiden. Her wyis took physical form once again in a string of dark energy that knocked Aiden's sword from his hand, then curled around his waist. He struggled to get free, but the energy around him tightened.

"Let him go." I pointed my sword at the Miyu. I couldn't risk using my tin-chai, but it didn't mean I'd go down without a fight.

"Please Aunt," Amika said. "Don't hurt them. There have been enough grievances between the Miyu and the Shyan. I don't want to add more to the list."

"Quiet." Hara pointed her free hand at Amika. A blast of energy released from her palm, sending Amika flying backward. The girl hit the back of the cage and fell to the ground, still conscious but dazed.

"Do not interfere, niece." Hara hung Amika's cloak on one arm. "I'll deal with you later."

Her attention focused upon me. "You are a Shyan female. I have no wish to hurt a woman. Lower your weapon, take your belongings, and you're free to leave my island. I left your kite undisturbed on the beach."

"I won't leave without them," I said.

Her lips twisted in a look of amusement. "You would risk your life for these males? Shyan men are the most controlling over their women as far as I've seen."

"Aiden's not like that. He's my friend. Daki, too. I'll defend them to the death." I refused to lower my sword.

"Friend? Foolish girl, I can tell you actually like this boy." With her energy twisted around Aiden, Hara lifted him into the air. "True, I suppose he is more handsome than the average male, and he would be enjoyable to have as a lover."

I yelled a battle cry and charged at Hara. But something grabbed at my sword, stopping me full force. I stumbled. The sword grew heavier. Hara had curled a second wisp of her dark energy around it. I fought against the weight, but she twisted her hand and swept the sword out of my hand. It clattered onto the ground.

I raised my fists to fight.

"You are stubborn—I give you that," Hara said. "But I still don't wish to harm another female. Listen to me, child. This boy is like any other man, pretending to be your friend but lusting after your body. He desires you as an object to win over and then discard when he grows bored. I watched the two of you before you entered my lair. This boy pretended he didn't see you bathing in the lagoon, but he watched without your knowing for many minutes before alerting you of his presence."

With a gasp, my gaze flashed to Aiden, trying to assess if what Hara said was true.

Aiden's cheeks reddened. That was answer enough.

I glared at him, but now wasn't the time to chastise him.

"The boy must have intentions to seduce you," Hara said. "And I have no doubt you'd give in to the temptation eventually, which will be your downfall. He's no different than the beast that seduced and abandoned me. I'm only doing you a favor. I'll show you how easy it is to sway him into becoming my lover. Then you can decide whether you still want to risk your life to save him."

"You're insane," Aiden said. "I'm not going to be your lover." He glanced helplessly in my direction.

"Oh, but you have no choice, just as I had no choice when one of your kind wanted me." She drew him closer to her and caressed his cheek with a finger. She looked into his eyes. "You will love none other than me until the day I'm through with you."

Aiden didn't move. His eyes glazed over. "I am yours. There is no other."

"See how easy it was to make him forget you? If a man was truly capable of loving only one woman, he would not give into a Miyu's hypnotic allure. If you're not convinced yet, maybe this will make you give up on him."

She tilted his head toward her and kissed him. A pang of jealousy stirred in my chest. I shook it off.

Amika's cloak dangled from Hara's arm. She was distracted kissing Aiden. Now was my chance.

I charged at her and snatched the princess's cloak.

"No!" Hara screamed. She threw Aiden aside, and he fell to the ground, unresponsive. His eyes were still glazed in hypnotic stupor.

I threw the cloak into Amika's cage. The princess rushed forward, grabbed her cloak, and draped it over her shoulders. She blasted a bolt of energy from her hand into the lock and burst out of the cage.

Amika threw a second energy bolt at Hara.

But Hara easily dodged it. She sent a wave of dark energy through the air and struck Amika's shoulder. Wincing, the princess fell. I ran to Amika's side.

Hara gave me a pitying look. "Since you've decided to go against me, I have no choice but to kill you." She regarded Amika. "And you, dear niece. Do you sincerely believe you can win against me? You are a mere babe. Isn't that why your mother wouldn't allow you out of her sight? I convinced her you'd be safe in my care because I knew it would be easy to trick you. You didn't even notice when I was leading you in the wrong direction. You're a sheltered weakling."

"I trusted you," Amika said. "I thought you believed in me."

"Believe in a weak child like you? You have never had to fend for yourself. Sentinels protect you. I never had the privilege. I had to fight all my battles on my own." Hara inspected her fingernails as though bored. "You may try to fight me if you wish, but you're dreaming if you think you've got a chance to defeat me."

I sensed the princess's confidence waver. She whispered to me. "We need to retreat. Follow me." Her gaze drifted to the waterway behind us, where we had first entered. The waters had been calm, but now they rose and stirred into fast-moving rapids. Amika dived in.

"Get back here," Hara screamed.

She lunged at me. I had no choice. I plunged into the canal. The cold surrounded me, and I went under.

# CHAPTER 16

✦ ✦ ✦ ✦ ✦ ✦ ✦ ✦ ✦ ✦

The current pulled at me, but I pushed above the surface of the water, took a gasping breath, and treaded against the tide. I grabbed onto the canal bank and clung to it. I wouldn't be able to hold on for long.

I had to use my tin-chai, the layer I'd learned before defeating Terran, to control the natural elements with my voice. *Please don't fail me now*, I prayed.

Breathless, I sang out three notes, commanding the water to obey me. A tendril of water wrapped itself around my waist. It was working.

A flash of red, draped on the shape of a large fish-like creature, rippled in the water. Princess Amika. She was here.

What if I harmed her? I couldn't use my tin-chai.

The water fell away from me as if I'd never sung at all. My hand slipped from the rock. I went down. My lungs threatened to collapse. I fought to swim, but as I continued to struggle, I quickly lost strength against the rapids. Something grabbed me around the waist and lifted me from the water.

I gasped for air, coughing and sputtering. Through my swirling vision, I saw a watery beast. A sea kaigon. It used its talon to scoop me up from the water. But unlike the sea kaigon that had tried to kill us back on the ship, this one wore a gentle expression and treated me with tenderness. It placed me on its back and carried me through the water channels. We went through the gushing waterfall. Then it deposited me onto the marshy banks of the lagoon.

I lay on the ground, breathing hard. My muscles ached.

Amika surfaced from the water and came up on land. Her fish tail transformed into legs. Then the sea kaigon dissipated into mist and reattached onto Amika's skin, forming a tattoo inked on her forearm.

"I take it you have a plan," I said.

"We need to get back to the shore before my aunt finds us," Amika said. "Then we'll take my sea kaigon and find my mother. She and the other Miyu sentinels will fight Aunt Hara."

"There's no time. Your aunt has my best friend hypnotized and my other friend turned into a bird. She may kill them before your mother has the chance to get here."

"But I'm not powerful enough to destroy her," Princess Amika said. "Not unless I have help."

"We have to get back to the cave."

Amika's eyes sharpened. She grabbed my arm, cutting me off. "Shh. My aunt's coming through the waterfall."

We both crouched behind the foliage, breath abated. Hara rose from the water and changed her tail into legs. She cried out in a singsong voice as she walked down the path. "I know you couldn't have gone far, my niece. And you must have the Shyan girl. Come out now before I lose my patience."

She stopped several feet away from us but close enough that I was sure she would be able to sense our presence behind her.

"You're mistaken if you think you can leave this island and find your mother," Hara said. "I've already employed my own sea kaigon to guard the shoreline. If you attempt to swim out to sea, they'll simply take you back to me."

Amika grimaced. So much for that plan.

"All right. Keep hiding then," Hara said. "I'll catch you eventually."

She headed in the opposite direction, which I knew to be the shoreline. Neither Amika nor I moved for another long minute, watching Hara's back until she was out of view.

I slumped to the ground, my muscles exhausted. "She was alone. This means my friends are in her lair, and they aren't guarded now. I have to go back for them."

"This might be one of her tricks," Amika said. "What if she wants us to think she's leaving the cave unguarded so we go back?"

"That's a chance I'm willing to take. I got your cloak back, so will you tell me now? How do I break your aunt's spells on my friends?"

"I can return the captain into his original form now that I have my cloak back. Then we take on my aunt. If we can steal her cloak, her powers will be drained. She won't be able to summon her sea kaigon or use any magic. She'll be easier to overcome then. Since she's away from the cave, your friend, the golden-eyed boy, won't be under her hypnosis. But she'll control him again once he's within hearing range. If we can find a way to drown out her voice so he can't hear her, he'll be able to break free of her spell. My mother might kill me for telling you this, but music and loud noises weaken a Miyu."

I thought about the flute in my cloak. Although I couldn't try using my singing voice in case I accidentally hurt someone, I could use the flute to subdue Hara. "You, a Shyan, are willing to tell me of your people's weakness?"

"I've no other choice but to trust you as you trusted me. It's my fault my sentinel was killed. She questioned why we were traveling north when we were supposed to go south to Exentria. But I told her she was being paranoid, and my aunt wouldn't lead us astray. I don't want anyone else to die at Hara's hands."

"We can defeat her if we work together," I said. "We need a plan."

Amika gazed back at the lagoon. "We'll plan on the way."

Her sea kaigon tattoo disappeared from her skin, forming what looked like dust in the air. This dust fell into the water. In another five seconds, a sea kaigon, his back long and silver, bobbed his head up from the water.

"Climb on," she said.

I did as she instructed and wrapped my arms around the creature's neck. The kaigon took off, paddling the water with his back fins and tail.

We went through the waterfall, and the spray drenched me again. The air was humid and muggy, so I didn't mind. It kept my skin cool.

Amika surfaced from the water and swam beside us. "I saw you attempt to use your tin-chai. You use your voice to control the natural elements, don't you? Perhaps if you sing loud enough, your voice will weaken Hara. Not kill her, if we can avoid it. She is still my aunt, and I believe there's some good left in her."

Amika was right. If Hara were purely evil, she wouldn't have tried to let me go free.

"Then I'm afraid using my voice would be too risky." My shoulders slumped. "While one of my tin-chai's layers is to control the elements, another layer is to afflict disease and to kill. Unfortunately, my tin-chai has been failing me lately, and I've accidentally killed people I didn't mean to harm. What if you sing? Would you be able to drown out her voice?"

She pursed her lips and grimaced. "I'm afraid Miyu voices are not effective in weakening other Miyu."

I took the bamboo flute out of my cloak. "Will this work against her?"

Amika's eyes brightened. "Yes, she won't be able to withstand the music of a flute."

"Why does your aunt hate Shyan men so much?" I asked. "And why would she be willing to betray her family to become queen?"

"A Shyan man broke her heart," Amika said. "Becoming queen is the only way she can bring about the destruction of Seracedar in a way she feels will bring justice for herself."

"I saw some of her memories through her tears. There was a man she saved from drowning. Was it him?"

"That's the one," Amika said. "I've picked up bits and pieces of the story from my mother. Hara was assigned to this region during the war. She used this island to kill sailors if they survived her attack on their ship, but there was a man who saved her from the spears of his comrades. When our sentinels sank their ship, Hara saved the man's life."

The water was calm, and the sea kaigon floated through the channels without creating a single wave. Aside from Amika's voice, all was quiet.

"The two of them lived on this island a year," she continued. "But he wanted to go home and tell his parents he was still alive. He promised to return but never did. Once she realized he'd deceived her, she went into a rampage against Shyan males. She's been trying to convince my mother to use our hypnotic powers to seduce Shyan men. We could easily make your kingdom stop attacking us, if we used such tactics, and perhaps even conquer your kingdom. But Mother does not believe in using our magic to make men, especially those who already have wives at home, fall in love with us. She says that would only make the entire world misunderstand us more."

"Your mother didn't have any idea that Hara wanted to take over the throne?" I asked.

"They may have had their disagreements, but they are sisters. They grew up together. Mother trusted her as did I." Amika's eyes grew downcast. "It took so long to convince my mother to allow me to leave our kingdom. Aunt Hara spoke on my behalf, and I believed she was on my side. Despite her hatred toward the Shyan, I never thought she would hurt her own family."

"I'm sorry the pirates killed your sentinel for her tail," I said. "There are too many cruel people in this world."

Her eyes sparked with anger. "The tail was not for the pirates but the Lotuses. The pirates arranged to acquire the tail for the Lotuses. In exchange, they would lead the pirates to some fugitives with a hefty price on their heads."

"Fugitives? That would be Aiden and me," I said. "What Lotus would want a Miyu's tail?"

"Their Dahlia," Amika said. "I saw her face. It was like porcelain."

Androgy Haming.

"When the pirates killed my sentinel, I saw the burns on the Dahlia's back. They even started crawling on her neck. Then she changed form into a man. But that didn't help with the scars. They seemed to be getting worse. He was in a lot of pain."

I remembered when Androgy Haming revealed himself at the inn. He had burn marks, and Teer protested his use of his tin-chai. It was as though doing so exhausted his wyis and pained him.

Those scars hadn't been on Haming when we'd parted ways after Limera's death.

We continued through the channel, Amika treading the water beside me. "The man, or Dahlia—whatever he is—asked the pirates and the Lotuses to leave for a moment so he could speak to my aunt alone. They made a side deal together. If the pirates failed to capture you, my aunt was to finish the job. In exchange, the man promised to locate my aunt's lover and bring him to this island. He was determined to stop you from sailing out of Yao Kingdom. Then he, the Lotuses, and the pirates went into the village to ambush you and your friends. My aunt brought me here, and then she waited to see if you'd managed to escape the pirates and Lotuses. It seems we both have battles to ensure the peace of our kingdoms. We cannot let my aunt or this Androgy Haming win."

Her words were backed by determination. It strengthened my resolve. Together, we would defeat Hara and venture on to Emberwood. There was no room for failure.

# CHAPTER 17

✦ ✦ ✦ ✦ ✦ ✦ ✦ ✦ ✦ ✦

We stopped at the mouth of the cave of Hara's lair and hid behind the wreckage of the ship. I held tightly onto the flute, ready to take on Hara whenever she came back.

I located Aiden sleeping on a lounge chair. Ropes bound his arms and feet to the chair. Amika had said as long as he didn't hear Hara's voice, he wouldn't be under her hypnosis. Fire would easily burn those ropes, allowing him to get away.

"Did your aunt drug him?" I asked. "Why would he be asleep instead of fighting to get free?"

"Being under a Miyu's hypnotic spell is like being drugged," Amika said. "It makes her victims tired even when she is not commanding them at the moment. Wake him up and untie him. As long as she's not here, he'll be himself. I'll open the captain's cage and change him back. Stay alert. My aunt will be back at any moment."

I kept my footsteps light as I inched toward Aiden. His eyes opened, and he saw me. He strained against the bindings. "Rilla? You can't be here. She'll be back at any time."

"I'm going to untie you," I said.

He gave me a wry look. "If that worked, I would have burned these ropes off myself by now. They also have her dark energy infused into them. Unless she removes her energy from the shackles, I can't break free."

I swore. "Then the only way is to get her cloak away from her. Weaken her magic."

Behind me, Daki screeched from his cage, diverting my attention to him. Amika had pulled him out of his cage, but suddenly, she jumped. "Rilla, watch out. My aunt is here. She's humming out of your hearing range, but I can hear it."

I raised the flute to my lips, but I didn't have time to play. Aiden's eyes had darkened. Flames formed in his hands, burning the ropes into ash in seconds. He rose from the chair.

I ducked and rolled across the ground as a blast of fire went over my head. I crouched, breathing hard. Aiden stood ten feet away. His pupils were dilated.

From behind the chaise, Hara emerged from the shadows. "Did you think you could sneak back in without my knowing?"

Daki flew above her head, attempting to peck her, but Hara merely swept him aside, sending him crashing into the cave wall. He fell to the ground, unmoving.

"Daki!" I cried.

Hara addressed Aiden. "Kill your friend. I'll subdue the princess."

Before I could blink, she sent a blast of dark energy at Amika. The princess barely had a chance to deflect it with her own energy. Aiden blocked my path. I was cornered, my back to the cave wall.

I raised the flute to my lips. He came at me and knocked it away, out of reach. I dodged again as another blast of fire hit the wall behind me. The smell of burnt hair filled the air. My hair.

I couldn't get too close to him. He could easily overpower me with strength alone. But I couldn't continue dodging his fire blasts either. "Aiden, it's me," I shouted. "You need to snap out of Hara's hypnosis."

The fire ball grew in his palms.

How was I supposed to fight fire? With more fire?

Blood magic. Sago's diamond on my necklace still contained a trace of Aiden's blood absorbed in it.

Dodging another burst from Aiden, I felt for my wyis, let it thread through all four channels, then reached into what remained of Aiden's wyis in his blood. Heat simmered through my veins, and a single flame burst from my palm then faded almost as instantly.

Aiden reached for me, but the flame in my hands distracted him. He jumped back, startled. I dropped to the ground, rolled toward the flute, and snatched it up. I placed the flute to my lips and played *The Lady of the Sea*. The notes of the flute had a breathy timbre, rich and sweet. The sound echoed through the cave.

The fire in his hands subsided to a small flame. It was working.

"How did you get that flute?" Hara's screech echoed in the cave.

I continued to play the flute. *Please remember me*. I willed Aiden to come back to himself. The black in his irises flickered to gold. I kept playing, trying to keep my focus and my gaze locked on Aiden.

But behind him, the fight between Hara and Amika raged on. The physical forms of their wyis were interlocked, two streams of energy clashing with one another. Amika took a step back. She didn't look like she'd last for much longer.

If music made all Miyu weaker, Amika was also affected.

Aiden groaned, forcing my attention back to him. His eyes were still glazed over and threatened to go completely black again.

"Rilla, keep playing," Amika shouted. "Don't worry about me."

I focused on my song, playing the flute as loud as I could.

Amika's screams echoed through the air. But I couldn't stop playing yet.

Then Aiden shook his head and blinked. His eyes were back to their golden hue. He looked at me with clarity.

Amika screamed again. Hara had pinned her to the ground and removed Amika's cloak.

"You'll not be getting your power back this time." Hara looked weary. Splotches of red dotted her face, and her breathing was heavy.

Amika groaned on the ground.

I continued playing the flute.

"Stop playing that blasted thing!" Hara screeched. She tried to form a thread of her dark energy in her palm, but it dissipated into the air. She grabbed a knife from her cloak and held it to Amika's neck. "I don't want to do this, but I will sacrifice my niece if you continue. I'll not surrender until I become the Miyu queen and save my people from the Shyan."

I stopped playing. "Don't hurt her."

"You can't harm her," Aiden said. "You still need her as leverage. Without her, the queen will never cede the throne to you."

He took a small step, making sure his back was facing me. Behind his back, he pointed to the water canal. Then he used his finger to make a twisting motion.

He wanted me to use my tin-chai to control the water and bind Hara. But what if my tin-chai failed again? No. I had to try.

"I'll pin the blame on you," Hara said. "Her mother will never believe a Shyan over her own sister."

Aiden considered this, then said, "You could blame us for her death. You can even kill us. I know we can't defeat you as long as you have your cloak. But it won't matter. They'll find Amika's pearl tears or the tears of the sentinel you betrayed. There's no way you can find and destroy all of them. Just one will show the truth as soon as the queen and her sentinels touch it, and I'll bet they already suspect you."

Hara wavered, and I seized the chance. I sang.

*"The lady of the sea lost her one true love*
*Beneath the stormy, billowing swell*
*She pled with the waters for his return*
*'Til the sea surrendered a silver shell."*

The water moved. A thread curled into the air.
Hara saw this and gasped. She charged at me, dagger in hand.

# CHAPTER 18

✦ ✦ ✦ ✦ ✦ ✦ ✦ ✦ ✦ ✦

Panic lurched in my chest. I sang louder. All my focus shifted from the water to Hara. The tendril of water fell into the canal.

Hara stopped midstep and shrieked in pain. She dropped the dagger. Her hands flew to her face, and she collapsed to the ground.

Her screams shifted from anger to alarm.

"Rilla, stop!" Aiden cried. "I think your voice . . . you're killing her."

I stopped my song. Hara writhed on the ground in agony, hands clasping her face.

"Aunt Hara!" Amika cried, crouching by her aunt's side. Hara's skin dissolved, fizzling into foam. The screams subsided. Nothing was left of her but white froth bubbling on the floor. Her cloak dissolved, turning to foam and then to water.

Once again, I hadn't been able to control my powers. I'd intended only to move the water to subdue Hara, but I killed her.

I fell to my knees. My tin-chai was out of my control. I took a sharp glance around the cave at Aiden, Daki, and Amika. "Did I hurt you?"

I could have killed them. My whole body shook at the realization.

Aiden shook his head no. "We're all fine."

"I didn't mean for this to happen," I said. "I didn't want to use my tin-chai to kill again."

Aiden placed an arm around my shoulders and hugged me. "We'll figure this out together."

I hung my head, addressing Amika. "I'm sorry. I know you wanted her to be brought back to your people alive."

The princess stood and gazed upon the last of the foam. "This isn't your fault. I wasn't strong enough to subdue her. If you hadn't killed her, she may have killed me. Without me as a witness, she would have been able to return to the Miyu, ambush my mother, and succeed in taking control of the Miyu throne."

A tear rolled down Amika's cheek and solidified into a pearl before hitting the ground. "She was too far gone. Consumed by her hatred. Thank you for not abandoning me. The Miyu will return the favor. I promise this."

Amika grabbed her cloak from the ground. White froth from Hara's remains still foamed in the dirt. With one last lingering look at the foam, Amika wiped her tears.

She placed her cloak around her shoulders. She walked to Daki, who squawked and flapped his wings impatiently. The princess murmured a chant, and Daki illuminated with light from within. His body elongated, and there he stood in his original form once again.

"Thank Old Grandfather Heaven," he said. "Here I always thought I'd want permanent wings, but now I may never wish to fly again."

We stood on the shoreline of the island, trying to decide if Daki should use his tin-chai to rebuild another ship or to mend the kites.

"It will definitely be faster for me to mend the kites," Daki said. "Although after being turned into a bird, I'd prefer to not fly."

"How long will it take to build a ship?" Aiden asked. "Haming's already a day ahead of us."

"I can finish it by evening," Daki answered.

He summoned his wyis. He lifted his hands, and a tree came toward him. The tree splintered into usable pieces, taking on different shapes. We watched in awe as he worked.

My attention wandered over to Amika, who sat in the sand, watching the tide ripple onto the shore. Then my gaze caught a glimmer of silvery bodies out in the sea, swiftly swimming our way.

I pointed. "Look. Are those Miyu?"

Amika stood. "Yes. It's Mother. They've found me."

"I hope they don't think we kidnapped you and try to kill us," Aiden said. "I can't take another Miyu attack."

"Nonsense. You are my saviors," Amika said. "They won't harm you. I promise."

She waded into the sea, transformed into her Miyu body, and swam toward the approaching pod. After a few minutes, Amika turned to the shore with one of the Miyu, the rest of the pod staying back. The other Miyu was older and wore a tiara made of pearls. *The queen.*

Mother and daughter transformed and walked toward us.

"My daughter explained everything to me," the Miyu queen said. "I am Yisa, the sovereign of the Miyu. I wish I had realized earlier how disturbed my sister had become. Thank you for coming to our princess's aid. Our people are indebted to you."

I bowed low. "Helping the princess was the right thing to do."

"I am sorry the Shyan have been such aggressors toward the Miyu," Aiden said. "My hope is that one day our future emperor will make amends to your people."

Queen Yisa nodded. "If only the Shyan were ruled by those as noble as both of you. My daughter has told me of your situation—that you need to get to Emberwood. Please allow the Miyu to escort you there. With our sea kaigon pulling your ship, we believe we can get you there faster than if you were to sail on your own."

"In that case, we'd be most obliged," Daki said. "Our journey has already been delayed by days, and we could use all the help we can get. I can finish rebuilding the ship by this evening. Would it be all right with Your Majesty to wait?"

"Of course," Queen Yisa said. "We shall start whenever you are ready."

"How long do you think it will take to get there?" Aiden asked.

"I believe we can get you to the coast of Emberwood by dawn."

Aiden smiled and thanked her. He turned to me. "Personally, I'm grateful we don't have to fly those kites again."

"Perhaps on our next adventure," I said.

He gave me a look. "Next adventure? Let's make sure we survive this one first."

# CHAPTER 19

✦ ✦ ✦ ✦ ✦ ✦ ✦ ✦ ✦ ✦

We boarded the ship, and the Miyu let their sea kaigons push us into the sea. The kaigons guided the ship through the waters, and we were off, gliding through the ocean with the sunset casting pastels over the horizon.

The ship Daki had built this time around was more spacious than the last. No one was required to steer the ship since the Miyu and their sea kaigons were guiding the ship. The journey to Emberwood would last overnight, and after our harrowing time on that island, I was looking forward to getting some sleep. Daki had even built each of us our own cabin for privacy and a cot to sleep on.

We sat on deck, grilling eight-legged seazhi and fish for supper. I remembered the bamboo flute and took it out.

Daki gazed at it. "We're lucky you had that. How did you know the music would weaken Hara?"

"Amika told me," I said. "I want you to examine it though. Do you recognize this instrument at all?"

Daki took it from me. "Why, should I?"

"It belonged to a man who used it to escape from Hara," I said. "He appeared in Hara's memories. He escaped using a kite like yours, and Aiden said your kites are one of a kind."

Daki inspected the flute. His lips curled into a frown as he concentrated. Then his gaze widened, and he gasped. "Wait a minute, the initials JW are carved here. This is Welder's flute. JW stands for Jelby Welder. He carried it with him when we fled the kingdom. Played it a few times as well before we parted ways. I recall thinking him quite talented."

"No wonder he had your kite," Aiden said. "And if he took the same route we did, it would make sense that Hara would have caused his ship to wreck, diverting him to her island."

"Yes, I gave him the kite as a parting gift in case he needed it," Daki said. "But he wanted to travel by boat alone. Said he wanted the solitude to think."

Aiden glanced back at me. "If you think Haming is formidable with his face-changing tin-chai, just wait until you meet Welder."

"I recall Daki mentioning Welder's tin-chai before," I said. "He can alter the appearance of any object."

"Yes," Daki said. "Welder is a survivor. If anyone can outwit a Miyu, it would be him. Thank Old Grandfather Heaven he dropped the flute when he escaped. It saved us from Hara."

"Maybe I should have kept playing the flute instead of singing," I said. "But it was also hurting Amika. I had to stop."

"You shouldn't feel guilty for killing Hara," Daki said. "She was about to kill all of us. And judging from all the skeletons in her lair, she must have killed hundreds of sailors."

Even though she would have killed us, it didn't stop the guilt from gnawing into my chest. She looked like she was in so much pain when her body dissolved into sea foam. I never thought I'd be using my tin-chai as a weapon of destruction when all I'd ever dreamed of was to use my tin-chai to heal people.

Suddenly, every bone in my body felt heavy and tired.

"Excuse me," I said. "I think I'll go to bed. Wake me when we're almost to the port."

I walked into my cabin and shut the door. Without bothering to pull the covers away from the cot, I flopped down and stared at the ceiling.

Why could I no longer control my tin-chai?

I closed my eyes, willing my mind to grow blank.

The next thing I knew, I stood in an icy forest. I recognized this place. It was the Winter Woods at Cedar Palace. This had to be a dream. I couldn't be here. I was traveling on a ship to Emberwood, wasn't I?

I sniffed the air. It was permeated with the sick stench of pine mingled with urine, sweat, and body odor.

My gaze focused on the path before me.

The cages. They were here. Each one an exact replica of those in Cedar Palace.

Beechwood, cedar, silver birch, cherry, and oak. Different kinds of wood formed the bars of each pagoda cage. Red trumpet vines ran the lengths of the tree trunks, standing out against the green and brown background like splotches of red paint on an otherwise gray canvas.

The cages were cloaked in sheer, white curtains. The wind parted the curtains. Radi stood in one cage, and my parents sat in another. My gaze traveled behind them to where my brother, Rell, and my sister-in-law, Nia, cowered in a corner of a third cage. They shielded their infant son.

In the cage neighboring them were Carrick and Aiden, sprawled on the ground. Blood streamed from their lifeless bodies. With a cry, I rushed to them. A dart was lodged in Carrick's shoulder, and poison blackened his skin. Aiden was soaked in blood from a slash through his chest.

I clawed at the door of their cage, pulled the lock, but it was no use. Vines whipped around, shackling my wrists and ankles. As I struggled to get free, laughter echoed in the chilly winds blowing through the pine trees.

The pirates we'd encountered at Tamika Village appeared. They gathered around the cages that imprisoned my family and friends. Their swords flashed as they lunged the pointed weapons through the bars. The sharp blades thrust repeatedly at my loved ones, skewering them dozens of times.

"No!" I screamed.

Terran materialized in front of me. He bent down, one hand grabbing hold of my chin and forcing me to look at him.

"Don't fight, my nightingale," he said. "You will sing for my pleasure alone, or not at all. I warned you already. My ghost remains to haunt you. I'll make sure you'll kill your loved ones every time you sing. Open your mouth, and you will be responsible for their deaths. This is your punishment for murdering me."

I shook my head. He no longer had control of me. This was a dream. His ghost wasn't real and couldn't hurt me. I would never allow myself to hurt my loved ones.

I spat in his face and took satisfaction in watching him flinch. White spittle trickled down his cheek. "Stay dead, you monster."

I sang, focusing on the pirates and Terran. The skin dissolved from Terran's face. The pirates were next. One by one, their flesh melted into powdered dust, leaving behind rattling skeletons that crashed onto the bare earth.

*"Oh, blossoms of June, sweet blossoms of June*
*How the love of our youth e'er did bloom*
*'Til the fading light of that autumn noon*
*And then, oh, those sweet blossoms of June*
*Died under the light of the Lavender Moon."*

But something was wrong. I was still singing.

> *"And then, oh, those sweet blossoms of June*
> *Died under the light of the Lavender Moon."*

I couldn't stop singing the same two lines. The words came from my mouth in an endless loop. The vines still held me in place, and I couldn't move, couldn't clamp my hands over my mouth, couldn't bite my teeth together. It was like someone was controlling me with strings, moving my mouth for me.

My loved ones writhed in pain at the sound of my voice. In horror, I watched their flesh wrinkle with age and disappear into dust until nothing was left of them but a pile of bones.

Only then did the vines retreat, and I could close my mouth. I fell to my knees, tears falling down my face.

Terran's voice rattled in wraithlike echoes. "I told you, my nightingale. Your voice belongs to me. You will never become a healer."

Radi spoke next, her voice bitter. "You couldn't save me. I thought you were my friend."

Then came Mama's chiding warning. "I told you to keep your mouth shut, but you didn't listen. Now look what you've done."

My gaze darted to my feet. The mutilated body of Carrick's androgy, Solar, lay there. His eyes opened. He spoke through decomposing gray lips. "You could have saved me, but you didn't. You are the reason I'm dead."

I lifted my hands, and to my horror, I saw that they were covered in blood. "I didn't mean to. I'm sorry. I wanted to save you. All I ever wanted was to help people. To be a healer. I never wanted to turn into a killer."

My eyes flew open, and cold sweat fell down my face. I got out of bed and fled the cabin.

On the deck, the fresh air hit my face. Instant relief. I inhaled a deep breath, and some of the tension left my shoulders. Leaning my arms against the railing, I watched the billowing waves roll, fluid and free as they swirled against the side of the ship. The glimmering tails of the Miyu and the ethereal bodies of their sea kaigons were outlined under the surface of the dark water. Across the horizon, majestic shades of purple and gold blended with the puffy clouds in a painting of mountains and rivers that seemed to be conjured from another world.

Aiden came out of his cabin and approached. "Mind if I join you?"

I fidgeted with my hands, still feeling the tension in my shoulders. "I appreciate the company."

"I'm guessing you couldn't sleep," he said.

"I . . . I had a bad dream."

"I know," he said. "I heard you."

My gaze flew to his face. I must have been screaming in my sleep, and Aiden's cabin was right next to mine. "I'm sorry. I didn't mean to disturb your sleep."

"Don't apologize," he said. "If you're not able to sleep, then neither will I. You can tell me about your nightmares if you wish. I want to help if I can."

My face reddened. I looked away, feeling embarrassed. "I dreamed I killed everyone I love. Including you."

He paused for a moment as though thinking about his words carefully. "The last time we talked about this, we ended up arguing, so I don't want to hurt your feelings again."

"I was the immature one then," I said. "I'm sorry. Say whatever is on your mind. It may not be what I want to hear, but you always say what I need to hear."

He nodded. "Then I'm going to repeat what I said last time. I don't believe for a moment you've lost your ability to heal. I know it's inside you because that's who you are. You are a healer, and you always will be. I think it's a mind block preventing you from using your tin-chai the way you wish. But I know you can."

"You have more faith in me than I do." I fingered the ship around my neck again, seeking its comfort. "If this is a mind block because of my fear, how do I get over it? I'm so afraid that when I do need to heal someone, I'll fail—just as I failed with my parents and with Solar. What worth do I have if I can no longer use my healing tin-chai?"

Aiden shook his head and took my hands in his, forcing me to meet his gaze. "Your worth isn't dependent upon your tin-chai. A person can have super strength, the quickest mind, and all the talent in the world, but if he doesn't have love for his family and friends, that's when he becomes worthless. You are worth everything because you love people with an open heart."

How had I been blessed with a friend like him? He'd always been there for me. Even in my darkest days in the novelty cage, he'd come to visit me when Carrick did not.

"I will always have faith in you. I will do whatever it takes to help you sing again," he said and patted my shoulder. "I'm going back to my cabin to get ready. You should do the same. We'll be arriving at Leihu Harbor soon."

He veered around and made his exit, leaving me to my thoughts. What was waiting for us in Emberwood? Whatever was in store, I hoped I had the strength to find my voice again.

# CHAPTER 20

✦ ✦ ✦ ✦ ✦ ✦ ✦ ✦ ✦ ✦

The morning light shone above the horizon as we approached Leihu Harbor. The Miyu needed to say their goodbyes before we reached the port. They didn't want any Embers to spot them and risk instigating any animosity. It was a pity the Miyu were so reviled and misunderstood by most land dwellers. I hoped one day more of us could see things from the Miyu's perspective and come to realize it was unfair to villainize them.

"I hope we meet again one day." Princess Amika waved at me from the water, and I waved back.

"We will," I said.

One by one, the sea kaigons dissipated into watery mist and reattached as tattoos to the Miyu's skin.

Queen Yisa bowed her head, and the other Miyu followed her lead. "The Miyu are in your debt. If you are ever in trouble and need our help, simply find a conch shell and play it. The songs of land dwellers weaken us, but the songs of the sea call to us. We will hear the music of the conch, and we will come to you."

"Thank you, Your Majesty." I bowed to her.

With one last wave goodbye, the pod swam away.

Daki took the helm. "Ready to meet the Ember king and queen?"

"I've been ready for years," Aiden said.

"I hope Haming hasn't gotten to Welder first," I said.

We steered into the harbor. As we approached the port, tiny dots took shape, forming the individual figures of busy Embers.

Leihu Harbor, the main port in Emberwood, lay on the north side of the kingdom. We still had to travel to the capitol city of Huohua and Linlang Palace, where the king and queen took residence. Aiden had said the journey would take another three days. But at least we were in Emberwood now.

The prospering economy of Emberwood was far different from that of Seracedar. The harbor was filled with ships loaded with cargo. The *clunk-clunk* of rudders echoed in the cool breeze, and horns blew like kettles as they left the port.

The moment we docked, a heady excitement hit me. It occurred to me that, after years of listening to my baba talk about his travels to Emberwood, I was finally here. I could experience this kingdom for myself.

Before we could pass the docks, the border officers standing guard had us sign some papers describing our reasons for coming to Emberwood and how long we intended to stay. If I didn't feel obligated to return to Cedar Palace, I might consider staying here permanently. A new life. It sounded so tempting.

The officer who had given us the paperwork gave us some privacy to fill out the documents while he helped someone else.

"You won't have to worry about hiding your scar anymore," Aiden said, now that no one else was within earshot. "People here aren't as superstitious against the number four, and it's considered rude to stare at someone's blemishes."

"What if someone recognizes me from the fugitive posters?" I asked.

"There are no posters here," he said. "If a Seracedarean here recognizes you, they can't force you to return to Seracedar now that you're on Emberwood territory."

"Even so," Daki said, "we need to be alert. If you think someone is following us, speak up right away."

I started to fill out the form. Name, height, age, hair color. Name? I wondered if I should make up an alias.

I glanced at Aiden's form. "Should we make up our names? What if the Seracedarean guards asked the Emberwood guards to hand us over?"

"Emberwood doesn't follow Seracedarean laws," Aiden said. "But if you feel more comfortable giving a fake name, feel free. They won't ask. Most fugitives want to start a new life here anyway, and many of them do give themselves new names."

I wrote Radiana Ying. The thought of my friend brought up a pang of wistfulness. I hoped she was okay. Once we brought the scepter back to Carrick, all would be well, and Radi could live a life of freedom just as she's always wanted.

I glanced at the next section. *Purpose of visit.*

Daki frowned. "Aiden, what should we—"

"Temporary protection with the hope of becoming a permanent Emberwood citizen," he said, anticipating the question. "As I said, they're friendly to fugitives."

Once we finished filling out the papers, we took them back to the border guard. He stamped a document, one for each of us. He didn't ask us a single question. Aiden was right. I'd been worried for nothing.

"Carry this document with you wherever you go in the kingdom," the border guard said. "It acts as a temporary proof of your identity. If you wish to stay here longer or apply for citizenship, you'll need to find one of our offices and fill out other paperwork. We're stationed in every city, just so you know."

The border guard had a friendly voice, which surprised me. I was used to guards who wanted to imprison me, but this man sounded like he wanted to invite us to tea. So far, I had the impression Emberwood looked kindly on foreigners who wanted to find sanctuary and a fresh start here.

The border guard let us through a low-barred gate. From there, we made our way from the docks to the main part of the city. It was far bigger than any town I'd been to in Seracedar, including the capitol of Senlin.

The streets were crowded with hordes of people, pushing past as they scurried to wherever they needed to be.

Aiden glanced at our surroundings and pointed to a yellow sign of an arrow pointing straight down the road. It had a picture of two parallel bars with several perpendicular lines connecting them. "In case we are separated, look for those signs." Aiden had to shout for Daki and me to hear him. "They'll direct you to Leihu Rail Coach Station. We'll find each other there if we get lost."

Getting lost was the last thing I wanted. I grabbed onto a corner of Aiden's tunic and stuck close to him.

We passed vendors selling everything from candles to blankets to fresh meat that lay on ice so it wouldn't spoil. Hanging paper lanterns seemed to float in midair. Though the lights were off now since it was day, I imagined at night it would look magical. Everyone seemed to wear genuinely bright smiles, and there was a certain buoyancy in the way they walked, like they had purpose. It reminded me of what the Cascasean sea market had been when I was a child—before the tidal wave had obliterated our economy.

The smells of fresh-baked pastries, fried meat pancakes, and steamed dumplings made my stomach growl. My mouth watered as I stopped by a hawker selling a curious dish of what looked to be crispy fried noodles drenched in a fermented chili and ground meat sauce. I didn't know the names of half the foods being sold, but it all looked so delicious I wished I could sample a bit of everything.

Aiden watched two men seated at an outside table as they slurped their noodles. He swallowed. "We need to convert our Seran into Em before we can buy anything. As soon as we do, we're coming back for knife-cut noodles and fermented chili sauce. I haven't had that dish since I was a kid."

I wasn't going to argue with him there.

We passed by several women on the street, and I caught myself staring, fascinated by what they were wearing: dark blue slacks and colorful, loose-fitting blouses. Their slacks were similar to what the men were wearing, and nobody seemed to care.

*How scandalous.*

"The women are dressed like men. They look so comfortable." My shocked whisper made Aiden chuckle.

"Actually, those clothes are meant for both women and men. The pants are made from blue cotton twill," Aiden said.

"We should probably all buy new outfits to blend in with the locals," Daki said. "Any vendor will take one look at us, know we're not from around here, and double the price of their merchandise."

I took a step forward to cross the street. Something fast and loud whirred past us in a flurry of black. I jumped back on the curb, my heart lurching into my throat. The black contraption looked like a gigantic metal carriage. It stopped as a crowd of people got in its way. Steam jetted from open vents on its tail end.

*Beep, beep, beep!* It barked like a temperamental godog, loud and impatient to hurry on its way.

Daki's eyes lit up with animation. "A steam-powered coach. I've heard of the Emberwood invention, but this is my first time seeing it."

"A steam-powered coach?" I repeated.

"They are palanquins or carriages that don't require magic or horses," Aiden explained. "They use steam to fuel them. These models look even more advanced than I remember."

The crowd cleared the street, giving way to the coach.

*Hisss!* It sped off, leaving a cloud of gray dust trailing behind it.

Everywhere I looked, there was something innovative to behold. But unlike in Seracedar, I didn't see people using their tin-chai in the open, nor did this town require the use of tin-chai to operate.

"Emberwood is so different from Seracedar," I said. "I don't see tin-chai or magic of any kind."

"But there *is* magic here," Aiden said. "Tin-chai developed the systems and operations that make Emberwood functional. It's just that the Embers used their tin-chai to make inventions that do the work for us. Doing so removed the constant output of the wyis required to use our tin-chai in daily living. Look at that hawker. He's got the same tin-chai as me."

The hawker formed a flame in his hands and lit a contraption that boiled water into steam. The steam then went into a box that converted powder into a fully cooked meal.

We stopped at a general store to convert our Seran into Em. We didn't get nearly as many Em coins from the Seran we had. I thought the store owner had cheated us until Aiden explained the value of the Em coin was higher than that of a Seran.

"Emberwood is a more prosperous kingdom at the moment," Aiden said.

"Rather unfortunate for us in this case," I said with a sour look at the ten Em coins in my purse. I'd traded thirty Seran for them. "I feel like we got robbed."

"Good news is we have enough money among the three of us for food and shelter for several days," Daki said. "Maybe we can look for temporary work until we can get to the palace and locate Welder." He grinned at Aiden. "You can also find your family in the capitol. Then we'll have a place to stay. Right, my boy?"

"Yes, of course," Aiden said. "There should be no reason we can't get to my family in one piece." Under his breath, he muttered something that sounded like, "At least I hope."

"What was that?" I asked, wondering if I'd imagined it.

"I said at least I hope we get food first," he said. "I can't go anywhere else when my stomach's this empty."

"Wait up," Daki said. "One more thing before food." He paused at the newspaper stand and picked up a copy of today's paper.

"Good idea," I said. Having been away from a town for so long, we needed to know Seracedar's situation now. My heart raced, hoping not to find any news that Carrick had been captured, or worse, dead.

We returned to the noodle hawker, ordered our food, then sat at one of the open benches to read the paper as we waited for our meal.

The headline read:

## SENLIN CITY, SERACEDAR CAPITOL, DIVIDED INTO TWO PARTIES AS WHEREABOUTS OF SACRED CEDAR SCEPTER REMAIN A MYSTERY

Aiden read the story out loud: "With Nelan still controlling the palace and the western part of Senlin, and Carrick's followers holding off the eastern sector, it has become apparent during this standstill that neither prince has the Sacred Cedar Scepter.

"Prince Nelan has declared that the scepter's disappearance is indicative that the Will of Heaven is an outdated tradition. Nelan continues to turn those who oppose him into terracotta statues. With Nelan in control of the army, Carrick's forces struggle to continue defending the eastern sector. However, Prince Carrick has made a bold claim that he has sent his people to locate the scepter, and he will have it in his hands soon. He maintains he will achieve tin-chai amplification. Whether he can prove this remains to be seen, but both princes are running out of time to claim their right to the throne.

While most noblemen have chosen to side with one of the princes, there are others who remain on middle ground.

"There are also talks among some noblemen and androgies who wish to begin their own campaign to locate the scepter and challenge both princes. But until one of them does indeed find the scepter and prove his right to rule through tin-chai amplification, Seracedar's next emperor cannot be officially named. Until then, the kingdom should be prepared for more civil unrest."

I folded my hands. My palms felt clammy. "What does this mean for Carrick?"

Aiden folded the newspaper. "It means Carrick and Nelan are still the main contenders, but it's only a matter of time before other competitors gain more supporters."

Daki nodded. "Sounds like Carrick has enough defense to hold up his part of the city for now. Let's fuel up first and then work on finding that scepter."

We stopped talking as the hawker came with our noodle bowls. He set them down on the table, and we dug in. The sauce was decadent; savory and sweet blended perfectly with the right amount of heat. I'd never tasted a bowl of noodles this good.

"Even the food in Emberwood is similar but different than Seracedar," Daki commented. "It's like sisters with similar features but different styles of dress."

That was an interesting yet accurate metaphor. The food did remind me of home in a way, but the sauce was cooked differently.

"My mama used to make noodles with fermented sauce," I said. "But this sauce is sweeter and darker. There's a slight difference in the blend of spices. Do you know what it is?"

Aiden didn't answer, which made me shift my attention from the noodles to him. He seemed distracted, though he kept his gaze on his bowl of noodles.

"Is something wrong?" I asked. "It's not like you to not comment on food, or to have so much left in your bowl."

"There are two men a few tables behind us who keep looking at us," he said quietly, "They're trying to be subtle, but I sense them observing us."

I started to turn. Aiden smacked my shoulder lightly, causing me to stop.

"Don't look. They'll know we're onto them."

"What do they look like?" I asked. "Do you think they recognize us from somewhere?"

Daki maintained his gaze on the cup of tea in his hand. "They look like scholars or aristocrats. They're wearing black and gold robes."

"The colors of Ember University," Aiden said.

"They aren't from Cedar Palace then." I exhaled in relief until another thought flickered in my mind. "Unless they're Nelan's men impersonating Embers."

"Shh, they're coming over," Aiden said.

A young man about seventeen or eighteen years old came from behind me. He was accompanied by a middle-aged man who looked like a teacher. Strange, but the student's hair was lighter in color like Aiden's, unusual for a Shyan. And there was a similarity in his golden eyes that reminded me of Aiden as well.

The younger man spoke directly to Aiden. "Excuse me. I must ask you a question. You share a striking resemblance to someone I once knew. Do you recognize me? My name is Sito."

Aiden paused a moment, studying the teenager's face. Aiden's gaze passed to the older man, and something distrustful flickered in Aiden's eyes. A second later, he masked it. "No, I don't know you. Why would I?"

"What is your birth name? I must make sure you aren't him."

"Jin," Aiden said. "Seeing as I only arrived to Emberwood this morning, I don't think it's possible we knew each other in the past. I'm from Seracedar. Never been to Emberwood before today."

Why would Aiden lie? Did he think there was a danger in telling someone that he was originally an Ember?

"I told you it couldn't be him," the older gentleman said. "I'm sorry, son. He isn't coming home whether you like it or not."

The young man's face fell. "I suppose it was wishful thinking," he told Aiden. "I'm sorry for taking up your time." They sauntered away, but I could still feel their stares.

"Are you sure you don't know him?" I asked. "Perhaps you were acquainted when you were children."

"We can't trust anyone," Aiden said. "How do we know he isn't working for Haming?"

It didn't escape my attention that he hadn't precisely answered my question. "But that young scholar looked genuinely disappointed. He must have really thought you were the person he knew. You were quite young when you left Emberwood. Perhaps you simply cannot recognize him any longer."

"I agree with Rilla," Daki said. "Anyone working for Haming would be trying to stop us from getting to the palace, not asking if you were a childhood friend."

Aiden shrugged. "I can't pretend to know what Haming is strategizing. We need to get to the palace without him knowing we've arrived in Emberwood."

Aiden continued to be evasive about his childhood, his background, and his family. But why?

It wouldn't do to pry. He couldn't avoid his past forever, especially since we were going to his hometown, Huohua, the capital city. I wondered what secrets about him we'd discover there. Whatever they were, I was ready to fight by his side no matter what ghosts from his past jumped out at us.

# CHAPTER 21

✦ ✦ ✦ ✦ ✦ ✦ ✦ ✦ ✦ ✦

After our meal, we decided to find a place to rest for the night. We tried several inns, but none of them had any vacancies, and all were far too expensive. Finally, we came to a teahouse.

Lady Nana's Teahouse was located in the middle of the hustle and bustle of the port. The bright orange paint on the outside was a happy color, reminding me of the sunset. It looked like a regular restaurant, but Aiden mentioned it might have a vacant room.

"A teahouse usually has private rooms on the upper level with a restaurant for tea, wine, and food downstairs," Aiden said.

"What makes a teahouse different from a restaurant or other inns that serve meals?"

"Teahouses are open late into the night," he said. "And there's entertainment."

"Are there teahouses in Seracedar?" I asked. I'd never seen one before. Then again, I'd rarely set foot outside of my village.

"Yes, but mostly in big cities," Daki said. "Many of my subordinates enjoyed frequenting teahouses during their off time, though I never have. I wasn't interested in that kind of entertainment. I'd much rather spend my time in solitude and surrounded by the sea."

I frowned. "What kind of entertainment?"

Aiden swallowed a nervous gulp. "Uhm . . . dancing girls."

"Like novelties and baubles?" My scowl deepened.

"Not at all like that," Aiden said. "I promise these dancers are here because they want to be. They regard dancing as their art. And unlike in Seracedar, it's against the law in Emberwood for a man to touch or solicit a dancer without her permission."

"Still," Daki said. "The idea of watching women dance for pleasure is something men came up with. And I think if there are dancing women, then there should also be dancing men."

"We don't have to go in," Aiden said. "But this might be our final hope of not sleeping on the street tonight. I don't mind either way."

"I suppose we can try," I said. It would be nice to sleep in a bed and have a roof over our heads.

Inside the teahouse, we waited for the hostess to greet us. She was a copper-haired woman in her mid-twenties. Several gentlemen guests addressed her as Lady Nana. She was probably the owner, though I wondered if she really was a lady of nobility, married to a lord, or just gave herself the title. She beamed at Aiden and Daki but ignored me.

"How may I help you gentlemen today?" she asked.

"We're hoping to stay here for the night," Daki said. "We need a room and some supper."

The woman gave me a side glance. "Is this little girl with you? The only females permitted entry into my teahouse are those who work for me, and they are all of legal age. Only they are allowed to entertain gentlemen guests. I won't have outside entertainment coming into my establishment."

"I'm not a little girl," I said with a spark of indignation. "And I'm not entertainment."

"Still, the rules are the rules," she said. "If you snuck away from home, I don't want to be responsible when your ah-fu and ah-mu come blaming me for allowing you to accompany two gentlemen alone."

"There seems to be a misunderstanding, Lady Nana." Aiden casually leaned against the desk, grinning with full-on charm. "We're only traveling companions, arrived in Emberwood this morning. You have my word, we're of legal age, even if my friend here looks young. All the other inns are full, and you're our last chance for a hot supper and shelter."

It was like watching ice melt in a vat of liquid gold. The woman stared at Aiden and giggled like a little girl. "In that case, I may be able to put you up for the night."

"Also, I'm afraid we don't have much money on us. But you seem like a savvy businesswoman and an accommodating hostess. Look at the crowd. Perhaps we can help you work tonight in exchange for a room."

As if giggling wasn't silly enough, Lady Nana twirled her hair. "I don't usually have men working in front, as gentlemen guests prefer the company of pretty ladies, but I do employ men in the kitchen. As it happens, I am short-staffed tonight. I'll let you stay free of charge if you gentlemen will help wash dishes. As for the lady, despite that horrid scar, you have a pretty face and a lovely set of eyes. I'll use makeup to cover it up. You can greet the guests, show them to their room or table, and take their order."

Aiden directed his gaze on me. "What do you think? Does this sound reasonable for you?"

"Fine," I said. "I can do that." I didn't like Lady Nana, but I also didn't want to be the reason we didn't get to sleep indoors.

"One more thing," she said. "Late in the evening, it gets quieter in the main dining room. Most guests go home while some retire to private rooms, where some of my girls are paid extra to dance for them. However, there are a few who remain downstairs, drinking in solitude. I need you all to monitor them while I'm busy upstairs. Usually my kitchen staff does so, but two of the boys are out sick today. Some guests may be reluctant to leave, but you must urge them to go home before closing for the night."

"I can help you get rid of those unwanted guests," Daki said, a gleam in his eye. "Dealing with drunk fools was my specialty back in the day."

Aiden winked at the woman. "That settles it. We're all yours tonight."

She left for less than a minute before returning to us with a full-fledged smile on her face. She fluttered her long eyelashes at Aiden. I bit my lip, repressing the urge to tell her she should be working instead of flirting.

"I made sure to reserve two rooms instead of one," she said. "I hope it will make your stay here more comfortable. I made my staff aware that you'll be helping out tonight. You're all set to attend your stations." Her attention shifted back to Aiden. "Has anyone told you that you could pass for royalty?"

Aiden tilted his head slightly, giving her a pleased look. "Do you think so?"

She bobbed her head up and down. "You have the look of a prince."

"Well, thank you, my lady." He beamed at her. "You are lovely for accommodating us. We'll start at once. Show us the way."

Lady Nana looked as though she might dissolve into a puddle. One would've thought Aiden was the sun itself.

She hollered at a tall young man, who I assumed to be one of the servers. "Show this delightful party of three to their rooms." Addressing us again, she said, "Go ahead and drop off your bags first."

I had a room to myself. I washed the dirt and grime from my body, finally feeling clean for the first time since getting shipwrecked and trudging through mud on the island. I changed into fresh clothes;

then, feeling refreshed, I met Daki and Aiden in the hall. They had also freshened up.

I noticed Daki rubbing his temples. His eyes closed as though he was having trouble staying awake. I read his wyis. It was still weak.

"Are you all right, Daki?" I asked. "You look tired."

"I'm fine. I must not have fully recovered my strength from when Hara turned me into a bird."

"Maybe you should stay in the room and rest," Aiden said.

"Nonsense." Daki shook his head. "I'm sure I'll wake up once we're working. I just need one good night of sleep, and I'll be back to normal in the morning."

We headed back downstairs. I took a glance around the teahouse dining area. At the center of the teahouse was a stage. A group of dancers delivered a graceful performance. They wore colorful costumes and headdresses, their movements flowing as though they were gliding.

Many of the tables were occupied with gentlemen who were eating and sipping on tea. At a few tables, some of the guests were already getting drunk on rice wine. The women workers who weren't dancers sat and conversed with the gentlemen. They made sure the gentlemen's wine cups were always full.

Aiden and Daki went back to the kitchen while Lady Nana took me to a backroom behind the stage. I sat in front of a dresser and mirror. She brushed some powder onto my cheeks, stood back, and looked at her handiwork.

"I can still see it," she said, frowning. She opened the top dresser drawer and took out a scarf, which she wrapped around the bottom half of my face. "Yes, that works. I like it. Adds an air of mystery about you."

She led me to the front entrance. "All you have to do is bow when a customer comes in, greet them, and show them to a table. Think you can handle it on your own?"

I nodded.

She gave me a tight-lipped smile and took her leave.

I didn't have to wait long for the first customer. Two minutes later, a man entered the teahouse. "Excuse me."

I bowed. "Welcome."

"I'd like a table for two. I'm meeting a friend here."

"Yes, of course," I said. "Follow me."

As the supper hour hit, more gentlemen guests streamed in. The teahouse filled quickly. Patrons occupied each of the round, wooden tables that surrounded the raised dais, where dancers performed. The high, lilting background music mixed with the sound of chatter. Soon there was a line of gentlemen waiting for empty tables.

A young gentleman entered. Wide-rimmed eyeglasses were balanced on his nose, and he had the pale complexion of one who rarely saw the sun. He wore a uniform with the words "Ember University" sewn onto the front. He must've been a scholar, like the ones we'd met earlier at the noodle stand.

"Hello there," he said. His gaze scanned me up and down. "First day on the job?"

I nodded. "How did you know?"

"It's the first time I've seen you here," he replied. "I'm a high scholar at Ember University and come here for supper at least three times a week. I only talk to the serving girls who I deem interesting."

He spoke as though I should be flattered to be getting attention from him.

"Well, let me show you to your table," I said, hoping he didn't mean to flirt with me. Thankfully, he didn't say anything further. I showed him to an empty table, and he sat by himself, watching the dancers from afar.

I kept busy, greeting other guests who came in, politely telling them it would be a bit of a wait for a table, and bowing to gentlemen who left, wishing them a good rest of the evening. In between guests, I wiped down tables.

Aiden came out of the kitchen and sat at one of the tables to converse with Lady Nana and two other female companions who worked there. The women were giggling and not so discreetly touching his arm. I scowled. Wasn't he supposed to be working in the kitchen? Instead, he was encouraging their flirtations.

The women all wore robes cut low at the bodice. Their breasts threatened to spill out from the fabric. Aiden made no secret that he appreciated the flaunting display of skin. I didn't know why I felt so disturbed watching him. It wasn't as though I hadn't known he was charming. But before now I hadn't seen him flirt with anyone but me.

His freedoms had been limited in the palace, so it was only natural for him to show interest in the girls he met now that there were no rules against it. As for our relationship, he'd already made it clear we were just friends. I was comfortable with Aiden.

That was it. Comfortable—the inevitable consequence of being in such close proximity to one another during our travels. It was easy to mistake the comfort of being with a friend for romantic attraction.

The young scholar from earlier beckoned me over. He already had a jug of rice wine on the table.

"What can I get for you, sir?" I asked.

Instead of answering, he grinned, then took up a cup filled with wine and tossed it down in one gulp. He winced as though it burned his throat.

"I must say, you have beautiful eyes, though I wish I could see the rest of your face. Could you take off the scarf for a moment?"

"Well, thank you for the compliment," I said, "but I'm not comfortable removing the scarf. It's part of my costume, and Lady Nana has strict rules."

I didn't appreciate how he was looking at me, but I couldn't be rude to a customer. Especially not at a place that was giving me lodging as payment for being a polite server. "What would you like to order?"

"The daily special. As well as the pleasure of your company when you're done with your shift." His gaze lingered on my bosom.

Now I was annoyed. "I don't—"

Aiden's voice interrupted me. "She's not interested."

I whirled around, finding him a hair's breadth away. He was fuming. Where had he come from? Where were Lady Nana and the other two ladies he'd been with? They were nowhere to be seen.

The man calmly stared back at Aiden. "The lady can speak for herself." He looked Aiden over in disdain. "And who are you to be speaking to a high scholar of Ember University?"

"Do your teachers know you're here breaking the university protocol?" Aiden retorted. "I know you scholars aren't permitted to frequent these establishments or ask young women to accompany you alone. I should report you."

The neighboring table had gone quiet, observing this exchange. My cheeks were boiling with embarrassment.

The man scoffed. "Go ahead. They'll let me off with a warning. Do you know who my father is? Lord Par Ting, the royal historian and part of King Ashbel's court."

If this gentleman's father was a lord, so was he. We couldn't afford to offend nobility.

Lady Nana came to the table. "Is everything all right here?"

"This guest made untoward advances at my friend and made her uncomfortable," Aiden said. "I know this is unacceptable behavior in your establishment, and it's against the policy of Ember University for a scholar to be here in the first place."

"Yes, it certainly is," Lady Nana said. "Young Master Ting, I don't want any trouble. If your father knows you're here again—"

"Relax." The man pulled out a pouch and dropped it on the table.

The heavy weight of it smacked on the table. "He doesn't have to know, does he? Besides, I didn't do anything wrong. I merely expressed interest in the lady. If she does not want my attention, she only needs to tell me herself."

Aiden moved to say something again, but I pushed him to the side.

I returned my focus to the man. "I'm sorry, my lord. I'm not looking for the attention of any gentlemen at the moment."

He shrugged. "All right. Thank you for your honesty. Are we ready to move on now?" He slid the pouch toward Lady Nana, who took it and smiled.

"Yes, enjoy your visit," she said. "I'll have more wine brought out to you in a moment."

"My lady," Aiden whispered. "You could get into trouble by allowing a scholar to stay here and drink. It's against the school's policy."

She whispered back, "A risk I'm willing to take. He brings in triple the amount of money than an average gentleman." Then she addressed the neighboring tables. "Sorry for the disturbance. Would you like me to bring you anything else?"

I spun around, narrowing my eyes at Aiden. "You turned that into a bigger scene than necessary. I could have refused him without your help."

"Did you see the way he was looking at you?" Aiden said.

"Yes, but I didn't need you to embarrass me." I glared at him. "I don't have time to argue with you."

Another customer waved me over. I walked away from Aiden, pasting a smile on my face to do my job.

Aiden and I didn't speak for the rest of the evening. He continued flirting with Lady Nana and the other girls.

I tried not to notice and focused on my job.

By closing time, most of the guests had either gone home or found private rooms. Only a few stragglers remained in the main dining hall to drink. I hoped I wouldn't have to deal with them, but I was the only one left.

Lady Nana and the women were entertaining guests upstairs. I could hear music and raucous laughter. Aiden was nowhere in sight. I wondered if he was upstairs, too, flirting with a dancer.

Daki came out of the kitchen. He looked on the verge of collapse. Black circles underscored his eyes.

I touched his forehead. "You've got a fever."

"Probably need to drink more water," he said, though his eyes threatened to close, and he slurred his words. "Maybe some sleep, too."

"Go upstairs and rest," I said. "I can handle it down here."

"Are you sure?" His voice sounded strained. "What if a drunkard tries to start a fight?"

"There are so few guests left here," I said. "I doubt that will happen. Besides, I've got Aiden."

At least I hoped he would be here if I needed him.

Daki nodded, lacking energy to refuse, and he stumbled upstairs. One by one, the guests either went upstairs to sleep in the rooms or went home until only one guest remained awake in the dining room.

I inwardly cringed, realizing it was the scholar who had tried to flirt with me earlier. I'd been too busy and too mad at Aiden to notice he had stayed the entire evening. I swallowed, and my chest tightened.

He was watching me and smiled as I took notice. He lifted his wine cup and called me over.

"Hello again." He slurred and didn't hide his leering at my chest. "Now that the crazy boy is gone, what do you say I show you what it's like to be with a real man?" He burped loudly.

"Sir, I believe it's time for you to go to bed. It's very late, and the dining room is closing."

"I'll only go to bed if you join me . . . *hic*."

His wandering hands grabbed the front of my dress. I lifted my knee, intending to dig it into his privates, but someone pushed me aside. Aiden slammed his fist into the man's face.

The young lord pulled himself up and spat on the ground. "Is that all you got?" His speech cleared. He sneered, and his eyes shone with clarity. Odd, but he seemed sober now.

He lifted his palms and waved them toward the tables I hadn't been able to clear yet. The discarded chopsticks and wine cups levitated from the tables and into the air. "Why don't you fight me with your tin-chai? Unless you're just a koong."

Fire formed in Aiden's hands, and in a blurred movement too quick for my eyes, the porcelain cups and ivory chopsticks caught ablaze before burning to char.

"I'll take you on," Aiden said, and another firebomb formed. "It'll be a matter of seconds before you're begging me to spare your life."

The young lord placed his hands up in surrender. "Forget it. I see I picked a fight with the wrong man."

"Get out," Aiden said. "Before I change my mind."

The man bowed low. "As you wish, Your Highness." His tone was laced with sarcasm.

"What did you call me?" Aiden asked.

But the scholar had already staggered out the door.

A few gentlemen and their lady escorts came out of their rooms and peered downstairs. Their curious whispers carried toward us.

"All is well," Aiden reassured them. "Just a drunkard, but he's gone. You can return to your rooms."

The gentlemen and ladies did as he said, and all was quiet once more. Other than Aiden and me, no one was downstairs in the dining room.

Aiden stared back at the door where the man had made his exit. There was something about his expression I couldn't read. But in the next second, he glared at me. "If a stranger starts flirting with you, you should come straight to me, not try to handle him on your own."

"Oh?" I raised an eyebrow. "You don't think I can take care of myself?"

"We don't know who might be following us," he replied. "You still don't have the advanced skills to defend yourself from someone who is as skilled as I am. You should not have let yourself be alone with someone dangerous like him."

Annoyance flickered in my chest. "That wasn't my fault. Daki needed to rest, and you left me alone to go flirt with Lady Nana and those other girls."

A crease formed between his brows. "What girls? The ones I was talking to with Lady Nana? I wasn't flirting."

I rolled my eyes. "Talking. Sure, that's what it was. Why don't you go back and finish *talking* to them, then? I don't need your help defending myself from anyone. Need I remind you that my voice has the power to kill? I would have taken care of that scholar even if you hadn't come along."

"For your information, I was in the kitchen, helping mop the floors. And earlier, I was talking to Lady Nana and those girls to get updates on Emberwood's current events."

"It sure didn't look that way to me," I said. "They were cozying up to you, touching you all over, and you showed no signs of not liking the attention."

Aiden looked into my eyes. His amused look made me even more annoyed.

"Rilla, are you jealous?"

Emotions burst within me "What if I am?"

Aiden's eyes froze in horror. "No, you can't be."

"Why not?"

"I've worked so hard to suppress my feelings."

My eyes widened. "Suppress your feelings? What do you mean?"

He rubbed a hand through his hair. "Blast the Lavender Moon. You're meant to be with him. I—I thought you loved him."

Him. Carrick. How I felt about each of them was completely different. Carrick had said he needed me, and it was nice to be needed.

It had also been burdensome. But it had never been so with Aiden.

"It was you who always remained by my side in my darkest times. You encouraged me to have hope. With you, I feel free to be myself for the first time in my life. I like you. And not just as a friend."

The confession was both shocking and not. To hear myself say the words out loud felt like a rush of adrenaline. I realized the feelings had been there in my heart all along, but I'd tried to deny it.

Aiden paced the room. "No, no, no. This can't be. You're confused. This is merely an infatuation. It's because we've been spending a lot of time together. Once you see Carrick again, you'll realize it's him you love, not me. You're meant to be with him."

"No," I said. "I did like Carrick, and I thought I loved him. But never once did I think we had a future together. Not when he's meant to be the emperor."

Aiden stopped pacing and leaned back against one of the tables. He crossed his arms. "You can't be saying this. Carrick loves you. We can't betray him."

"You have feelings for me, too," I said, my voice breathless. My heartbeat thumped in my ears.

The look he gave me was gut-wrenching. "I have had feelings for you from the moment we met. But it was because of Carrick that I couldn't act on my feelings. I thought you loved him, too. If you loved him in return, I could have put away my feelings. But what am I supposed to do now, knowing you feel something for me?"

He shook his head as though trying to dislodge something from his brain. "Back at the palace, you must have believed yourself in love with him. So, what has changed since then? I wouldn't believe your heart to be as fickle as that."

"What's changed is we both left Carrick's shadow," I said. "I always sensed you in the background back at the palace, but Carrick dominated my thoughts with his presence. He sucked me in with his vulnerability. It was manipulative. Away from him now, I realize I can't go back to being someone he needs. It would be stifling. I didn't love him. I pitied him."

"He loves you, though," Aiden said.

"Not enough to give up the throne," I said. "I don't harbor any resentment for that. His destiny is to become the emperor, but becoming one of his faela is not what I want for myself. I don't want any part of palace politics once we find the scepter."

Aiden looked away. "Just because you don't want to stay in the palace doesn't mean you don't love him. And what if I was like Carrick, destined to be in a position of power? Would you just as easily walk away from me?"

"You're not destined for power, though," I said. "And you're definitely nothing like Carrick."

"That's not what I mean. What if someday I'm no longer just Aiden, the bodyguard? What if I have to become someone you didn't expect me to be?"

The look in his eyes told me that for some reason this answer was important to him. Was he hinting that his true identity was someone with power?

I stepped toward him, closing the distance between us until I could feel the heat radiating from his body. Only a two-inch gap separated us. He didn't try to move away.

"I could survive life without Carrick," I said. "But I wouldn't be able to bear it if we were separated forever. I'd fight against everyone and everything to keep you in my life, no matter the consequences. Even with the threat of being imprisoned in the palace again, just to be with you, I would—"

I was cut off abruptly as he roughly pulled me into him. Our lips met, flooding me with heat. I pressed into him, wanting more. His kiss gentled, warm and sweet, searching deeper. He tasted of summer rain and strawberries. Our breath mingled, and his hands skated down my back. Pleasant shivers coursed through my body.

I burrowed closer into him, my own hands combing through his hair. I forgot who we were and where we were. Never before had I been kissed like this. I felt the echo of his heartbeat in his chest and in sync with mine.

For a second, he broke the kiss, allowing both of us to breathe, but then his lips skimmed my jawline and lowered to my neck. I gasped. Heat coursed through my body.

A single thought rushed through my mind: *I've been waiting my whole life for this moment.*

It was as though the music of his soul were singing in harmony with mine. It felt like, as long as we held each other, as long as I had his light, I'd never find myself banished to the shadows again.

He broke away suddenly, and I felt a chill. We stared at each other, both of us catching our breath.

"I'm sorry," he said and stepped back, placing his hands out as though warding me off. "I'm going for a walk."

He rushed away into the dead of night.

How could he just take off like that? Did he regret our kiss? I was so confused.

*Should I go after him?* I hesitated. Maybe he needed space.

But I needed to know what he was feeling. Plus, it must be hours past midnight, closer to morning than night, and we were in an unfamiliar kingdom. Even if Aiden was originally from Emberwood, he hadn't returned in over a decade. Not to mention, Haming was lurking about, and that scholar might have gone and gotten some of his friends to help him get revenge for earlier.

I ran after Aiden. The Turquoise Moon lit up the empty streets that had been bustling hours earlier. Now there wasn't even one straggler around. The street lanterns were lit up with fiery orbs of red and gold. Instead of hanging from posts, they floated on their own by use of magic. They were like ships floating in the night sea. If I wasn't so concerned about catching up to Aiden, I would have been awed by their beauty, and I would have taken the time to admire the scene.

Just ahead, Aiden crossed the street. I called to him, and he spun around.

"Why are you following me? I need some time to think. I can't talk to you when my mind's jumbled."

"We don't have to talk about us. Or Carrick or anything," I said. "Come back. We both need sleep, and it's late. It's too dangerous to be wandering alone."

He stared at me like I'd lost my mind. "I've fought off assassins and taken on a dozen men with powerful tin-chai at one time. If someone does attack, I can handle myself. Go back to the teahouse."

I ignored him and crossed the street to him. "If you're going for a walk, I'll follow from behind. It's for my own peace of mind. I'll get no sleep if I'm worried you might be attacked or vanish into the night."

He glared at me, clearly exasperated. "You're being paranoid. Nobody's going to be awake at—" He stopped, his gaze darting upward. He unsheathed his sword. "Damn the spirits straight to the underworld. It's so annoying when you're right."

Two shadowy figures jumped down from the roof of the building and blocked our path.

The first one spoke. "There he is, Mr. Rino. It's him all right. He has a fire tin-chai." I recognized the voice. It was the drunk scholar, Lord Ting.

Aiden swore. "That's why he picked a fight with me. I should have known."

A beam from the torch of the streetlight hit his companion's face. The middle-aged gentleman from the noodle stand ... what was he doing here?

I glared at them. "What do you want with us?"

The man who had been addressed as Mr. Rino laughed, the sound filling the air like a noxious gas. "Silly girl. You're not my target. He is." He pinned his gaze on Aiden.

I gasped. What business could he have with Aiden? I stepped in front of Aiden, shielding him. "I don't know who you are, but if you're his enemy, then you're mine, too."

Aiden pushed me back behind him. "This has nothing to do with you. Stand back. I can handle this."

Mr. Rino smirked. "I'd do what he says, little girl. Get out of my way, or I'll kill you, too."

I withdrew my sword. "Never."

"So be it." The metal of his sword glinted, reflecting the turquoise glow of moonlight. He addressed Aiden. "Thought you would have died in Seracedar, boy. but this was an oversight on my part. This time I'm not letting you get away alive."

Before I had a chance to reflect on what any of this meant, the two men attacked.

# CHAPTER 22

✦ ✦ ✦ ✦ ✦ ✦ ✦ ✦ ✦ ✦

Aiden immediately formed firebombs in his hands and aimed them at the middle-aged man. But Mr. Rino jumped into the air and onto the roof, escaping the flames. He flew toward Aiden.

The young lord came at me. His sword gleamed in his hands. I dodged the blow of the blade. It came so close it cut off a piece of my hair.

He attacked again.

I deflected with my sword. Time to see if the skills I'd been practicing would pay off.

Though he wasn't as drunk as he had pretended to be, the alcohol did make his reaction slower. I took advantage. I parried and ducked, then jabbed at him. My sword landed on his wrist, cutting through the fabric of his robe. He screamed and dropped his sword. I grabbed his other arm and flipped him over onto the ground.

Before he could stand, I had my sword to his neck. Then, as Aiden had taught me, I hit the back of the man's head, knocking him unconscious without killing him.

I looked back at Aiden. He had cornered Mr. Rino against a wall and unarmed him.

Quickly, I bound Lord Ting's hands with the sash of his robe. He wouldn't be able to make his escape even if he did wake up now.

I hurried toward Aiden. Rino held his hands up in surrender. I heard their conversation as I approached.

"I see you've grown stronger since you were a boy," Mr. Rino said to Aiden. "Go ahead and kill me then. I accept my defeat like a true gentleman."

A boy? Was it possible Rino had something to do with why Aiden had been sold as a slave to Seracedar?

"No," Aiden said. "That would be too easy. After what you did to me, I'm going to bring you to the palace and see you convicted. If you were a true gentleman, you'd face the consequences of your actions. If you were any kind of decent human, you wouldn't have given a child to the enemy, where you knew he might receive a fate worse than death."

The man shook his head. "If I go through a trial, Sito will suffer. He has no knowledge of what I did to you or of my plans for him. No one does. You should know he never lost hope of finding you. I don't want my boy to be humiliated. Kill me, or I'll do it myself."

They might as well have been speaking in riddles for all I could understand, but I tried to piece together the clues. Sito was the boy who'd been with Rino at the noodle stand. He'd recognized Aiden. He and Aiden had been close, then. Both Rino and Aiden cared about Sito it was clear to see. But why would Sito suffer if Rino were put on trial?

Aiden glared at the man for a moment longer, then swore. "So be it, then. Sito will never learn the truth. Neither will anyone else. My revenge ends with you."

In one swift movement, he gutted the man. I winced and bit back a scream.

Blood poured out of the man, seeping into the street and glistening under the turquoise moonlight. With one last bloodstained jeer, Mr. Rino tumbled forward, his face striking the pavement.

"Hey, you! Freeze, or I'll strike you down right there!" A voice called from the other street corner. Two uniformed guards quickly approached. One guard held his palms up, and two icicles grew out of them, so sharp they glinted under the streetlights. "Don't move, or I'll be forced to strike."

The guard's partner raised his hands to his mouth and yelled a high-pitched shriek that reminded me of Irica, my childhood bully. The sound echoed and carried through the air. "I need reinforcements. Location on the corner of Leihu and Huaflower Street."

"What do we do?" I asked Aiden, but he stood straight and tall, his demeanor strangely calm.

He threw down his sword and lifted his hands in surrender. "Put up your hands."

I did as he said. "They're going to throw us in prison."

"No, I promise that won't happen," he said. "Follow my lead. You may get angry with me in a moment, and I'm sorry for hiding everything for so long. But no matter what happens or who I'm supposed to be, remember that, to you, I will always be *Friend*."

What in the eighteen levels of the underworld was he saying? Who was he?

In a matter of seconds, an assembly of guards surrounded us, many already showing their tin-chai—ice crystals formed in some of their hands, fire in others, and stones flew into the air, threatening to bombard us.

"Identify yourselves," one guard shouted.

Aiden replied serenely. "Don't hurt the lady accompanying me. Her name is Rilla Marseas, and if there is even so much as a scratch on her, there will be consequences. I am Langdon Ai, son of King Ashbel Ai, and after twelve years, I have finally returned."

"What?" I whipped my head around and stared at him. Son of the king?

But Aiden didn't look like he was joking.

The guards murmured to each another.

"Th-that's impossible," the guard closest to us said.

"I have the proof on my chest," Aiden said.

Proof? Was he talking about his tattoo? The insignia of Emberwood inked on his chest? But surely any Ember could have that same tattoo on their skin. Couldn't they?

The head guard scoffed. "We have had many imposters over the years who forged the emblem. I warn you. It didn't end well for any of them, and it won't end well for you."

"I assure you I am no imposter," Aiden said. "If you will allow me to use my tin-chai, I can prove it. I know you're all aware it's the only way to discern the tattoo's authenticity."

The guards maintained their wary stances, keeping their swords ready. But the head guard motioned to Aiden. "Remove your upper garment then. If you are who you claim to be, it will be a miracle. Try anything, and we will attack instantly. Slowly now."

Aiden lifted his shirt, exposing his chest. The tattoo appeared ordinary at first, the dark ink barely visible in the dead of night. Aiden formed a small flickering flame in one hand. The ink on his chest illuminated, showing the flaming torch of Emberwood's crest. It glowed as though sunshine flowed from beneath his skin.

I gasped. I'd never seen anything like it. How was this possible?

Cries of astonishment echoed among the guards. In one rolling wave, all of them fell to their knees.

A choir of voices rang through the air. "All bow to His Royal Highness, Prince Langdon. Long live the crown prince of Emberwood."

# CHAPTER 23

✦ ✦ ✦ ✦ ✦ ✦ ✦ ✦ ✦ ✦

Back at the teahouse, Aiden and I sat in Daki's chamber, waiting for the guards to arrange our passage to the capitol.

*The lost prince of Emberwood.* I couldn't believe it, except Aiden had said he was someone I didn't expect him to be. How could he have kept his identity a secret all these years? Did Carrick know?

Daki sat on the edge of his bed. He rubbed the sleep from his eyes, still trying to take in all we'd told him.

Thankfully, he had recovered from earlier and no longer had a fever. He just must have been overtired. I was glad it wasn't anything serious.

"I'm still trying to process the fact that you kept this a secret and only revealed it because you'd have been arrested for murder otherwise," Daki told Aiden.

"Start from the beginning," I said. "How did you get from the protective walls of Linlang Palace to becoming the captive of your kingdom's enemy? I assume that old scholar was the one who sold you to Seracedar, but why?"

There were so many more questions I wanted to ask. Even Aiden's real name was different. Prince Langdon Ai. It felt like he had suddenly become a complete stranger.

Aiden sat on the floor and crossed his legs. "Yes, Mr. Rino was the one who sold me to Seracedarean slave traders when I was ten. He was my teacher. Instructed me not only in academics but also in martial arts."

"An idiotic move in my opinion," Daki scoffed. "Not that I'd condone this, but he would have received more money from the king and queen if he'd kidnapped and ransomed you. He must have had another motive."

Aiden looked at the door, where the guards stood outside. He spoke in a hushed tone. "You're right. He did have another reason for wanting to get rid of me. You must promise not to reveal what I'm about to say to anyone, as it would cause someone dear to me great pain."

At Daki's and my nods, he continued. "Mr. Rino wanted me gone because I was the heir to the throne as my father's only son. My parents could not have children after me, so my cousin, Sito, would be the next in line for the throne after my father's death. Mr. Rino wanted Sito to become king one day."

"Your cousin?" My eyes widened. "He was the young scholar at the noodle booth who recognized you."

"Does your cousin want you dead, too?" Daki asked. "He must have been a mere child when you were sold."

"Only Mr. Rino and my aunt, Sito's mother, were involved in the plot to sell me off," Aiden said. "I know Sito had no idea. We were best friends. Rino was going to kill me, but he had gambling debts and decided to sell me instead. Didn't think I'd stay alive for long."

"Did Mr. Rino work for your aunt?" Daki asked.

"They were lovers," Aiden replied. "She was married to my uncle, my father's brother. Before Mr. Rino sold me, I heard him and my aunt talking. I discovered Rino was Sito's birth father. Sito also holds Mr. Rino in high regard as his favorite teacher, and my aunt named Rino as Sito's godfather."

"So, if your cousin became king one day, Mr. Rino could potentially wield great power through Sito," I said. "No wonder Rino wanted you gone."

No matter the kingdom, there would always be power struggles. I thought about how Carrick's brothers had fought one another for control. It was no wonder Aiden had formed such a close bond with Carrick.

Aiden continued. "Sito will already be saddened to know Mr. Rino was responsible for my disappearance, but if he finds out the truth about his birth, he will be devastated. Not to mention the scandal that will result. The whole kingdom may ostracize him."

"What about his mother?" I asked.

"Dead," he said. "A few years ago, I tagged along with Carrick on his tour of Province Yupa. We came close to the Emberwood border, and I was able to find news of my family. Aunt Whin caught a sickness one winter and passed. There's no use giving up the name of a dead woman. I will only name Rino as the culprit for selling me to gain a few extra coins for his gambling debts, and I hope this will lessen the impact on my cousin."

I frowned. If Aiden had been able to leave Cedar Palace with Carrick, then with his skills in martial arts, he must have had an opportunity to escape and go home. Why hadn't he?

"Didn't you ever want to return home?" I asked. "Why did you stay with Carrick?"

"Of course, I wanted to go home," he said. "But I couldn't leave Carrick. I had a duty to protect him. He saved my life. I already told you that I would have become an androgy had he not interfered on my behalf."

Aiden was far too loyal to Carrick in my opinion. I thought about our unfinished conversation regarding our relationship. If Aiden hadn't left Carrick's side all these years even though he could have gone home, then it was no wonder why he'd never told me he had feelings for me. He put Carrick's life and happiness above his own.

Aiden's loyalty was a trait I liked about him, but it was also his weakness. No one deserved to have that much power over him, not even someone who had saved him from becoming an androgy.

"You have a responsibility to your kingdom as well," I said. "You are the crown prince of Emberwood. Don't you think your parents deserved to know you were still alive?"

"If I couldn't help Carrick become the emperor, then Terran or one of the other princes would eventually declare war upon Emberwood," Aiden said. "It was also for the sake of my kingdom and my family that I stayed in Seracedar, working behind the scenes. I didn't want my parents to know, not when the relationship between our kingdoms was tense. I didn't want to be the reason for the start of a war. I thought it best for all involved if I were to stay in the shadows as long as I could."

I wanted to ask more questions, but a knock sounded on the door. One of the Ember guards walked in and addressed Aiden. "Your Highness, I've received word that the security escort team assigned to take you to the palace is on its way. It will ensure your safety on the journey to the palace."

Aiden cleared his throat. "Was Ember University informed of Rino's death?"

"Yes, Your Highness. The university and the palace also know of his involvement in your disappearance and his attack on you."

"And my cousin?"

"He and the rest of the students will be informed in the morning," the guard said.

"Will Sito return to the palace?" Aiden asked.

"That remains to be determined," the guard answered. "But the king and queen wish to see you at once. You will be traveling by private rail coach as soon as the security escort team arrives."

Footsteps echoed in the hallway.

"That must be the head of the security escort." He stepped back and spoke into the hallway. "Ah, right on time."

A tall, broad-shouldered man with short, black hair entered the room. He didn't look more than thirty years of age, but there was a hard quality about him. His unsmiling, sapphire eyes were deeply set and dangerously narrow, as if he were constantly poised for oncoming battle. The bridge of his nose was slightly crooked, probably from being broken more than once in his past. Above his high cheekbones was a deep scar that crossed the arch of his right brow and ended at the start of his hairline. It glared white and red against his russet skin.

I felt his wyis. Stronger than the average man's, but nothing was off about it.

Aiden stood abruptly. "Blast the three moons."

At the same time, Daki let out an expletive, followed by, "I must be seeing things."

I looked between the men, wondering what the blazes was wrong.

"Is that really you, General?" Daki asked.

The newcomer also froze, and his brows lifted in surprise. "Montier? Aiden?"

And then it clicked. He knew Daki as Montier, and Daki had called him General.

I cleared my throat. "Is it possible that *you're* General Jelby Welder?"

He bowed. "At your service, my lady."

# CHAPTER 24

✦ ✦ ✦ ✦ ✦ ✦ ✦ ✦ ✦ ✦

"It is you." Aiden patted Welder's shoulder. "I can't believe our luck. Never in three dynasties did I think we'd cross paths so soon after landing in Emberwood."

"I am just as astounded, believe me." Welder closed his eyes, pressed his palms together, and raised them. "Old Grandfather Heaven, this must be your will for us to meet again." He opened his eyes. "And Montier, I'm so glad to see you safe and sound."

Daki grinned. "I'm called Daki now, my Yao name. Am I to assume you are assigned to escort us to the palace? Does this mean you managed to get a position with the royal guard?"

"Not exactly. Since we parted ways two years ago, I built up my own private security conveyance agency. The palace hires my men to transport precious cargo or people. I heard of the lost prince's return and requested to lead the return team, but I had no idea Aiden was the prince." Welder regarded me. "My lady, I'm afraid I didn't get your name."

I supposed it would be safe to give Welder my real name. Aiden wouldn't let anything happen to me in his kingdom.

"Rilla Marseas, sir. I know a lot about you. In fact, you're the reason we've come to Emberwood." I lowered my voice so no one outside of the room could hear us. "We think you stole the Sacred Cedar Scepter. Do you have it with you now?"

He furrowed his brow. "Just to be on the safe side, I'd feel more comfortable discussing that once we're in a completely private place and I'm sure there's no risk of anyone spying on us."

"That seems wise," Aiden said.

Welder gave a curt nod. "We must hurry and get to the capitol before news breaks of the lost prince's return. The guards are trying to keep it a secret for as long as possible, but news of this magnitude always leaks. Some scheming sensational news journalist will prey on a novice guard and get the lad to say something he shouldn't. Not one of my men, but probably one of the local guards. The crowds will swarm the streets then, and it will be a nuisance to avoid the other reporters."

Welder and his security escort moved efficiently. He hustled us out of the room directly into a coach while the streets were still dark. Within the next hour, we stood inside a rail coach station. I gawked at all the rail coaches in wonder. They were lined up on several railways, metal roads extending in both directions. I'd never seen a transportation system like this before.

The rail coaches were round vehicles. They were made of metal, each coach consisting of multiple units chained together, but the front unit looked like it had a circular face, and steam rose from the dome on top. Some passengers embarked on one that had stopped at the station, though there were few people given that it was still quite early in the morning.

We ascended some stairs that took us to a higher platform inside the station. There, a smaller, box-shaped coach was waiting. It was open, with no roof, and crates filled with barrels were loaded upon it. The labels on the crates had pictures of blueberry rice wine, so I was surprised when Welder gestured to this coach.

"This is the private royal rail coach," Welder said. "But I've disguised it as a cargo coach, so we needn't worry about anyone bothering us. This will be a half day's journey as opposed to three days if we rode by horse."

On the side of the coach, Welder lifted a latch to a door. Even though the coach appeared to be full of wooden crates, when I peered inside, there were just velvet cushioned seats, two rows on either side.

We boarded the coach and sat in the chairs. There was plenty of space to stretch my legs, and the velvet backrest was comfortable. As far as I could see, there were at least three other rail cars attached in front of this one, but they were all empty.

"Why are there so many rail cars?" I asked. "Aren't we the only ones riding?"

"It's part of the illusion that this is a cargo coach," Welder said. "Cargo coaches have at least ten cars attached to one another. Also, one of the rail cars in front of us has a kitchen and a hired chef. If you're hungry, I'll have him make you something." Sure enough, I smelled something good. Green onion pancakes, maybe?

"We should be going in a moment," Welder said. "Sit back, relax, and enjoy the ride."

Dawn peered through the window. I couldn't believe it was already morning.

"Maybe you can catch us up on what you've been doing since we parted," Daki said. "How did you come to be leading a security conveyance agency for the king? And what happened to the scepter?"

My eyes threatened to close. The lack of sleep was finally catching up to me. Still, I forced myself to stay awake. I wanted to hear Welder's story.

Welder settled back into the seat and crossed his legs. "As you know by now, my tin-chai allows me to camouflage objects, making it hard for a robber or assassin to distinguish his true target. I was quite successful, and the king soon began to hire me. I became His Majesty's preferred security agency to deliver important items to and from the palace."

"If I had that tin-chai, it would be easy to turn to a life of thievery," I said.

Welder's eyes twitched—whether from annoyance or from surprise, I couldn't tell. His face was unreadable. He glanced down at his watch and addressed his six subordinates. "One of you, check with the conductor and see what is holding us up. We should have started by now. The rest of you, make sure the coach doors are all secure. Even though our coach is in disguise, I still don't want to take a chance of anyone sneaking aboard."

They did as he asked, walking to the next attached coach in front of ours.

"Now that you've ensured our privacy," I said, "I think you can stop stalling and admit that you stole the Sacred Cedar Scepter."

Then Welder gave me a pointed stare. "Looking at you, I would never have guessed you'd be so blunt."

"After crossing two kingdoms and traversing the ocean in search of you, I'm not in the mood to waste more time," I said with a shrug. "The sooner you answer my questions, the sooner I get to take a nap."

Amusement flickered in Welder's face. The corners of his lips threatened to curve upward. "Well, you should be able to get your beauty rest soon, then. Because yes, I can confirm that you are indeed correct. I did take the scepter when I fled Cedar Palace. I didn't think anyone suspected. How did you figure it out?"

"I knew you had flattered Empress Limera into taking you into her bed for a season," Daki said. "Apparently before her death, she hinted that an ex-lover stole the scepter from her, and the timing of it worked out so it could have been you."

"Androgy Solar also gave us a clue to find you and the scepter in Emberwood," Aiden added.

"I should have guessed Androgy Solar knew," Welder said. "He caught me sneaking out of Limera's chambers the night I took the scepter, the night before our attempt to dethrone Terran went terribly wrong. I had intended on keeping it until Terran lost his power and word got out that he no longer had the Will of Heaven. Unfortunately—"

Welder's gaze sharpened, darting to the door of the adjoining coach. One of Welder's men stepped into our coach.

"I'm sorry to interrupt, sir," he said. "We haven't been able to take off yet because there's been an accident up front. A steam coach ran off the road and came onto the railway at the next station."

Welder got up, but Aiden tugged him back. "You can't leave. This could be Androgy Haming trying to separate us so he can change places with you. He's a face-changer who has been following us, and he's been looking for you. His goal is to find the scepter, too."

Welder sat back down and addressed his man. "Take care of it, Hu. Be on the alert. This could be the trick of a man who can change his face, trying to gain access to our security team. Anyone, even one of us, might not be who they appear to be. Make sure you aren't alone."

The man nodded and left.

Welder closed his eyes, bowed his head, and pressed his palms together. "Old Grandfather Heaven, protect us and grant us the wisdom to see through the schemes of evil men." He opened his eyes and looked at us. "We shouldn't discuss the scepter any further. Not until we're sure there are no threats. We'll wait until we're under the security of Linlang Palace."

Ten minutes passed. A whistle sounded outside. Shouts and a commotion followed. I looked out the window. "What's going on?"

Welder withdrew his sword and moved to the coach door. "Don't worry. My men haven't let me down yet."

Another few minutes passed. The coach door opened, and Welder's man, Hu, boarded with a second guard on their team. Both men were breathing hard. I immediately read their wyis. They felt normal, but I couldn't be sure. Haming had figured out my trick and masked his wyis the last few times we met.

Hu swallowed and cleared his throat. "You were right. The accident was a set up. The driver who drove on the tracks disappeared. I went to call coach emergency services to clear the road, and the man in charge attacked me. He was wearing my face. If I hadn't asked Vay to come with me, he would have taken me down. The man got away. I'm sorry."

The other guard, Vay, said, "He took off running when I blew my whistle, and the others came to assist." He picked at his fingernails.

Hu swallowed, and both Vay and Hu looked nervous as they waited for Welder to reply. "Wait, how can we be sure you're Welder's men?" Aiden asked. "Rilla, can you read their wyis?"

"It won't do any good," I said. "Haming knows I can read wyis, and he's been able to cover up his."

"I can confirm their identities," Welder said. "Vay always picks at his nails when he thinks he's disappointed me. And Hu swallows and clears his throat when he's conveying bad news." To his men, he said, "Unfortunate that he got away. I'm disappointed, of course, but we'll have to deal with the androgy later. We need to get to Linlang Palace with no further incidents. What's the status on our departure time now?"

"Emergency coach services is clearing the tracks," Hu said. "We should be on our way in a few minutes."

Welder peered outside the window and groaned. "They've figured us out."

I followed his gaze. A throng of eager men and women were outside the coach, pushing against the guards, who were the only barrier stopping them from rushing our coach. Pulses of light flashed.

I blinked, temporarily blinded. "What is that light?"

"The flashes come from the photography boxes they carry," Welder said.

Now I noticed the peculiar black boxes many of the reporters held.

"Those photography boxes capture the image of what's in front of them," Welder explained. "Word of the lost prince's return must already have gotten out, and with the scuffle between my men and Androgy Haming, someone must have guessed the high security means we're in a disguised coach with the prince."

Aiden shielded his face from the window. "The crowd is getting larger."

"Don't worry. They can't see inside," Welder said.

One of the men outside waved his arms toward the growing crowd. The earth split, coming up from the ground to form a wall blocking the crowd. I could feel the rumbling in my body.

Welder's team returned on the rail coach.

Another one of Welder's men bowed. "We're ready, sir."

Everyone settled back down in their seats. The rail coach started again. The sound of a *click-clack* pulsed, growing faster as the coach picked up speed.

Thank Old Grandfather Heaven. We'd escaped Haming and the curious onlookers. At least for now.

Outside the window, the roads ran parallel to the railway. Hundreds of steam coaches lined up front to back in traffic on the streets. They reminded me of fish tightly packed into the tubs of ice at the sea market.

"We'll be there in a few more hours," Welder said. "You should all rest. There will be a lot to do once we reach the palace."

He eased into his seat and spoke with his subordinates, though they kept their voices at a murmur.

A stillness descended, and my eyelids grew heavier. I let myself relax and drift off to sleep.

# CHAPTER 25

✦ ✦ ✦ ✦ ✦ ✦ ✦ ✦ ✦ ✦

When I woke again, the sun streamed through the coach's window. A delightful roasted aroma wafted into my nose, along with the scent of baked goods of some sort. My stomach gurgled. I realized I hadn't eaten since yesterday afternoon.

Aiden and the others already had plates of food in front of them. Aiden had scarfed down half of his.

"Oh, you're awake," Aiden said to me. "We didn't want to wake you." He gestured to one of the guards. "Miss Rilla will take her meal now."

A guard came out from the rail car attached to ours. He carried a fresh plate of eggs and savory scallion pancakes along with a bowl of steaming rice porridge. He laid out the meal in front of me.

I dug in. I had never tasted anything so delicious.

As I ate, Welder came back in from the adjoining coach behind us. He sat across from us and wore a frown. "I'm afraid there are already crowds of Embers gathered in the capitol, waiting for us to pass. We will still have to take a regular steam coach from the station to the palace. As a diversion, my men will ride in another steam coach that will have the royal emblem. Are there any other dangers you can think of that we should consider?"

"What about Prince Nelan's men or other mercenaries?" I asked. "There's still a reward for our capture and return to Cedar Palace."

"We will look out for anyone who might be working for Nelan," Welder said. "But with all that has been going on at the Seracedar capitol, I doubt Nelan is focused on either of you anymore."

"What do you mean?" Aiden asked.

"I happened to read this morning's newspaper," Welder said. "Your hero, Prince Carrick, has gained ground and captured part of Nelan's territory. After Nelan proved to have a fake scepter, half the army turned their loyalty to Carrick. They may launch an attack on the palace any day. This means Nelan won't waste any men or time on pursuing fugitives when he needs every man he has to defend the palace walls."

I was glad to hear that Carrick was not only unharmed, but he had gained some leverage over Nelan. I was anxious to get to the palace so we could finally address the Sacred Cedar Scepter with Welder. It was our only hope.

An hour later, we reached the capitol and disembarked the rail coach. We got into a steam coach, with Welder as our driver. Daki sat in front with Welder. The driver's compartment was outside, but the passenger seats, where Aiden and I sat, were in an enclosed space. It was compact, and the top of the compartment was low, nearly touching the top of Aiden's head.

I twisted my body to face Aiden. I wanted to talk to him about what happened between us at the teahouse, but he gazed out the window, seemingly lost in his own thoughts. *This must be a lot for him. This is overwhelming for me.* Not only had I revealed my feelings to the man I liked only to discover he was the prince of a kingdom, I was on my way to meet his parents. And if one day we decided to get married, I would have to win over an entire nation that might not think I was good enough for their future ruler.

But I was getting too far ahead of myself. We had to get to the palace first and let Aiden reunite with his parents. Now wasn't the time to discuss our relationship.

As we drove down the road, I watched the activity going on outside. Dozens of tiny shops and restaurants sat on either side of the road. Shopkeepers decorated their store windows with the kingdom's emblem and golden flowers. Banners of the kingdom's colors—orange and black—flew in the air on every street corner, and workers hung strings of lanterns down the main street. It seemed they were preparing for a celebration.

As we stopped at a traffic junction, I caught snippets of conversation through the window.

"Are you ready for the festivities?"

"Of course. I can't believe Prince Langdon has returned after all these years."

These decorations were to celebrate Aiden. I peeked at him again to see if he had heard the shopkeepers. He still stared out the window, but he said, "I can't believe Prince Langdon has returned either."

I touched Aiden's arm. "How are you feeling about all of this?"

He brushed a hand through his hair. "Nervous. I'm anxious to see my parents. For years, I imagined how this might play out, but I'm afraid now that it's actually happening." He looked away from the window and back at me. "I hope they don't hate me."

The coach took off again.

I frowned. "Why would they hate you? They're probably overjoyed to be reunited with you. It wasn't your fault that you were sold to slavers and brought to Seracedar."

"But I could have come home years ago," he said. "Carrick gave me the chance. I couldn't leave him. I believed in his cause. He needed me more than Emberwood needed their crown prince, so I chose him over my family." Aiden whispered the words like a shameful confession.

I didn't get the chance to reply as the coach came to a screeching stop. Loud horns blared from coaches behind and in front of us.

Welder slid open the glass window that separated the outside compartment from us. He called to us. "Looks like we won't be able to go any farther until this mess clears. We'll have to wait for my men to distract the crowd and the reporters."

I peered through the window. Hordes of people spilled out onto the street, blocking the coaches from continuing forward. Some of the coaches tried going around the crowd. Ember guards blew their whistles and shouted for people to clear the road, but there were too few guards to control that many people.

Sirens and horns screamed behind us. A booming voice shouted, loud enough for all to hear: "Make way for Prince Langdon."

I caught a flash of lights out the rear window. A coach bearing the royal emblem approached, driving slowly. Guards walked in front of and behind it. People came up to the coach, trying to look inside. Lights flashed from photo boxes. A wall of electric sparks surrounded the coach and its guards, preventing anyone from getting too close or they'd risk getting shocked. But that didn't stop the crowd from following the coach as though it led a parade.

With the people moving forward, the flow of traffic slowly began to move again.

We pulled forward, inch by inch. Now I could see what the crowd had blocked. In the distance, up the sloped street, iron gates surrounded a large, wide dome. It was so tall that it climbed into the clouds. I couldn't see the top of it. That had to be Linlang Palace.

The building was enclosed on all sides with walls made of white stone that sparkled under the sun. But where were the gardens and the pavilions? It looked nothing like Cedar Palace.

The traffic and the crowd continued up the street toward the palace, following the royal coach and the sirens.

Welder took a sharp turn down a narrow alley. "My men in the royal coach will be the focus of the crowd's attention. They'll pull up to the front gates of the palace. Someone will probably figure out it's a ruse by then, but it'll buy us enough time to slip through the back."

We drove down narrow roads, twisting and turning through the city as we made our way up the hill. We came to the white stone wall that surrounded the palace and followed it around a wide circle. The wall ended at a small, forested area, a row of oak trees that grew in front of us, blocking the road.

Welder stopped the coach and got out. He walked to the first oak tree in front of our coach and placed a hand on the trunk, emitting a jolt of his wyis. The oak trees shimmered and disappeared, transforming into the white stone wall protecting the palace. In place of the trees, there was an iron gate and two Ember guards standing watch.

Through the window, I heard Welder speak to them. "The coming of autumn stirs the golden leaves."

A password phrase? It must be. The guards said nothing in return and opened the gates.

Welder returned into the coach. "The camouflaging of the back entrance into the oak trees was my doing. People trying to trespass into the palace can't find the backway and eventually give up. It makes my job easier when I need to get in or leave but don't want to meet the nosy citizens and reporters crowding the front gate."

Clever, I had to admit. But I wondered if someone like Haming could still find a way inside if he found out Welder's password. Or maybe not. He wouldn't be able to find the camouflaged oak tree without Welder's tin-chai.

We drove down a long driveway, made of the same white stone. At the end of the driveway, a dozen steam coaches were parked outside of a small building bustling with Ember guards and uniformed servants.

We parked, and one of the guards opened our coach's doors. As I disembarked, loud noises came from the coaches in the building. I saw servants in blue uniforms working underneath the coaches. They carried metal parts and oil cans, tightening bolts and tinkering with tools.

A man approached us. He was dressed in a black uniform with a closed collar fastened together with an orange tie.

He bowed. "Your Highness. I am Attendant Bin, the personal attendant to the king and queen. Mr. Welder, it's nice to see you again. The king and queen are on their way home from a week-long trip to the northern cities. They were informed of the prince's return and are rushing back, but it will be another two hours before they arrive. In the meantime, please follow me."

He took us past the steam coaches and the building of workers. We walked into a domed tunnel and stepped onto a moving staircase that lifted us to the next landing. I had never seen a staircase that moved like this and had to hold onto the railing to keep my balance.

Cautiously, I stepped onto the landing. A wide glass door in front of us had black, curvy letters at the top of it that read, *Linlang Palace Eastern Entrance.*

Linlang Palace. Aiden had spent his childhood here. I wondered how he felt to be back after all these years. I glanced at him. He had a nervous expression. His shoulders were tense, and his eyes were alert, taking everything in.

The attendant walked up to the door, and it opened by itself. I wondered if this was possible through someone's tin-chai, or if it was some new technology that Emberwood had developed.

We followed Attendant Bin inside, where we stopped in front of a foyer. A long, white table made of smooth marble was positioned longitudinally, barring visitors from entering farther into the building. The marble table didn't have legs. Rather, it hung on a black chain attached to a metal pulley. Several men and women dressed in gold and black uniforms stood behind the table. Palace guards? They bowed at the sight of us.

"Your Highness," they said in unison.

Attendant Bin touched the side of the marble table. A pulse of light flashed three times. Then came the sound of chains jerking, and the pulley shifted on its own. The marble table parted in the center, lifting to clear an entryway.

We passed the guards as we walked into a long hall where golden lanterns hung from the ceiling. The light from the lanterns was beautiful and bright. A clanking noise brought my attention back to the pulley, which reversed itself, and the marble table shifted back into place.

When we came to the end of the corridor, there was a series of three glass double doors, with each door pulling open in the center. Within each door, pulleys held a compartment going up and down a vertical column. These vertical columns extended all the way up to the ceiling. The palace seemed to have many levels. It was quite marvelous. Linlang Palace had to be as spacious and extraordinary as Cedar Palace, but the two palaces couldn't be more different.

"Trolleys," Aiden said. "They transport people to wherever they need to go in the palace."

"Convenient." I watched one of the trolleys coming down the vertical column. The trolley had glass windows on all four sides. I estimated that around twenty people could squeeze into one if necessary.

The trolley stopped in front of us, and a bell dinged. The door opened, and three people, all teenagers, exited. They weren't dressed in the same black and gold uniforms as the men and women in the foyer. I wasn't sure if they were servants. Their gazes flickered to Attendant Bin and Aiden. They hesitated a moment before bowing. "Your Highness," they said as they addressed Aiden.

Aiden smiled. "I see you recognize me."

"We were told of your return," one of them said. "And you do look so much like your father, the king."

"Students," Attendant Bin said, "if you are on your break time from class, then please continue as you were."

"Yes, Attendant Bin." They straightened and continued down the corridor. The faint strains of their whispers echoed behind them. I couldn't make out the words, but they had to be talking about Aiden.

We stepped onto the trolley.

I noticed that, on the side of the trolley, there were five circular buttons, each labeled with characters from the ancient Shyan language. The button Attendant Bin pressed said *Water and Crystal.* As the trolley rose, I read the names on the other four buttons: *Spirit Mountain, Forest Heart, Gold Song, and Sun Fire.*

Aiden took note of my curiosity. "Linlang Palace consists of five levels. Each level houses a different courtyard with a specialty of sorts."

Outside the glass window, I caught a glimpse of a forested courtyard not unlike the Spring Gardens of Cedar Palace. Even though Linlang Palace was indoors, the space was so expansive it seemed like we were still outside. If I didn't see the windows on the far sides of the building, I would have forgotten we were inside. The architecture was spectacular.

Natural light streamed in from the windows, but that wouldn't be enough to illuminate a place this massive.

"How do they keep the palace so bright?" I asked Aiden. "I feel like we're outdoors."

"Those with a tin-chai to cast light insert their wyis into the ceiling, adding to the natural light," Aiden said.

In the middle of the courtyard, children sat behind desks and studied scrolls. In another area, kids were painting, and in another, a group practiced musical instruments.

"That's Forest Heart Courtyard," Aiden said. "I remember it well. I studied there as a child. But it used to be just my cousin and me. Who are all these children?"

Attendant Bin stroked his beard. "After your disappearance, the king and queen turned Forest Heart into a school for orphans and poor children who cannot afford an education. We built dormitories for them as well. Most of our older children have continued in our program through their teenage years. Many of the teenagers have been able to score high marks on the entrance exams, earning scholarships into Ember University. Some of the students from the palace's programs have even gone on to become doctors, teachers, legal counselors, and inventors."

It seemed the kingdom took their children's education quite seriously. I wished it had been so in Seracedar. If I'd been born in Emberwood, perhaps I could have continued going to school after my sixteenth birthday. If only I could've become a doctor and still be accepted by society . . .

The trolley rose another level. This courtyard looked like it was atop a mountain. The walls were made of rocks, which several men dressed in training garb climbed. One of them jumped from one wall to the opposite wall as though he could fly. There were also flat surfaces on the peak of the mountain where a group of men practiced martial arts moves in unison.

"Spirit Mountain Courtyard," Aiden said. "The training grounds for those who wish to join the ranks. I used to train here with Mr. Rino. Before he sold me off."

The next level was bright and contained free-standing pagodas that acted as rooms scattered in the open space. The doors were painted in gold. Other workers dressed in the same attire as Attendant Bin walked through the corridors between the pagodas. There was an outdoor kitchen in the center of the courtyard. Cooks handled giant black woks over open flames and firepits. The smell of barbecued meats and chilies carried through the air. It smelled delicious.

"Gold Song Courtyard is where the servants stay," Attendant Bin said. "The food is also prepared here."

We rose another level, and the door opened to a courtyard. The ceiling and the walls were covered in some kind of material that made it look like we were under a clear blue sky.

We followed Attendant Bin down the pebbled path and came to a lake in the center of the courtyard. Attendant Bin stepped onto the water, and I realized it was solid.

I placed one foot on the lake warily.

"No need to worry," Attendant Bin said. "It's made of a shatter-proof material."

It wasn't ice. Unlike a frozen pond, the surface of the lake was completely see-through like glass so we could see everything beneath the water.

"The Water Crystal Courtyard is where the family and their guests take residence," the attendant said. "Your private rooms will be here. When the king and queen return, I'll take you to see them. In the meantime, I'm sure you are all hungry. You can enjoy some refreshment while you wait."

Golden and black fish swam below my feet. In the middle of the lake was a stone pavilion that stood on the surface of the water. The pavilion's arched roof curled upward like a gentle smile. Within the pavilion were a circular stone table and two benches that curved all around.

"Please be seated, and your meal will be right out." Attendant Bin gestured to the table.

"Before we eat, is there a place I can wash my hands?" I asked.

"Yes." The attendant summoned a servant. "Show Miss Rilla to the washroom."

I followed the servant off the lake and onto pebbled ground. Through a small corridor was a washroom for men to the left and the ladies' washroom to the right. The room had a small basin and chamber pot. The space was clean and smelled of fresh lemons. The floor was clear here, just like on the lake, and I could see the swimming fish.

I finished washing up quickly and returned to the pavilion. Attendant Bin was no longer there, but Welder was seated at the table, already sipping tea. I sat next to him. "Where are Daki and Aiden?"

"Washroom." Welder leaned forward and poured me a cup of tea.

"Thank you." I noticed a sachet dangling from around his neck. Tied around the sachet was a red silk knot with a tassel—probably a protection charm. Monasteries sold such talismans for those who wanted protection from evil spirits during a long journey. I wouldn't have thought Welder would be the superstitious sort. He was proving to be quite an interesting character.

My attention shifted beyond the table as Daki and Aiden rounded the corner and approached. They sat across from me.

Attendant Bin returned with a tray of tea and dishes of food. He placed the dishes on the table. There were stewed meats, seafood, several kinds of fresh vegetables, and a clay pot of rice to share.

I spooned some rice into my bowl and topped it with food, sampling a bit of each dish. I took a sip of the tea. It was slightly sweet and floral.

The attendant bowed. "I'll leave you to enjoy your meal. When the king and queen return, I'll inform you right away."

"The washrooms, the food, everything here is like art," Daki said. "It's amazing."

Welder nodded absentmindedly. "I suppose it is."

I regarded him. "We're in the safety of the palace, and there's no one here but us. I think you can tell us now."

Welder gave me a blank stare. "Tell you what?"

Was he serious? "The Sacred Cedar Scepter," I said. "What did you do with it?"

"Oh, yes the scepter," he said, slapping his forehead. "Forgive me. I'm a bit tired." He withdrew a dagger from his cloak and placed it on the table.

It looked like an ordinary dagger. But a light glinted off it. In another second, it extended. This time, not only did part of it change, but also, the entire scepter formed.

I exhaled. The Sacred Cedar Scepter.

Aiden touched the base, tracing the intricate carving of the cedar tree. "You had it all this time, and no one suspected?"

"The safest hiding spot is where no one expects it to be. I used my tin-chai to make the scepter appear as this dagger, and I always carry it on me. My goal was to wait for Terran to lose his power and reveal to the public that he'd lost the Will of Heaven."

"But it's been two years since you fled Cedar Palace," Aiden said. "Terran is already dead. What have you been waiting for?"

Welder touched the scepter again, and it converted back into the dagger. "I've been searching for the next rightful ruler these past two years. Since my tin-chai was not amplified, I haven't been given the Will of Heaven. But I tested different candidates in Emberwood, let them hold the dagger without their realizing it was actually the scepter. If they received the Will of Heaven, this would have transformed back into the scepter, and their tin-chai would be amplified. But I've had no luck. I had thought to see if King Ashbel might be the one to reunite the two Shyan kingdoms, but the dagger did not transform when placed in his hands."

"I doubt my father wants to expand his kingdom by reuniting with Seracedar," Aiden said. He gave Welder a chiding glance. "Carrick is meant to rule Seracedar. You shouldn't have removed the scepter from Cedar Palace. While you helped to quicken Terran's fall, you also made it impossible for anyone else from Terran's line to test their right to rule. After all, it is tradition for the princes of the ruling family to be given a chance to attain Old Grandfather Heaven's blessing."

Welder's glance sharpened. "What makes you believe in Carrick so strongly? He might not be as corrupt as his brothers, but I find him lacking. But you have always regarded him as your savior, so you're blind to his darkness."

"I know he isn't perfect," Aiden said. "Nobody is. That doesn't mean he's lacking."

"Then explain this." Welder folded his arms across his chest. "Why does he always use you to fight his battles? A truly noble gentleman would not keep another man as his prisoner, nor would he send another in his place to find the scepter."

"Carrick never asked me to find the scepter for him." Aiden's lips curled in a displeased glower. "He has granted me freedom. It was I who decided to help him take the throne. He saved my life, and I know him. He wants to right the wrongs of his forefathers. Besides, who are you to take Old Grandfather Heaven's role and act as judge? You decided to take the scepter and find the next rightful ruler by yourself. That isn't your job."

His hands curled into fists, and he sat on the edge of his chair, glaring at Welder.

I reached across the table and placed a hand on Aiden's forearm. "There's no reason to start fighting. This is a discussion, and Welder's opinions deserve to be heard."

Although I could argue that Welder wasn't in a position to accuse anyone of compromising one's morals—after all, he had slept with Limera and stolen the scepter—I had to concede that he had a valid point. I understood that Aiden regarded Carrick as a friend and a brother, but Carrick still viewed Aiden as property. Carrick had forced Aiden to stay silent in my presence and he'd spoken to Aiden as though his opinion meant nothing.

Now that I had put some distance between Carrick and myself, I could see him more objectively. There was a darkness about Carrick that had always frightened me even though I had been fascinated by him at the same time.

"Rilla's right," Daki said. "We're all on the same side and want what's best for the future of Seracedar and the rest of Caliwyis."

Welder's features softened. "Yes, I don't wish to argue. Perhaps Aiden has a point. I suppose Carrick deserves a chance."

Aiden opened his mouth to speak but stopped, his gaze drifting to the distance. Attendant Bin approached our table. This conversation would have to continue later.

The attendant bowed. "The king and queen have returned and wish to see you immediately."

We followed him back to the trolley. One more level up brought us to Sun Fire Courtyard. The doors to the trolley opened. We walked into a beautiful open garden in the center of a quad of pavilions. We were on the highest floor of the palace, and high above us, there was an open ceiling to the sky. Dozens of glass windows surrounded the courtyard. I imagined in the daytime there would be a lot of natural light streaming in. Now it was after sunset, and the blue tint of light from the Turquoise Moon reflected on the glass.

In this garden, lanterns made of diaphanous red fabric floated in the air as they had in the Emberwood city streets. The flames burned brightly, tinged with the warmth of their red shade covers.

Bursts of colorful flowers bloomed on each side of the path where we walked. The entire garden appeared to be glowing as though lighting up in celebration for the lost prince's return I could feel heat emanating from them and realized that mini flames burned within their centers, colorful sparks reflective of the shade of the petals. Red, orange, purple, white, and blue. Streams of light glowed from the centers of the flowers. The lights from the flowers beamed up and formed clusters. They reminded me of fireworks.

"Fireflowers," Aiden said. "They only grow in Emberwood. The flowers' flames emit pollen into the air. That's what the light streams are. It's like a show, isn't it?"

"It's beautiful," I said.

The others continued walking ahead, but Aiden stopped. I paused as well, watching him.

He stared at the flowers, unblinking. "They're my ah-mu's favorite flower. We used to watch the lights together when I was a boy." A look of apprehension crossed his face. "What will they say to me? I was away for so long in an enemy kingdom, and much of that time was by my own choice. They might not understand. What if they question my loyalty to them and Emberwood? What if . . . what if they say I no longer belong here?"

His voice was a whisper of uncertainty.

I touched his upper arm. "I doubt they'll say that. The whole kingdom is rejoicing over your return, and your parents rushed back here to see you. But if that happens, I'll be here. The place by my side will always belong to you."

His gaze shifted from the flowers to me. We locked eyes.

"What are you two standing there for?" Daki's voice burst through the air, interrupting our moment. "Come on, the king and queen are waiting."

We walked across the path that took us through the fireflower garden. A pagoda structure stood on its own in the center of the fireflower garden. The pagoda had a wide archway forming an open entryway with no door. Attendant Bin gestured for us to go inside.

Spread on the ground and extending across the room was a gorgeous velvet red carpet, and at the end of that carpet was a divan. Seated there were the king and queen.

Aiden's gaze fell upon them, and he stilled. The king and queen, unable to contain their emotions, stood and rushed toward him. They stopped two feet away. All doubt fell away from Aiden's face then, and I could see why. The love in his parents' faces shone so brightly, it made me teary-eyed for them.

King Ashbel's shoulders trembled. "Is it really you?"

"It's me, Ah-fu," Aiden said. "Ah-mu."

Queen Leonora burst into tears. She embraced Aiden and sobbed into his shoulder. "You're home. You're finally home."

"Let's give them some privacy, shall we?" Welder said. "Whatever we have to discuss can wait for later."

Although I'd expected to meet the king and queen, Welder was right. The family needed time to reunite in private. Introductions could wait until tomorrow.

Welder, Daki, and I exited the room to return to our private quarters. Aiden and his parents didn't notice. I couldn't be happier for their family. They'd been separated for so long. I thought of my own family. How I missed Rell and Nia. One day soon, I hoped we could be reunited. But oh, I would give anything for my parents to be here again.

A tear rolled down my cheek. I wiped it away. I couldn't think about Mama and Baba now, or I might break down crying. After this was all over, I would find my brother and sister-in-law, and I'd finally meet my nephew.

One day soon, I'd no longer be a fugitive. I'd see Radi again, and she could live in peace without the worry of anyone using or hurting her.

We just had to get the scepter back to Carrick, and all would be well.

# CHAPTER 26

✦ ✦ ✦ ✦ ✦ ✦ ✦ ✦ ✦ ✦

Early the next morning, Attendant Bin brought Welder, Daki, and me to the Ice Flower Pavilion across from our rooms.

Inside the pavilion, the king, queen, and Aiden were seated around a large circular table.

We bowed. "Your Majesties."

King Ashbel nodded and uttered a brief grunt.

Queen Leonora gestured with animation, urging us to have a seat. "Please sit and make yourselves at home. There is a lot to discuss."

"Yes, and we'll talk over breakfast," King Ashbel said.

Servants bustled in, bringing platters of food.

Now I knew why Aiden loved food so much and why he seemed to have a bottomless stomach. All Embers did was eat, it appeared.

I took in the variety of refreshments on the large turntable at the center of the table: elegant tea cakes decorated with fruit slices, fried meat pies, even the curious street food dish of fermented chili and rice cakes I'd seen earlier on the streets of Leihu Port.

Once all the food had been spread out, the servants left the dining hall, giving us some privacy.

"I'm so sorry for our rudeness last night," Queen Leonora said.

"We ignored you, our honored guests, and we didn't even introduce ourselves."

"Under the circumstances, there are no apologies necessary, Your Majesties," Daki said.

Leonora maintained a hold on Aiden's arm as though she were afraid he might disappear. "Langdon, you must introduce me to your friends."

Langdon. Right, Prince Langdon was Aiden's real name. I still had to get used to that.

"Ah-mu, Ah-fu, this man is Captain Tae Montier," Aiden said, indicating Daki. "Though he goes by Daki now."

"Montier," Ashbel repeated. "I heard of you. Weren't you a captain of the Seracedarean Navy, charged with treason because you led the failed coup that brought Welder to Emberwood?"

"Yes, Your Majesty." Daki bowed his head.

"Daki. Is that a Yao name?" Leonora asked.

Daki hesitated, and his cheeks reddened. I knew it must be because it was considered shameful in Seracedar to be part Yao and the reason he'd hidden it for most of his life. "My mother was a Yao. After the failed coup against Terran, I escaped from Seracedar and went to live in my mother's hometown."

Leonora didn't look perturbed at all. "I've studied the Yao language and visited the northern coast a few times in my youth. It was beautiful. I hope to go again one day. Emberwood and Yao have been on good terms for most of my husband's reign, and I'm determined that our kingdoms continue maintaining our friendship."

The tension in Daki's shoulders loosened, and he smiled at Leonora. "If Your Majesties do visit Yao, I'd love to show you the sights."

"And what about you, young lady?" Ashbel asked me. "Rilla Marseas, correct?"

"Yes, Your Majesties," I said, tilting my head down in a slight bow.

Leonora beamed at me. "You are beautiful. Langdon has already spoken of you. He says you became his source of light the moment you met."

I blinked in surprise. Those words were exactly how I would describe my feelings toward him. "Aiden—I mean, Prince Langdon—is the one who has been protecting me. I would never have survived the palace or this journey without him."

"That is what he has said of you." Queen Leonora patted Aiden's head fondly.

Aiden wouldn't meet my gaze, but his cheeks reddened. We had yet to resolve what had happened between us at the teahouse. But we probably wouldn't be able to have some privacy for awhile.

"Ah-mu, stop embarrassing me," Aiden said.

"After a decade of believing you were dead, I think I have the right to embarrass and coddle you all I want," she said and heaped tons of food onto his plate. Then she did the same for me.

"Thank you, Your Majesty," I said. "But this is a lot of food. I'm not sure I can finish all of this."

"You need to eat more." Ignoring my protests, she placed another spoonful of rice cakes on my plate. "You're all too skinny, and I'm determined to plump you up."

I could see where Aiden got the rest of his vibrant personality. Queen Leonora wasn't the prettiest woman by societal standards. Her hair was a dull caramel shade that curled a little wildly like ribbons wrapped around a gift package, and she had a figure that most, at least in my hometown, would have considered plump. But there was a brightness to her face, and she had such a pleasant, welcoming smile that radiated with friendliness. She exuded charisma. Certainly, she had passed these traits down to her son.

As for Ashbel, even though his face was beginning to wrinkle now, and his hair was thinning, it was obvious he had been a handsome charmer in his day, like his son. From his wispy brownish-blond hair to his stunning golden eyes and slender but toned physique, he was what Aiden would look like in twenty years.

Welder tugged at the chain around his neck and absentmindedly played with the protective sachet attached to it. "Your Majesty," he said to the king, "I assume the prince has informed you that I carry the Sacred Cedar Scepter. We must decide what to do with it."

Welder took the dagger from his cloak. It elongated, taking the shape of the scepter again.

Ashbel scowled. "Yes, indeed we should. My son has already told me about his time in Seracedar and his mission in helping Prince Carrick ascend the throne. One thing is for sure—I want the scepter taken out of Emberwood as soon as possible. If Cedar Palace discovers the scepter is in Emberwood, they will assume I had something to do with it. We already have a tense relationship. I don't want them to initiate war with us."

Aiden munched enthusiastically, savoring each bite. "Ah-fu has agreed to provide the resources to help bring the scepter back to Carrick and Cedar Palace," he said between bites. "Welder, you will be assigned to lead the mission."

Welder bowed his head. "I'd be honored."

"And I'd be happy to assist you in any way, my friend," Daki said.

"I appreciate that," Welder said, nodding at Daki. And to the king, he said, "Thank you for this opportunity, Your Majesty. I won't fail you."

Ashbel glared at Welder. "You should know that, had I discovered you'd smuggled the scepter into my kingdom two years ago, I would have told you to leave Emberwood immediately. Don't think I've forgiven you yet."

Welder hung his head. "I apologize, Your Majesty. But I was trying to protect Seracedar."

"You did this only for the good of Seracedar, not for Emberwood, which is the kingdom you adopted as your homeland when you agreed to become a permanent citizen here." The king's chiding glare didn't leave Welder. "We broke away from Seracedar long ago, and we've no need to revive the old traditions of allowing a scepter to decide our fate. There are those who believe Seracedar should have control over us because they were in possession of the scepter for centuries after our split. Others might think I have ambitions to conquer Seracedar and reunite our kingdoms if they knew the scepter was here. That is far from my mind. I want my legacy to be that I was a ruler of peace, not of war."

I was surprised by King Ashbel's reaction. I'd thought all rulers wanted more power and more territory. I liked that the king wanted to be known as a ruler of peace. No wonder his son also had such a noble heart.

Welder nodded. "Again, my king, I sincerely apologize. I accept whatever consequences you deem necessary."

Ashbel folded his hands on the table. His eyes gentled. "Seeing as you've earned my trust these past two years, I will forgive you. Since it was Prince Carrick who saved my son from a life as an androgy, I agree with Langdon. Carrick should be given the chance to prove he has the right to rule Seracedar. Perhaps with him on the throne, the relationship between our kingdoms will be restored. You will locate Carrick and bring the scepter directly to him."

"Yes, Your Majesty." Welder absentmindedly played with the sachet around his neck. "But what if Carrick proves to not receive the Will of Heaven? Or what if he does, and Nelan won't give up the throne?"

"Hand Carrick the scepter and do nothing else," Ashbel said. "Only Old Grandfather Heaven has the power to be the judge of their kingdom's rightful ruler. We can only act as messengers."

Only the messengers. I didn't like the sound of that, yet the king had a point. We could try to help Carrick all we wanted, but if Old Grandfather Heaven did not give him the Will of Heaven, there was nothing else we could do. All of this would be for naught.

"Do you think Carrick will allow me to leave with the scepter again if he does not get tin-chai amplification?" Welder frowned. "He may try to keep it and feign the right to rule as Nelan has been doing."

Daki furled his brow. "Prince Taimin always told me Carrick was the only one of his brothers he respected. Would Carrick really do such a horrific thing?"

"Of course not," I said. But an unsettling feeling gnawed in my abdomen. I couldn't be sure Carrick wouldn't lie. After all, I had borne witness to his dark, manipulative side. Even he had admitted to being more like his father than he wanted to be.

Aiden's fists curled. "Carrick is a man of honor. If the scepter does not choose him, I believe he will give it up and leave Seracedar forever. But Ah-fu, you must help him if he receives resistance from Nelan or any other challenger."

Ashbel rubbed at his chin. "It still remains to be seen if Carrick's tin-chai is amplified. If he does indeed receive Old Grandfather's blessing, we can discuss whether it's in Emberwood's interests to ally ourselves with him."

Aiden's glower indicated he was not pleased with this answer, yet he remained silent. Once again, I took note of his loyalty to Carrick and hoped it wasn't misplaced.

"That closes the matter of the scepter," Ashbel said. "You will leave after the festivities."

"Festivities?" Welder raised an eyebrow.

"Emberwood is celebrating the return of our prince," Ashbel said. "We're having a banquet in my son's honor."

"Ah-fu, I already told you it isn't necessary," Aiden said.

"Nonsense. There are many important noblemen who will want to see you."

"But—"

"Don't argue with your father," Leonora said. "Here, have some more food."

Aiden pouted, but he stuffed his mouth full of rice cakes. "The only person I want to see is my cousin, Sito. Will he be here?"

The king's expression softened to something that looked like pity. "I've asked him to return, but he told me that he's too embarrassed to face you. He said he'll be back during the winter respite, and he hopes you'll forgive him for his godfather's actions by then."

"Nonsense. There's nothing to forgive," Aiden said. "It's not his fault Mr. Rino tried to kill me. I had hoped to see my cousin before I return to Seracedar."

Both the king and queen's faces darkened.

"Return to Seracedar?" Leonora said quietly. "What do you mean?"

"I'll be going with Welder, of course," Aiden said. "To witness Carrick's ascension to the throne and help him fight Nelan if it comes to that."

"No, absolutely not." Ashbel shook his head and glowered, his hands tightening into fists. His speech was clipped. "After all these years, you have finally come home. I will not allow you to go back into danger. Into the enemy's den."

"Carrick isn't our enemy, and I can't abandon him," Aiden said. "I promised to help him in any way I could. I've been his friend for over a decade and his bodyguard for most of those years."

"You may once have been Carrick's bodyguard but no longer." Ashbel's voice rose. He banged a fist on the table and rose from his chair. "First and foremost, you are and have always been the crown prince of Emberwood. You have finally come home and been restored to your station. After twelve long years of believing my son was dead, I forbid you to be so cavalier with your own life. I have already agreed to return the scepter to Carrick, but it is not our family's business whether or not he succeeds in ascending the throne."

I felt rather awkward witnessing this family argument and kept my gaze down. Daki, too, stared at his breakfast plate as though he had suddenly taken great interest in the scraps he hadn't cared to eat.

Welder cleared his throat and tugged at his sachet. He addressed Aiden. "Your Highness, you can trust me. I will get the scepter safely into Carrick's hands. There is no need for you to come with me. Since you believe in his character so strongly, you should have no doubts that he will achieve tin-chai amplification and the Will of Heaven. When this happens, he will naturally gain more supporters, enough to take Nelan on his own, with or without Emberwood's aid."

"Yes, that's right," Leonora said quickly. Her nervous gaze darted between her husband and son. "Mr. Welder has never failed a mission. Langdon, you only just came back to your mother. Please don't make me suffer again wondering if you'll return safely."

Guilt flickered on Aiden's face. "If Ah-fu and Ah-mu wish for me to stay, then I will obey," he said softly, though displeasure lingered in his eyes.

"Rilla and Daki," Leonora said. "You have the freedom to choose whether you wish to accompany Welder back to Seracedar, but you are also welcome to stay here at Linlang Palace for as long as you'd like. I do love having guests, especially ones as charming as you both."

If Aiden wasn't returning, then I didn't know if I wanted to leave him. But if I didn't go back, I wouldn't be able to see Radi. Not to say that I'd never return. It just wouldn't be as soon as I'd like.

Maybe it was best if I stayed here and let Welder take care of the scepter. But did allowing Welder to take over mean we had forfeited the mission? I'd always thought if Aiden and I succeeded in finding the scepter, we would personally witness Carrick's ascension and celebrate together.

"I'm going with you, Welder," Daki said. "I'm determined to see that order and peace be reestablished to Seracedar since I've always considered it to be my homeland."

With his answer, everyone regarded me, expectant to hear mine. I caught Aiden's gaze. He lifted an eyebrow in question.

"I—I'm not sure what I'll do yet," I said. "I'll have to think about it."

"Then it's settled," Ashbel said, standing from the table. "Langdon and Leonora, we have much to prepare for the banquet. Welder and Daki, you are free to do what you must for your journey. And Rilla, you have permission to visit any part of the palace you wish. The servants will provide anything you need. You have only to ask."

Aiden gave me another look. "I'll talk to you later."

We bowed as the king, queen, and Aiden took their leave.

# CHAPTER 27

✦ ✦ ✦ ✦ ✦ ✦ ✦ ✦ ✦ ✦

Welder and Daki left to make the appropriate arrangements for their departure that evening. I went down to the Gold Song Courtyard, where Attendant Bin said there was a music room. I thought I could play some music while contemplating whether I should return to Seracedar.

I didn't want to leave Aiden, not when there were unresolved issues between us. But I also wanted to see Carrick and watch him take the scepter. And I needed to tell him that although I'd always treasure our friendship and time together at the palace, I couldn't stay with him.

I passed through a free-standing stone pagoda, where a group of students a little younger than me were practicing calligraphy. The path glinted gold. On either side was a layer of gravel, with the Shyan character for "song" perfectly printed in lined patterns.

I continued down the pebbled path and stopped in front of a two-tiered pavilion. The doors were wide open, and sunlight streamed inside, catching on several displayed instruments. The music room.

A variety of instruments filled the room. Several zithers and lutes were in front on display. There were shelves of music books and sheet music. I picked a sheet of music up and placed it on a music stand.

I remembered the flute I'd found on Hara's island. Welder's flute. It was still in the pocket of my cloak. I had forgotten to mention it to Welder. I wondered if he wanted it back. It would be nice if I could keep it.

I took it out of my pocket and lifted the mouthpiece to my lips. Then I played, sight-reading the music in front of me. I hadn't sung in so long. Playing an instrument was soothing, and hearing the tinkling notes relaxed my heavy muscles. Music was like a familiar old friend I hadn't seen in ages, but once we gathered in each other's company, it was as if she'd never left.

I recognized the tune. It was a folk song Mama had hummed when she was in the kitchen, and sometimes she'd played it on her zither. But the lyrics written on the page were different than what Mama had sung. I hadn't realized Emberwood shared similar folk songs to us, but I shouldn't have been surprised. Our histories had been enmeshed once upon a time, dynasties ago.

A knock sounded on the door. I stopped playing as Aiden entered the room.

"I thought you were with your parents," I said.

"They'll join us in a few minutes, but I wanted to speak with you first. We need to talk about what happened that night at the teahouse, or things may get awkward soon. I don't want to leave anything unresolved between us."

"Yes, I've wanted to talk to you, too."

I put the flute back in my cloak. "Where did we leave off?" I tapped my chin, pretending to contemplate this. "That's right, you were running away from me because you didn't want to face your true feelings."

"I wasn't running away," he said, and he came across the room to me. "I needed time to think. I do want to be with you. It's what I've always wanted. But I promised Carrick I wouldn't get too close to you because he always feared I would take you away. Back at the palace, no matter how much I liked you, I couldn't act on my feelings. Now I realize I don't have the strength to keep that promise."

My heart skipped a beat to hear his confession. But I maintained my composure.

"We're not at the palace any longer," I said. "No one has the right to control us or decide who we end up having feelings for. I believe, as you do, that Carrick is an honorable man. If he regards both of us as his true friends, then although he may be hurt at first, he'll love us enough to accept this."

"Yes, you're right. I know you are." He averted his gaze. "Yet, he is my friend and savior, and I can't help but feel like I'm betraying him. If I can make sure he ends up on the throne, perhaps I'll feel less guilty about taking away his woman."

"Let's make one thing clear." I stepped closer until we were only a hair's breadth apart. I placed my hand on his shoulder, and I felt his warm breath on my cheek. "I was never his woman. I belong to nobody, though I choose to be with you, and I want you to choose me, too. Choose me over your obligations to Carrick. If that makes me selfish, so be it."

He gazed at me with such fierce eyes that it took my breath away. "I love you. I do choose to be with you." He pulled me into him and embraced me tightly. "I'll make this right with Carrick. Once I clarify things with him, we can be together. I promise."

"How will we tell him?" I asked. "You're not allowed to return to Seracedar, and I'm not leaving without you." I pulled away from his embrace but still interlaced my fingers with his.

Aiden kissed the back of my hand. "I will find a way to explain everything to him. I won't—"

"Oh!" A woman's excited voice squealed. "I knew I was right."

Aiden and I released hands and stepped apart. Queen Leonora

stood at the entrance of the room. Her face lit up with a bright beaming smile that could make the moons jealous.

"Ah-mu." Aiden's cheeks turned red. I knew my own face reflected the same shade of crimson. "What are you doing here?"

"I was told Rilla would be in the music pavilion," she said. "I didn't expect my son to be here as well. But you don't need to hide it from me anymore. I told your ah-fu I was sure as the sun the two of you are together. Now I have proof. Why didn't you tell us?"

"We only confirmed our feelings for one another moments ago, Your Majesty," I said. "I didn't mean to keep anything from you, and I assure you I have no ill intentions toward your son."

"I'm not angry," she said. "I'm overjoyed. Though if you wanted a moment of privacy, you should have closed the sliding door." She gestured to the door. Two giggling maid servants, who I hadn't noticed until now, stood at the entrance, listening to us. They whispered to one another. "Quiet, girls. I trust you to keep your discretion. The prince is not yet ready to announce his betrothal."

My cheeks grew more heated. "Betrothal? Your Majesty, we're not—"

"As I said, you are not *yet* ready," Leonora said. "But I will be patient. Come now, I must take you to prepare for tonight's banquet." She took my arm and pulled me toward the door.

"Wait," Aiden said. "I have more to say to her."

"Not now," his mother told him. "You should be preparing for the banquet as well."

She whisked me away. The serving maids followed us down the corridor and back to my room.

Twenty minutes later, I stood still with my arms out as the maids took my measurements.

Leonora regarded me in the mirror and smiled. She touched a curl of my hair. "You have such beautiful locks," she said. "The dream client of a hairstylist. You should know, styling hair is my tin-chai. It was my profession before I met Ashbel and he convinced me to marry him. Even so, I still often style some of the ladies' hair on occasion."

I dropped my jaw, astonished. "I didn't think a queen would be allowed to take on such a task."

"It makes me happy," she said. "Ashbel has never forbidden it. And no one would ever suggest it's beneath me. In Emberwood, no job is disrespected. No tin-chai is looked down upon. And no koong is considered beneath those with tin-chai. No matter who we are, we all have important roles to help our society exist."

"Her Majesty has even styled our hair before," one of the maids said. "I felt like a goddess." She and the other maid bowed. "We've finished with the measurements. We shall return with Miss Rilla's new outfit in no more than two hours."

Leonora nodded. "Thank you, Kita and Ti. I can't wait to see what you come up with."

They made their exit.

"A *new* outfit in two hours?" I said. "I thought I was getting something already made. How can they finish so quickly?"

"Kita's tin-chai allows her to sew quicker than anyone in the kingdom," Leonora said. "And Ti is a designer. She can assemble several outfits that fit a person's character and body type with one look. She never gets her client wrong. They always design my gowns, and I love their passion for what they do."

She smoothed out my hair. "I heard that you have a passion as well. Langdon says you wish to be a healer. He has described to me your tin-chai. Old Grandfather Heaven has blessed you with such a lovely gift."

"If only I could use it properly again." I sighed. "The way it was meant to be used. Now I can't sing for fear I'll kill someone by accident."

"Langdon never mentioned that." She smoothed her hand against my hair. "Dear child, I'm sorry to hear it." She paused as though trying to decide what to say. "I cannot tell you that your tin-chai will return to what it once was, but if your dream is to be a healer, then there's nothing stopping you from achieving that. At the very least, while you're here in Emberwood, you have my full support as well as the king's."

"Thank you, Your Majesty," I said. "That's very kind."

Leonora's warmth touched my heart. Her smile reminded me of Aiden, and there was an easiness about her that comforted me. She smoothed over the locks of my hair, and I remembered my mama doing the same soothing gesture when I was a little girl.

"You must allow me to do your hair," she said. "Langdon mentioned your ah-mu passed away when you were quite young. I always imagined doing my daughter's hair, but I wasn't fortunate to have been blessed with one. I'd be truly honored if you would allow me to style yours for tonight."

I could see this meant a lot to her. I did understand how someone could long to use her tin-chai to bring joy to others. I would do anything to be able to use my tin-chai that way again. "Thank you. I would love that. And the honor is all mine."

# CHAPTER 28

✦ ✦ ✦ ✦ ✦ ✦ ✦ ✦ ✦ ✦

I had come from my room to the entrance of the courtyard at precisely seven in the evening, as Queen Leonora had instructed when she left me to get ready herself. Sun Fire Courtyard was radiant. The floating lanterns were all lit up, illuminating the courtyard with firelight. Banners of words written in ink hung on the tree trunks. *Peace, longevity, joy*. Large, round wooden tables filled the courtyard. The tables were covered in pink embroidered cloth, and bouquets of red peonies acted as the centerpieces.

The guests were beginning to trickle in. The few who were already here conversed under the trees instead of sitting at the tables. The men wore colorful coats that buttoned down the front rather than the traditional robes most aristocrats in Seracedar wore. The rest of the men's outfits consisted of slacks that were comfortably fitted, not too loose or too tight, tied at the waist and the ankles.

The ladies wore beautiful kipa, all bright colors of pink, blue, and red. Emberwood kipa were a little different than those in Seracedar. Whereas the kipa in Seracedar were tight-fitting with a closed collar that fastened at the neck, these kipa had lower necklines and a hemline extending to the ground. Some even had longer trains that trailed after them. The fit was snug at the bosom and waistline but flared at the skirt. And each kipa was unique in design or pattern. There was a sequined kipa, one designed after a peacock's feathers, and another like a spotted maocat.

The women wore their hair in braided chignons, a style Leonora said was the most recent trend. She'd done my hair in a similar fashion, and I wore a silver Emberwood kipa that changed to blue depending on the lighting. The kipa had a short train, but the front of it was cut right above my ankles, and the lightweight material conformed to my movements. I had to admit, I liked this kipa far better than anything I'd worn during the showcase at Cedar Palace. Leonora had also covered the four-brand mark on my face with a painted flower. Even though the Embers weren't superstitious, it was still unsightly to me, and people might stare.

I didn't know any of the aristocrats here, and I didn't want to chat with strangers without being introduced, so I checked the guestlist for where I was to be seated. Table one. Aiden was supposed to be seated next to me. I was at the royal table.

I located my table, but Aiden wasn't there or in the courtyard yet. Near table one, someone was crawling on his hands and knees, seemingly searching for something on the ground.

"Welder?" I asked. "Did you lose something?"

Welder jerked up, nearly bumping his head on the edge of the table. He stood and bowed in greeting. "Oh, it's nothing important. Something fell out of my pocket."

"Do you need help looking for it?"

"No, you should go ahead and talk to other people," he said quickly. "Besides, you'd ruin your outfit. I can search on my own."

His gaze drifted behind my shoulder, and a flicker of annoyance entered his features before he masked it. "Great, we've got company."

Daki and a woman joined us. The lady stared at me like I was a rare specimen she wished to examine.

"Ah, Rilla," Daki said. "Lady Tu wanted an introduction. I hope you don't mind." He fidgeted, looking awkward.

"Oh, I'm sure she doesn't mind," the lady said. "I am pleased to meet you, Rilla."

"Lady Tu is one of the news reporters of the *Emberwood Daily*," Daki said. "She's also the wife of Lord Tu, a close friend of the king's."

I bowed. "It's a pleasure to meet you, Lady Tu."

"Indeed," she said with a smile. "So, you are the mystery girl everyone is talking about. The crown prince's betrothed."

"What?" It was impossible not to gawk. "I'm sorry, Lady Tu. But where did you get that idea? It's not true."

"Oh, but it must be. The maids are all gossiping about it, and they heard it from the girl who designed that kipa you're wearing. Which is beautiful by the way."

"Thank you," I said. "But I must clarify. I'm not engaged to—"

"There is no use trying to deny it," Lady Tu said. "Everyone knows already. You will be the talk of the banquet tonight."

I looked around and realized many stares were directed at me. But as I caught people looking, they averted their gazes quickly.

"Oh, there is Headmaster Vin," Lady Tu said. "I must go say hello. We shall talk again later, Miss Rilla. It was a pleasure." She scuttled away.

"This is terrible," I said to Welder and Daki. "What am I going to do?"

"Is it true?" Daki asked. "I mean, it's obvious you and Aiden love each other, but are you betrothed?"

"No." My cheeks heated. "I—I mean, he hasn't asked. And we just realized our feelings. No one goes from liking someone to proposing marriage overnight, right?"

"Well, at this rate, the news will be all over the kingdom by morning," Daki said. "And perhaps even travel to Seracedar. Though you never explicitly told me, I can guess Carrick's interest in you based on the snippets of conversation I've overheard between you and Aiden. I hope you have the chance to tell Carrick about you and Aiden before he finds out on his own."

Welder played with the chain around his neck. "I'm happy for both of you, but I do have a piece of unsolicited advice, if I may. I would suggest you and Aiden never return to Seracedar. Carrick may not forgive you and prevent you from leaving him."

"He's not that kind of person," I said, though a flicker of doubt crossed my mind. Every time I tried to defend Carrick, I couldn't help thinking of the night he'd told me in anger that he owned Aiden and he intended on making me his mistress. Though he'd retracted it later, a part of me knew he wouldn't have said it unless at least a piece of him believed it.

"I hope you're right." Welder tucked the chain under his shirt. I realized the sachet was no longer attached to it.

"Did you lose your sachet?" I asked and scanned the ground.

"It's not important anyway," Welder said. "I've got more important things to think about. We're leaving after the banquet."

"Why did you choose to leave at night?" I asked. "Why not leave tomorrow morning and enjoy the banquet?"

"There will be fewer coaches on the merchants' trail at night," Welder said. "It's a faster and more direct route by land, straight through Emberwood, unlike the way we came. It's not necessary to go by sea and through Yao Kingdom when we're no longer fugitives but going into Seracedar as Ember citizens. Daki has constructed a steam coach that can be converted into a palanquin once we reach Seracedar. It also travels at twice the speed of any existing steam coach, so we'll arrive at the Seracedar border by morning."

"You still need to be careful of Nelan's men once you enter Seracedar," I said. "And how will you find Carrick?"

"I have my ways," Welder said. "There's a reason I'm the best security escort in Emberwood and have never once failed a mission. Trust me. Besides, you'd be surprised how much information people will tell you when you're dressed like someone with authority."

I hugged my arms to my chest. Even though I'd decided to stay here with Aiden, part of me wished I could go with them. Make sure the mission was a success. Find Radi. "Could you do a favor for me? Look in on my friend, Radi. Carrick has been protecting her in his safe house, but I just want to know how she's doing. She went through so much."

"Of course," Welder said, but his gaze darted behind my shoulder, distracted. "Looks like the royal family is about to be introduced."

A trumpet blared. "All bow to King Ashbel, Queen Leonora, and Crown Prince Langdon."

Unlike in Seracedar, we didn't have to fall to our knees and kowtow. Instead, we bowed at the waist and lowered our heads respectfully.

"Everyone, at ease," Ashbel's voice carried around the courtyard.

All courtiers straightened their posture and remained silent, waiting for the king to speak.

"Tonight, we have many reasons to celebrate," Ashbel said. "My only son has been returned after a decade of obscurity. We thought him dead, but Old Grandfather Heaven kept him safe. Though he remained in enemy territory, he dared not reveal his true identity for fear all our attempts at maintaining peace would be for nothing. I weep for what he must have gone through, but the old emperor is gone now, and retaliation is useless. Instead, I call for unity in moving forward, focusing on building our kingdom and keeping peace. Let our enemy remain in darkness. Emberwood shall only burn brighter. Now let us feast."

Cheers erupted from the guests.

We went to our assigned table. Welder and Daki sat across from me. Aiden's seat next to me was still empty. So were Leonora's and Ashbel's chairs. It felt lonely without Aiden here despite being surrounded by so many people. I was accustomed to having him by my side.

The first course came out, a soup with seafood, vegetables, and flavorings of scallions and bean curd paste.

I looked for Aiden and saw him across the courtyard. He was busy talking to guests. Leonora and Ashbel were surrounded as well. It seemed everyone wanted to congratulate them.

We finished the soup and started on the second course, fried yaduck in fluffy pancakes. Aiden was still making his rounds at all the tables with his parents.

The third course came out. A variety of dishes decorated the table. Fish cakes stir-fried with tender stalks of greens. A clay pot with rice, meat, and mushrooms topped with a deep caramelized savory sauce. Crispy noodles slathered in fresh seafood.

Finally, Aiden took his seat next to me. Ashbel and Leonora also took their seats across from us.

Aiden unfolded his napkin and placed it on his lap. "That was tough—watching everyone eat and not being able to stuff my own face. You should know, they were most curious about you."

"Were they?" I frowned.

"I was trying to answer as best I could so they wouldn't bother you," he said. "But some of them might come up to you. Be prepared."

The servers brought individual meal plates, fresh and hot, to the royal family. These plates had a bit of all the courses we'd been served. Aiden picked up his chopsticks and dug in enthusiastically.

He took a few bites then stopped. His gaze darted behind my shoulder, and he groaned. "Someone else is coming to talk to us."

Aiden stood, and I followed his lead. A tall man with a thick beard approached us. I bowed my head in greeting.

The tall man bowed in return. "Prince Langdon, while I have already expressed outrage for all you've suffered at the hands of my colleague, Rino, I am overjoyed for your return." He regarded me and grinned. "And I must say, you certainly found a beautiful companion on your way back to us."

Aiden swallowed what he was chewing and put on a brilliant smile. "Headmaster Vin. May I introduce my friend, Rilla Marseas. Rilla, this is the headmaster of Ember University."

"Please allow me to offer a toast to both of you, not only for your harrowing escape from Cedar Palace, but for your upcoming nuptials." He poured wine into three cups for Aiden, me, and himself.

Did everyone think we were engaged?

"Thank you, Headmaster," Aiden said. He raised his cup, and downed the contents, then poured another shot for himself and the Headmaster. "And now I must toast you for all the good work you do." He picked up the cup again, but the wine sloshed out, spilling all over the front of his attire.

"Oh, no," I said, rushing to find a napkin. Though the wine was clear and wouldn't leave a stain, it did have a sticky residue.

"How clumsy of me," Aiden said. "Sorry, Headmaster, but you must excuse me. I should go change quickly. There are still many more toasts to come tonight."

"Then I'll speak to you later." The Headmaster nodded and took his leave.

"Rilla, I'm sorry," Aiden said.

"About everyone thinking we're engaged?" I said. "It's fine, but I'm not sure how to correct them."

"I promise I'll correct them when I return."

"Hurry and go change before you become a sticky mess," I said.

"I'll figure out how to endure any other awkward conversations until you get back."

His gaze lingered on me. "I'm so sorry."

"Stop apologizing and go," I said. What was he waiting for?

I watched him walk away, wondering why he looked like he was about to go to war rather than simply change his clothes. I turned and saw Daki and Welder speaking to the king and queen.

"Are you leaving already?" I asked. "The banquet isn't over."

"Change of plans." Welder glanced down at his watch. The lines around his eyes crinkled with impatience. "I want to take off a few hours early so my men might get some rest once we reach the border."

Daki shook my hand. "Wish us luck. I may not see you for awhile. I've decided, no matter what happens, I will stay and help the kingdom become strong again." He bowed. "It was an honor traveling with you, and I hope we meet again soon."

I hugged him back. "I hope so, too. Good luck to you, my friend."

The king cleared his throat. "Where is Langdon? Welder and Daki are leaving, and he must say goodbye."

"He spilled wine on his robe," I said. "He'll be right back."

"I'm afraid we can't wait," Welder said. "Give our regards to the prince."

He and Daki bowed and made their exit.

I sat and gazed at the entrance for any sign of Aiden. He was taking longer than expected.

The servants cleared the savory dishes away. We enjoyed a dessert course next. Sweetened round rice cakes with an almond paste filling. I ate it slowly and kept looking at the entrance. *Aiden should be back by now. He would never purposely miss dessert.* What if something was wrong?

No, what could go wrong in Linlang Palace? I'd never seen a

kingdom with such tight security. Unless . . . Haming had managed to break in.

Ashbel and Leonora were whispering to one another.

Leonora touched my arm. "Are you sure Langdon only went to change his clothes?"

I nodded. "I don't know what's taking him so long. I hope he's okay."

Leonora wrinkled the napkin in her lap. "What if something has happened?"

"I'll go look for him." I rose.

Ashbel gestured for me to sit back down. "Nonsense, you're the guest of honor. I'm sure there's no reason to worry. He probably got caught up in a conversation with someone. You know how much he loves to talk. I'll send someone to find him."

He jostled the table as he circled around to look for Attendant Bin, and his chopsticks fell to the ground. I reached under the table to pick them up. Not far from where the chopsticks had landed, something glinted next to the leg of Welder's empty seat. I crawled forward a bit and grabbed it.

Welder's protective sachet, but the silk knot and tassel had disappeared and half of the sachet itself had turned to gold, forming part of an earring with the stud in back. A gold earring. I recognized the part of the design that had been revealed. A bird with a sword in its mouth. This was Dahlia Nin's earring.

# CHAPTER 29

✦ ✦ ✦ ✦ ✦ ✦ ✦ ✦ ✦ ✦

My heart thudded in my throat as I stared at the earring. The truth hit me fast and hard like a tidal wave.

Androgy Haming had been here. Androgy Haming had been pretending to be Welder.

The sachet-turned-earring, must have been what he'd lost earlier, what he'd been searching for. He knew if someone found it, his identity would be revealed. No wonder he'd been in such a rush to leave.

Slowly, the sachet completely changed back into the earring, and I saw a tiny diamond in the center of the piece. It was stained with blood. This must be a Yao diamond, and Haming had used it for blood magic. Welder's blood. Haming had used Welder's tin-chai to make this earring appear as a sachet. Then he'd tricked all of us, changing the dagger into the scepter. But why? Did he have the scepter? Was the real Welder still alive?

I got up from the ground to show Ashbel the earring, but the king was talking to Attendant Bin. Judging from their serious expressions, they already knew something was wrong.

"Has something happened to Langdon?" Leonora asked.

"It isn't Langdon," Ashbel said. "The guards claim Commander

Welder is at the front of the palace, and he's badly wounded."

"But he just left," Leonora said. "Is Daki with him?"

"I think the wounded man must be the real Welder," I said, showing the king and queen the earring. "I found this on the ground. It belonged to Androgy Haming's other form, Dahlia Nin. He was pretending to be Welder. He used blood magic to borrow Welder's tinchai so we wouldn't suspect."

"I'll go assess the situation and make sure this Welder is not an imposter," King Ashbel said. "If I don't return before the guests start leaving, tell them I was feeling overtired."

Leonora trembled but maintained a calm expression and nodded. "And what about Langdon?"

"I'll go check on him," I said.

"Thank you, Rilla," Ashbel said. "I'll send Attendant Bin with you in case there's an issue."

I followed Attendant Bin to Aiden's room. The door was locked from the inside.

"Aiden, are you in there?" I called. I placed my ear to the door and heard a muffled sound.

"Get the guards," I told Attendant Bin. "Someone's in there."

In another minute, Attendant Bin came back with two guards. They kicked in the door. A man was tied up on the floor. He wore Aiden's garments, but it wasn't Aiden.

"This is Security Escort Hu, one of Welder's men," Attendant Bin said. He unmuzzled and untied him. "Where is the prince?"

"Prince Langdon knocked me unconscious," Hu said. "Next thing I knew, I woke up here, wearing the prince's clothes. I think he stole mine."

"He must have snuck onto Welder's team," I said. I should have known. "He's determined to return to Seracedar and help Carrick."

And he'd left me behind. A silent rage filled my chest. How could he? We were supposed to be partners.

"Go alert the king," Attendant Bin said.

Hu bowed and took off. The other guards searched the rest of the room.

"I've found something," one of them said. "A letter addressed to Miss Rilla and the king and queen."

I took it from him and read.

*Ah-fu, Ah-mu, and Rilla,*

*I'm sorry, but I had to go. Delivering the scepter to Carrick is my final mission for him, and with this success, I consider my debt to him paid in full. I will tell him that I intend on marrying Rilla and will ask for his blessing. But if there is a chance he does not give it, I could not risk taking you, Rilla. As emperor, he'd have the authority of forcing you to stay in Seracedar, and I know he can have a temper sometimes. I hope that I might appease him, but as I am restored as the crown prince of Emberwood, politics will prevent him from detaining me against my will. This is the best I can do for all sides, as my loyalties are split at the moment. I hope you understand.*

*Respectfully,*

*Langdon/Aiden*

My hands shook as I handed it to Attendant Bin, and he read it aloud. King Ashbel stepped into the room.

"Your Majesty," Attendant Bin said. "The prince disguised himself as a man on Welder's team. Does that have something to do with Welder's return?"

Ashbel wore a grim look. "No. Rilla was right. Androgy Haming was pretending to be Commander Welder. The real Welder has returned. He says Haming ambushed him just shortly after your arrival at the palace. He has been locked up since then, but he managed to escape hours ago. Haming is now in charge of leading our team to Seracedar, and they have no idea."

"Can we still stop them?" I asked.

"Unfortunately, no," Ashbel said. "They are long gone. Even if this Androgy Haming knows Langdon disguised himself, he won't interfere as long as Langdon doesn't know he's pretending to be Welder. I don't know what his intentions are, but he's in a hurry to get to Seracedar. The good thing is Welder has confirmed he never gave the real scepter to Haming."

"I don't understand Haming's motive," I said. "If he used Welder's tin-chai to transform a regular dagger into a scepter, then why is he taking that fake scepter back to Seracedar?"

A cough sounded behind me. "I may be able to answer your question." Welder, the real one I could only assume, hobbled in. His lip was cut, and a black bruise surrounded his eye.

"What are you doing here?" Ashbel said. "You should be resting, and a doctor should be tending to you. Guards, summon Doctor Ji. The doctor's herbal remedies will heal you within hours, guaranteed."

A doctor with a similar tin-chai to mine—or at least what mine used to be.

"I'll see the doctor later," Welder said. "Don't worry. I've had far worse. Besides, this mess happened on my watch, and I'm determined to fix it. I hope you don't mind if I sit."

Without waiting for an answer, he slumped onto the side of the futon with a wince. "Thank Old Grandfather Heaven for his protection over me."

"Why don't you start from the beginning?" Ashbel suggested. "Fill Rilla in on the details, so we can figure out what Haming is up to."

"First of all, I don't have the scepter," Welder told me. "I lost it two years ago on my escape to Emberwood. I was going to tell you when we arrived at Linlang Palace that first day. But Haming ambushed me when we were seated at the pavilion in Water Crystal Courtyard, waiting to speak with the king and queen. All of you had gone to the washroom. Remember?"

"That early? How did he get into the palace?"

"He disguised himself as Attendant Bin, and he had a maid with him, who I assume was one of his Lotuses. Caught me by surprise and knocked me unconscious. Then I woke somewhere that smelled like horse stables. When I escaped, I realized I was on palace grounds all along."

Ashbel nodded. "The old stables were abandoned after the new palace was built, and steam coaches became the main mode of transportation in Emberwood. Nobody goes out there for fear of it being haunted."

"Several Lotuses guarded me there," Welder said. "They locked all my pressure points so I couldn't move. Then Androgy Haming came and insisted I tell him where I had hidden the Sacred Cedar Scepter. I told him to go drown in horse shit. He didn't take that well at all."

Welder sneered and touched his swollen face, chuckling as though his torture had consisted of tickles and kisses. "I knew he wouldn't kill me, not until he got me to confess the location of the scepter. Ha." He spat, a look of disdain crossing his face. "Even if I knew, none of us can control fate or become someone we're not meant to be. He's a fool as I once was. I stole the scepter because I believed I could find a way to make the scepter grant me tin-chai amplification. But Old Grandfather Heaven removes the scepter from anyone who doesn't deserve it, and only the one he deems worthy will find it again."

"How did you get away from the Lotuses who guarded you?" I asked.

"I recovered my wyis, and with that, I was able to unlock my own pressure points. I killed two sisters. The other three fled, probably to tell Haming I'd gotten away. They had blood magic, used Haming's blood to disguise themselves. I wouldn't be surprised if they pretended to be guests at your banquet, but by now, they're long gone. Probably following the coach where Haming has my men, Daki, and Prince Langdon."

Ashbel's face turned gray, and his eyes flashed with fury. "But why? What does he intend to do with a fake scepter?"

Then the realization jolted me like I'd touched a too-hot surface. "I think he means to discredit Carrick. When Carrick touches the fake scepter, his tin-chai won't be amplified."

Welder nodded. "Exactly. All his followers and soldiers will desert him. Then Haming will do the same to Nelan, who is a stupid boy and will easily fall for the bait. Once the last of Terran's line fails, Haming will find a way to snatch up the princes' supporters if he can trick them into believing he has attained the Will of Heaven."

"Do you have any idea where you lost the scepter?" I asked. "If we can't get it to Carrick, then all hope will be lost."

"Unfortunately, the scepter dropped out of my cloak pocket when I was fleeing from a Miyu on one of the Unclaimed Islands in the Enyi Ocean. I used a contraption Daki had given me to fly away, and the scepter plummeted down. I couldn't go back for it."

I took a sharp breath and touched the flute in my cloak. Could it be?

Ashbel interrupted, his voice rising before I could ask the question. "I don't care about the scepter or Terran's sons. My only concern is for that foolish son of mine. His life is in danger, and knowing his loyalty to Carrick, he will not leave his friend, even if the prince is discredited and war breaks out."

"Not to worry, Your Majesty," Welder said. "I will go after them."

I took out the flute and raised it. Welder's eyes widened. "Where did you get that?"

"On one of the Unclaimed Islands in the Enyi Ocean, where a Miyu named Hara lived," I said. "She had it among her possessions."

He brushed his hand over it, not touching nor trying to take it from me. The flute elongated, growing into the scepter. But unlike all the fakes, it had a polished shine to it. This scepter felt sturdy and impenetrable, and it was heavy. I could barely hold it in my right hand and had to use my other hand to grab it. The moment I did, it became lighter as though it were adjusting its weight to accommodate me. How strange.

"I cannot believe you found it," Welder said.

King Ashbel stared at me like I'd grown horns. "I never believed in Old Grandfather Heaven or His Will, but perhaps I should adjust my thinking. Did your tin-chai—" He waved his hand in the air. "Do you feel any different?"

"What? No, surely you don't expect that I'm destined to rule Seracedar." I laughed. "If I were, then my tin-chai wouldn't have failed me after I found the scepter."

"Still," Welder said. "Old Grandfather Heaven led you to that island in the middle of the ocean. He had you find where the Miyu stashed it."

"Then perhaps Old Grandfather Heaven is showing mercy," I said. "With this, Carrick still has a chance to prove he has the Will of Heaven."

"Welder, are you sure you are up to this mission?" Ashbel asked. "I trust you more than any other, but you are still wounded. Perhaps I should ask General Gin to lead this time. He is a trustworthy man and can be let in on what's going on."

Welder shook his head emphatically. "I am well enough, and once Doctor Ji tends to me, I'll be mostly healed. I won't let anyone else take this mission away from me. It was my fault for getting caught by Haming. I will make this right. I will see to it that Prince Langdon and my men return home safely, and then I shall hang Haming's head on a stake."

"I will send a few of my best soldiers with you," Ashbel said.

"Not necessary. I only need my one man who was left behind, Hu. As well as one other person." His gaze fell on me. "Miss Rilla."

Ashbel frowned. "Langdon stated in his letter that he wants Rilla to stay here for her safety. And as Rilla is my future daughter-in-law, I am inclined to agree. Unless you have a legitimate reason."

"I do," Welder said. "Old Grandfather Heaven allowed me to lose the scepter only to lead Rilla to find it. If I take it from her, there is a chance it may be taken away again. Perhaps Old Grandfather Heaven has charged Rilla with the scepter for safekeeping until the true ruler is established on the Seracedarean throne. We cannot go against Old Grandfather Heaven's will."

Ashbel hesitated. "You don't know for sure that this is Old Grandfather Heaven's will."

"I want to go," I said. "I think Welder may be right. On that island, I heard a song. I didn't know where it was coming from. But maybe it was the scepter calling to me. Maybe it wanted me to find it. If it's my responsibility to carry the scepter until Carrick is given the Will of Heaven, then I can't ignore my calling."

"Are you sure?" Ashbel asked. "You are under my protection here. But once you return to Seracedar, I no longer have any power to defend you or your right to freedom. Even if I were to make you a citizen of Emberwood, the palace may not recognize it. Not only are you a fugitive wanted for Terran's murder, but Carrick may wish to keep you. I've heard from Langdon that Carrick considers you his property. While Langdon remains optimistic that Carrick wouldn't keep you against your will, no one really knows a person's true character until they are put to the test."

The king was right. Once Carrick became emperor, he'd have the power to stop me from leaving. Now that Emberwood knew their prince was alive and had been stuck in Seracedar for over ten years,

Carrick couldn't keep Aiden there without causing conflict. But I didn't have the same privilege. I was still a Seracedarean citizen.

"You don't need to worry, Your Majesty," Welder said. "I will make sure Rilla returns to Emberwood safe and sound. Unless, of course, she wishes to stay in Seracedar."

"No," I said. "Seracedar is in my past. Aiden is my future now. But this scepter is our last obligation to help Carrick. If our assessment of Carrick's character is wrong, then I believe he will not receive the right to rule in the first place. We'll know when he touches the scepter."

"And if he is not the honest man you and Aiden think he is," Welder said, "then you can trust I have a plan to ensure he cannot keep you."

"What is this plan?" I asked. "I don't like surprises."

"I'm afraid I cannot reveal it unless we must go through with it," he said. "Just know I never fail my missions; although, on occasion, I have one go unexpectedly. But I will always end up making it right."

"One more question," I said. "What if Haming tries to harm Aiden, Daki, or Carrick? They don't know he's disguised as you."

"Haming won't risk it," Welder said. "He won't want to cast suspicion until he's had a chance to prove neither Carrick nor Nelan has the Will of Heaven. While I'm not sure how he intends to publicly discredit them, I do know Haming won't let Carrick touch the scepter until there are enough witnesses. All we can do is try to get to them as fast as we can."

"So be it." Ashbel nodded. "We'll make the preparations for you to leave at once."

# CHAPTER 30

✦ ✦ ✦ ✦ ✦ ✦ ✦ ✦ ✦ ✦

It was nearly midnight before Welder, Hu, and I set off in the steam coach, with Hu driving. I'd had a quick goodbye with the king and queen, promising Leonora I'd get her son back and smack him for leaving without notice. Though I hadn't spent long in Emberwood, it already felt like my new home, and I already missed Leonora's warmth and Ashbel's protectiveness. It had been so long since I'd felt like I was a part of a family.

"It will be a long night, and I know you're tired," Welder said. "You can sleep until we cross the border. We'll need to disguise ourselves then."

"You should sleep, too, sir," Hu told Welder. "While you can."

"We'll change shifts in a couple of hours," Welder said. But he didn't close his eyes and instead focused his gaze out the side window.

Meanwhile, Hu drove with complete precision though we were going at an alarming speed. I could barely see the road despite the glowing lights of the floating street lanterns. I felt the scepter, now changed back into the flute, in the front of my bodice. There was no safer place to hide it than on me, where I could feel it at all times. Nobody could remove it without invading my personal space first. But because no one except Welder and Hu knew that the flute was the scepter, I didn't think anyone would try.

With this reassuring thought, I closed my eyes and drifted off.

When I woke, the late morning light already trickled through the coach's glass windows. I stretched and yawned.

"Good, you're awake. We're almost there." Welder sounded completely alert, and he now sat in the driver's seat, while Hu slept in the back seat next to me. Had he slept at all? After getting locked away for two days, subjugated to torture, and now on another mission without recovery, I wondered if the man was made of the same metal as this steam coach.

"Hu," Welder said. "It's time."

Hu opened his eyes and blinked away the sleepiness. "We've reached the border?"

"Still another hour, but we have to prepare," Welder said. He gave me a hair clip and a skintight mask. "Put your hair into a single bun and wear this. A temporary disguise. Unfortunately, the only thing I can't change is a person, but that's what masks are for."

I did as he said. The mask went over my head. Other than holes for my eyes, nose, and mouth, it covered the rest of my face and my hair. I found my reflection in the glass window and gasped. I had the appearance of a man with a moustache. There was no evidence of the scar on my cheek.

Welder touched the sleeve of my dress. I felt a spark of his wyis jolt through my clothes. My dress transformed into a man's tunic and twill pants. I was dressed as an Ember merchant, like the one who sold toys to me at the sea market when I was a child.

Welder and Hu also wore masks, disguising themselves as merchants. Then Welder touched the coach window, and the entire coach began to shake. The roof opened, and the metal evolved into wood. The front of the coach shimmered and morphed; the shapes of two horses sprang up from two shuroos from nearby trees, and they attached themselves to our coach. No, not a coach any longer. Now it was a carriage.

We trotted along at a much slower speed.

"We'll use this carriage the rest of the way," Welder told me.

"How will we ever catch up to Haming in time?" I asked.

"Unfortunately, we won't," Hu said. "It's impossible. It will take another four days to get to Senlin City once we cross the border into Seracedar. Haming and the others will reach Senlin City within two days."

Welder pulled the reins, and the horses slowed until we came to a stop behind a line of other carriages. We were parked outside a stone wall that extended in either direction as far as I could see. On our side of the wall were rows of steam coaches and stalls of horses, where people were renting or buying whatever means of transportation they needed. The majority looked like merchants.

On the other side of the wall was a barricade of tall trees, similar to the border outside Cedar Palace. Now I knew we never could have made it to Emberwood if Aiden and I had come this way on the journey. We would have been caught for sure without a disguise.

Seracedarean sentinels were staged atop the trees, and they all had bows ready to aim at any Seracedarean who attempted to escape across the border to Emberwood. Only merchants or those with permits were able to go back and forth between the kingdoms.

Our carriage pulled through the gates. The patrol guards up front were scanning each carriage's documents.

"Will they see through my disguise?" I asked.

"The guards all have tin-chai to check whether the paperwork is legitimate, or if someone used their tin-chai to forge it," Welder said. "As long as there's no trace of magic on the documents, they'll let us through. They won't look at us because we've got the authentic king's seal."

When it was our turn, Welder handed the patrol guards our paperwork, signed by the king. One of the guards put his index finger against the king's seal.

"All right, you're good to go." The guard gave us a nod to continue.

A tremor of fear still rushed through me, sending chills down my spine. Here we were returning to the kingdom of my birth, where I'd been stifled all my life and hiding in the shadows. I might never be able to cross this border again once we passed through.

I took a deep breath. No matter who became the new emperor, I wasn't going to let anyone stop me from living the life I wanted. As we passed through the arched gate, I made a promise to myself.

*I will never give up my freedom.*

# CHAPTER 31

✦ ✦ ✦ ✦ ✦ ✦ ✦ ✦ ✦ ✦

We traveled another two days, stopping for rest and food at small towns on the way to Senlin City. I couldn't stop worrying despite Welder's assurances that Haming wouldn't reveal his hand yet. Not until Carrick touched the scepter, and that wouldn't happen until Haming could arrange for the masses to witness his failure to receive tin-chai amplification.

On the third day, we stopped at a restaurant late in the afternoon for food. We were all famished.

Welder lifted his head toward the sky and squinted. "We have half a day's worth of light left for travel. It will take another full day for us to reach Senlin City. Keep your ears open. There must be news by now of the scepter's return and perhaps of Carrick's intentions to prove his right to rule in front of the noblemen in court."

We waited for the server to bring us our food and tea. At a nearby table, several village men were enjoying their meal. I listened in on the conversation between the men. They spoke of the weather, but the topic soon shifted, and I heard the words "scepter" and "Emberwood."

"There is talk that Emberwood has allied themselves with Carrick," one of the men said. "Seems that Carrick's bodyguard was the lost Emberwood prince, and he's brought back the real scepter."

"A bunch of nonsense," a second man said. "This gossip is meant to stir up trouble for Emperor Nelan. None of it is true."

"Nelan is not my emperor," a third man said. "It's been proven he carried a fake scepter. He lied to us, the Seracedarean citizens."

The first man grunted. "Well, tomorrow's meeting will determine if either Nelan or Carrick is granted tin-chai amplification."

I exchanged glances with Hu and Welder.

Welder cleared his throat and spoke to the men. "Excuse me, sirs. I couldn't help overhearing your conversation. What is happening tomorrow?"

The men gave us strange looks.

"Where have you been? Living in a cave?" the first man said.

"We were away on business and just came back to Seracedar," Welder said. "Haven't had time to catch up with recent news."

The man stroked his beard. "Well, while you've been gone, there have been some interesting political developments. Prince Carrick's bodyguard returned with what they claim to be the real scepter. The former General Welder and Captain Montier are back from exile as well. They are under Prince Carrick's protection. He's pardoned their crimes for the coup against Terran two years ago, and they helped arrange the meeting tomorrow. Nelan agreed not to arrest them for the time being."

Welder's eyes sparked. I wondered what emotions were running through him to know that Prince Carrick had pardoned him. "Then I assume the meeting is to establish once and for all whether Carrick or Nelan receives the Will of Heaven."

"Carrick and Nelan are to meet on neutral ground. Instead of a formal event in front of the noblemen to test who the scepter picks as the next rightful ruler, they will be on stage in front of the Seracedarean citizens as witnesses. Carrick and Nelan have agreed if one receives tin-chai amplification, the other will concede peacefully.

And if neither of them receives the right to rule, it is open to all challengers who wish to test if they receive the Will of Heaven."

"Where are they meeting?" I asked.

"At the Autumn Courtyard in Cedar Palace. They've already set up a dais and have invited anyone in the kingdom to be spectators should they wish to travel to Senlin City. A rare opportunity indeed. Only the first hundred people can enter Cedar Palace, but they're allowing viewers to gather outside the palace walls. The palace will be reporting the entire ceremony as it happens. Good luck getting a close spot. There are already hundreds camped out, waiting. You likely won't even get past the gates of Senlin."

This was bad. Carrick would touch the fake scepter in front of all those witnesses, and they would all see him fail to attain the Will of Heaven. Then the same would happen with Nelan, and Haming would discredit both of them in one day.

We would barely be able to reach the capitol by dawn tomorrow.

Welder thanked the men and turned back to Hu and me. "I didn't anticipate Haming would be able to make a move this quickly, even if he did reach Senlin City two days before us. It must have been his idea, telling Carrick to challenge Nelan in front of the masses and opening it to any challenger to test his right to rule. Not only will Haming be able to discredit both princes at one time, I wouldn't be surprised if he plans to feign the scepter's bestowment of the right to rule upon himself so he can seize the throne."

"Feign the right to rule? How would he do this?" Hu asked.

"It can't be that easy to fake," I said. "I've never seen an emperor receive the right to rule through the scepter, but I heard a light is transferred from the scepter to the next emperor. That this light glows within him."

"I've never seen it either," Welder said. "Witnesses say it's evident when a candidate receives the right to rule, that it's a grand display.

I'm not sure how Haming plans to fake it, but if anyone can figure out a way to trick the masses, it would be Haming."

"Then there's the matter of tin-chai amplification," Hu said. "How would he feign that?"

"Believe it or not, that part would be easier than figuring out how to make yourself glow with the scepter's light," Welder said. "Perhaps there is a layer to his tin-chai he has kept hidden. For example, I knew another face-changer who could take on the form of an animal in addition to a person. If Haming touches the scepter and demonstrates he can take the shape of an animal or even a non-living object, he may be able to fool the masses into believing his tin-chai has been amplified. People who are desperate for change will believe anything."

I hadn't even thought of the possibility that someone would hide a layer of his tin-chai for such a dishonorable purpose. This would be tantamount to challenging the authority of Old Grandfather Heaven himself. But Haming was devious enough.

Hu scratched his head. "But how would he prove he didn't have those layers of his tin-chai to begin with?"

"The Lotuses," I said. "There's a group of them who follow him. I don't know why they support him, but they will likely swear he has received tin-chai amplification. Many of the citizens are devoutly religious and believe Lotuses are incapable of lying."

"Can we make it to Senlin by dawn?" Hu asked.

"If we ride with no breaks," Welder said.

We were out of the town within half an hour, driving our carriage as fast as we could through the darkness of the forest. Except for the lantern that hung in front of the carriage and the glow of the Turquoise Moon, there was no other source of light. Still, we pushed on. Wise Grandmother Time was not on our side tonight.

Adrenaline shot through my body. I didn't feel drowsy despite lack of sleep. Dawn crept up behind our shoulders and highlighted the tips of the trees.

"Almost there," Welder called to me over his shoulder.

And then, there it was. The wall of hollowed trees stood tall against the blue sky. The gates of Senlin City. Climbing vines and gnarled branches weaved their way through the wall, leaving space only for the entry way, where carriages and carts pulled through.

We slowed our carriage as we came to the line of people trying to get into the city.

"There's no way we can get in if we have to wait here," I said.

"I have an idea." Welder held the reins out to Hu. "Stay here. Miss Rilla and I will continue on foot. Whenever you make it through the city, find us at the palace."

He touched my arm, and a zing of his wyis passed through me. I peered down at myself. I was garbed in the uniform of a palace soldier. So was Welder.

We got off the carriage, and we marched up to the walls of the city entrance. A team of palace guards stood by, letting some people enter but denying others.

As we approached them, Welder nodded to the guards. "We've got orders to help with the security at the stage."

"Go on through," one of the guards said, letting us pass the line.

Inside the city, we continued pushing through the crowds, but our disguises worked. No one questioned or stopped us.

As we drew closer to the palace, we came to the same circle of trees that barricaded Cedar Palace. I remembered the first time I'd entered. How lonely and afraid I'd been back then, wanting to retreat into the shadows. So much had happened since then, and I wasn't the same little girl as before.

Still, I shivered at the sight of the palace gates. The memories of being trapped flooded back.

But this time was different. I wasn't coming here as a prisoner but as a woman fighting for the betterment of my kingdom. I was here on a mission. To help others become free.

A man's voice reverberated through the air, carrying throughout the city. "The two candidates are now here, and we are ready to begin the ceremony."

"Oh, no," I said. "It's starting."

The voice carried on. "Prince Nelan may have already claimed the throne, but he has yet to prove his right to rule as his tin-chai was never amplified and no one witnessed the scepter bestow power upon him. The reason for this was recently discovered as the scepter he took from his father, the former Emperor Terran, was a fake. The prince insists he had no part in this deception."

Welder and I came to the throng of people that surrounded the entrance to Cedar Palace. In front of the crowd, a nobleman stood on a podium. He spoke to the people. "Challenging Prince Nelan is his brother, Prince Carrick, who says he has found the true scepter. Presently, the scepter is in the hands of a neutral party, Androgy Unther. Both princes will be allowed to touch the scepter in hopes of receiving tin-chai amplification and the Will of Heaven."

Despite the noise of the crowds and the sheer number of people, his words projected into the atmosphere, ringing loud and clear. He must have a tin-chai that increased the volume of his voice.

"If one of the princes is gifted with the right to rule, you will bear witness to the magical light of the scepter filling him with its power, causing him to illuminate from the inside out. This is an indicator that he has received tin-chai amplification, and he will demonstrate his new power to the crowd. Good luck to both of them, and may the victor live ten thousand years and ten thousand more."

There was a pathway separating the people into two sections, and the aisle kept the entryway into the palace clear. A team of guards wearing Carrick's colors stood around the noblemen and formed a border around both sections of the people. The guards scrutinized the crowd and prevented anyone from getting past them.

"Some of those guards are my men," Welder said. "And look who else happens to be here."

I followed his gaze to a familiar face. Haming in the guise of Welder. He barked orders at Welder's men and gestured for them to help Carrick's guards hold the crowd back.

"What do we do?" I whispered to the real Welder.

"Get into the palace. Find Aiden, Daki, and Carrick. Do anything to stop the ceremony. I'll take care of Haming."

Before I could ask him what he intended to do, he strode into the cleared path. He removed his mask and shouted at the guards in front of the entire crowd. "That man is an imposter." He pointed at Haming. "He has been posing as me all this time."

The crowd gasped, and the guards surrounded Welder. But the men looked at him, then back at Haming, hesitating.

"He's lying," Haming said. "Arrest him."

"Ti, Mun, Vay." Welder named his men. "I am the real Commander Welder, and I can prove it. Ti, I know when you sleep, you place a portrait of your girlfriend under your pillow. Mun, before every mission, you chant *Old Grandfather Heaven be with us* three times because it was your grandmother's superstition, and Vay, you pretend to listen to my lectures, but I know when your mind is wandering when you pick at your nails. I am trained to perceive details like this, just as I've trained you to notice details. Think hard, and you'll differentiate the real Welder from the imposter."

Welder's men spun around, focused on Haming. They pointed their swords at him. The androgy swore. He changed from wearing Welder's face to his own and ran.

"After him." Welder shouted at his men. They and Welder chased after Haming.

People in the crowd pointed and gasped, but the remaining guards settled them down.

"We have everything under control," a guard called out. "Continue observing the ceremony."

But I had to get inside the palace. Still in the guise of a guard, I managed to get through the gate. The other guards were too busy trying to regain control of the crowd to notice me. I entered through the hollowed-out tree trunk and came into the Autumn Courtyard. Aristocrats, androgies, and commoners stood in a semicircle around a dais.

On the dais, Carrick stood on the right with Aiden and Daki next to him. They wore blue and gold robes. On the opposite end were Nelan and two noblemen, all dressed in black. On the right side, the spectators wore blue and gold, while on the left, they wore black. Those dressed in blue and gold outnumbered those in black at least two to one. I glanced down at my own black robes and wished I wasn't wearing Nelan's colors.

In the middle of the dais, an androgy stood with the scepter—Androgy Unther, the one I'd been instructed to kill during my preliminary test at the showcase. I never would have expected to see him again, especially not under these circumstances.

I broke into a sprint, pushing past the spectators despite their angry protests and stares.

The announcer's voice carried throughout the atmosphere. "Both candidates will now step forward. Rise and move up to the scepter. In five . . . four . . ."

I continued pushing forward, reaching the edge of the dais.

"Three . . two . . ."

But the distance to climb the stage was two seconds too far.

"One."

Nelan and Carrick reached for the scepter, touching its base at the same time.

# CHAPTER 32

✦ ✦ ✦ ✦ ✦ ✦ ✦ ✦ ✦ ✦

Lightning illuminated the sky, and electricity surged through the air.

Carrick shouted, emitting his wyis into the atmosphere. Thunder rippled like the sound of glass breaking. Bolts struck the ground, eliciting screams from the crowd. The sky opened up, pouring rain in rivulets.

What was going on? Was Carrick using his tin-chai? But I thought he could only summon lightning. This was a full storm.

Another lightning bolt lit up the sky, and Carrick raised his hands to the heavens. The lightning struck him. I screamed, but he went unfazed. The electricity merged into his body, illuminating him and the scepter. His body appeared to be glowing.

Between his palms, he conjured sparks.

"Carrick's tin-chai has been amplified," a soldier shouted. "And the scepter has transferred its light upon him."

No, it wasn't the scepter. It was the lightning. Somehow, Carrick was controlling it to make himself appear illuminated. But if I didn't know that he carried a fake scepter, I'd be deceived, too. The spectacle was so grand it appeared real.

"No," Nelan screamed. "The scepter means nothing. Old Grandfather Heaven is a myth, and I don't need a fictional god to approve my right to be emperor. The throne belongs to me."

Nelan drew a dagger from his cloak and charged at Carrick. But Carrick raised his hand, and lightning illuminated above him, sending a bolt through Nelan's chest. Nelan shuddered and seized. A horrible burning smell filled the air.

Nelan fell to the ground, and his body thrashed like a nageel out of water. Foam gathered around his mouth. His eyes remained open, but he moved no more.

Nelan was dead.

For a moment, there was complete silence. No one dared move. Then Carrick raised his hands into the sky, and the storm stopped. Clouds retreated, and the sun returned, shining its radiance upon the prince. Carrick bowed to his dead brother as though saying a prayer, and then he took the scepter into his own hands. He rose, showing it to the crowd.

But how could this be? The scepter in Carrick's hands was a fake. How had his tin-chai been amplified? Unless . . . the thought was unbearable. Yet it was the only logical explanation. Carrick had feigned the amplification of his tin-chai.

"Heaven has bestowed upon me the right to rule," Carrick said. "Does anyone dare challenge the decree of Old Grandfather Heaven? If so, state your objections now, and I will allow you to leave the kingdom in peace. But if not, then I command loyalty from all my subjects henceforth."

Those in blue and gold fell to the ground and bowed their heads to Carrick. Aristocrats, androgies, and soldiers alike.

Reluctantly, those in black kneeled, one by one.

On the dais, Aiden, Daki, and Nelan's men bowed as well.

I followed suit and kneeled. My head reeled. Carrick was lying to everyone.

The chorus of voices flooded the atmosphere. "Long live Emperor

Carrick. May he live ten thousand years and ten thousand more."

Several seconds passed. Carrick walked off the wooden dais.

The herald called out. "Emperor Carrick has left our presence. All rise."

Soldiers and aristocrats rose from the ground, still arranged in an orderly fashion.

Androgy Unther stood in front of us. "By decree of His Majesty, today is declared a day of rest. Return to your families. Tomorrow will be the official coronation of His Majesty, followed by a royal banquet. Dress in your finest robes. You are all invited."

Aiden stood on the dais. I had to tell him about Haming and about Carrick's deception. I yanked off the mask and shook out my hair.

"Aiden," I shouted. "Over here." I jumped and waved, trying to catch his attention.

The voices around us were loud, everyone chattering about the ceremony and Carrick's ascension, but Aiden spun around, and through the crowd, his gaze met mine. His eyes widened in surprise. He jumped off the dais, worked his way through the dispersing spectators, and came to me.

"What are you doing here?" he asked.

"I have to talk to you."

But before I could say another word, Daki ran up to us. His brow rose at the sight of me. "Rilla, if you're here, then it must be true. I'm hearing reports from the soldiers that a man who looked like Welder showed up, claiming the man who journeyed with us from Emberwood is an imposter."

"What?" Aiden reared up.

"It's true," I said. "Haming has been impersonating Welder all along."

"Where are they now?" Aiden asked.

"Thankfully, Welder's men believed their commander, and they all took off after Haming."

"Since Emperor Carrick has granted you temporary military authority, Daki, you can tell the soldiers to find them," Aiden said. "Then go inform the emperor that Haming is lurking about."

Daki bowed and made his exit.

Aiden took my hand. "Come with me. Let's go somewhere more private."

I followed him behind a maple tree. While the noise of voices was still loud, at least we didn't have to shout to be heard.

"What's going on?" Aiden asked.

"Haming held Welder hostage and took his place the day we arrived at Linlang Palace. But Welder escaped and showed up the night of the banquet. We came after you at once, but we didn't have Daki to make us a fast-powered coach."

"I don't understand." Aiden shook his head. "What are Haming's intentions? If he wanted the scepter, why didn't he stop us from bringing it back to Seracedar?"

Welder's deep, booming voice stopped me from answering. "Haming planned to discredit both princes during the ceremony. He didn't expect either of them to receive the Will of Heaven. But it looks like he was wrong."

We looked up. Welder approached us. Or at least he wore Welder's face.

# CHAPTER 33

✦ ✦ ✦ ✦ ✦ ✦ ✦ ✦ ✦ ✦

"Stop right there," Aiden said, holding up a hand.

Welder smirked at Aiden. "I understand. It's wise to remain vigilant."

Welder picked up a stone from the ground. In the palm of his hand, the simple rock transformed into a rose. "Haming can't do that."

"Unless he's using blood magic," I said. "I want to make sure you're not wearing Yao gemstones."

"Fair point, my lady." Welder removed his cloak and slowly circled around, hands lifted in a gesture of surrender.

Aiden scrutinized Welder and patted him down. "No Yao gemstones." Aiden's wary glower altered into a smile. He clapped a hand on Welder's back. "I can't believe you let Haming best you, old man. I hope you were able to catch him."

"Unfortunately, no," Welder said. "One of Carrick's lightning bolts struck a tree near us, and Haming used the smoke from the fire to escape. My men are still looking for him, but I came back to warn you and the new emperor."

New emperor? Welder had to know Carrick's deception. Why was he covering it up?

"There's something else," I said. "The scepter that Haming gave to Carrick is a fake."

Aiden froze. "A fake? You must be mistaken. We all saw Carrick receive the Will of Heaven and tin-chai amplification."

"Rilla speaks the truth," Welder said. "The scepter never made it with me to Emberwood. I lost it on the way."

"Fortunately," I started, "I found—"

Welder coughed loud enough to drown me out. "We should talk about this later."

I gave Welder a questioning glance, which he didn't return. It was obvious he didn't want me to tell Aiden that I had the real scepter. But why?

Aiden stared into the open air as though trying to piece things together. "But if the scepter is a fake, then that implies Carrick used tricks to deceive us into thinking he received the Will of Heaven. I don't believe he would behave so despicably. I won't believe it." His face was pale with shock.

Welder touched Aiden's shoulder. "Listen to me. We can deal with Carrick and the scepter later. Right now, finding Haming is the priority. I need you to find Daki. Let him know that my men are still on the lookout for Haming and they need assistance from the palace guards."

Aiden shook out of his stupor. He still looked stunned, but he nodded. "Yes, you're right. We have to find Haming before he causes more trouble."

He rushed off, leaving Welder with me. I gave Welder a frown.

"Why don't you want me telling Aiden that I have the real scepter?" I asked.

"He's still processing that Carrick lied," Welder said. "He doesn't believe it yet. If we tell him that you have the scepter, he might still insist that we give Carrick a chance to touch it. Aiden needs time to come to terms that Carrick is not the man we thought he was."

"You mean, not the man Aiden and I believed he was," I said. "You questioned Carrick's character from the beginning, or you wouldn't have removed the scepter from the palace."

"You're quite perceptive." Welder lifted his gaze to the trees. He wore a solemn expression. "During my time in the palace, I saw the conflicted nature in Carrick. How similar he was to his father. Don't tell me you've never sensed the darkness within him."

I couldn't deny it. I had seen the darkness in Carrick—when he treated Aiden and me as his possessions, when he forced his kisses upon me and ripped my clothes in his anger.

But I'd also sensed the conflict in him. The part of him that wanted to be good, that needed his friends to believe in him. I might not love him the way he wanted me to, but I had once promised to believe in him.

"Feigning the amplification of his tin-chai is a grave sin against Heaven," Welder said. "Carrick would know this from his studies, and if he was still willing to do this, it reflects the true state of his heart. It confirms my belief that he cannot be the next emperor."

"We should confront him," I said.

But Welder shook his head. "Not yet. There's no telling what he may do. We can't tell him you have the real scepter. He may take it from you and imprison all of us. The wisest course of action would be to return to Emberwood as soon as we can. I believe Old Grandfather Heaven will expose Carrick as a fraud in time."

A fraud. I couldn't believe it of Carrick, no matter what he'd done. Becoming emperor had always been his goal—and to change Seracedar for the better. He'd been so passionate about overturning his father's dirty laws. Perhaps Carrick had thought the only way to defeat Nelan was to secure the throne first, then figure out how to gain the Will of Heaven. Though it didn't make his actions right, I did understand why he would have done it.

"What if I get him to admit to his sin?" I asked. "Perhaps he will be sorry. He might still have a chance of receiving tin-chai amplification when I let him touch the true scepter."

Welder gave me an impatient look. "I don't think Old Grandfather Heaven will forgive him for this. If you tell him you know what he did, he will feign repentance only because he got caught."

No sooner had he said this than Daki strode up to us. "I've let Aiden lead the search to find Androgy Haming, but unfortunately, it's impossible to know what new disguise he's taken on. At least his plans have been foiled for now. Rilla, I have informed His Majesty that you are here. He has absolved you and Aiden of all crimes you were accused of against the former emperor, effective immediately. You no longer have to worry about anyone chasing after you for murder and treason. Also, His Majesty requests for you to join him in his chambers for a brief meeting before tonight's celebratory feast."

I started for the Royal House on the other side of the courtyard, but Daki stopped me. "Where are you going?"

"The emperor's residence," I said. "Isn't it where Carrick is staying now that he's emperor?"

"Traditionally, yes," Daki said. "But Carrick wants you to go to his old house. That's where you'll be living while you're here."

Treehouse 8. Between the Dark Court and the Spring Gardens.

Welder and I followed Daki down the forested path. When we came to the entrance of the Dark Court, I shivered. It was still cold and ominous, with no light coming from any of the windows. What had happened to all of Terran's faela? Did they still live here? Or had Nelan forced them out of the palace when he'd taken over these past few months? And what about the novelties and baubles?

A commotion sounded from within the Spring Gardens. Wood being sawed through and clanking metal. Several guards strode out of the gardens. Trailing behind was a group of women in silk robes.

Novelties. They looked confused and moved like they were swimming in a pool of molasses.

"Come along now," one of the guards said, urging them to hurry.

I breathed out a gasp and started for them. "What are you doing to these women?"

The guard looked at me in surprise. "We've been instructed to relocate the novel—I mean, women."

Daki touched my shoulder. "Rilla, it's all right. The guards are only taking them to see the doctor."

"What?"

"Carrick's first decree," Daki explained. "All caged novelties and baubles are to be released at once and brought to the doctor for proper medical care. He refuses to start the celebratory banquet until all of them are free."

"Oh." My anger dispersed.

Daki nodded to the guards. "Carry on."

"Well, it is a noble act, but has Carrick thought through what will become of these women?" Welder asked. "There are hundreds of them, and not all of them can return to their families after they may have been sold to the palace in the first place."

"Those who have families can choose to return home if they wish," Daki said. "Or they can stay here to live and work respectably. And those who are too sick will be taken care of for the remainder of their lives."

Carrick had kept his promise. I remembered him saying his first act as emperor would be to free the baubles and novelties. Although he'd lied about receiving tin-chai amplification, maybe he still deserved another chance to make things right and touch the real scepter.

Seeing those women reminded me of Radi. "Have you seen Radi?" I asked.

"Not personally, but I did inquire after her," Daki said. "His

Majesty said she is doing well and has been recovering. Rest assured, he has been taking care of her."

I murmured low for only Welder to hear. "See? Carrick's advocacy for these women and for Radi proves he still has a good heart despite the flaws. I think there's hope for him yet."

This was more like the Carrick I knew. Welder simply shrugged. His expression remained unreadable.

We entered Treehouse 8. Carrick stood in the center of the living area, his presence filling the room. He wore the robes of his father, gold silk with the kaigon icon. And upon his head, he was adorned with the same headdress I recognized from Terran's portrait. It made Carrick appear larger and taller, an intimidating figure.

We kneeled and bowed until our foreheads touched the ground.

"You may rise," Carrick said. "Did you find Androgy Haming?"

"Unfortunately, he has escaped," Daki said. "But Aiden and a few men continue to search."

Carrick's gaze flashed to me and gentled, but instead of addressing me, he spoke to Welder. "It's been awhile, General."

"I'm no longer a general," Welder said. "Simply a commander, Your Majesty. But please call me Welder."

Carrick nodded. "I cannot believe I allowed Haming to fool me, but I'm glad the truth has come to light and you are well. Any idea what his motive was in trading places with you, and why he would bring me the scepter instead of taking it for himself?"

"I was telling Rilla that he must have believed both you and Nelan would fail in receiving Old Grandfather Heaven's blessing," Welder said. "We are fortunate this was not the case, and you triumphed over your brother and Haming."

I watched Carrick's face for any telltale signs of guilt, but there were none.

"It has been a long two months of battles with Nelan," Carrick said. "But he could not hide that he had a fake scepter all along, and this was his downfall in the end. Many of his supporters felt betrayed by his lies and ended up coming over to my side. I was fortunate that, for whatever motives Haming had, he brought the scepter to me when he did."

I cleared my throat. One question was on my mind. "Where is Radi? Is she all right?"

"She's fine. I can't say the same for my mother." Carrick looked away, his eyes reflecting sadness.

Daki whispered in my ear. "Lady Cirisa was killed along with many other faela when Nelan took control of the palace."

"I wasn't able to get her out in time," Carrick said.

"I'm sorry." I bowed my head.

"It's all right. She knew I loved her and wanted to save her." A solemn smile flickered on his face as he regarded me again. "But I know you're concerned for your friend. You always have been. Radi has been the most protected of all of us these past few months. Other than myself and a handful of my most trusted men guarding the safe house, I've allowed no one else near its vicinity in case Nelan was tracking them. The only way to see through the invisibility shield is by using blood magic I received from Androgy Solar." He touched a sapphire stone set in a chain around his neck. A Yao sapphire. "I was able to shield myself whenever I went there, and the house remains invisible to anyone who doesn't channel this blood magic."

For the first time, I noticed how tired Carrick looked. White hairs peppered into his sideburns, which was certainly unusual for a young man in his early twenties. I remembered how Sago had warned that blood magic could not be used by those who weren't pure in heart without devastating consequences, and this was why Terran and Limera dared not use it. Could it be that Carrick was facing those consequences?

"His Majesty wouldn't even allow Aiden or I to visit the safe house," Daki said. "But since Nelan is no longer a threat, there should be no problem to allow Rilla to visit her friend. And your men stationed there should be informed that you have received the Will of Heaven."

"Yes, I will personally go there after the banquet," Carrick said.

"After the banquet?" I repeated. I looked around for Welder's and Daki's reactions. Daki's eyebrows lifted in confusion, but he didn't question Carrick. Welder seemed observant, his face wiped clean of emotions.

"I would think that they would be invited to celebrate with us," I said.

"Unfortunately, Radi is recovering from a chill," Carrick said. "A few more days of rest will be good for her, and my men will be paid for their extra time on duty. I promise I'll take you to see her after the coronation banquet. Now, enough of that. I must speak to you of other matters. In private." He cleared his throat and gave Welder and Daki a look.

"I'll be right outside in case you need me," Welder told me. He and Daki bowed and exited the treehouse.

As soon as they were gone, Carrick stood, came toward me, and pulled me into his embrace. "Thank Old Grandfather Heaven you are here. I thought I might never see you again. When Aiden came with the scepter and told me all that had transpired . . . I can't tell you how many emotions ran through my head. Anger that you would endanger yourself instead of going to Fauxhemia as I instructed. Relief that you were all right. And gratitude for what you've done. And to Aiden as well."

I tried pulling away from him, but he wouldn't let me. "We searched for a way to help you become the emperor because we believe in you. I hope you don't let us down."

A frown flickered on his lips. "Now that I'm on the throne, I will make sure Seracedar becomes strong again." His gaze gentled. "I told you that I need you. These past few months have been miserable without you. I couldn't keep the nightmares away. I kept dreaming that I had become him. My father."

He inhaled my scent and breathed out. The goosebumps that formed on my skin were not pleasant. I wanted to escape.

"Now that you're back," he continued, "I already feel lighter. Like the tension has left my body. You keep me in check and drive the darkness away. I need you to stay by my side forever. I've decided you will become my empress."

He finally loosened his hold, and I took two steps away from him.

"Empress? Wait—"

"No waiting. We will marry in a month's time."

"Carrick, I will always be your friend, but I realized over the past few months that I don't feel for you the way you want me to. I don't want to marry you."

His expression didn't change. It was almost as though he hadn't heard me. "You must be tired, and it's making you confused."

"I'm not—"

"We'll talk tomorrow when you aren't as emotional," he said.

"But Carrick, I need you to understand. Aiden and I—"

"No," he said, his voice an abrupt bark. "Not another word. If you fancy yourself in love with another, I will simply have to change your mind. And if you have betrayed me already, I forgive you. We need never speak of it."

My eyes widened. He already knew about Aiden and me. He just refused to recognize it.

"I assure you," he continued. "You will never leave me again." He exited the door. I lunged forward, but he shut the door in my face. I grabbed the handle and pulled. It didn't give. I could feel Carrick's weight pushing against the door, preventing me from opening it. A lock snapped into place.

Was I to be Carrick's prisoner now? I banged on the door, shook the chain, and shouted. "Let me out."

Footsteps sounded, and I heard Daki's voice from the other side. "Are you locking her up? She's done nothing wrong."

"Of course I'm not locking her up," Carrick said. "Rilla needs some time to rest before the banquet. This is to keep her safe. With Haming on the loose, I don't want anything to happen to her."

Welder cleared his throat. "Your Majesty, I have a responsibility to the Emberwood king. I promised to keep both Rilla and Aiden safe."

"Rilla," Daki called through the door. "Are you okay?"

"Let me out," I shouted again. "He's keeping me here against my will."

"I can't hear anything," Welder said. "Rilla, tell us you're all right."

Why couldn't they hear me? Had Carrick done something to the door? Used some kind of magic to keep the treehouse soundproof to the outside?

"I told you she's resting," Carrick snapped. "She's asleep. I don't appreciate your insinuation that I would hold her against her will. I would never harm my friends, even if they betrayed me." This he said louder, emphasizing the words.

"Of course not, Your Majesty," Welder said. "But—"

"Commander Welder, if you continue these protests, I can easily have my men remove you from Seracedar."

"I apologize, Your Majesty," Welder said. "I mean no disrespect. I defer to your judgment."

Their footsteps and voices faded.

I slid to the floor and sat with my chin propped on my knees. Carrick wouldn't even let me broach the subject of our relationship being impossible. Would he hurt Aiden? And what about Radi? I didn't buy Carrick's excuse that she wasn't feeling well. Something seemed suspicious. Why didn't he want her at the banquet?

Never once during our conversation had he shown the least bit of guilt about faking tin-chai amplification. When I'd realized he'd abolished the novelty and bauble cages, I'd hoped it was a sign he would overcome the shadows and step into the light.

But after that conversation? I was no longer sure.

A knock sounded on my door. The lock rattled. Someone was setting me free. Was it Welder?

The door swung open. It was a serving trifle. In her hands, she carried a basket covered with a tea towel.

"I've been sent here by Miss Radi," she said.

# CHAPTER 34

✦ ✦ ✦ ✦ ✦ ✦ ✦ ✦ ✦ ✦

The trifle looked to her left and to her right down the corridors connecting the treehouses. She lowered her voice to a hoarse whisper. "I've come from His Majesty's safe house. Miss Radi sent me to find you."

I frowned. "Wait. Emperor Carrick told me no one has been allowed in or out of the safe house."

The trifle held out a basket. "Lotus cakes. Miss Radi made them. I cannot say more, and I must go before anyone sees me."

I took the basket from her. "Radi made them? But how does she know I'm here?"

"I can't answer that," the trifle said. "I think you'll find the filling in the cakes delightful. Don't leave until you've tried them."

She closed the door, but she didn't bolt the lock. What was going on?

I placed the basket on the table and stared at it.

I picked up a lotus cake and broke it in half. Something caught midway. A piece of paper had been baked into it.

*Don't trust Carrick.*

I remembered now a story my baba had once told me.

A general, who was spying on enemy forces, learned that the leader of the rebel band planned to invade the city he was responsible for protecting. But he couldn't alert the king or the city, or the enemy would learn his identity and know he was onto them. Instead, he rallied all the bakers he could find, and he had them bake cakes with the message of the impending attack. The bread was sold all over the city. When the people opened the bread and read the message, they rallied together and were able to defend their city from the rebel attack.

Did the other cakes have messages? I opened the other three. Each of them had a note in it. When I compiled them together, they read:

*Need to talk.*

*Silver Tears Lake.*

*Make sure no one sees.*

*Meet when the Turquoise Moon hangs above the cherry trees.*

I peered out the window toward the grove of cherry trees. The Turquoise Moon shone its ominous blue light upon the treetops, making them glisten.

I tested the door. Sure enough, the trifle hadn't locked it. The door swung open. In the courtyard, two guards lay on the ground. I gasped. They had been knocked out.

Radi must have heard of my arrival. She must know something about Carrick. Perhaps that was why he had her locked away at the safe house.

She must have sent her trifle to help me. If she wanted me to meet her at Silver Tears Lake, then she must have escaped as well. Why endanger herself by coming to the palace?

Did she know he'd faked his tin-chai amplification? Or was there another secret he was hiding?

I exited Treehouse 8. Other than the two unconscious guards, there was no one else. Strange. I'd have thought Carrick would have put more security on me.

I strode down the path. The stars blinked above me, but the Turquoise Moon took over the sky, full and bright. I came to the banks of the lake and remembered when Radi and I had come here to swim. The night we'd broken palace rules for a taste of freedom. It was also the night we'd met Carrick.

So much had changed since then, but many things felt the same. This place still held the weight of imprisonment. Of forbidden secrets. Dangerous secrets.

Several feet away, a still figure stood tall under a tree. Radi. Her back faced me. Her hair had grown out, now past her shoulder blades. She spun around.

I almost cried seeing her face.

"You're here," Radi said. "I didn't think it would be so easy to distract the guards. Then again, my people are far more capable than the fools who bow to an unworthy ruler."

Her body shimmered, beginning to morph. It was Haming.

*Fainting faela!* This was a trap.

Something invisible restrained my arms. Three more Shyan became detectable, materializing from nothing. Invisibility tin-chai. They were all Lotuses. The sign of the bird with a sword in its mouth was tattooed on the base of their necks.

Two of the Lotuses held my arms back. The third stood next to Haming. She was the trifle who had given me the lotus cakes.

Lotus cakes. The significance did not elude me.

I should have seen it earlier, should have known. In my eagerness to reunite with Radi, I'd let down my guard.

"What do you want with me, Haming?" I refused to cower, no matter how much I trembled inside. "I could kill you now with my voice."

Haming laughed. "Spare me the lies. I know you haven't been able to control your tin-chai properly."

"The only layer of my tin-chai I *can* control is the ability to kill," I said.

"Oh, but you won't want to kill us," he said. "And I no longer wish to kill you. I see greater potential in uniting our powers."

"Joining forces with you?" I spat. "You have to be joking."

"You might as well hear me out," he replied. "I should mention my people have infiltrated Carrick's safe house, and if you don't want your friend Radi or Lady Arlyn's bastard child to get hurt you'll come with us quietly. Kill us now, and my people have instructions to kill them in an hour's time."

I paused. "Arlyn's baby is with Radi?"

"You know so little," Haming said. "But we must hurry. If they die before we arrive, it will be your fault for dallying."

I had little choice. Carrick would eventually discover Haming had broken into the safe house, but I couldn't risk endangering Radi or the baby.

One of the Lotuses touched the ivory beads she wore around her neck. They were smeared with blood. Blood magic again.

She grabbed my arms. The moment she touched my skin, a zing of wyis entered my body. When I looked at my feet, they had a translucent quality. They'd turned me invisible.

The Lotus carried me on her back as though I weighed no more than a single rose. She jumped into the trees and scaled over the palace walls and into the surrounding forest. She landed on the path and deposited me onto the ground. Haming was right behind her, easily climbing over the walls as well. Like Aiden, they were all well-trained fighters, their bodies built to be agile and athletic.

"It's not far from here," Haming said. "I trust you care enough about your friend's safety not to run. We'll walk the rest of the way. I want to talk to you."

I set my pace but didn't look at him. "Excuse me if I have no desire to converse with bloodthirsty villains."

Even so, I was curious to find out what he was up to. I would go along with him and not resist for now.

The trail was dark, and the trees stood tall all around. It was hard to tell what was ahead and how far behind the palace was. A sliver of moonlight peeked through the forested canopy, the only source of light illuminating the path. I followed Haming, and the three Lotuses tailed me.

"We aren't the villains, Miss Marseas. We want what's best for this kingdom. I don't want to hurt you, either. I want you to listen to our side of the story. As I said, I no longer wish to be enemies, and I believe we can work together to make Seracedar strong again."

I scoffed. "Why would I want to work with you? You have no qualms about killing innocent people. You tried to make me kill Androgy Unther during the showcase preliminary test, and now you're threatening to kill my friends. I don't think you'll earn the right to rule, either."

"Oh, and you think your precious Carrick will earn that right? You know as well as I that he faked his tin-chai amplification."

"That isn't to say he won't attain the Will of Heaven with the true scepter," I said.

"He won't. Because I will."

My heart beat faster. I hoped he couldn't sense it. Couldn't sense the scepter was in my cloak right now. I swallowed and said, "How are you so sure? No one knows where the scepter has disappeared to. How are you so sure you'll find the scepter when no one has yet?"

Haming straightened his collar. "I will scour the seven kingdoms until I do. I won't ever give up. Old Grandfather Heaven will recognize my right to rule, and if he doesn't, I'll destroy the scepter and make the worship of Heaven an outdated tradition. I'll prove to everyone that it is I, and not Terran's line, who is worthy of the throne.

It has been me all along, and Old Grandfather Heaven was wrong to overlook me."

The man was mad. There was no other way to explain his twisted sense of logic.

I gaped at him. "How does that make you better than Carrick? Than Terran? Or the emperors before them?"

"I wouldn't betray those who are loyal to me," he snapped. "I'd protect the ones I love. You have no idea how many other dark secrets Carrick's been hiding from you and Aiden. How he's deceived both of you. I'm not only talking about faking his tin-chai amplification."

I faltered. "What are you talking about?"

"I knew you'd be curious," he said, smirking. "I'll tell you one secret now. The rest will be revealed at the safe house where there's evidence of Carrick's lies. I know that, during the showcase, your family was threatened if you did not participate. Carrick had them relocated to Fauxhemia for your sake."

I glared at him. "Yes, you spied on all of us for Lady Limera. Thank you for reminding me of another reason to not trust you."

He ignored that jab. "I used to pretend to be one of Carrick's guards in the Spring Gardens. Aiden thinks he's good at sensing a spy, but no one ever catches me. I heard them arguing about what to do with your family. Carrick must have told you he was responsible for helping your family—that he sent his androgy to bring them to safety. But that's not the true story."

"I know my family's safe. Aiden confirmed it."

"I'm sure they are. That part wasn't a lie. But Carrick took credit for it when in fact he couldn't have cared less."

I shook my head, confused. "Why would he lie about that?"

Haming looked at me as if I were the village idiot. "So, you would love him. But the truth is, Aiden's the one who advocated for your family. Aiden asked if Carrick could send Solar to your family. Carrick wouldn't have done it if Aiden hadn't insisted."

A wave of surprise struck my chest. But I narrowed my gaze at Haming, not wanting him to catch my reaction. "Why are you telling me this?"

"I want you to know his true character. He lies and uses people as pawns. Anything to get what he wants. He knew Aiden was beginning to fall for you, and if you became a trifle after the showcase, Aiden would have been allowed to pursue you. Carrick didn't care about your family. He wanted you for himself. He made Aiden promise never to speak to you in exchange for agreeing to send Solar to relocate your family."

The blood rushed to my head. All this time, I'd truly believed Carrick had shown a kindness to my family and to me.

Reflecting now, I didn't know why I was surprised. More than once, Carrick had spoken of Aiden and me like we were his possessions, not his friends. He'd only saved Radi because Aiden and I had gone to rescue her first.

Haming's hands formed into fists, and angry creases marked his brow. "That doesn't even begin to scratch the surface of his betrayals to people he claims to care about. You'll find out soon enough. I'm almost sorry to be the bearer of bad news, but I'm determined to expose that fraud to everyone in the kingdom, starting with you."

What other secrets would I discover Carrick was hiding? I was almost too scared to find out. But I had to know the truth. No matter how much it hurt.

"What do you gain by telling me all of this?" I asked. "I know you're only using me to trap Carrick. But why do you want me to know all of his secrets?"

"Because I want you to join my side," he said. "I could use a tinchai as strong as yours. And . . . I feel responsible for you in a way."

I gaped at him. "What? Why?"

He looked away. "I knew your mother. Before I became the person

I am now. Seems a lifetime ago. She had a powerful tin-chai, much like yours."

Not even I had known my mother had a tin-chai.

"How do you know my mother? Who are you? Before you became Androgy Haming?"

He smiled. "That is a secret I prefer to keep for now." He stared ahead at the path. "Enough talk. We've arrived. It's time for you to be reunited with your friend."

The Lotuses stood silently behind me, waiting for Haming. The trail appeared to have come to a dead end, blocked by the uncleared forest. Tall redwoods towered to the sky. *But the safe house must be here, past Solar's shield.*

"How did you do it?" I asked Haming. "From what I understand, only Carrick and his androgy, Solar, could access the safe house. Even though Aiden had the coordinates, not even he would be able to penetrate the protective invisibility shield without Carrick's or Solar's approval."

"I have many talents," Haming said. "All I needed was Solar's blood. I collected a sample when Solar was still alive. Then, I used blood magic to penetrate Solar's shield. Watch and learn."

Androgy Haming revealed a jade brooch pinned to his inner garment. I wondered how much he had stolen from the Yao. Many of his followers had Yao gems and precious metals, and though he had lost his gold earring, he'd still managed to get his hands on Yao jade.

"After penetrating the shield, all I had to do from there was pretend to be Carrick," Haming said. "His men let me in right away. My Lotuses, with their invisibility tin-chai, took care of them."

From his pocket, Haming took out a small vial no bigger than my thumb. He dipped his finger in it, coming away with blood, and he dabbed this on his jade brooch. The air was charged with his wyis and the wyis from the blood.

The redwoods disappeared, revealing a small cabin nestled in a clearing. Wisps of smoke swirled out of the chimney.

Haming groaned as though in pain, and a Lotus held onto his arm, giving him support. A burn scar formed on the back of his neck, but five seconds later, it disappeared, and he straightened.

"You've been using a lot of blood magic," I said. "Is that why you're suffering from burn scars and needed a Miyu's tail to heal yourself? I've heard there are serious repercussions if you have evil intentions while using blood magic."

"My intentions are not evil," Haming said. "Though you may disagree, I want what is best for this kingdom and my followers. I'm willing to bear whatever consequences Old Grandfather Heaven gives to me. And if not for a previous injury, the pain wouldn't be this great." He sounded bitter.

The Lotuses urged me forward.

Around the cabin was a wooden gate that creaked when Haming pushed it open. As soon as I stepped across the threshold, I saw dead bodies littering the ground. I recoiled.

I counted eight men. They wore Carrick's colors. These had been Carrick's guards.

Three Lotus sisters guarded the house, standing straight and tall. When they saw Haming, they bowed in greeting.

"You killed them in cold blood." I growled at him. "And you still say your intentions are pure?"

How could it be that the blood magic he used hadn't turned him *three* decades older?

"Sacrifices for the greater good," Haming said. The Lotuses standing behind me pushed me forward. Their fellow sisters, who stood guard, opened the door to the house, and we entered.

Another Lotus, a buxom woman, sat in the entryway, blocking the door to one of the rooms.

"Have they been behaving?" Haming asked her.

A baby wailed from the room.

"That is a demon child," she said. "Hasn't stopped crying. I tried using my tin-chai to quiet her, but she resisted. She must have some kind of shield tin-chai making her immune to my power. The only way she'll shut her mouth is if she's with Lady Radi."

"Interesting," Haming said. "Already so much potential for a baby. I hope I don't end up having to kill her."

The Lotus stood away from the door, letting us into the room. Inside, Radi sat on the corner of the bed closest to the wall. She didn't notice us coming in. Her attention was on the baby she carried, about five months old in my estimation. But the baby was still smaller than average for her age. After all, Lady Arlyn had given birth prematurely.

Another Lotus was in the room. She held out a cup to Radi.

"You haven't had any nutrition for over a day," the Lotus said. "At least drink some water."

Radi spoke harshly to the Lotus. "I don't trust anything you offer me. You should be ashamed of yourself, a holy messenger of Old Grandfather Heaven, working for that face-shifter."

"Lady Radi," Haming said. "Are you giving these poor holy sisters a difficult time? If you don't eat, they'll take the child again. Force feed you. Perhaps a friendly face will persuade you."

He pushed me forward.

For a brief second, Radi's eyes lit up to see me. Then she scowled. "Why did you bring her? Don't you have enough hostages?"

"I brought her here, so you could reveal the truth to her, Lady Radi," Haming said. "So both of you will stop having delusions about Carrick."

Why did Haming keep referring to Radi as a lady as though she were married to royalty?

"Carrick wants to marry her and make her empress," Haming said. "What do you say to that, Lady Radi? After all, you are his wife."

# CHAPTER 35

✦ ✦ ✦ ✦ ✦ ✦ ✦ ✦ ✦ ✦

Wife? The blood rushed to my head. It couldn't be.

"You and Carrick are married?"

"You face-shifting bastard," Radi spat at Haming. "I don't believe for a moment that Carrick would betray me."

"Believe it," Haming said. "Ask Rilla."

Radi sent me a desperate look. "Please tell me the androgy is lying. Carrick couldn't have asked you to be his empress. He promised to protect and cherish me as his wife for the rest of our lives."

I couldn't meet her gaze. "I'm sorry, Radi. He did ask me, but I turned him down. I don't love him, and I would never do anything to get in the way of your marriage."

"I don't believe it," Radi said. "This stupid androgy is trying to stir up trouble and create strife between us."

She regarded Haming with a glare. "I don't care what you say. If you think you'll get either Rilla or me to turn on him, you couldn't be more wrong. He'll be a better emperor than you any day."

Haming laughed. "There are many more revelations about Carrick to come. I've already sent Carrick the alert that we've taken over his safe house and have all of you as our guests. In exchange for your lives, he must come here alone and surrender himself to me. I'm willing to bet he won't risk his own life. You'll see he's nothing but the selfish, rotten seed of the monster that sired him. Then you can tell me if he still deserves your loyalty."

"Even if he doesn't come, I'd rather die than have you use me for my tin-chai," Radi said.

Haming gave her a look of pity. "I wish you would come to your senses. He isn't worth dying for. If Carrick doesn't show, and if you still don't come to my side, I'll take the baby and give her to a family to raise. You'll never see her again."

Without another word, he and the Lotuses left the room. The snick of a lock sounded on the other side of the door, preventing our escape.

I stared at Radi. I'd been so worried about her, but now my attention focused on the baby she bounced on her lap. The baby had stopped crying, and a gurgling laugh escaped her lips. Her features resembled Lady Arlyn's, except for her eyes. Those piercing, dark eyes reminded me of someone else. A suspicion weighed in my stomach. Lady Arlyn had refused to name the father, but the baby had the same eyes as Terran and all his sons. Including Carrick.

"I didn't think you'd come back here," Radi said. "Carrick told me that you were going to Fauxhemia to be with your family."

"That was the plan, until I thought I could help Carrick find the scepter," I said quietly. I nodded toward the baby. "What is her name?"

Radi looked me directly in the eye. "Cirisa. After her paternal grandmother."

"After Cirisa? Carrick's mama?" I choked back a gasp, overcome by emotions I couldn't name. "Carrick is the baby's father?" My voice trembled. "Carrick left Lady Arlyn to deal with the pregnancy on her own?"

Radi rocked the baby back and forth. Risa quieted. "Carrick said it was a mistake, but there was no way he could admit his guilt without jeopardizing his position. Terran would have killed him."

Everything made sense now. I remembered how he had been waiting for me at the Dark Palace so many afternoons. But he hadn't been waiting for me. He'd been with Arlyn, and he must have accompanied me on those walks to give Arlyn time to get rid of evidence that he'd been there. Then when I'd found out about Arlyn's pregnancy, I remembered he'd wanted me to give Arlyn medicine to make her miscarry. He said it was for my sake, so I wouldn't be embroiled in Arlyn's drama. But his real motive had been selfish.

My hands clenched into tight fists. "Limera killed Arlyn. Even then, Arlyn didn't reveal his name. She carried his secret to her grave."

"Arlyn knew giving up his name would ruin any hope of his succession to the throne," Radi said. Her tone was so practical. "Carrick kept his secret from everyone, including his bodyguard and androgy."

"Aiden doesn't know?" That surprised me, though I hoped it was true. If Aiden had known and never told me, it would be even harder to take than Carrick's betrayal. "But he followed Carrick everywhere in the palace."

Radi shook her head. "Not everywhere. There were times when Carrick assigned him on other missions. Aiden wasn't even involved in rescuing baby Risa. Carrick brought her here on his own. He asked me to look after her. That's when he confessed everything to me. He couldn't keep it quiet anymore. He felt so guilty about what happened to Arlyn."

"It doesn't make any of this right," I said.

I could never let Carrick take the scepter after this.

"You can't believe that," Radi said, the sparks of annoyance filling her tone. "You can't seriously be using one mistake to judge Carrick. You're letting Haming get to you."

"Did you know he faked his tin-chai amplification?" I asked Radi.

She paused, a hint of surprise in her gaze, but she shook it off. "And so what if he did? The Will of Heaven is an outdated tradition anyway. Would you rather see someone like Nelan take over? Or that despicable androgy?"

I shook my head. "No, but that doesn't mean Carrick is a right fit, either. Not after all the lies he's spouted."

Radi glared at me. "Are you saying this because you're angry he married me? He told me that you fell for him. Said there was no future with you, and he would tell you so if you came back. But I never expected you to actually return."

I rolled my eyes. "Of course, he would say such things to you."

"You have no right to be jealous of me. Not after everything I went through." A tremor broke through Radi's voice. "It can't be true what Haming said. Carrick can't make you his empress. You can't take him away. He is the one good thing that's happened to me. He promised he wouldn't have a harem like his father. Tell me you won't say yes to him."

"Oh, Radi." I wondered if the old Radi would ever return. This Radi was a stranger. "I have no plans to marry Carrick. Maybe I thought I was in love with him during the showcase, but now I see it was only a girlish infatuation. Besides, I've moved on. I only wish you hadn't believed—"

Tears streamed down Radi's face. I broke off. It wouldn't do any good to speak ill of Carrick now. Radi wasn't in the right mental state.

"I'm curious. How did you come to be married to him?" I asked.

"He married me to protect me and this child. If Nelan had won the throne, Carrick had instructed us to escape to Exentria, where family members on his maternal side are prominent government officials. If I presented our marriage certificate as evidence, he promised they would take me into their care. Then by Exentrik law, no one could force me to return to Seracedar. And if everyone believed the baby was my child, she wouldn't grow up ostracized."

Radi's gaze met mine. "No matter what anyone says, I know Carrick is a good man. With him, for the first time in my life, I feel wanted. And this baby makes me feel needed. They have become my family, and I will do anything to protect them."

"Don't you care that Carrick lied?" I was exasperated. Didn't she see how wrong he was? "He didn't receive the Will of Heaven, but he's pretending he did."

"If that's true, he did it out of necessity. I once told you we can't play by the rules if we're going to survive. The enemy doesn't care about fairness. I stand by Carrick's actions."

"What about asking me to marry him without telling me he's already married to you? Do you think he'll keep his promise of not having a harem?"

She winced. "I still don't believe he'd keep a harem. Even if he does, and even if he can't forget about you, I don't care. I don't need to be loved. Carrick wants me in his family, as his partner to raise his child. And Risa needs me. That's enough."

Was Radi so foolish to believe that? As emperor of Seracedar, he would be expected to take on concubines for political alliances. Was being needed without being loved truly enough for her?

"You don't understand how important it is to be treated like I still have value," she said. "After being trapped in that cage, my body no longer felt like mine. I still get trapped in my mind. Every night, I wake from the nightmares." She broke off, a sob choking in her throat, but she held me off before I could say anything and continued, her voice breathy and hollow. "After—after I got out, I reviled myself. No amount of washing made me feel clean enough. I felt like trash. I wanted to die, and there was a time I tried to end it all."

Tears pricked at my eyes, but I fought them back. She wouldn't want to see me cry for her. She wouldn't want to be pitied.

Radi had changed so much since our days in the showcase. I missed the bold friend I used to know. She had gone through so much trauma. I wished I could take away her pain.

"I'm so sorry, Radi." I didn't know what else to say.

"Carrick saved me," she said. "He got so angry at me for attempting to kill myself. Told me I owed him my life and I was more valuable to him alive than dead. He said all his friends were gone, and he felt alone. I was the only one he could talk to after the long days and nights of battles. He said he wanted to marry me, not just for my protection, but because he needed me. He wanted me to be Risa's mama. It's because of Carrick and Risa that I feel like I have a reason to keep living."

Needed. Wanted. That longing to be both was so familiar. I did understand the draw Carrick had on people. He made them feel like his life was intertwined with theirs, and without them, he was nothing. It was why Aiden felt loyal to him, why I had been caught up in his vulnerability and made it my duty to help Carrick ascend the throne. I couldn't fault Radi for how she felt. I wished Carrick had proven himself worthy. Believing Carrick needed her gave her life purpose. I couldn't contradict her.

We were silent. The child sat on Radi's lap and cooed. Radi made baby noises, and Risa giggled.

"I know it may sound strange, but I feel like I was meant to be her mama," Radi said. "I have never loved anyone this much. What was her mama like? I would like to know so I can preserve Lady Arlyn's memory and tell Risa one day."

"She was eccentric and mercurial. But she was kind. She helped me paint over the brand on my cheek that Limera gave me." I pointed to the number four on my face. "Most of all, she loved her child. I think she would be happy to know you're here to love Risa the way she would have."

Radi nodded. She brushed the tears away from her cheeks. "Let's not waste any more time arguing about Carrick. We have to break out of here. If not for our sake, then for Risa's. I refuse to let Haming hurt her. If we die, he might take her and use her tin-chai for his purposes, as Terran intended to do with us."

"I agree," I said. "We need to figure out a plan to escape."

Radi gave me a meaningful look. "I heard from Carrick that you were able to stop the vines in your novelty cage from whipping you. And I overheard Haming telling the Lotuses not to underestimate you because you defeated Irica and Terran by mastering the elements with your voice. What if you control the tree branches surrounding this house? You could break down the door and tie up the Lotuses."

I shook my head. "I haven't been able to control my tin-chai lately. I killed a family of moonrabbit shifters by accident. And the last time I sang, I unintentionally killed a Miyu. I can't take the chance of hurting you or Risa."

Radi regarded me for a moment. "The only way past Haming and those Lotuses is to use our tin-chai. Mine won't be helpful at the moment. You need to at least try."

"You don't understand. What if I kill you?"

"What if I said I trust you not to kill us? In fact, I know you won't." She peered down at the baby, her eyes filling with gentleness and protectiveness. "I discovered Risa's tin-chai. She's immune to other people's tin-chai. One of the Lotuses tried to use her tin-chai to make Risa fall asleep, but Risa kept crying. Didn't faze her at all."

That must have been what the Lotus had meant about the baby's crying.

"That doesn't make you immune," I said.

"The Lotus's tin-chai didn't work on me either. As long as I hold onto her, she will protect me, too."

I frowned. "Are you sure?"

"Why would I lie? I'd like you to try using your tin-chai, but not enough that I would jeopardize my own life. Attempt it on something small first." She pointed to a wooden hair stick that lay on the dresser next to us. "Move that."

I hesitated.

She scowled impatiently. "Unless you have any other ideas about how to escape Haming and the dozen Lotuses surrounding us, all of whom have powerful tin-chai, you need to stop doubting yourself."

Radi was right. I could see no other way of getting past them. Knowing I couldn't hurt her or Risa gave me some confidence.

Focusing on the hair stick, I sang a stanza.

*"The lady of the sea lost her one true love*
*Beneath the stormy, billowing swell*
*She pled with the waters for his return*
*'Til the sea surrendered a silver shell."*

The wooden stick twitched, then moved through the air. I caught it in the palm of my hand.

I gaped, my jaw falling open. *I did it.*

Looking back at Radi, I noticed her face was paler than it had been. "Are you okay?"

"Couldn't be better. Now we have a chance at escape."

It dawned on me. "Risa's shield tin-chai won't really protect you. You tricked me."

"Yes, you dummy," she said. "If I hadn't, we'd still be sitting here not knowing your tin-chai is actually functional. I was willing to bet you could do it, but if you killed me, I knew you'd be guilt ridden and take care of the baby for me."

"Thank you," I said.

"Stop wasting time talking. Summon tree roots, break through the door, and let's send those Lotuses into the underworld where they belong."

I concentrated on the tree roots that made up the house, placing my wyis into the words I sang. I had been able to move the hair stick, used my tin-chai without hurting anyone. I could do it again.

*"The lady of the sea waded through the tide*
*To seek the one comfort she could find*
*At long last the sea yielded to her request*
*The weeping waves heaved one final sigh."*

Vines curled up from the foundation of the house and burst through the front door.

My heart pounded, and I wanted to cry in relief. My tin-chai was coming back to me.

The Lotuses jumped and whirled around, rushing toward us. With newfound confidence, I sang louder.

The tree roots tied themselves around both Lotuses standing guard and ripped them limb from limb. Their dying screams filled the air. I grabbed one of the dead Lotus's swords from the ground.

We took off for the surrounding forest. Shouts sounded behind us, but we didn't wait to see who was chasing us. Dawn pushed into the horizon, spreading its light through the tips of the trees.

But a shadow descended, blocking our path. Androgy Haming.

We turned the opposite way. Too slow. Haming twirled through the air and landed in front of us. His attention was aimed at Radi.

"Watch out!" I shouted.

Radi wasn't fast enough. Haming pushed her, and the baby fell from her arms. Haming caught Risa. A Lotus grabbed Radi, and the two of them scuffled.

A second Lotus charged at me. No longer did I fear using my tin-chai. I sang at a tree root and used it to trip her. Before she could get up, I bound her with it and pointed my sword at her.

"Enough," Androgy Haming said. He stood fifteen feet to my right. Behind him was another Lotus.

The androgy raised Risa in the air. "I'd hate to use this innocent child to force you to stop."

I froze. "Don't harm her." The Lotus who had been fighting Radi had cornered my friend behind Haming. The Lotus put a knife to Radi's neck.

I turned back to the Lotus I'd bound, but she'd disappeared. Yet, the tree root was still tied tight. I thrust my sword forward and heard a grunt. The Lotus was still there, but she was invisible.

"Let the sister go," Haming told me. "I promise she won't hurt you, and I won't restrain you again. I just want you to listen to me without interruption. Without singing. But try anything, and I'll have Radi killed."

The Lotus I'd tripped revealed herself again. I pulled the sword away from her and unbound her. She scrambled up and shuffled toward Androgy Haming. Now he had three Lotuses, including the one who held a knife to Radi. There was no way I could take them all down.

"There. That wasn't so hard, right?" Androgy Haming said. He tickled the baby's belly. She stopped crying and let out a giggle instead.

"Please don't hurt Cirisa." Radi struggled against her captor. The sister Lotus brought the blade closer to Radi's neck, making her wince.

"Stop moving," the Lotus growled. The other two Lotuses grabbed Radi's arms, further restraining her.

"I never said I'd harm this innocent child," Haming said. He bounced the baby in his arms. She giggled again. "See? She likes me. I would never kill such a cute thing. But if you don't cooperate with me, I'll take her far away, never to be seen again. She'll never know her true identity. Don't test me."

I debated whether to try singing anyway, but there was too much at stake. I wouldn't be able to sing fast enough to summon branches to attack them all at once. "I won't sing, I promise. But you need to let Radi and the baby go."

"All in good time," Haming said. He smiled. "I think our guest is here. Soon, you'll hear the truth from his lips."

Behind Haming, the trees moved, and a man jumped down from the branches.

Carrick. He'd come for us after all. His low dangerous voice echoed through the forest. "Release them."

# CHAPTER 36

✦ ✦ ✦ ✦ ✦ ✦ ✦ ✦ ✦ ✦

The prince stalked toward us silently, glaring at Haming.

Haming pivoted to face Carrick. "Ah, Your Highness, so you've finally come to join us. I was starting to doubt that you would."

Carrick spat. "You didn't give me any choice, did you? Don't hurt my daughter."

Haming rocked the baby in his arms. Amazing enough, Risa cooed at him. The androgy made a clucking noise back at her. "I have to admit, the baby princess is adorable. I think we may have bonded. It's too bad her father is a liar and a coward. In that respect, she and I are similar. Perhaps I'll take her to another family to raise after all. She'd be better off."

"Give her back to me," Carrick said, moving forward.

"Nah, ah." Haming shook his head. "Not another step. I wouldn't hurt a baby, but I can't say the same about your wife. Lay down your weapon. If you make one false move, Radi will die."

Radi made another sound of pain. Blood trickled down the blade that the Lotus held to her neck.

"Carrick, just do what he asks," I said, curling my hands into fists.

Carrick stopped ten feet away from Haming and the three Lotuses. He unhooked the hilt of his sword from his belt and laid the weapon on the ground, then stood slowly and raised his hands in surrender. "I'm here as you requested. Let them go."

Haming laughed. "Are you certain your loyal bodyguard didn't come with you? Excuse me. I forget, he's not your servant anymore but the lost Emberwood prince. Who would have known his position is as elevated as yours? Some may say even higher than yours, since he isn't just the son of his father's concubine."

"I told no one," Carrick said, not rising to the bait. "Not even Aiden."

"It would not be wise to trust a liar." Haming continued scanning the trees behind Carrick. "But I can't feel his wyis. Unless he has learned to hide it as I have."

"Stop wasting time. I've already told you, he isn't here," Carrick said. "Tell me what you want."

"I want you to admit all your sins," Haming said. "First to the women you claim to love. I want to watch them turn on you. Let them hear your confessions in your own words. How you let Lady Arlyn die and refused to acknowledge your own child. And how you promised to make Rilla your empress even though you already married Radi."

"Radi and I already talked about that," I said. "We know Carrick is far from perfect, but we aren't going to turn on him or let you harm Cirisa."

"I want the shameless bastard to admit it himself," Haming said. "I want him to admit he's as monstrous as his father. That he's not deserving of the throne."

Carrick's face was filled with shame and guilt. "I couldn't tell anyone about Arlyn. It was a mistake. I'll never forgive myself for what happened to her." His eyes focused on me. "Rilla, I only married Radi because I thought it was the only way I could protect her. And Cirisa needed a mother to raise her."

Tears fell down Radi's face. Carrick couldn't meet Radi's gaze.

"I'm sorry, Radi. I mean to keep my promise to care for you, but I love Rilla. I shouldn't have led you to believe otherwise, but I didn't think you could take it."

I wished I could scream at Carrick.

But calling him names would do nothing to save us now. Haming wouldn't be satisfied until he had turned me to his side, and he thought Carrick's confessions would convince me. I had to make him release Radi and Risa.

A breeze picked up behind me, and a faint smell reached my nose. The menthol from carob bark balm. I'd know it anywhere. That was Aiden's scent. He was here.

Had Carrick told Aiden to come with him? Or had Aiden followed him secretly?

It didn't matter as long as Haming didn't suspect. If I could make Haming release the baby, then I had to trust Aiden would take on the Lotus holding Radi captive. That left Carrick, but he could handle himself.

Carrick gazed at me with sad eyes. "You must forgive me. I hope you understand. Radi is your best friend, and I thought you'd want me to—"

"Enough," I said.

"I won't keep a harem like my father or grandfather. It will only be the two of you."

"You're delusional if you still think I'll marry you," I said. "I already told you that I don't want to marry you. I don't love you. But I thought I could support you as a friend and help you take the throne. Yet that's no longer possible either. You're a chronic liar. We already know about how you faked your tin-chai amplification. You might as well admit that, too."

Carrick's gaze sharpened. "H—how did—never mind. I don't need to explain myself to anyone. I did what I had to do for the sake of this kingdom."

I heard Radi's barely audible whisper: "No. It can't be true."

"Haming gave you a fake scepter," I said.

"What?" Carrick jolted in surprise.

Haming laughed. "I foolishly thought you'd play by the rules, and once everyone saw that you and Nelan both failed to acquire the Will of Heaven, it would be the end of Terran's line. I could fake my own tin-chai amplification and take the throne. I didn't expect you to have the same idea. Guess I underestimated you."

I glared at Haming. "He admitted all his faults. Let them go."

"Oh, but I saved the best for last." Haming's gaze narrowed on Carrick. "I have a theory. One I developed after you faked your tin-chai amplification. But I need you to confirm it. I think it was years ago when you discovered you could summon a full storm and direct it to the location of your choosing. Yet you hid this ability from everyone, making them think you aren't as powerful as you truly are and that your tin-chai only has one layer—the simple ability to summon lightning."

"Fine, I admit it," Carrick said. "But as I said, I did what I had to for the sake of the kingdom. If I had revealed the full extent of my power, my brothers would have thought I was a bigger threat. They would have targeted me even more. I had to keep it a secret to survive all these years."

"I'm not finished," Haming said. "During my years of pretending to be an androgy for your father, I collected a lot of information about all the princes. Eight years ago, you journeyed to the south alone, after your mother became a novelty. You tried to free her, so Terran punished you. Sent you away for four months. You stayed at a monastery, under another name, to train your physical fighting abilities and strengthen your wyis. It was also the same year of the tidal wave that destroyed Cascasea Village. Everyone believed it was because the three moons aligned, but that wouldn't have created a tidal wave so destructive on its own. Not without the misfortune of an added storm at the same time."

"What exactly are you implying?" Carrick said. I took note that although he tried to maintain his cool, a quiver of nervousness entered his tone.

"As a prince of Seracedar, you have studied the kingdom's history inside and out. You must have learned how natural disasters occurred around the time of a dynasty's end, signaling Old Grandfather Heaven's displeasure. Someone with a storm-summoning tin-chai could have created the conditions to exacerbate the tidal wave."

"Stop talking *now*," Carrick growled.

Storm summoning tin-chai? The air in my lungs felt like it had been sucked out completely. I knew where Haming was going with this, but I couldn't believe it.

"No, I don't think I shall stop," Haming replied. "Because I think Rilla should know what I think. I'm sure she's curious."

"I said, shut your mouth," Carrick shouted.

Haming looked me in the eye. "Carrick made sure to create a storm that would generate a tidal wave big enough to flood the Port of Cascasea. All for the sake of discrediting his father. He killed all of those innocent people."

# CHAPTER 37

✦ ✦ ✦ ✦ ✦ ✦ ✦ ✦ ✦ ✦

I shook my head, stunned.

"Don't listen to him, Rilla," Radi said. "I don't believe it, and you must not either."

She gasped in pain as the Lotus jostled her. "How many times must you be warned to hold your tongue?"

I didn't want to believe it, but the guilt on Carrick's face said everything.

"How could you?" I shook my head. "So many innocent people were killed. My family would have died if we'd gone to the port that day."

"I did it to make everyone see my father's time in power needed to come to an end," Carrick said. "I did it for the good of the kingdom."

"You did it for yourself," I said. "You don't deserve to sit on the throne."

"Don't say that." Carrick's desperate eyes searched my face. "You know my goal has always been to bring prosperity back to this kingdom. I'm nothing like my father. You told me that once."

"You've proven me wrong." I gave him a cold look. I did hate him for what he'd done but not enough to align with Haming. I just had to sound angry enough to fool Haming into believing I'd turned to his side. "Haming is right. I should have never aligned myself with you. You deserve to pay for all the lies and the deaths you caused. For betraying me with Arlyn and now Radi."

I sang two notes, breaking a branch off a tree behind Carrick, and before he could react, I twined it around Carrick's neck.

"Finally, you've come to see reason, child," Haming said. "I knew you would." He came to stand beside me.

Carrick stared at me in disbelief. "You would kill me and side with Haming? He's threatened to kill my child. She is innocent."

"I don't care," I said. "She is the product of your betrayal with Arlyn. All that time, you played me as a fool. I fancied myself in love with you, and you let me think you came to the Dark Palace to see me. You made sure I'd never suspect you were there for Arlyn."

"It happened before I realized I was in love with you," he said. "You have to believe me. I never loved anyone the way I love you. I need you. Without you, I'll lose myself."

"You used me, is what you did. I risked my own life for Arlyn, for you, and for this bastard child, and you didn't care about me at all." I sang two more notes and let the branch tighten around him. His face turned red.

"End this now," Haming said. "Kill him. Do it." His grip on Risa loosened. He stepped forward, coming toward me in his excitement and away from the Lotuses.

Now was my chance.

I sang two notes, then screamed, putting all my power into the branch around Carrick. It twisted and turned, whipping toward Haming's face. Surprised, he whirled away. At the same time, I directed my wyis at another branch from the tree behind Carrick. It snapped off with little effort, and I directed it toward Risa, wrapping it around her tiny body. The branch caught her up and grabbed her away from Haming. I caught her in my arms. I barely had time to check that she was unharmed when an arrow zinged through the air and pierced the Lotus carrying the knife through the heart.

The other two Lotuses holding Radi's arms shrieked and let go of her to shield themselves.

The Lotus who had been shot gasped and gurgled. She released Radi and fell to the ground. Radi screamed and ran toward me. Blood pooled from the fatal wound and mingled with the dirt, turning it crimson.

Aiden jumped down from the trees. He shot an arrow at Haming, but the androgy dodged.

"You followed me?" Carrick asked. "How much did you hear?"

Aiden growled. "Enough to know I placed my faith in the wrong person and wasted my loyalty. But don't worry. Like Rilla, I'm not about to let Haming win either."

"Wrong decision, both of you," Haming said. "No matter. I'll kill the bastard myself."

Haming flew at Carrick. Carrick dove to the ground, grabbed his sword, and met with Haming's blade with not a second to spare. Aiden fired a blast at Haming, but the androgy dodged low. His blade deflected the firebomb, and he rolled onto the ground, managing to avoid Carrick's descending blow. Haming jumped into the trees. Aiden and Carrick pursued.

Carrick was no match for Haming alone, but with Aiden, the two of them might have a chance.

The two remaining Lotuses had recovered from the shock of their sister's death. They approached Radi and me. I sang, summoning two roots to spring from the ground. The sisters disappeared. The invisibility tin-chai.

"I've got this," Radi said. She raised her hands to the sky and moved her feet back and forth quickly. Sparks of light dusted down, and like magnets, they gravitated toward the two Lotuses, outlining the tops of their heads.

I redirected the roots and heard the sisters trip and fall. They turned visible again. I used the roots to tie them up.

"Impressive," I said to Radi.

"You're not the only one who discovered more layers to their tin-chai." Radi, tossing her hair back on her shoulders, was a semblance of the old, confident Radi I'd once known.

She picked up the blade the Lotus had held to her neck and pointed it at the two women. "I'll kill you quickly if you answer my questions. But if you refuse to talk, I'll drag this out with great pleasure. I thought the holy Lotuses and Crocuses are not supposed to involve themselves in politics. Why and how many of you have joined forces with Haming?"

"Hah, like we'd tell you," one of them said and spat onto Radi's shoe.

"Wrong answer." Radi sliced the dagger against the Lotus's cheek. The sister shrieked.

Blood dripped through Radi's fingers, but she merely wiped it off on her clothes.

The other Lotus trembled. "Don't kill me. I'll answer. There are others like us around the kingdom. Only Lotuses qualify to become Haming's followers, and he chooses us. We share this mark to know who we are, Haming's disciples." She nodded to the brooch pinned to her lapel. It was shaped like a bird with a sword in its mouth.

"There are no Crocuses?" I asked. "Why not?"

"Because men would never identify with our suffering. Only women know the burden of being a woman. Both of you would understand. You have more in common with us than you believe."

"What are you talking about?" Radi said.

"We've suffered at the hands of Yikan and Terran. We were the lucky ones who escaped. The monastery was the only place we could go to be safe. Although we have taken our vows, we set ourselves apart from the Lotuses and Crocuses who only swear to Old Grandfather Heaven. They don't even know of our existence or that we've made a separate oath to Androgy Haming. Then he chose a select few of us to follow you. We went to Tinsai Monastery, drugged the real Dahlia Nin and a few of her Lotuses and took their places right before you came so we could spy on you. None of the sisters already in residence took notice until we were long gone and on your trail in the mountains."

I saw blood on her brooch. These Lotuses had used blood magic, too. But I saw no signs of age on their faces, unlike the consequences of Carrick's hair whitening or Haming's scars. Was it because they believed in their cause? Because they truly believed they were doing the right thing, and therefore, their intent was not evil or selfish?

"The design of the brooch on your robe—" I said, "—it's not on all of the Lotuses, only on the Lotuses who follow Haming. Which means the Lotuses Haming has chosen have one thing in common. That bird represents what you once were, doesn't it? Trapped in cages in Cedar Palace for the pleasure of the emperor."

Radi's hand shook, and the blade slipped from her grasp. "You were baubles?"

The Lotus nodded. "Some of us were baubles, and others were novelties. This bird represents our shared trauma. We support Haming because he understands. He was one of us. He was a bauble."

"A bauble?" I repeated. "I've never known men to be caged."

"He didn't always exist in his current form," the Lotus said. "He was born as royalty—a princess, the older sister to Terran. It was Terran who put his own sister in a cage and then burned her alive. But the princess escaped and took on a new identity at the monastery to help others like us. She became a Lotus. A few years later, she took on

Haming's form to spy on Terran. That is why we follow Androgy Haming. He is the last remaining descendant of the royal family who actually deserves the throne."

"Princess?" Mama had been rescued by a princess who could change faces. And Haming told me that he had known my mama. The pieces all fell into place. Haming was the princess who had traded places with Mama. If not for him, Mama wouldn't have survived. I wouldn't have been born.

"I don't care who Haming was in the past," Radi said.

I barely heard her, but I forced myself to focus. Even though Haming had saved Mama, it didn't mean he wouldn't harm us now. He had tried to kill us many times.

"Whatever good you think you're doing, it doesn't excuse killing innocent people," Radi said. Her voice shook. "Threatening an innocent baby. Haming worked with Empress Limera. Helped her torture and kill. And you supported him." She glared at the Lotuses. "I won't let you destroy Carrick. Not when he's worked so hard to take the throne. I'm going to kill you and expose all of you across the kingdom. Anyone wearing that symbol. Once the real Crocuses and Lotuses realize you've betrayed your oath to Old Grandfather Heaven, they will renounce you. You won't be able to hide any longer."

"Please don't," the Lotus cried. "If you expose the others, they won't have anywhere to go. No one will take them. They will be scorned for their past. They'll be penniless. They'll die of starvation. A ruined woman has no place in society, even if she had no choice in what happened to herself. I thought, of all people, you would understand."

The Lotus gave Radi a pleading look. "I heard you cry out. The nightmares never go away."

"If he helped you, then why didn't he help me?" Radi shook and fell to her knees. "I tried to escape from the showcase. I would have succeeded, but Haming caught me. He turned me in. He's the reason I was punished and became a bauble. Why would he let that happen to me if he chose to save others?"

Tears fell down her cheeks. I had no words.

Shouts came from above. Haming jumped through the trees past us. Close behind were Aiden and Carrick.

"Take the baby back to the palace, and tell them to send reinforcements," I told Radi.

"What about you?" Radi asked.

"I'm going to help them catch Haming."

"And them?" Radi gestured toward the Lotuses.

"We'll leave them tied up here."

Radi gave me a look, and before I could stop her, she grabbed both Lotuses' heads and bashed them against one another, knocking them unconscious. "We can't take the chance of them getting loose. Now we can leave them."

She took off down the path.

I raced toward the fight. Haming matched Aiden and Carrick, blow for blow, but he was slowing down. His face was pale and dotted with sweat. Perhaps he was the superior fighter if he fought Aiden or Carrick one on one but not when they worked together. I couldn't let them kill him. Didn't he deserve a chance at redemption? After all, he had saved Mama and taken on her punishment for himself.

"Stop fighting," I shouted, but the three were too engrossed in battle to hear.

I harnessed my wyis into the ground and sang. The earth shook. Pebbles rose into the air and swirled around the battle scene. The three men stopped and stumbled as the ground quaked beneath them.

I redirected my wyis into the trees, bringing a vine to wrap around Haming's legs. He tripped and fell to the ground. I disarmed him, and his sword fell.

Carrick charged at him, but I wrapped another branch around his sword, taking it from his hand. He glared at me. "What are you doing?"

Aiden let his sword fall to his side. "Rilla, it's not that I don't trust you, but I'm wondering the same thing. Why are you stopping us?"

"Now's our chance to finish him," Carrick said. "Unless you've changed your alliance."

"I'm not on his side or yours," I said. "You and Haming both lied and killed for the sake of power. I'm willing to give you a second chance, just as I think Haming deserves. Not to take the throne but to live."

I directed my gaze at Haming. "I know you're the princess who saved my mama's life. You took her place in the cage, and Terran must have turned you into a bauble."

Aiden gaped. "That must be why you hate him so much."

"You figured it out," Haming said. His skin shimmered and shifted, his muscles stretching. The androgy's face grew grotesque. Burned flesh. Disfigured. I stifled the surprised sound in my throat and tried not to look alarmed.

"Don't bother covering up your disgust," Haming said. "I know I look revolting. If I do not consume the flesh of a Miyu's tail once every five years, these scars will show no matter whose face I wear. Using blood magic worsens the pain. But this is my true form. I once was known as Princess Muriella."

"Muriella?" Carrick said. "Father Emperor's older sister? It can't be. You were killed in an accidental fire."

Haming snarled. "That fire was no accident. I was supposed to marry an Exentrik official with the hopes of an alliance. Yikan was already near his last days, but he wished to form political ties with Exentria. When Terran found out I had changed places with a trinket from his father's showcase, he burned my cage with me in it. If Yikan would have found out Terran had ruined me and his ambitions, Terran would have been killed."

"But you escaped," I said. "And you went to the monastery. You've been helping others who escaped the palace. That was noble. I don't understand why you didn't let Radi escape when you knew what her punishment would be."

"I needed to catch Radi so Limera would continue to trust me," Haming said. "My only mistake was actually falling for Limera. She had once been a kind woman. I allowed the image of her old self to get in the way of who she had become. I let her lead me on with promises that she would reveal the scepter when I should have threatened her early on. Then, I might have figured out she no longer had it."

The former princess laughed a bitter sound. "My goal was to ruin Terran and any of his remaining sons. And to take the throne for myself. I deserve it. If I had been born a son, I would have taken the scepter and proven my right to rule instead of Terran."

"But that's not how the scepter works," Carrick said.

Aiden nodded. "Even if you were born a son, Old Grandfather Heaven may not have bestowed the Will of Heaven upon you."

"I don't care," Haming said. "Old Grandfather Heaven is a myth. As long as I had the scepter, I could have tricked the fools in this kingdom into bowing to me."

I shook my head in pity. He didn't hear the hypocrisy in his words. "You saved my mama, and I am thankful. But you have become like Terran as much as you try to deny it. You certainly are no better than Carrick."

"You've won," Haming said. "All I ask is that you don't let Carrick kill me. You do it yourself. With your voice. You sound like your mama. She could heal and kill like you."

I gasped. "She could?" I had the same tin-chai as Mama? No

wonder she had always feared it. She must have foreseen all the trouble I'd have once I exposed it to the world.

Haming smiled, and a distant look came into his eyes. "You look so much like her. I remember her with fondness. We became fast friends. She encouraged me to run away and make my own path. I would have escaped, but I came back for her when I found out she was thrown into a cage."

Aiden shouted. "Rilla."

A glint drew my eye back to Haming. He moved so fast, I barely saw the hidden dagger he slipped out from his sleeve. Barely registered the shimmering diamond embedded in it, covered in blood.

Not until he disappeared from sight.

Aiden charged at where Haming had been, but his sword met empty air. The root that had bound his legs had been cut.

"No!" I screamed, running to get to Carrick. The last of Terran's line, he would be Haming's first target.

Aiden got there first. The horror played out, seemingly in slow motion. Aiden blocked Carrick, and an invisible dagger plunged into Aiden's chest.

Blood poured from his body. *No, not Aiden. Please no.*

With the dagger embedded in Aiden, Haming let go of the hilt and became visible again.

I roared a song, anger filling my words. This time, I aimed to kill.

*"You remain in your dark cave,*
*But I'll shine with the stars above*
*Your sins will hold your heart a slave*
*Until you finally learn to love."*

Haming froze, his skin melting away to expose blood, then muscle, and then a skeleton. He was dead. Crumpled bones, paper-thin like autumn leaves.

I kicked away Haming's fallen dagger and rushed to Aiden. "You cannot die. Do you hear me, Aiden?"

Carrick kneeled by my side. He ripped a piece of cloth from his robe and handed it to me. "Use this."

I placed the cloth on the wound and applied pressure. Blood soaked my hands and clothes.

Aiden's eyes opened, the barest of slits. I touched the pendant around my neck. He had put it together for me. I couldn't imagine a world without him.

"You'll get through this," I said. "Stay with me."

"I was there behind you all along, and my spirit will be with you from now on."

"No!" I said. "I want you. Alive."

Aiden's breathing grew more ragged. "Rilla, I . . . lo . . . lo . . ."

His head fell limply to the side.

"Aiden!" I screamed.

He was still breathing. He could still make it.

"Carrick," I shouted. "Help me carry him. We have to get him to a doctor."

"There's no time to take him to a doctor," Carrick said. "He's fading."

He stood, looking away.

"He saved your life," I said. "He regarded you as his friend. But I suppose you only ever regarded him as your slave. A life to be sacrificed for your benefit."

"Do you believe me to be that callous?" Carrick slowly rotated back toward me. Tears streamed down his cheeks. "If we move him now, he won't make it. There's only one person who can save him. *You.*"

I hesitated. I had to sing. But could I do it? What if I killed him?

"It's the only way," Carrick said. "If you don't, then he will die.

Hurry, we're running out of time."

I replayed the memory of when Aiden and I were traveling together, how he'd encouraged me when my tin-chai failed, and all the times he'd believed in me when I hadn't believed in myself.

Aiden's voice rang clear in my head: *"I don't believe for a moment you've lost your ability to heal. I know it's inside you because that's who you are. You are a healer, and you always will be."*

"I love you," I whispered. I kissed his forehead. "I won't let you die."

# CHAPTER 38

✦ ✦ ✦ ✦ ✦ ✦ ✦ ✦ ✦ ✦

I detected Aiden's wyis and pulled it into me, letting it flow into my soul, bright and sunny, always giving. When I parted my lips, the words of a familiar song poured into my head.

*"The lady of the sea waded through the tide*
*To seek the one comfort she could find*
*At long last the sea yielded to her request*
*The weeping waves heaved one final sigh."*

I paused, watching him closely. He hadn't turned into dust. But there was still so much blood. I continued singing, praying the words to Old Grandfather Heaven.

The gaping hole in his chest closed. The blood faded, evaporating into the air like morning mist. Aiden's skin regenerated, the blackened, mutilated pieces smoothing out until there was no trace of a scar. But he still looked pale as death.

*"The lady of the sea saw her love again*
*He called her name, and she took his hand*
*They waltzed into the sunset, ne'er to look back*
*At the treasures left buried in the sand."*

I heard the beat of his steady pulse, felt the strum of his heartbeat beneath the palm of my hand. His cold skin turned warm once more.

His breathing eased. Finally, those golden eyes fluttered open.

"Aiden?" I called.

His clouded gaze focused, and he homed in on me. "Well," he said, his voice still hoarse, "that didn't go at all as I'd planned."

I embraced him tightly and kissed his neck. Tears of relief streamed down my cheeks. I never wanted to let him go.

Carrick's hand dug into my arm. "Enough," he said, pulling me away from Aiden. "You forget your place. You belong to me."

I whirled to face him. "I am not yours. I will never be yours."

Carrick's grip on me tightened. "I know you're angry about the things I did to secure my rightful place on the throne. I had no choice. But I won't let you leave me. You are mine whether you like it or not."

"No, she is not yours." Aiden struggled to rise. He grabbed Carrick's arm, pulling him off me.

"This isn't your place," Carrick said. "You saved my life. But I wouldn't expect this betrayal from one who I considered a friend."

"Friend? Betrayal?" Aiden scoffed. "I thought you regarded me as your friend, your brother. But how many secrets have you hidden? It's clear I placed my trust in the wrong person."

"If you believe that, why did you bother saving my life?"

"I thought you had enough honor to admit your faults. Today was my last act of friendship. I have paid my debt."

Carrick stood taller, crowding Aiden in. "But I am the emperor of Seracedar."

Aiden didn't move. He looked Carrick straight in the eye, and in a clear, calm voice, declared, "And I am the prince of Emberwood. Let Rilla go, or you will find Emberwood your enemy. You cannot afford a war when Seracedar is so weak."

Carrick laughed. "Your father would not agree to go to war over a woman." He grabbed me again.

"I suggest Your Majesty let go of the lady." A new voice broke through the stillness. I turned to find Welder sauntering toward us. "Rilla is the future princess of Emberwood, consort to Prince Langdon, known to you as Aiden. If they do not return to Emberwood, this would certainly be a reason for King Ashbel to wage war upon you."

"Consort?" Carrick looked between us. "You are married?"

I couldn't mask my surprise either. True, the gossip in Emberwood was that Aiden and I were betrothed, but how was lying about a fake marriage going to make Carrick let me go?

Carrick dropped my arm, shock overcoming his features. "You must be bluffing."

Welder waved a document in his hand. "I have a copy of their marriage document. The king and queen have the original copy with them."

It was indeed a document of my marriage to the prince of Emberwood. My signature, as well as Aiden's, was scrawled upon it. The seal of Emberwood was stamped at the bottom. It couldn't be real, but it looked authentic. He must have used his tin-chai to make it.

Welder rolled the parchment back up. "I am certain the palace advisors and aristocrats would not approve of your politics or of their emperor stealing the consort of another kingdom's leader. Emberwood has long been at odds with Seracedar, but with Aiden as their newly returned prince, your kingdoms have a chance at rebuilding your relationship."

"I know you have the ability to transform objects," Carrick said. "The marriage document has to be a falsification. Look, Rilla seems as surprised as I am."

"Well, believe it," Aiden said, not missing a beat. "In case something happened to me, I wanted to ensure she would be well taken care of. I signed all the marriage documents before I left Emberwood and tricked Rilla into signing them, too. She had no idea."

"How could you?" Carrick growled. "You promised you wouldn't act on your feelings. You knew she was mine."

I finally found my voice. "I was never yours. I never wanted to be trapped in the palace as your empress, unable to fulfill my dream of becoming a healer."

"What if I didn't make you give up your dream?" Carrick said.

I shook my head. "I don't want to marry you because I don't love you. You aren't the man I thought you were."

I regarded Aiden, my eyes shining with admiration. "But I *have* fallen in love with my friend, a man who has never tried to control me."

Aiden stood tall, coming up to Carrick. "I shouldn't have yielded to you. I'm done being the one you blame when things don't go your way."

Aiden looked directly into my eyes. "I won't hide myself or my true feelings again. I declare my love for her loudly and proudly."

Welder stepped in front of Aiden and me and spoke to Carrick. "While we can't prove the scepter in your hands is a fake, gossip can do enough harm if spread through the kingdom."

Carrick growled at him. "I don't appreciate your threats."

"Not a threat. The truth," Welder said. "I am saddened to see the boy who tried to escape the shadow of his father has failed. But you are no longer my concern. I have been charged with protecting the prince and his bride, and I shall not fail."

The echoes of footsteps sounded around us. Boots marching. *The palace guards must be here.*

Welder smirked. "My men and your palace guards will be here in a few seconds. For your sake, I suggest you grant us safe passage from your kingdom. You have enough on your hands with trying to locate the real scepter. I doubt you have time to instigate a tiff with Emberwood at the same time."

"You are free to go," Carrick said. He looked defeated, but he whirled around to face Aiden and me. "From this day forward, I have nothing to do with either of you. We are no longer friends, and if any Ember comes into my kingdom again, they will be considered an enemy."

With those words, Welder's men and two dozen Seracedarean soldiers marched in and came around us. Welder's men also brought the carriage.

Daki came up to Carrick. "Where are Haming and his followers?"

I pointed at Haming's skeleton.

Daki stopped at the sight and winced. "I see you took care of the threat on your own. That's a relief."

"The Embers must return to their kingdom at once," Carrick said. "My men will escort me back to the palace."

He flipped his robe and strode away without a backward glance. The palace soldiers followed, some looking bewildered.

Daki hesitated, glancing at us with uncertainty. "I've chosen to stay and rebuild Seracedar."

"Are you sure you've thought this through?" Welder asked.

"I will see to it that Seracedar is restored to its former glory," Daki said. "I know you told me Carrick has lied, but I still have hope in him."

Welder shook his head. "I think you're making a mistake."

"Perhaps he will change for the better," Daki said. "For his older brother's sake, the honorable Prince Taimin, I cannot forsake Carrick yet."

Aiden nodded. "So be it, my friend. If you change your mind, Emberwood is open to you."

Daki bowed and turned around, following the Seracedarean soldiers.

Welder gestured to his men. "It's time to go home."

# CHAPTER 39

✦ ✦ ✦ ✦ ✦ ✦ ✦ ✦ ✦ ✦

We rode on horseback as we returned to Emberwood through the forest. Although we had a carriage, I needed the fresh air. Aiden rode alongside me. He didn't say a word. Welder and his team of seven men rode in front of and behind us, with one of the men driving the carriage.

I hated to leave without saying goodbye to Radi, but it couldn't be helped. We had to leave in case Carrick changed his mind. Besides, Radi was Carrick's legitimate wife, which now made us enemies as well.

Welder came up to us on his horse. "We should talk. I highly advise we make this marriage a truth as soon as possible. It's the only way to ensure Rilla is protected from Carrick."

"I do not appreciate being manipulated," Aiden said. "I refuse to let anyone, including you, use my relationship with Rilla for politics."

"It was the only way he would let go of Rilla, and you know it." Welder rode tall and straight-backed, his expression unrepentant. "All marriages, especially those made in a royal family, are political."

"Political or not, whether Aiden and I end up married doesn't affect you unless you've got another motive," I said. "What is it you really want?"

Welder made a sound that was half surprise, half laughter. "You are quite direct now, aren't you?"

I looked straight into his eyes. "Forgive my skepticism, but I want to make sure you're not pretending to be our friend. I find it hard to believe you'd care this much about getting me back to Emberwood and married to Aiden if it wasn't for the scepter."

I didn't know what his intentions were, but I'd be a fool to trust him so easily. He could want to find the chosen ruler and grow his own power. A man like him might have ambitions to control the ruler behind the scenes. After all, he'd stolen the scepter to try to control the Will of Heaven on his own. Tried to play the role of Old Grandfather Heaven.

"What are you talking about?" Aiden asked. "I thought Welder lost the scepter. What does it have to do with you?"

I brought out the flute from my cloak. "I have the true scepter. The flute I found on Hara's island is the scepter. Welder lost it when he fled from Hara. He believes Old Grandfather Heaven charged me with finding it so I could bring it to the next rightful ruler."

Aiden stared at the flute. His jaw dropped. "Why didn't you tell me?"

"I told her not to," Welder said. "I thought you would have insisted on bringing it to Carrick. In fact, you wouldn't have believed him capable of all his sins had you not heard it from his lips for yourself. At first, I was angry that you took off alone to follow Carrick. By the time I read your note and assembled my men to follow, I feared it was too late. But now I see that the timing was impeccable."

"Impeccable?" Aiden repeated. "I almost died. I know it was my decision to follow Carrick alone, but you might have come a little sooner, before Haming nearly killed me."

"In the end, it was fortunate. Old Grandfather Heaven always has a reason for the way things turn out. Rilla recovered her healing tin-chai, and both of you are no longer under Carrick's manipulation. I've accomplished my mission. And in answer to you, Rilla, I'm not pretending to be your friend because of the scepter. I have no designs for power. I am simply trying to do what is best to protect you and Prince Langdon because it's my job. Whether you believe me or not is your choice."

With that, he rode up to the front, leaving us behind.

I watched Aiden's face. His eyes were puffy with exhaustion, and his lips pressed together in a thin line.

"I won't bother asking if you're okay because I know you're not," I said. "But if you need to talk about what happened, about Carrick, I'm here for you."

Aiden didn't return my gaze. He closed his eyes and breathed out a long exhale. "I don't know what to say. He was my best friend. I—I thought I knew him. Did you know I could have left the palace years ago? Escaped on my own. But I chose to stay because I believed in Carrick and his cause. I don't know what hurts more, his actual betrayal, or knowing I was a fool for trusting him."

I rode closer to him and touched his arm. "You are no fool. You're a better man than anyone I know. Loyal, honest, and caring. He is the fool."

"Perhaps so," Aiden said. "Which makes it all the worse. Because even though he broke our trust first, I still admit I care about what happens to him. I don't want to see him continue down the wrong path and bring Seracedar to ruin. And I hope Emberwood never goes to war with him. I don't wish to fight him, but these are my people and my family at stake. They are my responsibility, and I regret not placing them as a priority earlier. I should have been serving my own kingdom instead of devoting myself to Carrick's cause. I won't make that mistake any longer."

He still didn't return my gaze. He picked up his reins. "I'm sorry,

Rilla. I need some time to myself." With that, he urged his horse forward, leaving space between himself and the rest of us.

I couldn't blame him for his melancholy over Carrick's actions. We'd both lost a friend today, and it must be worse for Aiden, who had fought for Carrick for most of his life. I would let Aiden have his space.

In four days, we safely reached the border of Emberwood. It would take another day to reach Linlang Palace. I was relieved Carrick hadn't changed his mind and pursued us. We occupied the rooms of a small inn in Candlelace Village.

The inn probably didn't have many visitors, and the auntie who owned it was quite pleased to host us, especially after Welder paid her a hefty sum. But once she made sure we had everything we needed, she left us alone.

I had a separate room from Aiden, but I wished I could talk to him. We'd both already confessed our feelings for one another, but I knew what had happened with Carrick affected things between us. I wondered what he thought about Welder's idea that our marriage should take place sooner rather than later.

I didn't want to marry Aiden because of politics. I didn't want either of us to be forced. I didn't even know if he wanted to marry me.

There was a knock on my door. I opened it. Aiden came into the room without hesitation.

"Rilla, I've been thinking a lot, and I'm ready to talk." He paced the length of the room, gesturing with his hands as he spoke. "You do not need to marry me despite what Welder says. He does not get to decide our lives. I will protect you no matter what in Emberwood. As long as you wish to stay, and—"

"I—" I waved my hands to get his attention, but he wasn't looking at me and continued to pace, his words coming out fast.

"I'm so sorry about Carrick. I know you were in love with him once. And even though you told me you love me now, I know it must have still hurt when you found out he married Radi and had a child with Arlyn."

I touched his shoulder. "It doesn't matter."

He stopped pacing, but he continued talking faster and faster. "If I'd known he was carrying on an affair with Arlyn, I would have told you. I would have chastised him regardless of my position. You have to believe me."

"Aiden—"

"I have loved you since the beginning. I only stepped aside because Carrick was my friend. I should have fought for you despite Carrick's objections. If I ever acted like he was more important than you, I'm sorry. I shouldn't have left you behind in Emberwood either."

"Be quiet for a second and listen to me." I touched his cheek.

He finally lifted his head and stopped talking.

I stepped forward and gazed into his bright, golden eyes. "I want to marry you. As soon as possible. Not because of Carrick or Welder. But because I love you."

He blinked. "What?"

"I love you."

"I don't want you to feel pressured. I know you have dreams to be a healer, and—"

"Shut up, will you?" I moved in and kissed him.

He stilled, then deepened the kiss.

We broke away, breathing hard.

"Is that the only way to stop you from talking?" I stroked his cheek. "I can marry you *and* become a healer."

"Yes. Yes, that works." He smiled. "I love you. I've loved you from the start."

I touched my forehead to his and closed my eyes, enjoying the feel of him. "You taught me what real love is. As a friend and as a partner. I can't imagine ever being separated from you. I want to be with you for the rest of my life. Not for protection, not because anyone says we have to, but because I want you." I kissed him again and unbuttoned the first two buttons of my cloak.

His eyes bulged. "No, we can't. My parents would kill me."

"Are you going to change your mind about me? Perhaps you wish to take a harem for yourself."

He scrunched his brow. "Don't be ridiculous."

I popped open another button.

"Stop doing that." His voice was hoarse.

I hid a smile. He was giving in.

I took off my cloak and tossed it on the chair behind me. I placed my fingers on the first button of my silk dress. I looked at him, asking the question with my eyes. He nodded and swallowed. I undid the first button, then the rest, until my dress was open.

I slid it off my shoulders and let it fall to the floor. "I'm offering myself to you."

He pulled me into him. Our lips met, and he stroked my back. He whispered, his warm breath caressing my ear. "After tonight, you'll be mine and I'll be yours forever."

For the rest of the night, we knew nothing else but each other.

I lay in Aiden's arms and bathed in the luxury of his warmth. Never had I known such bliss. He kissed my shoulder and pulled the blankets around our bodies.

"I never thought this happiness was possible." Aiden pulled me closer. He looked at me in wonder. "What did I ever do to deserve you?"

"Don't question it," I said. "For as long as I live, I'm yours."

"But seriously, I can't believe—"

"You talk far too much, and I know of only one way to shut your mouth. Now let me show you how much I love you so you'll never question it again." I cast him a coy smile.

A wicked grin crossed his face. He pretended to lock his mouth with an imaginary key and throw it behind his shoulder. I kissed his chest, and he groaned.

# CHAPTER 40

✦ ✦ ✦ ✦ ✦ ✦ ✦ ✦ ✦ ✦

The lilting and beautiful song of a flute played in my sleep. I dreamed of Aiden and myself on the beach of my village, and the song played as we walked on the shore.

*"United in love, the two shall become one*
*He shall be fire who bears the flame*
*And she who sees life's future present*
*Shall further give or take away."*

I woke in Aiden's arms, bedsheets tangled around us. Morning light streamed through the windows. I stared at Aiden's sleeping profile and fought the urge to trace his eyebrows. His eyes opened, and he smirked.

"You can't get enough of my pretty face, can you?"

I averted my gaze, embarrassed to have been caught staring. He stroked my hair and kissed my head.

"I can't get enough of you either," he said. "I dreamed of you. We were in your hometown. I've never been there, but somehow, I knew it was your village. A flute was playing."

"I had the same dream," I said in surprise. "How can that be?"

Again, the song played in my ear as audible as if someone were playing the flute right next to us. From Aiden's expression, I knew he'd heard it, too.

A light shone through my cloak, which lay on the chair, where I had discarded it the night before.

"It's the scepter," I said.

We dressed quickly. I grabbed my cloak and reached into the pocket for the scepter, which still took the shape of a flute. It shook in my hands, and the force drew me forward. Aiden caught me.

The flute stopped shaking, and it transformed, elongating into the scepter. The light shone through every intricate carving in the base of the scepter, traveling to the head. It grew brighter and burst into the air, then transferred into me, through me, and into Aiden.

I gasped. "What's going on?" A zing of energy rushed through every nerve in my body. Then the light died, and the scepter remained in my hands. Aiden still held me tightly.

A knock sounded on the door, and Welder barged in. "I felt some extremely powerful energy." He stopped as his gaze fell upon the scepter. "Is that—how did—"

"It transformed on its own," I said.

"The Sacred Cedar Scepter," Aiden said. "The carvings are similar to the fake one Carrick had, only I can sense something different. Powerful. It's as though the scepter has its own wyis."

"I know exactly what you mean," I said.

"Something happened when I touched you after you held the scepter," Aiden said. "I know you experienced it, too. Let me try something."

He moved away from the bed and from us, then closed his eyes. He took the form of fire. His whole body set aflame.

I jumped back. A flame sparked off his body and lit the top bed cover on fire. Welder pulled off his cloak and smothered the flame.

Aiden flickered off, coming back to normal.

Welder stared at the smoke from where he'd put out the fire. His gaze traveled to Aiden, and a slow grin broke out on his face. "Aiden, you are the next Seracedarean emperor. Old Grandfather Heaven has spoken, and the scepter has amplified your tin-chai."

Aiden shook his head no. "Not just me. The light went through Rilla, too. Both of us had our tin-chai amplified."

"Me?" I gaped at him.

Welder tossed his scorched cloak onto the bed. "But the scepter has never before chosen two rulers at once, nor has it amplified a woman's tin-chai."

"Doesn't mean it can't happen. It's all in the song." Aiden repeated the lyrics. "The two shall become one, and he shall be fire who bears the flame. She who sees life's future present shall further give or take away."

"Give or take away," I repeated.

"You already know how the scepter amplified your tin-chai," he said. "Just think about it."

I thought back to the moments leading up to Irica's death. I thought I had taken away her tin-chai, that I'd developed another layer to my tin-chai and could steal someone's tin-chai for myself. I hadn't been able to do it since then, but maybe now I could. Was that the tin-chai amplification the scepter had bestowed upon me?

Life's future present. Present had two meanings. The here and now was the first meaning. But what if it was the other meaning? Gifts. Powers. Tin-chai.

I gasped. What if the scepter had granted me the ability to take away tin-chai *and* to give another tin-chai layer to someone else? It made sense. I was able to heal *and* to kill, to make the elements move *and* to stop them. Every layer to my tin-chai had a dual nature to it.

Aiden grinned and touched my cheek with his hand. "It looks like you might know what gift you've been given."

"Impossible." My voice trembled as I spoke. "I'm not worthy of such power."

"No one is truly worthy, but if we're called to bear that responsibility, all we can do is try our best," he said. "We are in this together."

"Don't keep me in suspense," Welder said, impatience tingeing his voice. "What power has Rilla been granted?"

I barely heard him. All my attention was on Aiden. He was the light to my inner darkness. Without him, I would have succumbed to the darkness completely.

"I think the scepter has granted me its own gift," I said. Then I placed my hands upon Aiden's back and sang the song of the flute.

*"United in love, the two shall become one*
*He shall be fire who bears the flame*
*And she who sees life's future present*
*Shall further give or take away."*

I let my wyis flow through him. When I lifted my palms away, heat radiated from his skin. He turned into fire and then into something else. He disappeared, but his energy raced and pulsed. Light illuminated the room. Sparks generated through the air.

Then he was back. His eyes widened. "I—I believe I just changed into light. See, there's no denying it anymore. Welder, do you understand now? Rilla amplified my tin-chai."

Welder stood there, his jaw stretching wide. "Rilla—you have the gift of the scepter itself. To amplify tin-chai. Which also means you can take tin-chai away."

"My voice has the scepter's power." I sank onto the bed, unable to believe it.

"But my love, I think my tin-chai has been amplified enough for one day," Aiden said. "If you need someone to practice on, you'll have to use someone else. Don't want Old Grandfather Heaven to think I'm being greedy."

"This is all too much. I'm not sure I want this responsibility." I held Aiden's hand for reassurance. "What do we do? If we have the right to rule Seracedar, will we have to challenge Carrick for the throne?"

"Whether you want it or not doesn't matter." Welder's voice reverberated through the room. A spark of triumph lit in his eyes. "We now have the means to expose Carrick. You are destined to be the next rulers of Seracedar, and the Shyan kingdoms will finally be reunited." He lifted his palms and cast his gaze upward. "This must be Old Grandfather Heaven's will. May it be accomplished."

Aiden quickly sobered. His hand tightened around mine, and he whispered, "That means war with Carrick is inevitable. Even if we reveal we've got the scepter, Carrick won't surrender. He'll be the first to declare war with Emberwood."

"So be it, then," Welder said. "But do you have what it takes to go against your former friend? For the sake of your family, your kingdom, and your future bride? Because if you don't accept the duty that the scepter has bestowed upon you, Old Grandfather Heaven can just as quickly take away his favor from you as he did with Terran. You must commit to this mission. Fail and you could lose everything and everyone you love."

A fierce expression came across Aiden's face. "No, I'll never let that happen. I'll do whatever is necessary to defend Rilla, my family, and Emberwood. My loyalty lies here with you all now. If anyone threatens those I love, I will kill them."

I looked Aiden straight in the eye. "And I will kill anyone who threatens you." I raised the scepter and held it up to Aiden. He clasped the scepter, his hand over mine, a symbol of unity.

With that, I made him a promise. "Whatever battles come our way, we will fight them together."

# GLOSSARY

✦ ✦ ✦

## CHARACTERS

AIDEN LANG—(EY-den LAHNG) *Prince Carrick's loyal bodyguard*

AMIKA—(ah-MEE-kah) *The Miyu princess*

ANDROGY HAMING—(AN-dro-gee HAH-meeng) *Emperor Terran's former advisor*

DAHLIA NIN—(DAH-lee-ah NIN) *The head of a monastery of sister Lotuses*

DAKI—(DAH-kee) *A shatooth Yao and ship captain*

HARA—(HAH-rah) *Amika's aunt*

JELBY WELDER—(JELL-bee WELL-der) *Former general in Seracedar*

PRINCE CARRICK—(KEER-ick) *The emperor's son*

RADI YING—(REY-dee YEENG) *Rilla's best friend*

RILLA MARSEAS—(RILL-ah MAR-see-aahs) *The story's protagonist*

SAGO—(SAY-go) *A fox Yao and overprotective mother*

TEER—(TEE-ehr) *A Lotus-in-training*

WYLE—(WHY-el) *A fox Yao kit; Sago's son*

✦ ✦ ✦

## SEVEN KINGDOMS OF CALIWYIS

(CAL-uh-WEES)

AILO—(EYE-low) *Kingdom of Ailo, a race of rock dwellers who were conquered by Seracedar and became a tribute kingdom*

EMBERWOOD—(EHM-ber-WUD) *Kingdom of Embers, also of the Shyan race who that rebelled and started their own kingdom two hundred years ago*

EXENTRIA—(ex-EHN-tree-ah) *Kingdom of the Exentriks, technologically advanced people who can banish ghosts and demons with their magic*

FAUXHEMIA—(fo-HEE-mee-ah) *Kingdom of Fauxhemian race, artists and storytellers with magic*

MIYU (MEE-yoo) ISLANDS—*Sea nation of fish- shapeshifting women warriors said to descend from the sea goddess Mi* (MEE)

SERACEDAR—(SEER-ah-SEE-der) *Kingdom of Shyan people, a race born with tin-chai, unique magical abilities controlled through four channels*

YAO—(YOW) *Kingdom of Yao, a race of animal spirit shapeshifters conquered by Seracedar and who became a tribute kingdom*

✦ ✦ ✦

## PLACES IN SERACEDAR

CASCASEA VILLAGE—(KASS-kah-SEE-ah) *Protagonist's Rilla's hometown. A fishing village in Province Ca*

JAILONG VILLAGE—(JHAI-loong) *Village in Province Yupa*

PROVINCE CA—(KAH) *Province where fishing is the main industry*

PROVINCE PEON—(PEE-AHN) *Province where agriculture is the main industry*

PROVINCE SEN—(SEHN) *Province that is the kingdom's main trading hub and home of Imperial Palace (Cedar Palace)*

PROVINCE YUPA—(YOO-pah) *Province where textiles is is the main industry*

SENLIN CITY—(SEHN-leen) *Imperial City*

TAMIKA VILLAGE—(tah-MEE-kah) *A coastal village in Yao Kingdom*

TINSAI VILLAGE—(TIN-sye) *A ghost village devastated by a previous pestilence*

✦ ✦ ✦

## OTHER SHYAN TERMS

DAI CHANNEL—(DYE) *Body channel. Magic through this channel controls physical elements*

DOFEI—(DOH-FAY) *A playful sea creature with an arched body and fins*

GODOG—(GOH-dawg) *A furry land creature that can be a faithful pet to its master*

HA CHANNEL—(HAA) *Soul channel. Magic through this channel controls health, wellness, and healing*

JI CHANNEL—(JEE) *Mind channel. Magic through this channel controls telekinetic abilities*

KAI CHANNEL—(KYE) *Heart channel. Magic through this channel controls emotions, desire, and passion*

KIPA—(KEE-pah) *The formal dress of Shyan women*

KOONG—(KOHNG) *A Shyan born with no magic*

MAOCAT—(MAOH-kat) *A land creature often kept as a pet, though more finicky and disobedient than a godog*

SHATOOTH—(SHAH-tooth) *A sharp-toothed fish that preys on weak and bleeding animals*

SHUROO—(SHOO-roo) *A forest creature with a bushy tail*

SIHAI—(SEE-HYE) *A sea creature with a sleek body and whiskers*

TIN-CHAI—(TIN-chhye) *A Shyan's magical ability*

WYIS—(WEES) *Spiritual energy*

# ACKNOWLEDGMENTS

Another episode of Rilla and Aiden's journey is complete. This second installment was initially the second half of UNDER THE LAVENDER MOON until I realized it was two arcs that had to be broken into two parts. It's funny how the growth of my characters always seems to be parallel to my own growth. Rilla's self-doubt reflects my own, but she continues despite the fear and imposter syndrome, motivating me to do the same.

Rilla needs her friends to remind her that her voice matters, to remind her to harness the power that has always been and will always be within her. And like Rilla, I'm so blessed to be surrounded by beautiful souls who remind me everyday that my voice matters. Without their encouragement and support, I would not be here doing what I love, and this book would not exist.

Of course, I'm always thankful for my family. My parents, David and Lily, and my brother, Daniel, I know you are my biggest supporters. Thank you for loving me.

To my grandma, Alice Lee, who recently left this earth and is now reunited with my grandpa, thank you for showing me true strength. I'll always continue writing in honor of your memory.

To the Chatta Monkees, Wing Ning Yung Taketa, Cindy Shao, Jean Tseng, and Judy Liang, I'll always cherish your friendship, and I appreciate all the encouragement you've given me over the years. Rie Takata, I am eternally grateful. Not only are you a great friend, but your artwork is inspiring, and I'm so lucky to have you as the artist behind all my bookmarks.

My girls, Tiffany Wong, Esther Kim, and Christina Colorina, there are no words for how much I love and appreciate you. Thank you for reading my drafts, for giving me honest feedback that I need to hear, and for telling me to keep going. Christina and Ron Colorina and kids, you are the most generous and loving family ever, and words can't express how much I appreciate you. I am better with you guys in my life. Esther, you are the sweetest lady ever, always ready to be a supportive friend whenever possible. Tiffy, I love you so much! Who would have known that our shared love of literature and deep talks about symbolism after English class would continue on for more than two decades? Oops, did I just reveal how old we are?

Jordan Duncan, thanks for being my cheerleader and for believing in me from the start. You saw my dream and helped me to own it.

Melanie Hooks, I'm so thankful for your friendship. I don't know what I'd do without you, my ENFP friend.

Laura Perkins, the greatest editor ever, you have always understood my voice, and this book wouldn't exist without you.

NJH, thank you for listening to me talk about my writing and letting me process the difficulties of revisions. You are a true sweetheart and such a good man with a kind heart. Like Aiden, your presence shines as bright as autumn gold. I hope you find happiness wherever life may lead you, even if it's not with me.

Holly Kammier and Jessica Therrien, thank you for letting me continue with Rilla's story and for putting it out into the world.

Molly Lewis, my editor, thank you for turning my crazy mess of a story into a finished novel I can be proud of.

Last, but not least, I'd like to thank everyone who has read Rilla's story and supported me in any way. This story is for anyone out there who wants to take a step into the light to achieve their dreams but may be scared to do so. Rilla grows into her power and takes ownership of her true self. It's no surprise that this has been my journey as well. So, I hope Rilla's story inspires all my readers to do the same, to find their power and to own it. Despite the fears and the uncertainties, take the jump anyway.

# AUTHOR BIO

After graduating from UC San Diego, Christina Fong built her career as a food scientist, but she never gave up on her true calling, writing poems and YA fantasy novels based in Asian American culture. She especially loves reading and writing about underestimated good girls who are pushed too far and must embrace their dark side to kick some butt. When Christina isn't writing, she's probably stuck in LA traffic, jamming out to her girl crush, Taylor Swift.

www.ingramcontent.com/pod-product-compliance
Lightning Source LLC
Chambersburg PA
CBHW020555310726
48979CB00008B/1225/J

* 9 7 9 8 8 8 5 2 8 0 1 0 5 *